HOW TO MARRY A GHOST

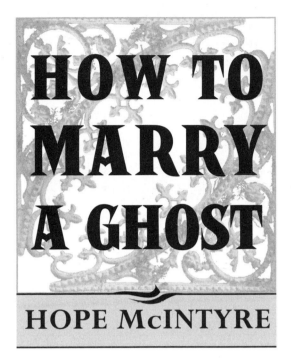

HOW TO MARRY A GHOST

HOPE McINTYRE

NEW YORK   BOSTON

Mysterious Press
Hachette Book Group USA
1271 Avenue of the Americas
New York, NY 10020

Visit our Web site at www.mysteriouspress.com.

Mysterious Press is an imprint of Warner Books, Inc. The Mysterious Press name and logo are trademarks of Warner Books, Inc.

Printed in the United States of America
First Edition: January 2007
10 9 8 7 6 5 4 3 2 1

Library of Congress Cataloging-in-Publication Data

McIntyre, Hope
   How to marry a ghost / Hope McIntyre. — 1st ed.
      p. cm.
   ISBN-13: 978-0-89296-014-9
   ISBN-10: 0-89296-014-0
      1. Ghostwriters—New York (State)—Long Island—Fiction.
   2. Weddings—Fiction. I. Title.
      PS3571.P33H67 2007
      813'.6—dc22   2006018562

For Joy Harris and Michael Brod, who met the summer I began this book, and who were married at Laurel Hollow, New York, in the presence of many friendly ghosts, the summer I finished it.

For Drew, Bumper, Tess, Seppi, Chula, Smilla, Augie, Jackson, and all the other dogs who came to visit while I was trying to write *How to Marry a Ghost*, and barked till I took them for a walk. And in memory of Hattie and Billy who died in Devon.

For Johnny Davenport-Handley, who first introduced me to R&B back in 1963, wherever he is.

And in memory of Crispin Meller, of Whitchurch Canonicorum, Dorset, born the summer of 1947, who as a young man designed and made his own guitars, and who died, much too young, just after Christmas 2004.

Author's Note

Many of the places featured in this book actually exist on the East End of Long Island, including the Old Stone Market. But I hasten to add that its proprietor at the time of the writing of this book, Karen Vaucher, bears no resemblance to my character Franny Cook and that the store has always been run with considerably more efficiency and professionalism than Franny displays in *How to Marry a Ghost*. The real Old Stone Market is a welcome haven for all the residents of Barnes Landing, catering to both gourmet and simple tastes alike. My thanks go to Karen for all her help in giving me a behind-the-scenes look at how a store like hers is established.

HOW TO
MARRY
A GHOST

CHAPTER 1

ON THE DAY THAT MY MOTHER ALMOST COMMITTED bigamy, the body of a man wearing a wedding dress washed up on the beach.

Maybe the use of the word "bigamy" is a little extreme but my mother *is* still married to my father. The fact that she was having a commitment ceremony rather than a wedding is neither here nor there. Actually it's on the end of Long Island, New York, where I found myself heading on a humid September afternoon the week after Labor Day.

"What's a commitment ceremony?" I asked her and by way of response she thrust a copy of the *New York Times Style* section into my hands.

"Here's where I got the idea," she said. "Look in the back. You'll see loads of them."

I glanced through the announcements of marriages that had taken place, complete with photos of couples smiling at the camera. And every now and then I read about a couple that had not married but who had instead affirmed their partnership. I couldn't help noticing that all these couples were gay.

My mother and I are British but the man with whom she intended to affirm her partnership was an American called Philip Abernathy, whom she had known for all of six months. She was committing to Philip and his portfolio of several billion dollars—

I dubbed him the Phillionaire before I'd even met him—barely a year after my father had left her for a French divorcée of whom, I might add, he had quickly tired. Now he wanted my mother back. But after an initial bout of understandable depression she had surprised us all by plunging cheerfully into midlife sexual freedom with a string of aging lotharios. These days the last thing she was interested in was a reunion with my father.

I was traveling in the Phillionaire's helicopter to the Hamptons where the ceremony was to take place. But instead of looking down at the breathtaking view below me of the breakers rolling in across the Atlantic onto a seemingly endless stretch of beach, I was sitting rigid with fear. My eyes were tight shut and my arms were wrapped around my body in what I called my security hug. The noise was deafening, otherwise I would have shouted to the pilot: *Can't you see? We're flying much too low. The ground's rushing up to meet us. We're going to crash at any minute. I want OUT!* Okay, I'm a big wimp, I'll admit it, but I'm scared of flying and the closest I'd ever imagined getting to a helicopter was watching *Apocalypse Now.* On television, so I could turn the sound down when it got too scary.

On our arrival at East Hampton Airport the weather gave no indication that the day would end in tragedy, that somewhere out in the warm, inviting waters a body was drifting slowly toward the shore. It was a glorious day, the brilliant sunshine giving everything the kind of hazy gloss that fools you into thinking the quality of your life has been raised a couple of notches. And God knows, mine certainly had and I knew I should stop delving into the negative and get with the program. The Phillionaire had sent his stretch to meet me and it was parked at an angle just a short walk across the tarmac, with a chauffeur holding open the door. This was my mother's new American life, I realized with a jolt. I was still trying to come to terms with the fact that the new man in her life was seriously rich.

The Phillionaire's house at the beach was a surprise. If there was anywhere a person had a chance to be conspicuous with their wealth, it was the Hamptons, but Phil's house turned out to be north of Montauk Highway—not fashionable with the ostentatious set. Its waterfront location was not the ocean or Georgica Pond but the bay side of Napeague, midway between the Devon Yacht Club and the Cranberry Hole Road fish farm.

It was an ugly house, a complete mishmash of styles. The main part was stucco fronted by a rather formal colonnade. It had the whole bit: sweeping circular driveway, manicured lawn, shuttered windows, balconies, turrets, a wraparound veranda with deck chairs that looked like relics from the 1920s. *It's a mausoleum,* I thought, wondering how my mother would survive in such a miserable-looking place.

I was about go inside when my mother came roaring up the drive at terrifying speed, sitting bolt upright in a little Jeep with a line of fishing rods in holders attached to the hood. They were swaying from side to side in such a violent fashion I thought they might snap at any moment.

"Darling!" she cried leaping out of the Jeep and coming toward me. My mother always greeted me as though she were about to fling her arms around me and I fell for it every time. I moved toward her, my own arms outstretched, but at the last minute she evaded me as she always did, stepping away and leaving me flapping at her in a bereft and clumsy fashion. I could count on one hand the number of times she had actually allowed me to embrace her. After almost forty years of being her daughter I'd finally accepted that while she clearly had a problem showing it, she really did love me. Up until very recently I'd imagined that I was a real disappointment to her. I was convinced that she would have preferred a wildly gregarious creature like herself for a daughter, someone who had married in their twenties and given her a brood of grandchildren to chase after and use up some of her seemingly inexhaustible energy. Someone like me, who actually chose to live alone and spend more time at home than going out on the razzle, was an alien to her. Nor did she understand my choice of career as a writer. To lock yourself away in a room and write for hours on end was incomprehensible to someone who had spent years as a high-profile ad executive. But when my father deserted her, after she had given it all up to accommodate his desire to go and bury himself in the French countryside, her vulnerable side had surfaced and I was there for her. It had taken the disintegration of my parents' marriage for the two of us to draw a little closer to each other but I was thankful for at least that one small mercy.

Now she stood before me, her skin pinpricked with beads of sweat, dressed in some kind of expensive gym gear—sleeveless tee, skintight spandex cycling shorts, and her new snow-white urchin cut half hidden by a sweatband. And she looked fabulous. She had always been stick thin but the rather hunched and scrawny demeanor of her depressed state following my father's departure had been replaced by a distinct firmness, slender thighs, and none of that underarm flab that is the hallmark of most middle-aged women. And yet, at sixty-two, could she even still be considered middle-aged? Was I not looking at someone bordering on an *old*-aged phenomenon?

Then it suddenly dawned on me. I'd been too jet-lagged to notice before but now I understood. She'd had work done—quite a lot of it by the looks of things. And there was something about her teeth—were they not considerably whiter than they had been? That's what all these trips to America had been about. Each time she'd come back to London looking glowing and rejuvenated and I'd put it all down to meeting the Phillionaire (at the bar in the British Airways first-class lounge at Heathrow—his Gulfstream was getting its cabin redecorated or something). But then why had she been going to America in the first place? She'd been pretty secretive about it all and again I'd assumed she didn't want to reveal his existence until she was sure the relationship was going somewhere. But maybe she'd met Phil much later than she'd said, *after* she'd had the work done? Indeed, maybe her makeover had resulted in him noticing her in the first place. I took a step forward and peered at her, trying to figure out exactly what she'd had done.

"Best not to get too close to me," she said quickly, backing away again. "I stink a bit. I've just spent an hour running along the ocean. Now I've got a ton of things to do so I'm going to leave you to find your room on your own. It's up the main staircase, turn left, and go all the way along to the end. It's the door on the right and you'll have a view of the bay."

I looked around for my bag but it was already being whisked inside by one of the posse of servants hovering on the doorstep. And then out of their midst emerged the Phillionaire.

"There you are," he said and engulfed me in a welcoming embrace that made up for my mother's pretend version. Even though his tall slim frame was encased in casual beachwear with an old straw hat perched on the back of his head, he still managed to look as distinguished as he did in the elegant tailored suits he wore in the city. If I'd ever been asked to guess his profession from his appearance I'd have said "Latin American diplomat" right away. He was always so impeccably dressed that I retained the fantasy that he kept a tiny Lilliputian tailor in his pocket at all times, ready to climb out and attend to his sartorial needs.

I followed him into the house under the ugly stone portico and let out an involuntary shudder as I noted the gloomy predominance of wood paneling. I had the sense that dust sheets had been whipped from the furniture only seconds before we arrived. It didn't say beach house; it said wealthy Long Island mansion suitable for resale as a retirement home.

"Your mother loathes this place," he said, noting the look of horror I was unable to disguise. "It's been in my wife's family for years." He explained, "She inherited it but we both felt it was a bit like being in a mausoleum at the beach. Still when my boys came along we made good use of it for summers out here. But your mother hates it."

"Oh, I'm sure she doesn't," I said quickly, cringing at the thought of what my mother must have said about it. Had she hurt his feelings?

"It's understandable," said Phil, "it was my wife's. Your mother wants us to start afresh. She wants to oversee the installation of a brand-new home so I'm building something totally modern along the bay. It'll be steel and glass and minimalist, nothing like this except that it'll have the same spectacular view."

"Do you own the whole bay?" I asked him, not entirely joking.

"Not quite but I wish I did. I bought up as much as I could on either side of my wife's house, probably around eleven acres. Paid under ten million dollars quite a few years ago, a real steal. It's my favorite area around here because you can keep a low profile. I never say I have a place in the Hamptons, because I don't. This whole area is a kind of no-man's-land. In fact it's called Promised Land and it's pretty far removed from the dreadful scene that goes on in East Hampton all summer. The only bit of fancy action is at the Devon Yacht Club over there." He pointed to a cluster of buildings with a flagpole and a jetty in front at the far end of the bay. "In the old days they said that if the wind was blowing the wrong way, the snooty crowd at Devon complained about the stench of the fish factory right here at Promised Land. The fish used to be shipped straight to the Fulton market in the city; you can see the remains of the railroad running through the dunes. I remember the bunker operation they had here. It was shut down in 1968. Now there's a fish farm on the same site, see? Over there?

"Oh yes," he sighed, "those were the days. All I do out here now is go for long walks along the beach and take my boat out in the bay to fish. Don't catch much besides blues but I'm never happier. I've told your mother, if she wants to go rushing off to the Hampton Classic horse show and all those fancy parties and benefits, she's going to have to do it without me. I get enough of that in the city. This commitment ceremony's the only event in which I'm going to participate. After that she's on her own." He put his arm through mine. "Come on, let's go down to the beach and see what she's up to."

My mother had called in a ton of markers from her advertising days to plan her waterfront ceremony, roping in all her former Madison Avenue contacts, and preparations were already in full flight for the ceremony that would take place at the end of the day. A team of stylists with whom she had worked on commercials was in the process of transforming the beach. They were raking sand, picking up litter, and setting out rows of white church-supper chairs with an aisle in the middle leading to a bamboo archway that had been draped with white tulle. Here my mother and the Phillionaire would exchange their vows at sunset. Tall zinc planters bearing a variety of ornamental grasses were being carried out and placed along the edge of the dunes. Tents were being erected on the lawns, tables were being laid for the dinner following the ceremony. Giant seashells formed the centerpiece of each table.

"Total waste of time." A man had appeared at Phil's side.

I noticed the Phillionaire didn't even turn to look at him.

"Lee, this is my son, Scott. Scott, this is Lee, Vanessa's daughter. Flown over from London."

My mother had told me about Phil's sons by his late wife. Scott, the elder, was an orthopedic surgeon with a thriving practice in East Hampton. He looked a lot like the Phillionaire only he had more hair, spiky black tufts of it sticking straight up. But he wasn't distinguished like his father. Far from it. He had the same long legs but he was even thinner than Phil and it gave him a mean look. He had a hooked nose where Phil's was straight and a curious habit of hunching up his shoulders almost to his earlobes, and then suddenly relaxing them in a jerky movement.

"Pleased to meet you, heard a lot about you." He said it very fast, making it obvious he wasn't and he hadn't. "Waste of time putting up all this stuff. We're going to get another bad storm in a few hours and it's going to blow it all away."

What was he talking about? There was no sign of a storm. I looked up at the royal blue sky and the sun beating down. There was a slight breeze but it was so gentle that it didn't even disturb the rose petals that were now being strewn between the chairs and along the sandy aisle.

"Well, don't tell Vanessa," said Phil, "she'll be devastated. I heard there was a storm coming up the eastern seaboard but I thought it was going to blow itself out over the Atlantic."

"Oh, I already did," said Scott, "and she was. A beach ceremony after Labor Day, what does she expect?"

I think that was when I had my first ominous feeling that there was something sinister lurking beneath the idyllic surface of the day. But I dismissed it quickly. I've always had a curious belief that mayhem is just around the corner waiting for me. Imagining myself being sucked out to sea in a tidal wave just because someone had mentioned the word "storm" was a pointless exercise. I wouldn't give it another thought and besides, I really resented the way Scott was pouring cold water on my mother's excitement.

Except he turned out to be right.

By early afternoon torrential rain was pelting down, the wind raged, and occasional gusts of up to sixty miles an hour raced along the beach, tossing the white supper chairs in the air, dismantling the bamboo arch and carrying it and the uprooted tents out to sea. It flared up so suddenly, only one or two of the table arrangements were saved. It was all over within a couple of hours but the damage had been done.

I found my mother standing alone at one of the upstairs windows and I could see there were tears in her eyes. I went to put my arm around her shoulders, searching desperately for words of comfort.

But as usual she didn't need them. She shrugged my arm off with an imperceptible movement and clapped her hands together.

"Right," she said and though her eyes were bright, her voice was strong and determined. "Slight change of plan. We can't cancel at this late stage. Most of our guests will have traveled a fair distance to the East End of Long Island and we mustn't disappoint them. We'll just have to go ahead without the props."

And that was exactly what happened. When the guests began to arrive at around six o'clock, some of them wearing galoshes and bundled up in rain capes to protect their finery, they were directed to the veranda at the back of the house overlooking the beach. Here they were served a warming punch from a recipe my mother had given the kitchen staff at the first sign of the storm. I had been instructed to be dressed and ready and waiting at the bottom of the sweeping staircase in the great hall. When I arrived, feeling very sophisticated with my hair swept securely into an elaborate updo by my mother's hairdresser, I found the Phillionaire standing there with Scott.

"You look quite beautiful, my dear," said Phil. As he held me in his arms for a second, I heard his sharp intake of breath as he looked over my shoulder. "But not as beautiful as your mother."

She was coming down the stairs in a white satin dress with a high round neck and long tight sleeves that set off the shape of her toned arms to perfection. The narrow body buttoned up the side and had a dropped waistline that descended into a full and softly pleated skirt ending at the knee. Tossed around her neck was a long white garland of gardenias. She was regal and serene and she carried a posy of white gardenias to match the bloom attached to the side of her headband just above her left ear.

When she reached the Phillionaire she didn't say a word, just looked deep into his eyes, took him by the hand and led him out via the French windows onto the veranda where everyone parted to let them through. Scott and I made up the rest of the family party and we followed. The rain had stopped but the wind was still howling and the waves were pounding onto the shore.

My mother turned and instructed us to take off our shoes and then she gave a slight nod to someone waiting at the far side of the deck.

"Watch," she whispered to me. "Something for Phil. He used to be a great surfer in his day, so I'm told. Here's his other son, Rufus."

Around each corner of the house came a procession of barechested hunks bearing surfboards. They lined up at the bottom of the steps to the deck and raised their boards to form an awning under which we picked our way barefoot across the eroded beach strewn with debris from the storm. We stopped at a small patch of sand that had been raked clean right at the edge of the sea. The surfers were the groomsmen, forming a semicircle around my mother and Phil, and holding their boards upright in the sand beside them like monuments. To look at, Rufus was as unlike his brother as he could possibly be. He was blond and cheeky with an upturned nose and freckles. He was quite short but his upper body was strong and muscled. He had a knapsack on his bare back from which he extracted two long garlands of white gardenias. He hung one each around my mother's neck and the Phillionaire's and then took his place by my side. Scott was trying to look cool in a lightweight gray suit and bare feet but he didn't stand a chance next to his buff and tanned brother.

My mother and the Phillionaire stood facing each other, barefoot in the sand, hands clasped, and suddenly I realized that we would not be able to hear their vows above the roar of the surf.

But it didn't matter. From the expression on their faces, there was no doubt that what they were exchanging were declarations of love.

And then I stopped abruptly because a figure had appeared on the horizon, walking toward us along the shoreline, and once again I sensed a portent that something disturbing was approaching. As it came closer, I saw it was a woman, not in the first flush of youth, long gray hair flowing past her shoulders. She was a beauty, whoever she was, but her appearance was as unkempt as my mother's was groomed and elegant. She was dressed hippie style in a loose flowing caftan and an Indian shawl was tossed around her shoulders. Hard lines of disappointment were etched in her strong face but there was no escaping the fierce intensity of her eyes.

The Phillionaire had told me that he didn't own the actual beach—anyone could walk along it—but it was surprising to see someone out for what appeared to be a leisurely stroll in the wake of a tropical storm. I expected her suddenly to sense she was intruding on a private ceremony and turn back but she kept on coming until she was near enough that a stranger might have mistaken her for one of our party. Then she stopped and stood there, watching and smiling at us in an eerily familiar way.

Rufus winked at me. We hadn't actually been introduced but he seemed to know who I was. "That's all we need," he muttered to me, grinning.

"Who is she?" I asked.

"Some woman who wanders the beach. Everyone calls her Miss Havisham. The word is she was left standing at the altar many years ago and it sent her around the bend. She never married anybody else and she frequents beach weddings because they're the only ones she has access to. But it's what they say will happen if she shows up at your wedding that's the killer."

"What do they say?"

"That she puts a curse on the wedding to avenge what happened to her, that the marriage won't last."

"Well, that's okay," I said, "because this isn't a proper wedding."

"Yeah, you're right," said Rufus, "and it's all a crock anyway."

But he didn't look too sure and I was relieved when "Miss Havisham" didn't make any attempt to follow us into the house for the dinner.

One good thing about the gloomy stucco mansion was that it had a ballroom. When I saw the Phillionaire lay down his cigar and lead my mother out onto the dance floor, I took the opportunity to slip out to the veranda to see if Miss Havisham was still wandering along the beach. But there was no sign of her. The surfers, now wearing sleek black wetsuits, were gathering up their boards in the moonlight and Rufus told me they were going over to the ocean to take advantage of the post-storm swells.

"Midnight surfing under the full moon," he said. "You want to come along?"

"Absolutely!" I was amazed at my spontaneity. Back in London my natural British reticence and neurotic terror of the unknown would have stopped me taking off so quickly with a bunch of near strangers. Yet riding through the dunes in the back of a pickup truck, dressed in nothing but a bit of black silk chiffon with my hair unraveling in the wind, I experienced a sense of sheer exhilaration and began to feel excited about the new person I might become in America.

For about twenty seconds.

As the trucks with their four-wheel drive sped along the wide ocean beach, an ambulance and a police car began to give chase behind us and, looking up, I saw a police helicopter whirring overhead. The surfers pulled over allowing the ambulance to overtake us and we followed at a discreet distance, everyone standing up in the back of the truck and craning their necks to see what was going on.

Farther up the beach appeared to be floodlit. At least a dozen vehicles had beaten us to it and crowds had already gathered at the water's edge. There was a body lying facedown on the sand illuminated by the headlamps of parked trucks. A familiar feeling of panic began to creep over me and my first instinct was to ask Rufus to take me back, but when everyone else got out and I found myself alone, I followed. I was drawn by a morbid fascination and, feeling sick with dread, I jostled with the crowds to get a closer look.

It was so weird that at first I thought I was hallucinating. The body had clearly been pulled from the water and I thought it must have somehow come to be wrapped in the tulle that the storm had whipped from our bamboo arch. Then, as the ambulance men lifted it onto a gurney, the head rolled toward us and I could see it was a man's face. Bloated and mottled and strewn with seaweed, but definitely a man's.

But he wasn't wrapped in something, he was wearing it.

It was sodden and crumpled and it clung to his body like the spoiled plumage of a magnificent bird washed up on the beach, but there was no mistaking it for anything but a wedding dress.

"White taffeta and gold brocade over layers of tulle," whispered a woman behind me with an air of reverence. "I sold a dress like that at Saks once."

"Some guys from the Town Shellfish Hatchery just reported that they found the veil over in the bay near our house," said Rufus. "It was caught up in a clam raft they were towing. Man! The press are going to be all over this one."

"Don't get too many men in wedding dresses washed up on your beach, I suppose?" I was being flippant to cover my nerves. That was a dead man lying there and without being aware of it, I had raised my hands to my face in horror.

"You don't get it." Rufus looked at me. "As far as the press are concerned, this isn't just any man. Someone just told me. It's the son of that British rock 'n' roll guy—Shotgun Marriott."

My knees gave way and I flopped down onto the sand before Rufus could catch me. There was another reason besides my mother's ceremony that had brought me to New York.

I was here to interview for the job of ghostwriting Shotgun Marriott's autobiography.

CHAPTER **2**

THAT NIGHT AROUND 3:00 A.M. I JERKED AWAKE, trembling with the jolt of a nightmare still reverberating vividly inside my head. I'd been swimming, plunging through the water for what seemed like forever, and my legs were on the verge of giving out from exhaustion. Finally I'd reached the shore and lain there, recovering on the wet sand as the tide ebbed over me, and after a while I'd become aware of another figure that had drifted in beside me.

It was the body in the wedding dress and as I reached out to touch it, the eyes opened wide and stared at me and the shriveled lips parted to speak.

I sat up in bed and realized that it was a dream and I never would hear what they said to me. My instant reaction was to reach for the phone on the nightstand and do what I always did when my insanely overactive imagination convinced me that danger was lurking in the shadows waiting to pounce.

I called Tommy.

I actually got as far as dialing his number in London, congratulating myself for remembering the country code without having to look it up, before it hit me at the sound of the first ring.

Tommy wasn't in my life anymore.

My relationship of almost nine years with a certain Tommy Kennedy was complicated. Complicated by me, I hasten to add.

Given that my natural inclination is to spend much of my life alone I had, until very recently—like about a year ago—insisted that Tommy and I live separately. Poor Tommy, a chubby forty-three-year-old radio engineer at the BBC, was warm, affectionate, and gregarious. He was desperate to get married, settle down, and have loads of little Kennedys and it was just his bad luck that he had fallen in love with someone for whom that appeared to be total anathema. As we often used to joke, I was the one with the biological clock but he was the one keeping time. He never could figure out why I banished him from my life for several days a week but being the devoted rock that he was, he accepted it.

Just as he accepted my irrational fear of violence and my belief that around every corner someone was lurking to kill me. When an arsonist started setting fire to buildings in my neighborhood with the result that those inside were barbecued, he moved in with me the minute I summoned him, so convinced was I that I would be the next victim. The only way I could feel remotely safe was to have his hefty bulk beside me every night.

The impossible happened. I got used to having him around. I fell in love with him all over again. And I asked him to marry me.

Yes, *I* asked *him* and he said yes and I spent the best part of a year planning our wedding to coincide with the Notting Hill carnival. We were going to be transported amidst the carnival revelers down Ladbroke Grove from the church to the reception on a float bearing the colors of Chelsea, the football team who were neck and neck with me when it came to receiving Tommy's unswerving devotion.

But in the end, Chelsea won.

He didn't leave me at the altar or anything. He's the sweetest, kindest man so he would never do anything like that. All he did was change his mind, something he was perfectly entitled to do.

We were having breakfast when he told me. I'd had to make the most enormous effort to incorporate his existence into my daily routine. My normal writing practice was to tumble out of bed, make myself a quick cup of coffee, and go straight to my desk before the inspiration and energy that came from getting a good night's sleep evaporated. Sometimes I didn't bother getting dressed until lunchtime.

In order to preserve that precious period of solitude for as long as possible I encouraged Tommy to go running every morning. "We have to get you in shape for the wedding," was my reasoning. The first morning, he agreed with enthusiasm and set off wearing a pair of ludicrous baggy shorts and a T-shirt that proclaimed he was a vegetarian, which was a total lie. After seven minutes he was back, clambering up the stairs to the bathroom where he spent *forty*-seven minutes in the tub, singing his favorite country and western songs at full volume. Then he demanded a full English breakfast, something I haven't eaten, let alone cooked, for several years.

I didn't say a word. After years of thinking I absolutely had to live alone, that I needed my space, that I didn't want to share my life with anyone, I had suddenly got the point of having someone else around. I had begun to find that I looked forward to sharing whatever thoughts I had during the day with Tommy when he came home in the evening. All right, it nearly drove me crazy having him disturb my early morning peace yet I was prepared to compromise. And that's a word that was not even part of my vocabulary six months ago. But I was changing and I was proud of it.

It took several weeks to persuade Tommy that for it to do any good at all, he would have to run for at least half an hour.

"That jacket you're going to wear for the wedding, it's fitted—it's not loose and floppy like most of your clothes," I pointed out to him. "If you lose ten pounds—even five would help—you'll look sensational in it."

"These scrambled eggs are disgusting," he complained, "and I'm not going to be wearing the jacket at the wedding."

"That's because they're made with egg substitute," I told him. "We've got to do something about your cholesterol. What do you mean, you're not wearing that jacket? You've had it made specially. It's beautiful."

"I meant I'm not going to be wearing the jacket at the wedding because I'm not going to be at the wedding."

"Oh really, Tommy? Where are you going to be? Prior arrangement at Stanford Bridge maybe?" Stanford Bridge was the Chelsea football ground, Tommy's home away from home. I think if it could have been arranged, he would have liked us to get married standing in the goal post with the stadium filled with our guests.

"I'm not going to be at the wedding because I don't want to get married anymore."

He was mumbling now but I heard every word as distinctly as if he had been bellowing.

I swallowed and held my breath and waited for the "just kidding." Tommy was a practical joker with a childlike sense of humor. But he didn't say anything.

"Any particular reason?" I decided to keep it light and cheery even though my state of mind was bordering on panic.

"Don't think I'm ready for it." More mumbling.

"That's not what you've been telling me for the past eight years." I turned on him. "You've always been the one who was desperate to get married."

"Changed my mind."

I resisted the urge to throw something at him. Tommy behaved like a small boy most of the time but when he thought he might be in the wrong, he was almost infantile in the curtness of his answers.

"Are you going to tell me why?" I sat down now. I was maintaining amazing calm but I knew that later the storm would break and I would collapse and wail in agony.

"All right, I'll tell you," he said, as if he really didn't owe me an explanation but he'd do me the great favor of giving me one. "I thought I wanted to get married but now I realize I don't."

"Tommy," I said, fighting hard not to raise my voice, "that's not good enough."

He sat there for a moment in silence, the jowls in his handsome open face collapsed like dewlaps and his huge hands resting palms-down on the table making him resemble a giant golden Labrador waiting to be fed.

"I know," he said finally, "I know. I've got to work out exactly how to tell you. But you know, it's these morning runs that did it."

"Running makes you antimarriage?"

"I had time to think about getting married while I was running. I'm not sure it's the right time."

"Ah," I said, trying my utmost to be patient with him. "I see"—although I didn't see at all—"and when do you think might be a good time for us to get married, Tommy?"

"About two years ago." Now he was looking very sheepish.

I didn't say a word. I just looked at him. Sometimes that was the only thing to do with Tommy. I'd just stare at him until he grew so uncomfortable that what was really bothering him bubbled to the surface and spewed out. It was a bit of a mean tactic but it always worked.

"Well, it was different. You needed me then."

"I need you now, Tommy."

"Not sure you do," he challenged, going red. "You're so independent, there'd be nothing I could do for you."

This was true of our relationship to a certain extent. Tommy didn't lead, he supported, he followed, and he always left the big decisions to me.

"You don't need my money, it's your house and—"

Ah, so this was what all the fuss was about.

"Tommy, it's not about possessions. I need *you*. It's about caring for each other and being there for each other when we have problems."

"But you don't have problems anymore."

I stared at him. He stared back looking sad and awkward.

"Don't look at me like that," he pleaded. "It's true. When I first met you, you were neurotic and frightened and jumpy and I was able to help you and understand you and I felt I was really important to you. Now things have changed."

Was I hearing him correctly? Could I translate what he was saying to mean I had grown up and he hadn't? Now I was no longer as needy, it didn't work for him anymore? Of course, in the beginning I had fallen in love with him because he was the only man I'd ever met who seemed to understand my insecurities, my fear of the world outside. He didn't judge me, he didn't question my need to be alone and to hide myself away. He just hung in there waiting for me to come to my senses. Except that now that I had, he didn't seem to want to celebrate my newfound maturity. He didn't seem to understand that now I needed him in a different way—as an equal partner and, more, as someone who could accept my help for a change.

But that would prove to be something he just couldn't bring himself to do. It turned out that there were problems at work, a reshuffling of his department and the possibility that he might lose his job. He'd been bottling everything up and now it all came tumbling out every night just as I was about to fall asleep. I lay beside him stiff as a board with tension because he would not allow me to comfort him, offer him the support he had always given me, and I wanted to scream *It's not fair!* at him. He was just telling me his problems as a way of explaining why he couldn't marry me. It wasn't just a case of cold feet or last minute nerves; he genuinely didn't think he was a worthy husband for me any-more, and no matter how much I tried to persuade him, he stuck to his guns. Which meant that I felt like a total failure because it was clearly insecurity about the future that was making him feel this way and I was unable to reassure him that I still wanted to marry him no matter what.

So this was the state I found myself in when my mother called to tell me she was planning to affirm *her* partnership with the Phillionaire. I was the one who was supposed to be walking down the aisle but at the moment it looked like a strong case of *always a bridesmaid . . .*

Now, in the early hours of the morning following my mother's ceremony, I struggled to come to terms with the fact that I could no longer turn to Tommy for reassurance. As I slowly hung up the phone, I realized I was on my own, sitting up in bed in a far-flung wing of a house I had likened to a mausoleum.

I didn't dare to attempt sleep again in case I had another nightmare. I lay, rigid with tension, until seven o'clock when I forced myself to get up and go downstairs in search of a cup of coffee.

To my surprise, I encountered Rufus padding about the kitchen in sweats and an old pair of sneakers, leaving a trail of sand wherever he went. A maid was anxiously monitoring his progress, poised to sweep up after him.

"Lucia, chill. I'll clear it up, I promise. Don't I always clear up after me?"

"No, Mr. Rufus. Never."

"Well, at least I try, which is more than Scott ever does. Hi Lee, how'd you sleep?"

My face must have given me away because he pulled out a chair and took my arm, guiding me into it.

"Not much, huh? I'm not surprised. What a night! I was down at the beach already and let me tell you, the rumors are starting to fly about the guy in the wedding dress. He was going to be married and his fiancée jilted him at the last minute so he took her dress and waded into the water in it. Or maybe he was a cross-dresser and he wandered down to the beach drunk after a party. You name it, they're throwing it all out there."

Rufus grinned at me and I began to relax. I'd had the distinct impression that he was his father's favorite and I could see why. "Rufus is the wild one," the Phillionaire had told me. "He was an afterthought, came along fourteen years after Scott. Bit of a shock to the system for his mother, we were both in our forties. He dropped out of college and spent a year on the draggers— fishing," he'd added when I'd looked bewildered. "Then he settled out here—although settled isn't exactly how I'd describe him. He works all over the place, clamming, landscaping, chopping wood, carpentry, construction, I can't keep up."

I was thinking how different he was from Scott, who his father had told me had been through an acrimonious divorce and now rattled around in solitary splendor in a palatial mansion on the ocean, when Lucia approached me with a coffeepot.

"You want?" she asked me.

"No, she doesn't. I'm taking her out to breakfast. Lucia, can we put these in the washing machine?" Rufus was holding up a bag of laundry. "They left, by the way."

"Who did?" I asked.

"Your mom and my dad. They took off last night when the

party ended, went back to the city to start their committed life or whatever you call it. But don't feel you have to rush off. You can stay as long as you like and I'll be at your disposal."

I felt suddenly rather awkward. Now that my mother was no longer around I wasn't sure how much longer I could stay without being in the way. I had spent the previous week in New York cooling my heels at the Phillionaire's apartment while I waited to be summoned for my interview with Shotgun Marriott. But it hadn't happened and now with the tragedy of his son's death, who knew how long it would be before my fate was decided.

Rufus saw my hesitation.

"It's okay, really." He assured me. "You're family now."

He smiled at me and I relaxed a little. He was right, I supposed. He and I were almost related in some way. I was an only child and all of a sudden I had a "little brother."

I smiled back at him. "Thanks," I said. "As a matter of fact, if I could stay a couple days until I sort myself out, it would be great. Do you live here?"

"I crash in the pool house when I don't have anywhere else to go." He nodded his head toward the window. I could see a pool and beyond it a small shingled building.

"Does Shotgun Marriott have a house round here? I thought he lived in New York." I wondered if my mother had mentioned that I had hoped to be working for him.

"Oh sure, I think he's got an apartment on Central Park West or someplace but he spends a lot of time out here, probably because he can keep a low profile. He transplanted a couple of giant barns into the woods along the bay—maybe they even came from England originally."

"You've been there?"

"Oh, no. No one gets invited there—socially, I mean. He keeps himself to himself. We only know he's there because people had to go there to clean and maintain the house and the word got out it was his. You'll see him around now and again—walking on the beach or grabbing a bit of late night sushi at Mount Fuji. They give him a table in back and leave him alone. But that's it, pretty much. You won't see him at any fancy parties or anything."

"Sounds like your dad," I said without thinking.

"Right. Sounds like my dad," he echoed. "You've gotten to know him a bit then?"

"I have," I said, "just a little and I have to say I love what I know. He's a sweetheart. I prejudged him before I even met him and I was totally wrong."

"How come?"

"Oh, I suppose I was just being protective of my mother. I sort of freaked when I heard he was so rich, I thought he'd be odious and ostentatious and I wouldn't have anything in common with him." I suddenly realized what I was saying. "I mean, nothing personal about your family. I'm just weird." I shrugged and grinned at him. "Don't ask me why but being around too much money makes me uncomfortable."

"You don't have to say another word. I get it. I'm here to tell you having money can cause as many problems as not having any sometimes. And you know what? I had the same doubts about your mom. I thought she might be like all the other women who tried to snare him. They never got the point of *him,* they just wanted his lifestyle. I think they just liked the idea of putting 'wife of Philip Abernathy' on their résumés. He and my mom had such a terrific marriage, he was devastated when she died. I never thought he'd find anyone to replace her but I can see he's totally smitten by Vanessa."

"Has he told you why?" I was curious.

"He loves how she's so down to earth, he loves her energy, but he says she's also got a vulnerable side. He figures she's been re-pressed emotionally for years. Now I would never say my dad was one of those touchy-feely kind of people but he seems deter-mined to help her—as he puts it—learn to love herself and ex-press her love for others."

I didn't say anything. I didn't feel comfortable admitting to Rufus—whom I had only just met—that I had always had a prob-lem relating to my mother emotionally. But it seemed he knew without my telling him.

"You don't get on with your mother?"

"We get along fine but we're not close." I decided to trust him. He was my "brother" after all. "We're just so different. It's like our roles are reversed and I'm her mother rather than the other way round. You mentioned her energy. She puts me to shame and I'm over twenty years younger. She has style, she keeps up with the world far more than I do—"

"I'm sure you do all right," he said gently. "Family members don't have to be identical. Look at Scott and me."

"Tell me about Scott—" I began. He was my "brother" too, so I had better start getting to know him.

"Maybe later," said Rufus. "He's not my favorite topic of con-versation. C'mon, we have to go get breakfast. I need an egg sandwich bad. We'll take Dad's Jeep and go along the beach.

"You'll like Mickey's," he told me as we bounced along the dunes, "although I shouldn't really be calling it that. Old Mrs. Mickey ran it as a little mom-and-pop convenience store. She died recently and left it to her niece, Frances Cook, and Franny's renamed it the Old Stone Market because it's situated right on the Old Stone Highway. She's got big plans for it, wants to give the place a total makeover. She's already overhauled the kitchen so she can cook food to go."

He swung the Jeep off the beach and onto a road and suddenly I was glimpsing houses dotted here and there in the woods.

"And this little community we're just coming into is called Stone Landing. I like to think it's not really part of what people call the Hamptons. It prides itself on being a quiet, peaceful neighborhood—you got retirement couples here as well as people who want to raise a young family far away from urban chaos."

He rambled on about Stone Landing, telling me how it was hidden away and balanced, a touch precariously due to the erosion of the bluff, high above Gardiner's Bay. It was comforting listening to him describe the area with such affection and I marveled that someone so young wasn't tempted by the "urban chaos" he had mentioned, just a hundred miles away in Manhattan.

We drew up to a parking area outside a sprawling wooden building with a white picket fence running off to the side. Pickup trucks were parked at random. Rufus whistled.

"Never seen so many cars here on a Sunday morning. Franny must be doing well."

But then the screen door banged shut and a construction worker came out of the store shaking his head.

"Wouldn't go in if I were you. It's bedlam in there. She don't know what she's doing."

When we stepped inside, I couldn't see Franny Cook for the throng of men shouting orders at her. I caught glimpses of her frying eggs, flipping bacon, plucking toast from the toaster, and lining up the orders on the counter.

"Hey Rufus," she shouted above the crowd. Her voice was gravelly, as if she'd just smoked a pack of Camels. "Jesus didn't show this morning. I've gotta take care of everything myself. Anything you can do to help would be appreciated. Hey, sir!" she yelled at a man who was pushing his way in front of the others. "Line forms on the right. Wait your turn like everyone else."

"Jesus is her breakfast cook," said Rufus. He pronounced it *"Hayzoos."* "I'd better get in there and help out. Franny, coming through! Hang in there. Listen everybody"—he turned to the construction workers milling about—"it's a beautiful day. Go sit outside and I'll bring you your orders."

I was impressed by how quickly they obeyed him. The store emptied as they streamed out to the picnic tables, and as she came around the counter bearing a plate of bagels with cream cheese high above her head, I had my first proper look at Franny Cook. She was about six feet and rangy with the longest and most shapely legs I had ever seen. In fact everything about her was long and shapely—her arms, her neck, her fingers. She had the kind of shoulders on which you could hang an old sack and it would look good and her head was tiny with a close cropped poodle cut that emphasized her large brown eyes. She was wearing a pair of skintight denim shorts and a cutoff tee that revealed her nut-brown abs.

"It was bad enough when she took over her father's care-taking, now she's got to ruin Mickey's as well." An old lady had just come in and was waiting in line beside me. My eyes appealed to Rufus to rescue me and he beckoned me outside.

"Here, have a muffin. Banana and oat bran, Franny bakes them herself. I'll bring you a coffee."

He returned and sat down opposite me.

"Franny's poor old dad worked his fingers to the bone trying to pay his property taxes and then he dropped dead at fifty-two. He was the caretaker around here, watched people's houses in the winter, mowed their lawns in the summer, and when he died Franny stepped in and carried on where he left off. You'll see her splitting wood and blowing leaves in the fall yard cleanups later on but the old folks around here don't like the idea of a woman caretaker any more than they like Mickey's being turned into the Old Stone Market."

"She runs this place *and* takes care of people's yards?" I was astounded.

"Oh, you haven't heard the half of it. She used to clean their houses too before she had the baby."

"The baby," I repeated.

"Six months old. And she's got an eighteen-year-old from a disaster of a relationship with some guy in the city."

I stared at Franny as she went by, balancing plates of toast on her forearms. What was this woman's secret? She'd had a baby six months ago and here she was walking around with a bare midriff and a stomach like a washboard.

"Hey Roof, can you come give me a hand here?" Franny was distributing the toast to the various tables. "I've told the SLRA they can hold their monthly board meeting in the back room. I hate their guts but I figure it'll be good for business if people see they've given me their stamp of approval. I need to set up a table in back."

"What's the SLRA?" I whispered as Rufus prepared to follow her.

"The Stone Landing Residents Association. Mostly New Yorkers with weekend homes around here. It's the same story wherever you go. They're some of Franny's best customers but she resents the hell out of them. Most of them have barely been here ten years whereas Franny's lived here her whole life. The Cooks have owned property in Stone Landing longer than any of us and Franny's the eleventh generation. Her family was among the original settlers. They have nine fucking acres whereas most of the SLRA members only have quarter-acre lots."

When I walked back inside, Franny was coming toward me carrying a trestle table upturned and balanced on her head. As she lowered it to the ground, there was a demanding wail from behind the counter.

"Damn!" Franny brushed past me. "Eliza's awake. I'm going to have to feed her before the SLRA arrive."

"You keep the baby in the shop?" I blurted out.

"Where else am I going to keep her?" Franny looked at me and shrugged. "We live above the store but I can't keep running up the stairs to check on her. Hey Roof, you want to take her up and change the diaper?"

"Can't say I *want* to," said Rufus amiably enough. "Eliza's explosions are mega stinky. Franny, this is Lee Bartholomew. She's over from England. She's the daughter of a friend of my dad's."

Well, that was one way of putting it.

"Pleased to meet you," said Franny, giving me a quick smile and handing the baby to Rufus. "The diapers are beside the changing table in the bedroom. Bring her back down when you're done and I'll feed her at the till. I'm a real pro at working that cash register with one hand while I cradle her."

Which, to my amazement, was exactly what she did, perched high on a stool behind the counter while the baby suckled at her breast. I found myself waiting with bated breath to see what would happen when a customer came in and caught a glimpse of her bare breast. Was I a prude to expect her to breast-feed in private? And how often did you find guys in their twenties who were prepared to change diapers? But then as I was fast discovering, Rufus was quite an unusual young man.

He was in love with Franny Cook. I'd known it the minute we walked in the store, maybe even before that from the slight catch in his voice when he mentioned her name. Now it was unmistakable as he stood watching her while she fed the baby. He had the same soft tender expression in his eyes as his father did when he looked at my mother. Franny might be a good ten years older than Rufus but he just couldn't take his eyes off her.

It was clear she took advantage of his devotion. When she finished feeding Eliza, she put her in her baby carriage and took her for a walk, taking it for granted that Rufus would mind the store in her absence.

"Who's the baby's father?" I asked him.

He looked at me hard for a second as if unsure whether to tell me. Then he said: "Scott. Eliza's my niece. But my father doesn't know so you have to keep it to yourself. Franny refuses to let me tell him."

"But Scott knows?"

"Oh, Scott knows all right but he won't do a damn thing about it. Says he's not interested in being a father. And to be honest, Franny likes it that way, says she wants Eliza to be a Cook not an Abernathy."

"But how did it happen?"

"Nobody ever told you how babies get made?" Rufus winked at me. "One-night stand after the Fourth of July picnic on the beach last year. Franny was drunk. Scott took her back to his place—I saw them leave together. But something wonderful came out of it. We have Eliza."

At that moment a customer demanded his attention and he left me to go to the cash register.

The bell began to *ping* repeatedly as the screen door opened and shut several times and half a dozen people converged on the store, helped themselves to coffee, and crowded into the small space in front of the cash register to pay for it. I became aware of a man standing beside me, scanning the shelves. I saw his hand, large and ugly with fingers like sausages, reach out and pluck a packet of Oreos. I was annoyed because it was the last one and I had been planning to buy it myself. I turned to see who had thwarted me and I saw him open his jacket and place the Oreos inside against his ribs. I watched, stunned, as he zipped up the jacket and looked straight at me for several seconds before walking out the door.

He'd had black hair brushed forward to frame a hard, brutal face in a style reminiscent of a Roman emperor, and a Roman nose to match. I suppose he was handsome if you went for the Tony Bennett type but he'd scared me and I'd behaved like a complete wimp. I'd let him walk out of the store and I hadn't said a word.

When Franny walked in a few minutes later I knew I had to tell her she'd had a shoplifter.

"What'd he look like?" she asked me.

I described the man and she nodded.

"You know who it was?" I said. "Listen, Franny, I'm sorry I didn't do anything. I was just thrown. I don't know what came over me."

She nodded again. "Yes, I know exactly who it was," she said slowly, "and I totally understand why you didn't do anything. If it makes you feel any better, it's not the first time it's happened and I've never done a thing about it."

And then before I could say anything else, she pushed past me to wheel the baby carriage behind the counter just as the members of the SLRA arrived for their meeting. The president, Louis Nichols, was an attractive well-preserved man who I guessed to be in his middle fifties. Rufus whispered to me that his family had been one of the first to build a vacation home in Stone Landing in the late fifties. In fact his parents had started the SLRA. Some people felt there was an element of droit du seigneur in the way he had assumed the presidency when it became vacant but no one could deny that he had worked tirelessly to keep the Association going.

He summoned everyone to the table and opened the meeting. "I was going to put forward Franny Cook's name today since she's been so kind as to let us use her store."

"Did I hear my name mentioned?" Franny sauntered over to them.

Louis got up and offered her a chair. When he reached out to take her arm, I sensed that maybe Rufus wasn't the only one interested in her. "Join us for coffee," he said. "We need another person on the board."

"Yes, I heard." Franny ignored Louis's hand and remained standing, turning to one of the other members. "Abe, you left a message about some logs. How many you want? Half a cord do you?"

"What are we going to do about the teenagers drinking on our beach at night?" an elderly woman interjected, getting down to business. "It's disgusting what you find when you go down there in the mornings."

"Condoms?" Franny asked, looking up at the ceiling.

"Same thing we're going to do about the beach vehicles that are causing all the disturbance to the beach grass. Write a letter to the town supervisor and the trustees asking them to restrict beach vehicle access. And we're going to ask for a ban on Jet Skis in the bay. I've got a draft right here if anyone wants to read it." Louis waved it in the air. Nobody took it from him.

"What's the point? They'll say the same thing they always do," said Abe. "The fishermen need to be able to launch their boats from there and if someone has a heart attack, or gets eaten by a shark, they need to be able to drive the ambulance along the sand."

"And they'll be right," said Franny. "So there are people launching Jet Skis and racing SUVs and disturbing your peace. That's the price you pay for turning Stone Landing into a vacation spot. It wasn't like this when my dad was growing up. Now it's a weekender's paradise. I know, I get to watch their homes all winter. Seventy-five percent of the homeowners are from the city. They're the ones who bring the SUVs and the Jet Skis."

"And they're the ones who'll keep you in work," said Abe sharply as Franny towered over him in such a rage that for one second I thought she was going to strike him, but then she wandered back to the cash register.

"Oh God," whispered Rufus, "when will Franny learn *not* to bite the hand that feeds her."

"Lou, I think you'll have a hard time getting us to vote *her* in," I heard Abe say. "She's not one of us, now is she?"

I wanted to tell him to keep his voice down but too late— Franny had turned on her heel and was marching back.

"What do you mean, not one of you? I've never heard such a crock. I'm a Stone Landing resident, I pay my taxes. I'm—"

A cell phone started ringing. Everyone fumbled in their pockets until I suddenly realized the sound was coming from Rufus who was standing right beside me. He turned away and began to walk out of the store, his phone clamped to his ear. Franny had abandoned her tirade to go back to the cash register yet again and I followed Rufus, worried he would leave without me. But we almost collided as he came back in again, the screen door banging behind him.

"They've found another one," he yelled. "Another body. A woman and they found her on his property."

"Whose property?" Franny leaned across the counter.

"Shotgun Marriott's," said Rufus and my blood ran cold. "First his son is washed up on the beach and now there's a woman lying facedown in his woods and they're saying someone shot her in the back with a bow and arrow."

SHOTGUN MARRIOTT HAD ONCE BEEN HUGE!
You couldn't write him off as just another aging British
rocker. He'd been a superior bluesman in his time and a leg-
endary womanizer. What's more, they were classy women, by all
accounts. A Shakespearean actress, a lawyer, a prize-winning
photojournalist who spent more time in war zones than with him.
I'd always wondered whether they actually called him Shotgun in
moments of intimacy. Of course there were plenty of scrubbers
crawling all over him in nightclubs and his band, the Suits, were
rumored to have trashed hotel rooms the world over but even so,
Shotgun Marriott had always had more style than your average
rock 'n' roll artist.

It was a woman who had brought him down, ended his career
and dispatched him to oblivion where he'd been for almost fifteen years. A groupie, found dead in his bed after a concert. He
wasn't charged with anything, but he had never revealed what
had happened that night. It had become the rock 'n' roll Chappa-
quiddick and if he told the whole story in his autobiography, it
would be dynamite.

I was desperate to land the job of working on that autobiography because it might well turn out to be the plum job of my
career. I'm a ghostwriter. I am the "as told to" or the "written
with" you see in small type underneath the celebrity's name. For

the past ten years I've worked in my native London coaxing reminiscences—or in some cases mentally blocking my ears to a torrent of sentimental fabrication—from showbiz personalities, sports stars, a medium, a fashion entrepreneur, you name it. My beloved agent Genevieve kept the work coming on a regular basis and all I had to do was show up, listen—and then go away and write, of course.

But recently I had encountered a problem in the form of a certain Bettina Pleshette.

I had always been aware that Genevieve had other clients besides me but until she'd taken on Bettina about eighteen months earlier, I had never been remotely interested in them. Providing Genevieve found me work, I didn't care a fig what her other clients were up to. But Bettina presented me with something I'd never encountered before: competition. I was used to the interviews Genevieve set up for me being merely a formality. Then, suddenly, whenever she put my name forward for a job, I'd find Bettina was also in the running.

"They asked for her, they knew about her, what could I do?" was always Genevieve's excuse. The problem was Bettina invariably got the job.

I found I wasn't comfortable being competitive. It comes naturally to some people but I had never even thought about it until Bettina entered the fray. I suppose I should have been grateful to her for single-handedly putting ghostwriters on the map. Until she came along we were backroom people both by nature and profession, content to suppress our egos and remain invisible. But that just wasn't Bettina's style. She'd hired a publicist and made herself a star as well as her subjects, so that whenever she ghosted a book, it immediately raised the stakes. This went against every single ghostwriting grain in my body and I hated her long before she ever came up against me for work.

Cards on the table: She's twenty-eight, eleven years younger than me. She's incredibly well-connected. She's sexier, firmer, and her hair is thicker. She seems to go out with a different guy every night and while Genevieve has never let on, I'm convinced Bettina commands a much higher rate than I do.

I faced up to the fact that I felt threatened. There was a new breed of ghost for hire and for the first time I felt just a little bit past it. To begin with I could rationalize Bettina's success by telling myself that the jobs she landed were the fluff stuff, writing the memoirs—*Memoirs? Ha! More like the teenage diaries*—of MTV chart toppers or someone hailed as the next Paris Hilton. There was a role for her as ghost for the youth market. But then she snatched a job I coveted from right under my nose, that of ghosting the autobiography of a respected BBC newscaster with an addiction to painkillers. That certainly wasn't a good fit for the youth chronicler niche and I felt the unfamiliar stirrings of rivalry, so much so that the first thing that came out of my mouth when I went to Genevieve's office for a meeting to discuss future work was:

"What's Bettina working on at the moment?"

Genevieve is a treasure. She is always brisk and efficient but she is also mumsy. There's no other word for it. She mothers me in a way my own mother never has. There I'll be in her tiny Covent Garden office, 5' 8" tall with my long Madonna (not the singer!) face and my willowy frame inevitably encased in the most minimalist clothes I can find, fretting about what my next job will be. And there she'll be, 5' 2", fussing around me in pastel-colored suits. And even though she is tiny, with dainty feet and hands, she is also *enormous,* like a pretty little hippo in sugary camouflage. But she is so comfortable with her bulk that she almost makes me want to gain thirty pounds.

And she is the only person, apart from Tommy, who understands that I'm neurotic and antisocial and that I prefer to live vicariously through other people, which is why ghostwriting is so perfect for me. But ever since Bettina had been on her books, I'd had the sense that she wasn't quite as *there* for me as she had once been.

"What's Bettina doing?" she echoed, lifting a little bottle of Evian to her rosebud lips and taking a tiny sip. "Nothing, dear. She's just finished the newscaster book and she's currently in New York for an interview. She's been there awhile actually, two or three weeks. Went there for a holiday and then this job came up."

"Genevieve, I want you to put me up for it too," I said.

She blinked in surprise and immediately protested. "You don't even know what it is. And it's not right for you, Lee. Anyway, as I just said, it's in New York."

"What's that got to do with it?" I was feeling very tetchy. "I know New York. I'm going there next week anyway because my mother lives there now and she's getting—" I let it dangle because I couldn't say she was getting married and I still hadn't quite got to grips with the partnership affirmation thing. "I could stay with her." I made eye contact with Genevieve and held it until she looked away. "So who is it?"

She shrugged. "Shotgun Marriott. Not your thing at all."

"Why should it be Bettina's thing and not mine?" I leaned forward to stare in outrage at Genevieve across her desk. "Well?" I said when she didn't reply.

"Oh all right," she said finally, "it might be something for you but Bettina does have a history with this guy."

"She knows him?"

"Not exactly. When I first took her on as a client she told me the one person whose book she wanted to ghost was Shotgun Marriott's. She said she'd tried to nail him—her words—once before a few years ago but he wasn't interested in doing a book. She said she was alerted to the idea of doing his story when she was ghosting the tell-all book by Patsy White, Smokey White's wife, remember?"

I nodded. Smokey White, another rock legend, had made the mistake of dumping his wife who had promptly dished the considerable dirt on their marriage to Bettina.

"Well, Patsy had been on the road with Shotgun and his wife and she hinted to Bettina that there was a story to tell about the Marriott marriage."

"So what happened?"

"Nothing as far as I know. Bettina said she did some digging around at the time but since neither Shotgun nor his ex-wife would talk to her, she didn't get very far. So it's understandable that when a rumor started to spread about a month ago that Shotgun wanted to do a book, she was determined to be first in line to ghost it. She said she was going to America on vacation but I shouldn't be surprised if she went there just to be strategically positioned geographically when he was ready to start interviewing."

"But she hasn't actually got the job yet?"

"Well, I haven't heard anything," Genevieve conceded.

Well, that was it! I'd been dithering at the thought of attending my mother's ceremony, telling myself I shouldn't go out of some kind of deep-rooted loyalty to my father, but the next day I called my mother and told her I was on my way.

But now, as I wandered about the mausoleum a couple of days after my mother's ceremony, dwelling on the drama of not one but *two* bodies being found with a connection to Shotgun Marriott and fretting about the fact that I still hadn't had a summons for an interview with him, I began to give up hope. Bettina had got there ahead of me and yet again she had landed the job.

I wished it could be me all alone in the pool house instead of Rufus. I needed a place where I could hole up and be on my own for a while. I'd had enough socializing and excitement over the last few days to last me a lifetime and if I didn't get some space and private time to recharge my batteries, pretty soon I'd begin to freak out.

I was right about the dust sheets in the mausoleum. The day after the beachfront ceremony, all the furniture on the ground floor had been covered up except for the breakfast room beside the kitchen. I set up my laptop there and settled down to wait. I went for long walks from one end of the sweeping curve of the bay to the other, cursing the fact that I had not brought a swimsuit. I had no car in which to explore the area and while Rufus was an angel, coming back from work in the evening bearing steaming aluminum cartons of delicious take-out food to share with me, during the day I felt somewhat cut off from reality.

He brought tantalizing bits of gossip about the recent deaths.

"There's no freakin' word on who she is," he said, plunging his hand into a pile of barbecued ribs with such relish that he evoked a painful vision of Tommy who had a habit of getting more food on his face than in his mouth. "Shotgun Marriott's place is off limits to the world. There are police lines wherever you look."

"Is he there?" I asked.

"They say he is but no one's seen him. The press are camped out on Cranberry Hole Road but no one's given them anything yet."

The next day I went for an early morning walk along the beach to the far end of the bay where I caught a glimpse of something yellow in the woods. The mist was still coming in off the water and I thought maybe I had imagined something but looking closer, I saw it was a police line. This had to be the edge of Shotgun's property. I hung about for a few minutes feeling edgy and then I saw them searching the area, dogs straining at their leashes. One man looked up and saw me and said something to another and they started coming toward me. I turned and ran. It was pure instinct and after a few seconds I slowed to a jog, imagining it must look very suspicious. Were they coming after me?

But when I looked around, the beach was empty. I arrived back at the Stucco House, as Rufus told me they called it—I thought "mausoleum" a much more appropriate name—and found a note on the kitchen table from Lucia. "Jenny called." Who was Jenny? Oh, *Genny,* as Genevieve liked to be called.

"So," she said triumphantly when I called her back, "it's a go. You got the job."

"I did? But I haven't even had an interview." Now that it had happened I was amazed. "He didn't want Bettina?"

"Apparently not. You know, I'm not talking directly with him. With someone like him, you deal with their 'people.' But now I come to think of it, they didn't mention Bettina. It's odd. I've been calling them every day for some kind of reaction about either you or Bettina and the last time I spoke to them, I mentioned that you were out in East Hampton. I said you'd need two or three hours' warning if you had to go into the city to meet with him. Anyway, it turns out he's out there too. They called back pretty quickly and said he wanted you. And he wants to see you right away. Have they buried his son yet? It's all over the papers in London this morning. Dreadful!"

"He's being cremated this morning," I said, repeating what Rufus had heard on the grapevine.

"*This morning?* Good God, and he wants to see you the same day!"

"For an interview?"

"They were talking as if you were already hired," said

Genevieve. "Call his office in the city and they'll tell you where to go."

"What time?" I reached for a pen. My hand was shaking slightly. Going to meet a subject for the first time the day he had cremated his son. It was almost unthinkable.

But Genevieve was moving right along. "Two o'clock and if you find out where Bettina's got to, let me know. She seems to have vanished off the face of the earth. Her cell phone's been turned off for days. For once I'm going to have to tell her she hasn't got the job."

This should have been music to my ears but when I hung up I was feeling weirdly uneasy.

For good reason.

Rufus swung by the house about an hour later.

"I came by to show you this." He flashed the *New York Post* in front of me. I caught the headline: GAL PAL DEAD IN SHOTGUN'S WOODS. WOMAN'S BODY FOUND 24 HOURS AFTER SON DIES IN WEDDING DRESS.

And below it was a blurred but easily recognizable photo of Bettina.

I sat down suddenly. I hadn't exactly been Bettina's biggest fan but I was deeply shocked and when I told Rufus about the connection, I could see that he was too.

"She was there for a job interview? The stories in the press make it sound like she was there on a date. Anyway, I'd better draw you a little map of how to get to Shotgun's place," he said. I guessed he was being practical to cover his nervousness. "It's quite complicated. I mean you could walk along the beach and through the woods but it's probably more professional to arrive via the front entrance."

"Assuming I really do have the job," I said, hesitating a little at the very thought of what it might entail, "I'm going to have to find somewhere to live around here."

"You mean you don't want to stay in this cozy little nest?"

"I'm not sure I—"

"Just kidding." He smiled. "When I was a kid I was always outside on the beach. I never noticed what a miserable place it was. Don't worry, we'll find you somewhere."

Later that day I mentioned the possibility that I might be staying out on Long Island in a phone call to my mother and she whooped in excitement.

"But Lee, that's utterly perfect. You can oversee the building of my house because God knows I won't have the time to come chasing out there every five minutes."

I noticed it had now become *her* house even though the Phillionaire was paying for it—and what exactly was it that would keep her so busy that she couldn't take a quick helicopter ride to monitor progress herself?

"I'm going to redecorate Phil's apartment," she said by way of explanation, "it's so fuddy-duddy. I'm going to gut it and start from scratch."

"What does Phil say about that?" I had thought his Fifth Avenue apartment the epitome of good taste and how anyone could say his state-of-the-art kitchen was fuddy-duddy was beyond me.

"Oh, Phil thinks it's a blissful idea. We're going to take a suite at the Carlyle. Now let me ask him what you should do about a place to live out there and get back to you."

As it turned out it was Phil himself who came back to me within the hour.

"It's a bad business," he said, referring to Bettina's death. "You sure you want to get mixed up in the life of this character?"

"I can't afford not to," I told him, glad that we weren't face to face so he couldn't tell how shaky I was about the possibility of being even remotely involved in a murder investigation. "Shotgun Marriott's story will be red-hot material now and I'll be right in the thick of it. I have a chance to make my career take off into the stratosphere and I can't afford not to take it." I was rather pleased about the *career taking off into the stratosphere* bit. I waited for Phil to be impressed by how ambitious I had become.

"You're a ghost, not a ghoul." He said it so quietly I had to strain my ear to the receiver. "It's the type of assignment that Bettina woman would have relished by the sound of things but you're too nice, Lee, too"—he paused—"too gentle."

"I—am—not!" I shouted down the phone, offended that he should think me less able to do the job than Bettina. "I'm very tough. I can handle it, easy. I'll do a terrific job."

"I'm sure you will," he said. "I'm just not so sure you'll come out of it unscathed. But anyway, it's your decision and Vanessa tells me you need somewhere to live. Listen up, I've got a suggestion. Put Rufus on the line, will you, please?"

Rufus listened for a while and then smiled. "Sure thing, Dad. I'll take her over there right away. Come on," he said when he'd hung up, "I'll show you where you're going to live."

I followed him out of the back of the house, stepping off the veranda and down a trail through the beach grass to the bay. Then we turned left and took the walk along the beach I had come to know so well. But after about seven minutes, Rufus suddenly turned inland again up another sandy trail through the dunes. And there in a clearing midway between the beach and the road, and hidden from both by tall bamboo, was a little wooden shack.

My first impression was of a pioneer log cabin—a twenty-first-century version, at least. This was no quaint, shingled beach cottage. It was a simple, relatively modern design—about the size of a two-car garage—with a flat roof, wide cedar planks, glass sliding doors leading to a deck. The little Jeep my mother had been driving was parked over to the side, the fishing rods still protruding from the hood.

"Who lives here?" I asked him.

"No one. Dad built it a couple of years ago as his own little private retreat. He comes here to be on his own, to read, to fish—I don't know, maybe he meditates. I'm the only one that knows about it but right before they left, he said he might want me to show it to you. You know, they're taking off on a trip, your mom and my dad—Venice, and maybe London. I guess he knew he wasn't going to be using it for a while. Even if you don't want to live here, he said you should use the Jeep."

But when we went inside I knew I did want to live there. More than anywhere else in the whole world. I fell in love with it instantly. It was just one room with a shower and a john behind a curtain but what a room! One corner was taken up with a state-of-the-art kitchen—Viking stove, Sub-Zero fridge, stainless steel cabinets, their clinical look warmed up by butcher-block countertops. In the opposite corner stood a wood-burning stove with a couple of inviting easy chairs in front of it and in the remaining space a bed, a nightstand, and a desk area surrounded by built-in, floor-to-ceiling bookshelves.

"And here's the keys to the Jeep," he said handing them to me. "Come back to the Stucco House with me and I'll give you some sheets. Maybe Lucia can come over and make the bed up for you."

"No, no, I can manage," I said quickly. I couldn't wait to move in.

I packed up my belongings, took a shower, and changed into a pair of clean pants and a sweater for my meeting with Shotgun. When I returned to the cabin, the Jeep beckoned me, and I decided that before anything else, I would drive to the Old Stone Market and stock up on provisions. I'm never entirely comfortable unless I know I have a well-stocked fridge. I'm not that big an eater, I just need to know it's there. You never know what might be right around the corner. Hurricanes, tornadoes, four feet of snow that could keep me housebound for days on end.

"Oh, we get all of the above," said Franny cheerfully when I explained why I wanted to stock up on a mountain of provisions. "So you're planning to be with us for a while, huh?"

She had been feeding the baby at the till when I walked in and now she was rocking her in her arms, the soft maternal gesture at odds with a tattoo of a snake I could see on her bare shoulder now exposed by the sleeveless undershirt she was wearing.

"I think I'm going to be working with Shotgun Marriott on his autobiography," I explained, wondering if I was being a little indiscreet. I wasn't too sure how public Shotgun had gone with his intention to do a book. "I'm going to be staying in Rufus's father's house."

"That miserable old place? Can't say I envy you."

I wondered if her bluntness ever let up. "No, he has a little cabin further up the beach."

"Oh." She looked up and smiled. "That's a cool little house. I've checked it out a few times. That'd be a perfect place for Eliza and me."

Well, tough, I thought, *beat you to it.* "So I need a whole load of stuff, all the basics," I said, running my finger along a shelf containing a line of bottled salad dressings, Skippy peanut butter, packets of granola, Uncle Ben's rice. "Where's the coffee and butter and eggs, that sort of thing?"

"Over there." She nodded in the direction of the back room. "But if I were you"—she stood up and carried a sleeping Eliza to her baby carriage behind the counter—"I'd do my bulk buying at one of the bigger markets, maybe even up the island at Costco. This is a small convenience store. My markup is a total rip-off but what am I going to do? I've got to make the place pay. See, I got two kinds of customers here. The guys you saw the other day, the construction workers picking up their breakfasts, their lunchtime sandwiches, and maybe their dinners to go—meatloaf, spaghetti and meatballs, Italian wedding soup, whatever, they eat pretty well for about eight or nine bucks."

She pointed to a blackboard where the menu of the day was written up.

"Then you got the weekend crowd popping in for whatever they've run out of and those people, they don't even notice they're paying three times what it costs at the IGA. But you—if you're going to stock up a whole house, you're better off going somewhere else."

"Thank you," I said, and I was genuinely grateful.

She shrugged. "You're a friend of Rufus. I don't want to rip you off." She pulled a face. "Although if I've got any sense, I should. I gotta do *something* to drag the customers in here. Somehow I don't think the Stone Landing Residents Association is going to be holding meetings here anymore." She picked up a copy of the *Post* and tapped the photo of Bettina. "So, you're stepping into a dead woman's shoes. You sure about that?"

This was uncomfortably close to the Phillionaire's reservations.

"I'm sure," I said firmly.

"You know him?" she asked. I shook my head. "I mean, you're going to be going in there right after he's lost Sean and—"

"Sean? That's his son? Did you know him?"

"Not real well. He was a lot younger than I am. Matter of fact, his mother was here earlier. Came right from the cremation and believe me she was in a truly bad way. She was so devastated she even left him here. I can introduce you."

I looked around without thinking but the store was empty.

"Here," said Franny, pointing to an object beside the doughnuts on display by the cash register. "Oh, I know I should have more respect for the dead but she came rushing in carrying this urn, drank a quick cup of coffee, and then she was gone. She left this behind. I figure it has to be him. Oops, he's got a little powdered sugar on him." She gave the urn a quick wipe with a cloth.

I felt sick. It was hard to think that the body I had seen lying in a wedding dress could be reduced to fit into the tiny urn.

"Any word on what happened to him—how he died?" I asked her.

"No, but if they've released the body for the funeral they must have determined the cause of death."

"What was he like?"

"As far as I know he was sweet and he never hurt a fly." She paused. "And I got this from Rufus—Sean was gay. He kept that on the down-low because he thought it didn't exactly fit in with his father's womanizing image but given that he was found wearing a dress, it's a cinch it's all going to come out. Maybe Shotgun will wind up putting it in the book. That's the kind of stuff folks are going to want to know."

"So what is his mother like?"

"Shotgun's ex? Well, you'll get to find out for yourself when she comes back to pick up her son." Franny gestured to the urn.

"I will? She'll be back soon?"

"Who knows? But you'll be here because I'm going to ask you to watch Eliza while I run out and do some errands. You see, I was nice enough to tell you where to do your shopping so I thought maybe you'd like a chance to return the favor."

"Oh, you're good!" I smiled. "But I've absolutely no experience looking after babies."

"She's asleep," said Franny, grabbing her purse and heading for the door. "How hard can it be?"

Not hard at all if Eliza stayed asleep but Franny banged the screen door so hard behind her that her baby woke up and began to bawl. Two women chose that moment to come in and begin gathering groceries.

"Don't pick her up," said one as I moved toward the baby carriage. "You've got to leave her. Never let her think she's the boss, that way she'll grow up spoiled."

"Oh, that's nonsense," said the other woman. "Poor little thing. She needs a cuddle and maybe her diaper needs changing. You don't want her to think she's abandoned, do you?" She looked at me sharply.

I didn't know what to do so I compromised by rocking the baby carriage back and forth and then I went into a state of panic as I realized these women would want to pay for something and I had no idea how to work the cash register. When I said as much, the first woman reassured me.

"Oh, for goodness sake. We just leave money in that can over there"—she pointed to an empty Maxwell House tin perched on top of the freezer—"and we take the change if we need it. Franny leaves the place to run itself half the time while she's off checking people's yards and stuff."

Eliza was still howling when they left and as I bent over her, I caught a pungent whiff that told me the diaper-changing theory was definitely the correct one. I recalled how Franny had sent Rufus upstairs to find a diaper in the bathroom but when I tried the door to the apartment above, it was locked. I didn't know much about babies but I could hazard a guess that Eliza would not shut up until I changed her.

And then I saw the solution. Boxes of Pampers were lined up on the top shelf in the back of the store. I couldn't see a step-ladder or a chair but there was a broom propped against the door so I used the handle to knock one of the boxes off the shelf.

I had never changed a diaper before and the countertop covered in powdered sugar was not the best place to start but I had no option. Eliza wriggled and screwed up her little features until she was red in the face. She knew I didn't have a clue what I was doing. The smell was overpowering and what on earth did I do with the old diaper? There was no convenient bucket or trash can close at hand. Then I realized I hadn't broken open the box of diapers before removing the old one. While I wrestled with that, Eliza would probably roll off the countertop and crack her skull open. And wasn't I supposed to wipe her clean with baby lotion or something? I saw the magic words "baby wipes" on a package over on a far shelf. I reached for them and just as my hand closed over the package, out of the corner of my eyes I saw Eliza begin to roll over.

"I think you need some help there."

The voice was quiet and low and the accent was British with a mid-Atlantic inflection. She was a tall woman somewhere in her fifties. She was wearing a tailored black pantsuit and a white shirt, and her eyes were obscured by a pair of oversize dark glasses. Her mouth was a slash of dark red and some of her lipstick came off on Eliza's forehead as the woman raised her and kissed her briefly.

"You're a little treasure, aren't you?" She snapped her fingers at the package of baby wipes my clumsy fingers were trying to open. She plucked several from the wad and went to work, expertly wiping all around Eliza's little pink bottom. "You're a little darling, yes you are. What are you, six months? Maybe eight?"

She turned to me and I said quickly, "Oh, she's not mine. She's Franny's."

"And you're English," said the woman. "Here, take this." She handed me the dirty diaper. "Take it outside and bury it or something."

I found a garbage can around the back of the store. When I

returned, Eliza was sitting on the edge of the counter in just her fresh diaper, banging her little heels against the side and chortling as the woman held her hands and brought them together as if to clap.

Suddenly I noticed that the urn was no longer where it had been. The woman had moved it to stand beside her purse.

"You're Angela Marriott," I blurted out, and then, because I had to say something: "I'm so sorry about your son."

"So am I," she said and choked. I noticed tears were running down her face below the dark glasses. "This baby—when Sean was a baby, he was so"—she took a deep breath—"adorable. Here, you take her now. I'm going to crack up completely if I spend much more time with her. So who are you, anyway?"

Her tone was a little abrupt but it was understandable under the circumstances. I felt at a disadvantage because I couldn't see her eyes behind the sunglasses. I couldn't read her expression or how she was reacting to me but I knew I had to grab this opportunity with Shotgun Marriott's ex-wife. I'd have to wing it a little because I knew next to nothing about her. They'd been separated for about fourteen years and the press clippings on Shotgun that I'd studied in a tearing rush before leaving London had focused mostly on his career rather than his personal life. Even so, there was something oddly familiar about her and I had the distinct feeling that maybe I'd met her somewhere before.

"I'm Lee Bartholomew. I'm minding the store for Franny—and the baby, as you can see. And I can't thank you enough for rescuing me there. Actually, it's a bit of a coincidence meeting you like this because I'm in America to work with your ex-husband."

She took off her glasses and stared at me for a few seconds.

"What are you doing with Kip?"

"Kip?"

"Well, you don't think he was born 'Shotgun,' do you? His name's Christopher. 'Kip' for short. But I think probably only his family calls him that."

"Oh. I'm going to be helping him with his autobiography. I'm a ghostwriter."

"Are—you—really?" She said it slowly and she leaned forward as if to take a closer look at me. "You're going to take over from the woman who was murdered?"

Eliza reacted at the sudden sharpness of Angela Marriott's tone and her little face puckered. There was a pause while we waited to see if she would cry. When she didn't, Angela repeated in a whisper, "Murdered. Just like my son."

"What?" I couldn't believe what she'd just said. "I thought he drowned—that it was an accident." I saw her mouth begin to crumple. "Oh, I'm sorry. I don't want to put you through this."

She had gone white and she was shaking but she managed a faint smile.

"It's okay. I need to talk about it. Yes, you're right, his body was pulled out of the water but before that he was shot and his killer cleaned him up, dressed him in a wedding dress, and threw him in the bay. Underneath that dress there was a gaping hole the size of a dinner plate in his chest. Have you any idea what a shotgun can do to you?"

I shook my head and I was pretty thrown by her question. Did she think I encountered bodies blasted by shotguns on a regular basis?

"Well, the fact that he'd been drifting in the bay for twenty-four hours probably meant most of his blood had drained out of him but what I really found horrific was that they told me the wound was plugged before he was dressed in the wedding dress."

"What do you mean, 'plugged'?"

"I don't know—filled in with cotton, bandages, some kind of dressing, whatever you do to stop blood flowing from a wound."

"Do they have any idea who killed him?"

"I don't know," she said. "There's a detective on the case and he's a pretty mean bastard by the looks of things, comes to us from the city and he was originally a patrolman in the South Bronx. He's new out here so he's going to be working this case pretty hard to prove himself. You're going to come across him if you're working with Kip, and good luck. He got nowhere with me but then I'm pretty tough myself. Anyway, I told him who I think he should regard as his prime suspect."

"You did? Who?"

"Oh, you'll find out soon enough," she said mysteriously. "So you've met Kip?"

Her abrupt switch threw me for a second and thinking of Shotgun as Kip was not going to be easy.

"Not yet," I said.

"You'll like working with him. He's a very nice man, decent, kind. A wonderful man." She was on the verge of tears again.

Oh my God, I thought, *she still loves him.*

"How long since you and he—" I faltered, not quite sure this was an area I ought to be getting into.

"Split up? I left him fourteen years ago."

"You left him?"

"Oh yes. You haven't done your homework, have you? Your predecessor was pretty thorough by the sounds of things."

"You met her?"

Angie shook her head. "No, but a few years ago she tried to get Kip to do a book and she was pretty persistent then, sent me a ton of e-mails to which I never replied. Apparently he wasn't interested and she thought she could get me to make him change his mind. But she didn't get anywhere with me either. And now I hear she's been sniffing round here for a few weeks, talking to people, trying to get them to tell her stuff about Kip."

"Did she speak to your son?"

"I'm guessing she did."

"Did you ask him about her? I mean, before he——"

Angela Marriott turned away from me so I couldn't see her face.

"No," she said, "I never asked him. You see, my son and I didn't speak for a very long time. When Kip and I split up, he stayed with his father. He was——" Her voice broke. "He was only ten."

I laid Eliza in her baby carriage and moved toward Angela, thinking she was on the point of collapse, but her back remained rigid and she didn't buckle.

When she turned around she had regained her composure to the extent that she was able to smile at me. She had replaced her dark glasses and they added to the overall glamorous image she presented. To me, she didn't look like the wife of a rock star—more like a corporate businesswoman, authoritative, decisive, very much a leader. I wondered what her life had been like since the breakup of her marriage.

"I'm sorry," she said, "I got a little out of control there."

Oh God! Here was someone who *really* resented loss of control. She hadn't seen her son in fourteen years and then he winds up murdered. Nobody would blame her if she went into a month-long total freak-out, whereas here she was apologizing for a five-second tremor in her voice.

She was a tough customer all right but then I thought of how tender she had been when changing Eliza's diaper. Maybe that's what being around a baby did to people, because in spite of her tattoo, her wood-chopping, her lawn-mowing, and *her* tough-guy attitude, Franny too had demonstrated a soft and utterly feminine side to her nature with Eliza in her arms.

"I have to get going," said Angela, picking up the urn.

"Wait," I said as she moved toward the door. There was something I had to ask her. "Will you talk to me for the book?"

She shook her head firmly. Then she paused at the door and turned to me. "Actually, I might. It depends."

On what, I wondered.

"Where can I reach you?" I said.

"I don't know if I'm going to be around here much longer and if I am, I don't know where I'll be. If I decide to speak to you, I'll find you."

After she left I sold four tomatoes on the vine, a couple of lemon cream doughnuts and a tub of crème fraîche to people who were in and out before I could even notice what they were like. I put the cash in the Maxwell House tin and when Franny came back, I handed it to her proudly with a list of the items I'd sold.

I drove home wishing I'd had a chance to talk further with her about Angela Marriott before Eliza claimed her attention. Back at the cabin I made up my bed, made sure my tape recorder was in my bag, and checked Rufus's directions to Shotgun Marriott's house. The press were still camped out on Cranberry Hole Road and when they saw me turn into the lane leading to Shotgun's house, they started to stir. But the cop who let me through when I gave him my name waved them away. The lane ended in a circular cul-de-sac and between two of the driveways facing me, Rufus had told me to look for a hidden dirt track.

"You get on that," he'd said, "and you'll find it'll take you deep into the woods—the woods where Bettina's body was found—and you keep going and finally you come to the house. I had to drop someone off once but I never got as far as the house. Apparently he doesn't like strangers getting too close so my passenger walked the last bit."

As I drove down the dirt track, I began to feel queasy with nerves. Okay, so part of it was due to the fact that since I'd arrived in America two people indirectly connected to me had wound up murdered, but the main reason was that I was about to come face to face with Shotgun Marriott and I wasn't prepared. I was hopelessly ill-informed about the rock music world and probably the last person who should be attempting to chronicle the life of one of its former giants. He'd probably cite umpteen points of reference and I'd have no clue as to what he was talking about. But most of all I was apprehensive about spending time with a hell-raiser. I have the worst stamina of anyone I know and if he expected me to stay up carousing with him every night, knocking back Southern Comfort and supping off illegal substances instead of a nourishing bowl of pasta and a salad, then I'd be in big trouble.

As I drove up Shotgun's endless dirt track, I caught a glimpse of more yellow tape in the woods and realized I was passing the spot where they'd found Bettina's body. I swallowed hard and looked the other way. I didn't want to do this. I wanted to get as far away from a murder scene as I could.

And then Bettina Pleshette reached out from beyond the grave—or, more likely, a slab at the morgue. I had a momentary vision of her body lying there with horrible cavities exposed by knives and rib spreaders, and her blood trickling away down runnels or whatever they have as a drain, and of course I nearly drove into a tree. But the weird thing was that she actually came to my rescue. I found myself thinking *What would Bettina do?* And the thought that she might have already shown Shotgun that she could go the distance with him, chemically fueled or otherwise, stirred me into action. I propelled the Phillionaire's Jeep—surely Shotgun would be impressed by my wheels?—a little faster down the track until we came into a clearing and once again I nearly veered off into the woods in surprise.

The dirt track had become an avenue lined with magnificent oak trees and there before me, standing majestically across an expanse of lawn, was an English manor house.

As I drew closer I saw that in fact the house was a mishmash of several different types of architecture. The two wings of the house looked to be Jacobean, flanking a more solid, almost fortified central building with a tower. There were additional outbuildings—stables, a coach house with a weathervane on the roof, and a bell tower on one side and a glass-roofed conservatory on the other. I saw that the dirt track continued on beyond the house toward the two barn buildings Rufus had mentioned off to the right.

But what really gave the house its English look was the mass of ivy covering virtually all the walls, climbing high to the attic windows below the eaves. Beneath it, here and there, I glimpsed a beautiful dusky pink stone on the frontal facade. Despite its assorted periods in style, this was, I decided, an unbelievably romantic house.

My immediate problem when I approached the main entrance was how to make anyone aware of my arrival. There was no bell, no door knocker, just a solid block of medieval paneling that looked as if it would take a battering ram to break down. But then when I touched it, it gave a little and when I gave it a push, it swung open, not with the groaning wrench of a horror movie but with inviting well-oiled ease, and a shaft of sunlight gave me a path to follow on the flagstone floors inside.

I found myself standing in a great hall with a magnificent Jacobean staircase rising up out of it to a gallery running around the upper level. A stag's head above a doorway to the left had a host of baseball caps hanging from its antlers. In the gloom I peered at several oil paintings that lined the walls and saw that they appeared to be ancestral portraits of men who bore a strange resemblance to Shotgun. Maybe they had been purchased specially for this reason.

I cleared my throat. "Hello?" It came out as little more than a squeak and I tried again. "HELLO?"

A door opened above me and a figure emerged through one of the doors leading from the gallery.

"Can I help you?" the man called down to me but he was standing too far back for me to see his face clearly. Was this Shotgun? The accent was American so probably not.

"I have an appointment with Sho—with Mr. Marriott."

"And you are?"

"Nathalie Bartholomew."

"What's your business with Shotgun Marriott?"

I sensed hostility in his tone.

"I'm here to meet with him about a book he wants to do. It was set up by my agent."

"Hold on a second."

The man disappeared and I heard mutterings. Then he reappeared and leaned over the banister and now I had a clear view of him.

"I'm Detective Evan Morrison and I'm in the middle of interviewing Mr. Marriott but he asks if you will wait downstairs till we're done. Go straight ahead"—he pointed to a door directly below him across the hall—"make yourself at home in that room, there. Okay?"

I nodded, too stunned to speak. Not because I'd walked in on an interview that was obviously connected with the murder but because Detective Evan Morrison was the man I'd seen shoplifting in the Old Stone Market.

CHAPTER 4

IF HE RECOGNIZED ME, HE DIDN'T LET ON.
I didn't like him and not just because he'd stolen from Franny. And what was that all about? A detective who shoplifted? Whatever it meant, and it couldn't be good, I didn't like his fleshy face with its mean eyes—too narrow and no eyebrows to speak of so they appeared like hard little raisins in a mass of dough. I didn't like his huge nose, his thin strip of a mouth below it, and most of all I didn't like the supercilious expression on his face. This was the second time I'd seen it and I knew it was part and parcel of him.

So what would I make of Shotgun Marriott? Only time would tell but maybe I could get a head start by checking out his home.

The room Evan Morrison had told me to wait in was a shock. There was nothing wrong with the room per se. It turned out to be a small L-shaped sitting room combined with a bigger library area at the far end. It was warm and inviting with a fireplace and a couple of high-backed sofas, the kind you more or less had to climb into like a dog. It was just that if you'd asked me whose home it was a part of, I'd never have said a rock star. I'd have told you a middle-aged country gent. A hunting, shooting, and fishing type. All right, so Shotgun had to be middle-aged by now and maybe he hunted and shot and fished but this wasn't a room with a "look" to that effect created by a decorator. It wasn't an American's idea of shabby chic that somehow always managed to look brand new. This was the real thing, straight out of an English country house that had accumulated centuries of family belongings. It was a room that was lived in and cluttered, brimming with personal possessions abandoned at random on surfaces and chairs. The furniture looked genuinely worn and the faded rose chintz on the sofas had some seriously threadbare patches. A couple of rather battered looking trunks served as end tables on which perched two jade green china lamps, one with a distinct crack zigzagging down the bowl. A cricket bat was propped up against a log basket by the fireplace. The oak floors, well-polished I noticed, were intermittently covered by a motley collection of rugs, worn kilims, colorful Indian dhurries, a jute runner, and what looked like a rather garish prayer mat. They were not at all in keeping with the rest of the room and their cheekiness made me smile. Whoever used this room clearly didn't take themselves too seriously.

As I regarded my reflection in the mirror above the marble fireplace—a sheet of mottled but wistful old glass in an ornate gold frame—I became aware of the murmur of voices above me and one in particular was quite distinct. Instinctively I stood on tiptoe, drawn toward the source of the sound, and I saw that it was an open heating—or air-conditioning—duct. I looked around and saw some library steps in the corner. I placed them below the duct and climbed up so I was as close as possible to the opening above, and I listened.

I realized they were moving about the room—or at least one of them was—because I could hear footsteps. I identified the voice I could hear as that of Detective Morrison. He appeared to have settled in one spot because I heard him quite clearly whereas Shotgun—for it had to be he—was merely a murmur that came and went.

"Okay, Mr. Marriott, I want you to listen," I heard Evan Morrison say, "it seems there are some discrepancies in your statements—the one you made following the discovery of your son Sean's body and the one you made at the time the body of Bettina Pleshette was found on your property.

"We now know," he went on, "that your son Sean was killed with a bullet to the chest from a twelve-bore shotgun on the night of Friday September tenth between the hours of eight P.M. and midnight. You have confirmed that you own a Purdey shotgun."

There was a murmur from Shotgun to which Evan Morrison replied: "Yes. We have that. It has not been fired for some considerable time.

"Now, on the night in question, Friday, you say you were alone here because you were expecting Bettina Pleshette to arrive for a meeting with you at seven thirty. You say you have no idea whether your son Sean was home or not. He lived in an apartment above the stables and the two of you rarely saw each other. We have established that Sean was in Manhattan the day he died and returned that night on the jitney, leaving Fortieth Street in the city at six and arriving in Amagansett around eight forty P.M. He called a cab on his cell phone and the cab driver confirms that Sean asked to be dropped off at the bay so that he could walk home along the beach and through the woods. The driver said he seemed to know exactly where he was going even though it was pitch-black. We can assume that it was on this walk that he was shot. Maybe he had an assignation on the beach. Was it a problem for you that your son was gay, Mr. Marriott?"

Evan Morrison was speaking loudly. This was a bonus for me as it meant I could hear every word, but I winced at the harshness of his tone with the last question, which came out of the blue and, to me, seemed unnecessarily personal. Shotgun said something but I couldn't make it out.

"Okay, so you didn't have a problem," said Detective Morrison, "but you weren't close to your son, were you, Mr. Marriott? He lived with you and yet you led totally separate lives. Can you explain why that was?"

Again there was a murmur and from Evan Morrison's reply, I deduced that Shotgun had declined to explain.

"Well, we can return to that later," said Detective Morrison. "I want to go over your movements the night of September tenth. You say you fixed yourself a drink and waited for Miss Pleshette in the room below this one, that you were listening to music so you would not have heard her car if she did arrive. But that is not the reason you didn't hear anything, is it, Mr. Marriott?"

I didn't hear Shotgun's reply.

"You didn't hear anything because she never came here that night, did she? We have a witness, a Mr. Scott Abernathy, who came forward after *her* body was found to say that she'd spent the evening and indeed the night of September tenth with him."

Shotgun said something very quickly.

"No, it was definitely that night. Mr. Abernathy was quite specific," said Evan Morrison with exaggerated patience. "He took Miss Pleshette to dinner at eight o'clock at the Palm in East Hampton. We have this from the maître d', the waitress who served them their steaks, and several other diners. On the way home they went into BookHampton where the manager observed Miss Pleshette pointing out to Mr. Abernathy several books she had ghosted. Then they had a drink at the bar Cittanuova, several drinks in fact. This takes us to past eleven o'clock. Are you saying she turned up for her meeting after that, Mr. Marriott? No, I thought not."

I shifted my balance on the steps to ease a certain stiffness that was creeping into my neck while I strained to listen. Shotgun said something but I didn't catch it.

"Ah!" said Evan Morrison. "So here we have a problem. Suddenly you remember that you canceled her but you just forgot to mention that. You knew she wouldn't be coming here that night. So this places you alone here on the night your son was killed—with no alibi."

And then I heard Shotgun's voice for the first time. I imagine they could have heard him five miles away in East Hampton, so loudly did he shout at Evan Morrison. But it was not the volume that surprised me. In the few interviews I recalled having watched with Shotgun Marriott, he had always spoken with a rather grating London accent, not really East End Cockney, but going west along the Thames to Isleworth or Twickenham maybe. The voice speaking above me was a rich baritone, smooth and educated and totally without regional intonation. It was raised in anger but without the taunting hostility of Evan Morrison's voice.

"Are you seriously suggesting that I killed my own son?"

"I'm not suggesting anything. I'm merely stating the facts as I have them. Which brings me to the night Bettina Pleshette's body was found in your woods. Do you own a bow and arrow, Mr. Marriott?"

I couldn't hear Shotgun's reply.

"Okay, so you do not—as indeed you stated at our last meeting. Did you by any chance have access to hunting equipment of this nature?" Was it my imagination or did Evan Morrison sound as if he were trying to catch Shotgun out in another lie? "Did your son hunt deer, for example?"

This time I heard Shotgun's reply. He had raised his voice again. "To the best of my knowledge, my son did not hunt and he certainly did not have a bow and arrow. I used to shoot in England years ago—with my Purdey—and at one time I did indeed have an interest in archery. My wife and I took lessons for a while. Then I had a bow and arrow but it was years ago. *Years!* I suppose you're going to say you found one on my property, and that Bettina Pleshette was killed with that."

"I am," I heard Evan Morrison say and I tensed in amazement. "How did you know? She had a wound consistent with an arrow being shot in her back. So you were here Saturday night when Bettina Pleshette was killed in your woods. Were you here alone?"

I couldn't hear Shotgun's reply.

"Oh," said Detective Morrison. "You're saying he was here that night, was he? I find it odd that you would say that, Mr. Marriott, because his mother says he was with her. What does *he* say? His own story is he can't remember where he was but he's a real slippery character. *And* he owns a bow and arrow, as I'm sure you know."

"Oh shit!" said a voice behind me. My body jerked in shock and I almost fell off the steps. Someone had come into the room and crept up behind me with astonishing stealth. I turned my head and saw it was a gangling youth, well over six feet tall. He was wearing denim shorts, a sweatshirt, and his long and extremely hairy legs ended in giant Timberland boots. Tufts of blond hair sprouted from beneath a cap turned back to front framing rosy cheeks and piercing blue eyes. One look at his face told me he was related to Franny Cook. The fine beautiful bone structure of his face was identical to hers.

"Who are you?" His question was blunt and sounded almost rude.

"Who are *you?*" I retaliated.

"I'm the guy he's just been talking about. I work for Shotgun. You found that listening hole, huh?" He grinned at me. "Cool, isn't it? Shotgun had an under-floor hot-air system put in last year and you get this flow-through of sound in quite a few of the rooms. Then he changed the ducts and forgot to fill in the ones in the rooms upstairs. You got to be standing over by the window, though."

"Who *are* you?" I descended the steps slowly. I was angry at being discovered spying by a teenager who seemed to think he had more right to be there than I did.

"Dumpster." He wiped his hand on his shorts and held it out to me.

What kind of a name was that? I shook his hand and smiled. "I'm Lee, and I'm also going to be working for Shotgun Marriott, on his book. What do you do for him?"

"Caretaker. Chop his wood. Mow his lawns. Check out his trees, blow his leaves, plow his driveway in winter. Plus I fish for him and bring him venison. Poor guy, he's been in a pretty bad way these last couple of days, let me tell you."

"You knew Sean?"

"Sure. I work here, don't I? Nice guy. Shy, like a rabbit. Scared of everything."

"What do you suppose he was doing out in the woods in the middle of the night he was killed?"

He hesitated, looking at me with suspicion for a moment but then he shrugged.

"Taking a walk. One thing he wasn't scared of was being out in the woods. He knew every inch of them. I'd find him out there all hours, rain or shine, wandering about on his own, reading po-etry and shit. Once, when his dad was away, Sean had a guy to stay. He was, like, you know, and the guy was one of *his* type, and he used to take him out to the woods. I stayed well away. I came across 'em lying on the beach buck naked and I ran a mile. I mean they can do what they want long as they don't do it to *me*!"

"So you've got to be related to Franny Cook," I said. "You look just like her."

"You know my mom?" He smiled and seemed to visibly relax.

I nodded. "Rufus introduced us. She's a terrific person, and your baby sister."

"She's not my sister," he said quickly.

"You have the same mother."

"Yeah, we do," he conceded. "But, like, I'm part of her old family. Eliza's her new family."

I thought I caught a note of resentment in his voice.

"Were you here those nights—when Sean died, and the other . . . ?"

"Why do you want to know?" He eyed me warily.

I shrugged as if to indicate no particular reason. But if he wanted to tell me, I was all ears. I needed to make this kid my friend if he'd been close to the action.

"Sure I was here," he said slowly. "Sean had gone to the city the night before he was killed. That's where he had his real life if you ask me. Out here he was too much in his father's shadow. He didn't like being the son of a rock musician, a *famous* rock musician."

"Did they get along?"

"No, but it was Sean's fault. I don't think he took the time to figure out that his father really was a nice guy. He had it fixed in his head that he was never going to measure up to what his father wanted him to be, but Shotgun used to tell me how it was cool with him that Sean was gay. He just wanted Sean to be happy. I tell you, I'd trade Shotgun as *my* father any day of the week."

"So, did Shotgun know Sean was in the city?"

"Who knows? They didn't communicate. All I know is that he was expecting this woman who kept calling him about his book to come and see him and then he called and canceled her."

I stared at him. "How do you know this?"

"I was right outside the door, I heard him on the phone with her. He had me putting up more shelves for his cookbooks in the kitchen and I was coming and going from the stables, bringing in the wood. I had so much to do during the day, I couldn't get to it until the evening and Shotgun doesn't care if I work at night. Cookbooks! Jesus! Guy fancies himself as a gourmet chef or what?"

I was about to quiz him further about the night Bettina was killed when I heard movement above us, footsteps crossing the room. Dumpster's arrival had curtailed my eavesdropping and I realized I'd missed the rest of Detective Morrison's interview.

A few seconds later the door opened and Shotgun Marriott walked into the room. He stopped dead, surprised to see Dumpster.

"The detective's out there?" Dumpster asked him.

"It's okay, he just left," said Shotgun and then held out his hand to me.

"Christopher Marriott. How are you? Sorry I've kept you waiting."

I recognized him from his photographs and the extensive television coverage when the dead groupie had been found in his room—but only just. The curly dirty blond hair that had flopped over his collar fourteen years ago was now shorn and fashionably layered to a crop of almost military severity. His face, lean and somehow rather poetic, had now acquired a certain cragginess and, until I saw it at such close quarters, I hadn't realized it was such a noble face. He had a long straight nose, slightly pointed like a fox, and a very sensuous wide mouth with, I noted, a trace of a mustache snaking above it as if he hadn't shaved properly. But his eyes were what arrested me the most. They were hooded with perfectly arched eyebrows high above them and they appeared to be mocking me.

But then he smiled suddenly and the five-o'clock shadow around his jaw line that had given him a sardonic, and faintly piratical, appearance seemed to recede.

"Dumpster, I despair of you sometimes," he said. "Couldn't you even have offered her a cup of tea? You know your way around my kitchen better than I do."

"Oh, I didn't need anything," I began as Dumpster mumbled an apology and shuffled out of the room, ducking as he went through the door.

"He always does that," said Shotgun, "even when he doesn't need to, I've noticed. I think he must have hit his head once too often when the door wasn't high enough to accommodate him."

"He is awfully tall," I said.

"He was a basketball star, so I understand—at school, when he lived in New York City. He could just reach up and dunk the ball in the net. Hence the name."

I looked blank.

"Well, okay, it was Dunkster originally."

Now I was even more confused.

"He *dunked* the ball, you know, slam dunk?" Shotgun raised one of his own long arms in the air and mimed dropping a ball in the net. "So first it was Dunkster and then he told me it got changed to Dumpster when his mother started throwing fits about the state of his bedroom."

I finally got it and smiled. "It's a good nickname. Speaking of names—"

"What are you going to call me? Don't worry, everyone has the same problem. I'm Shotgun to the media and always will be but I'm Kip to my friends. 'Christopher' is a bit formal. Could you live with 'Kip'?"

"If you'll call me Lee," I said. "My name's Nathalie but it's the same thing—too formal. What did Bettina call you?" I couldn't resist asking.

He looked at me in surprise. "She didn't call me anything. I never met her. Never even spoke to her apart from a few quick phone calls brushing her off."

"Oh," I said, "I heard she'd been around here for a week or two."

"Well, yes, I heard that too and she did talk to Sean. He was pretty anxious that I talk to her but the thing is I never liked the sound of her. I hope she wasn't one of your greatest friends?"

I shook my head.

"You see, it wasn't the first time I'd heard about her. She wanted to do a book with me a few years ago and I checked her out with a few people. She sounded altogether too pushy, not my kind of person—and in any case I didn't want to do a book *then*. But even recently—when I started thinking seriously about telling my story—I discounted her. I just didn't realize *how* pushy she was. I told my people to rule her out when we were drawing up a list of possible ghostwriters but that didn't deter her. She kept asking to meet me and then she came out here and started calling me."

"Have you told Detective Morrison all this?" I asked Shotgun. Of course, now that he'd suggested I call him Kip, I found I could only think of him as Shotgun.

"Till I'm blue in the face but he doesn't believe me. The trouble is I *was* expecting her the night Sean was killed. I thought if I told her face to face that I didn't want her to write my book, it might actually sink in and I could get rid of her once and for all."

Be careful what you wish for, I thought. Someone *had* got rid of her once and for all.

"But I canceled her," he went on. "I just couldn't face it. The problem was, for some reason, I never told Detective Morrison that the first time he interviewed me and this left him with the impression that I was waiting for her but she never showed up. Whereas in fact I lied by omission. Purely an oversight. But of course he doesn't see it that way. Anyway, look, I'm truly sorry you've walked into the middle of this."

"Listen," I said quickly, "*I'm* the one who's sorry. I'm only here because my agent told me to come. I'm afraid she's the same agent Bettina had. I couldn't believe it when she said you still wanted to do the book. I'll go now."

"No." He was on his feet with his hand out to stop me. "She was right, Miss Ten Percent. I do want to do the book."

"It's fifteen percent actually," I said.

"They'll bleed you white!" he said with a grim smile. "Anyway, now I've made up my mind to do it, I shouldn't let anything get in my way. There's a story I really want to tell in this book and I'm not getting any younger. If I put it off any longer, I'll never do it. Besides"—he turned away from me—"it'll help take my mind off all of this. Every second I'm alone, I start thinking about Sean. I know I have to mourn but I also know that someday I'm going to have to get past this. The truth is, if you'd agree to start work on the book, you'd be helping me"—he hesitated and looked away for a second—"more than you could possibly know.

"Now what can I get you?" He stood up suddenly and I could see he was embarrassed at having shown me how needy he was. "Nice cup of tea, coffee? I've got a secret stash of Bourbon biscuits and Jaffa cakes in the kitchen, or maybe you'd like a Marmite sandwich? We can pretend we're back in London."

"That would be great," I said, "but there's something I don't quite understand."

"What's that?"

"You're talking like I already have the job and I know my agent has already been discussing terms but don't you want to ask me a few questions before you make up your mind?"

"I've already made up my mind," he said, smiling now. "Don't worry, I did my homework. They gave me your name and just like with Bettina, I checked you out too. I called a few people back in England and I liked what I heard. You did an old girlfriend of mine." He mentioned the name of an actress whose lifestyle book I had helped put together a couple of years ago. "She said you'd be perfect, that you'd be very good for me. And as I just said, I want to get on with the book but look, if you're having second thoughts, I'd understand completely. Wouldn't blame you for a second."

I'd been having second thoughts, all right. And third, fourth, and fifth thoughts. Driving through the woods to his house had terrified me. What if the killer came back one night after the police search had been exhausted and Detective Morrison had pulled his men from the area to work another crime? What if I had to work late here with Shotgun and then drive home alone? Did I *really* need this job? It wasn't as if Bettina was still in the running as my rival so what did I have to prove?

But having met him, I knew that I had to tell Shotgun Marriott's story for him for a very simple reason.

I liked him.

He interested me. I wanted to know how he had managed not to become just another aging rocker, desperately trying to hang on to the image of his glory years. I liked his style. He was wearing a beautiful pale blue linen shirt with the sleeves casually rolled up to the elbow, and a pair of well-cut beige corduroys resting gently on his slim hips with the help of a brown leather belt, Italian and expensive, I guessed, like his shoes. He was a man approaching sixty making no attempt to disguise his age yet he looked both elegant and relaxed.

I wanted to know about his marriage to the control freak I had met at the Old Stone Market. I wanted to know what his son had been like and why they had led such a separate existence way out here on the East End of Long Island. I wanted to know what had really happened that night a groupie had been found dead in his bedroom and I was sure when he had spoken about "a story" he "really wanted to tell" he was referring to this.

But most of all I wanted to know about *him*. I realized with a start, having spent only a few minutes in his company, that I wanted to help him.

"I'd love to do your book," I said. "I can start whenever you want."

"That's fabulous!" The slight frown on his face, the only visible sign of the considerable strain he was under, disappeared for a second and he smiled at me in obvious relief. "That really is incredibly kind. Now, follow me to the kitchen while I go and make us a pot of tea. This way." He guided me through an archway. "The kitchen's a bit of a trek, I'm afraid. Thank God, the detective's gone although I fear he'll be back—and sooner rather than later, I expect. Do you know what his first question was for me when I'd identified Sean's body? *Why do they call you Shotgun?* My son's in the morgue, killed with a bullet from a shotgun, and he has to ask that."

Of course, now that he'd brought it up, I too was curious to know why he was called Shotgun.

"Well, I'm afraid it was because I was a pretty good shot in my youth and the rest of the band found this out," he said, reading my mind. "They used to unearth details of what they called my posh background and taunt me with them. So when our then manager said we had to come up with a better name for me than Kip Marriott—too wet and weedy for a hell-raising rock 'n' roll singer apparently—we went for Shotgun. I liked it because it had a kind of bluesy feel to it, you know, like Sonny Boy Williamson or Muddy Waters but our manager felt it had sexual connotations and there was a good publicity angle there."

And did it? I wondered.

"Anyway, I'm afraid I let Detective Morrison have the sexual version." He made a face to show what he thought of Evan Morrison. "I rather felt he was the type to appreciate it."

We had arrived at the kitchen and I was astonished. It was a bit like standing in a dungeon in which someone had placed an industrial-size stove and state-of-the-art stainless-steel appliances and flooded them with pools of recessed lighting. Hanging above the stove, a row of copper pans cast a reddish-brown metallic glint over the area. Several pewter tankards were lined up on the granite countertop. The floor was old flagstones and the walls behind the rows of glass-fronted cabinets also appeared to be stone. The overall effect may have been a touch gloomy, and I'm never very comfortable in those minimalist kitchens where absolutely nothing is left out on the surface, but it was certainly dramatic. I was wondering where the wooden shelves Dumpster was making were going to go when Shotgun pulled open a tall stainless-steel door to reveal a walk-in larder complete with wall-to-wall pine racking. The way the items were stacked floor-to-ceiling reminded me of Franny's store. Long planks of pine were propped against the far wall, evidence of Dumpster's industry.

"Lapsang souchong or PG Tips?" he asked me.

"PG Tips," I said, "always!"

He laughed. "Great minds think alike. Shortbread from Fortnum and Mason, Bourbons, or ginger nuts? I made the ginger nuts myself."

"Well, bring them on," I said. "This is quite a kitchen. I almost feel like I'm standing in a castle. Tell me how you came to find such an English house out here."

"I didn't so much find it as bring it with me," he said. "And you've hit the nail on the head about the castle. I grew up in one and in parts of the house, I've tried to re-create it. I've even given its name to this house: Mallaby."

"Did you really grow up in a castle?"

"Well, okay, it wasn't really a castle but it felt like one. It was a rambling slate manor on the edge of the Yorkshire moors, an old farmhouse with bits added on to it, but it had a tower at one end and there was a wide stream surrounding three-quarters of it that felt like a moat. I always thought of it as a castle."

"I don't really know Yorkshire," I said. "I grew up in London and I've lived there ever since."

"Oh, you're a 'townie,' poor thing." He was unplugging an electric kettle and pouring boiling water into the teapot. "I'm a country boy, in fact I was a nursling of the moors, filling my little lungs with the bracing air of the north wind every day. It's probably why I'm drawn to the bleakness of the Atlantic coast here."

"I didn't think the Hamptons were supposed to be bleak," I said.

"Try being here in February," he said darkly, "which you might well be once you get stuck into my book. Anyway, the house—it started with the central bit. Some tycoon from Ohio built himself a folly—a Norman tower. When I first came out here to look for a place, the real estate brokers couldn't wait to show it to me because they said it was English. Well, it was no more English than they were but it gave me an idea. I loved the isolation of the property, it was exactly what I was looking for, set way back here in the woods. I thought whatever the tycoon started, I could finish but I knew I'd never be able to re-create an old house by building it."

"Well, I don't know how you managed it," I said, "but this house really does seem old. It feels like it was built hundreds of years ago."

"That's because it was," he said. "Instead of getting a builder I hired a structural mover. They move houses lock, stock, and barrel from one place to another. We scoured New England and I bought two houses, each over three hundred years old, and then we moved them here and placed them either side of the folly."

As I followed him out of the kitchen, I was happy to see the strain on his face was lifted, if only temporarily, by his enthusiasm in explaining the house's restoration to me. In my mind, I started to plan a chapter that would deal with his experiences in putting together his house and then almost immediately I started to wonder how much control he would allow me in the structure of the book. Some subjects allowed me a free rein, others thought they knew exactly how to tell their story. Which they didn't— otherwise why would they hire me?

I heard voices up ahead of us. As we emerged from the gloom of the long corridor into the great hall Detective Morrison came toward Shotgun. He wasn't alone. Behind him were two other cops and through the windows I could see police cars lined up down the drive.

Evan Morrison was holding a shotgun.

I saw Shotgun's hands clench by his sides but his voice gave no sign of tension.

"Detective Morrison, back so soon?"

"Good afternoon, Mr. Marriott. This shotgun was found yesterday, buried in the sand on the beach just beyond your property. As you will see, it's a Purdey."

"So it is," said Shotgun. He wasn't looking at Detective Morrison. He was staring through the open front door as if he were fixated on something at the far end of his driveway.

"When I interviewed you the first time a few days ago, Mr. Marriott . . ." Evan Morrison was advancing toward him and as he did so Shotgun backed away, still without looking at the detective. They were performing a kind of bizarre dance around Shotgun's hallway. "I asked you if you owned a shotgun and you said you owned a Purdey twelve bore. You showed me where you kept it, we examined it and determined it had not been fired. What you omitted to mention was that it was one of a matching pair that was made by Purdey's for your father in 1937. When we found this gun"—he held it aloft—"naturally we ran the serial number past Purdey's in London and when I got back just now I found they had come back to us with the details. You never told us it was one of a pair."

What Detective Morrison said next gave me such a shock I felt as if I had been blasted by a shotgun myself.

"Christopher Marriott, I am arresting you for the murder of Bettina Pleshette. You have the right to remain silent. If you give up the right to remain silent, anything you say can and will be used against you in a court of law. You have the right to speak with an attorney and—"

I had only ever heard these words spoken in the movies and I watched in horror as an officer holding handcuffs stepped forward to stand beside Shotgun, who stepped away from them with his palms held high.

"You heard what the man said." He whipped out his cell phone. "I have the right to speak with an attorney before you can come up with any more fantastic scenarios. If you ever think about writing fiction, Lee"—he turned to me—"book in for a lesson with Detective Morrison here. He seems to have a highly inventive streak in him."

He made his call, then they cuffed him and took him outside to one of the waiting cars. As I followed them in the Phillionaire's Jeep, I watched the back of his head outlined in the rear window of the police car and saw it sink lower and lower as we drove slowly down the dirt track to Cranberry Hole Road.

CHAPTER 5

ON THE WAY BACK TO THE CABIN I WAS SO CON-sumed with worry about Shotgun that I paid no attention to the road. Pretty soon I had totally lost my way and eventually I found myself at the end of a spit of land with water on all sides. I got out of the car and went to lean against a rock on the beach. The sun was beginning to go down across the bay in a huge ball of crimson and for a while I drank in the breathtaking view. Normally if I stare long enough at water it calms me and enables me to empty my mind but this evening the astonishing beauty just seemed treacherous. I watched fishermen coming in across the bay, approaching the launching pad to my right, and I wondered if Sean had been tossed from a boat. Were there more bodies in these little skiffs approaching the harbor, lying in the bottom beside the catch of the day?

Of course there weren't! Why did I do this to myself? Why did I always have to imagine the darkest possible scenario? To force myself to get a grip, I checked my cell phone messages. There was one from Rufus that seemed to end in midair, saying he couldn't meet me tonight because he had to go to Riverhead to get his truck serviced and wouldn't be back until late. He'd see me in the morning at Franny's for breakfast at seven thirty and would I please—and then nothing. There was a very simple reason for this. Now that I came to think of it, I had not recharged my battery for at least two days—another sure sign I was losing it.

The mention of breakfast made me realize that after Franny warned me off paying her extortionate prices at the Old Stone Market, I still didn't have anything to eat for supper. It was getting dark and I'd already lost my way once so I approached a fisherman and asked for directions to the market. When I got there, Franny wasn't around but a Latino with the soulful brown eyes of a Labrador was lurking behind the counter. He told me his name was Jesus so I pointed at myself and said "Lee Bartholomew," and he clapped his hands in apparent delight and asked how he could help me. I remembered what Franny had said about the cooked dinners and within minutes I was driving home with a steaming aluminum foil dish containing a chicken pot pie.

Driving back to the cabin, I was a little nervous going along Cranberry Hole Road because it was a lonely stretch and until that moment it hadn't dawned on me just how isolated the cabin was. I was mildly comforted by the fact that Rufus was staying in the pool house just a short walk up the beach. But what about the nights when he stayed at a girlfriend's?

An unfamiliar light was blinking in the dark as I walked in and because I'm such a panic princess my immediate thought was that I'd set off some kind of alarm. Then I flicked a switch and saw it was the answering machine by the phone. I sat at the island and chomped away on my chicken pot pie ("I make," Jesus had announced with pride on handing it to me and I had to admit it was delicious), while I wondered whether or not to pick up the Phillionaire's messages. They had to be for Phil, I reasoned, because this was his retreat. Anyone wanting me would call my cell phone. But unless I passed them on, Phil wouldn't get these messages for quite a long time. What if they were urgent?

Procrastination was another of my special talents so of course

I had a shower in order to have more time to consider my options and while I was rejoicing in the force of the water pressure and the way it sweetly kneaded my shoulder muscles, the phone rang again. I heard my mother's voice.

"For God's sake, Lee, where on earth are you? This is the second message I've left."

There was an abrupt *click* and she was gone before I could pick up.

In fact both of the previous messages were for me and they were back to front. The first made me sit down suddenly on the bed.

"Hi. It's me. I've been texting you but you haven't come back to me. I've just seen your mother and she gave me this number. Anyway, I thought I'd give you a call."

That was it. Tommy was never much good on the telephone at the best of times and this kind of abrupt message was typical. The idiot had probably been texting me on the mobile I'd left in London. I switched off the tape quickly. The sound of his voice was enough to make me throw a wobbly in any case but hearing it so uncharacteristically gloomy made it even worse.

Suddenly I remembered my mother saying she had called before.

When I turned the machine back on I had to listen to Tommy's message again and then my mother began to speak. And speak and speak, until I began to wonder if she'd ever shut up. I wished it had been the reverse. I wished it had been Tommy who had left me a long and rambling message, using up most of the tape, and my mother who had shut up after three sentences.

"Lee, darling." Uh-oh, this was a bad sign. Her use of "darling" usually meant she wanted me to do something. "Phil gave me this number because I can't raise you on your cell phone. You've turned it off or something. We're in London, on our way to

Venice, and you just will not *believe* the state of Blenheim Crescent. It's a complete and utter pigsty and I cannot imagine what induced you to let Cath stay here. She's reduced the place to a kind of squalling day care center. We walked in on a gaggle of mothers and screaming babies. I just cannot imagine what Phil must have thought."

This was a bit rich! First of all it was my mother who had suggested Cath Clark and her boyfriend Sgt. Richie Cross, together with their baby Marcus, move into our house in Notting Hill Gate while their flat in nearby Shepherd's Bush was being renovated. Cath and I had been friends since we were kids, growing up in the same neighborhood, going to school together. We'd always had our designated roles. I was the hopeless one—the neurotic, willful, self-indulgent one who treated Tommy badly and didn't deserve him. Cath was the caring, responsible rock who always stood by me and gave me advice on how to get through life without alienating absolutely everyone.

Of course my mother has always thought Cath was completely wonderful and whenever she was in despair over my antisocial ways, Cath's name would be invoked as a paragon of everything she would wish for in a daughter. Now don't get me wrong, I have always adored Cath and she is my best friend, no question. But recently I have begun to feel that her judgment of me can be a little unfair. I just don't think I am as bad as she makes out. I suspect that under the surface Cath might just be as neurotic as I am and the only difference is that I am quite upfront about it whereas she pretends her life is eternally perfect.

Well, it isn't. Cath has been in and out of rehab for a drinking problem that, until quite recently, she kept secret from me.

"I was very good about it, darling," my mother's voice continued, "because she is your friend but I do think you might call her and have a word. And there's another thing. Why haven't you been in touch with poor Tommy? He didn't have the slightest clue you were even in America. Phil and I came back from the theater one night and found him sitting at the kitchen table with Cath. He was pretty far gone, I'm afraid. At least half a bottle of whiskey and before you say a word, Cath didn't touch a drop. It seems he's lost his job at the BBC and he doesn't know what to do with himself. His first thought was to come and tell you about it. You can imagine how utterly miserable he felt when he discovered you'd gone to America without telling him."

Why should I tell him? He was the one who called off the wedding.

"But before you jump on a plane and come rushing back to him—" my mother continued. She was joking, right?—"let me tell you that Cath was doing a fine job of consoling him. She really is the kindest person and—"

I wasn't sure I liked the sound of this. A while ago, in an unguarded moment and long before she'd got together with Richie, Cath had confessed to being in love with Tommy.

"—she told me you hadn't been in touch with her either. What is the matter with you, Lee? These people are closer to you than anyone and you appear to have just walked away from them."

Well, *hello!* There was the little question of the subject of my latest assignment being caught up in a murder investigation. Even if Tommy didn't grasp the significance of that, Cath was married to a detective, a *murder* detective, and if my mother had spared a moment to fill them in on where I stood work-wise then Cath would understand that I was probably a little preoccupied.

"Anyway," said my mother, "I gave them both your numbers so no doubt you'll be hearing from them. Now, Lee, what's happening with the construction of the beach house? Have you met the contractor yet? Have they cleared the ground? I want to know when they will be pouring the foundation."

I wasn't really listening. I was trying to work out why Tommy had not mentioned that he had lost his job in his message. He said he was calling after he'd seen my mother. I guessed what must have happened. He would not have wanted to admit he'd been fired in a message. Even if he'd reached me, I would probably have had to coax it out of him having heard in his voice that there was a problem.

I vaguely registered my mother droning on for another minute or two about her travel plans and when they would be returning and what she expected me to do about the beach house. Her voice followed me around the one-room cabin as I placed my plate in the dishwasher, switched off the lights, and turned down the bed. I would have an early night. I needed sleep to harness my energy to deal with the beach house and Tommy and Cath and what on earth I was going to do about my elusive assignment with Shotgun Marriott. Tucked up in bed, my thoughts turned to Tommy. I wondered if it was too late to call him. I switched on the light and dialed his number.

No reply.

It was three in the morning in London. Where was he? I left a quick message—"I'm sorry I wasn't here when you called. I'm sorry about your job"—and then, before I changed my mind—"I love you, Tommy." And then I hung up. Should I have mentioned that I knew he had lost his job? Should I have waited for him to tell me about it himself? How I wished it had been I rather than Cath who had been there to console him. But was it not a good sign that he had come around to tell me the news, an indication that maybe he did still see a future with me?

And then, as I switched off the light and the cabin was plunged into darkness, I saw a flicker of light outside. Suddenly I realized that there were no curtains or blinds on any of the windows. I got out of bed and crept through the darkness to the back of the cabin where I had seen the light and, peering through a window, I saw it came from the headlamps of a car in the distance along Cranberry Hole Road.

The car turned into my road and the headlamps were coming toward me. If the lights had still been on in the cabin I would have been clearly visible.

And then the headlamps went out. Whoever was out there had parked halfway down the dirt track to the cabin.

Was it Rufus? And if so, what did he want at ten thirty at night? Well, if it was, he would be here any second.

I grabbed my robe and sat huddled in it on the bed waiting for a knock on the door but it never came. I waited for the sound of the car starting up and driving away but after a while I found that the sheer silence all around me unnerved me more than anything. I went around to all the windows checking that they were firmly locked and I turned the key in the door. Then I crept back to bed and reached for the TV remote.

I watched *Letterman,* aware that the flickering of the TV screen must be visible through the window to the person in the car outside. And finally, about twenty minutes later, I heard the sound of the engine and, peering through the darkness, I saw the car back up and drive away.

I lay awake for nearly an hour telling myself it was nothing to worry about. People probably turned down deserted dirt roads at ten thirty at night and parked for half an hour all the time out here in the Hamptons. I was a city girl, what did I know of the habits of beach folk?

The next morning I overslept and woke up to find the television still blaring into the room. I didn't get to the Old Stone Market till eight o'clock and Rufus was just leaving.

"What happened to you?" he called from his truck. "I can't hang around now. I'm late for work. Call me later."

"Wait!" I yelled at him and rushed over to tell him about the parked car.

"Kids probably," he said, very matter of fact, "teenagers. Where else they got to go to make out?"

Then he was gone, leaving me feeling somewhat relieved. It was a perfectly reasonable explanation, after all. I just had this weird instinct that it wasn't the right one.

Inside the store Jesus was serving breakfast to a couple of construction workers.

"Your pie was delicious," I told him and he beamed.

"Franny, she in back." He nodded his head toward the far room.

I found Franny wandering around the shelves with a clipboard in her hand.

"Hi," she said, "you see Rufus? He waited forever for you."

"I overslept," I said.

"He asked me out on a date," she said. Her head was down and she was studying the shelves so I couldn't see her face.

Well, this was interesting. "Did you say yes?"

"He's gotta be ten years younger than I am."

"So you said no."

"I said if he found me a babysitter, he could take me out for a drink tonight." She looked at me sideways. "I told him you might be a good bet."

"He didn't say anything about it," I said.

"Oh." She sounded disappointed.

I felt a tiny bit of resentment that she should take it for granted that I would help her out but I decided to ignore it.

"I expect I could come over for an hour or two. What time?"

I was totally unprepared for her long arms reaching out to envelop me in a hug. My natural loner's reserve kicked in and I backed away from her. I wasn't the most tactile person until I'd had time to really get to know someone.

But she didn't seem to notice my lack of response. "*Thank you!*" she said. "I really do need to get out. You have no idea. This place is beginning to get me down. See, I'm doing a stock check here and it depresses the hell out of me. It's always the same old boring things that sell—candy, potato chips, cookies, sodas, and you know the only things most people come in for?"

I shook my head.

"Cigarettes and the newspaper. I make a dime on a newspaper if I'm lucky and maybe eighty cents on a pack of cigarettes after I pay all the taxes. How can I raise Eliza on that? And I had such high hopes when I first took this place over. I hired Jesus because he was able to bring in all the Hispanic clientele—the construction workers and their families. They know him and they trust him. He cooks them the Mexican food they like and that's all fine, but the rest of the locals, they don't seem to be comfortable with me trying to bring the place into the twenty-first century. They don't like change, they want it the way my aunt used to have it when the most exciting thing you could buy was a bologna sandwich. Look at this"—she pointed to a row of packets in front of her—"sea salt from Brittany in France, sesame rice crackers, Thai noodles, anything out of the ordinary and it never moves off the shelves. Meanwhile I've got the New Yorkers coming in at weekends and turning up their noses because I don't have *enough* of what they want."

She kicked an apple on the floor.

"And that's another problem. People pick up the produce and drop it on the floor so it's bruised and then I can't sell it. You would not believe the amount of stuff I have to throw away. You can only buy cheese by the case not by the piece. I got a case of

Brie wholesale last week and so far I've only sold three pieces and it'll only last two weeks."

I was half listening to her. I was standing right by a notice board and I was intrigued by the ads for secondhand sewing machines, surfboards, garden equipment, and services as varied as psychic readings, house cleaning, and dog transportation to and from New York. There was one particular card that really caught my attention. It was turning brown with age and had clearly been hidden for some time by another card pinned over it. It was only because someone had torn a phone number off the card on top that two words could be read on the card underneath. WEDDING DRESSES. I lifted up the top card and read: SECONDHAND WEDDING DRESSES, ANTIQUE, DESIGNER, ALL SIZES, ALTERATIONS OFFERED. MARTHA FARRELL and then a phone number. An image of Sean Marriott's body lying on the beach in drenched white tulle flashed before me and I shivered.

Before I could ask who Martha Farrell was, Franny said: "So I hear they arrested Shotgun Marriott."

"News travels fast around here."

"My son told me. He says you were over there yesterday."

"I was," I said. "And I met Dumpster—and Evan Morrison," I added. "Why didn't you tell me your shoplifter was a detective?"

Franny didn't say anything so I persisted. "Why do you let him get away with it? You told me it wasn't the first time he'd done it."

Still she said nothing.

"*Franny!* Just because he's a cop—"

"Exactly!" she said, suddenly turning on me. "It's *because* he's a cop."

"I don't get it," I said.

She sighed and gestured for me to sit down with her on one of the benches at the long table in the back room. "I'll tell you because you seem like a nice person and Lord knows I need to talk to someone. Plus Rufus says you're okay. But I'd appreciate it if you'd keep what I'm about to tell you to yourself."

"I won't say a word," I said, wondering what was coming.

"You met my son, Dumpster?" she said. "Well, it's because of him that I go along with Evan Morrison. When I got together with Dumpster's dad, I was just a kid and I thought living in the city was so exciting. But then when it came to raising Dumpster as a single parent, it became a little too exciting. I moved Dumpster back here because he had a problem. He was doing so many drugs, there was no way I could control him. There was a time when he could have had a real future in basketball but he got in with some delinquents at his school and he went downhill from there."

"Wasn't his father any help?"

She stared at me. "You have to be kidding. I don't even know where he is anymore. Anyway, I don't know why I thought it would be any better out here. We hadn't been back five minutes before Dumpster started hanging out with some Colombians in Montauk. Evan Morrison busted them dealing cocaine in a parking lot—it was all tied in to a homicide investigation. He did a deal with me over Dumpster. In exchange for keeping Dumpster's name out of it, Dumpster had to become his informant."

Now it was my turn to stare. "What does that mean exactly?"

"He's supposed to rat on his friends. Any drug action he sees, he's supposed to tell Detective Morrison who passes it on to the narcs. Morrison's after this dealer who allegedly killed one of his clients when he couldn't pay for his supply and Morrison thinks Dumpster might get him a lead."

"And Dumpster works for Shotgun."

"And Shotgun's been arrested," said Franny. "I see where you're going with this but there's two things you should know.

Dumpster worships Shotgun Marriott. There's no way he'd sell him out even if he was standing right beside that woman when Shotgun killed her. And the second thing is that Dumpster was here with me both nights, when Sean was killed *and* that woman."

"All night? Her name was Bettina Pleshette, by the way."

"All night." Franny tapped the table for emphasis. "He wasn't working for Shotgun those nights."

"Not at all?"

She shook her head.

Well, this didn't match what Dumpster had told me about the night Sean was killed. I had distinctly heard him say he was putting up shelves for Shotgun that night and had overheard Shotgun canceling Bettina. And what Shotgun had said later had confirmed this. So if Franny wasn't telling the truth about that night—maybe she was lying about the next one, when Bettina was killed. She wanted to protect her son and that was perfectly understandable but it would only complicate matters if she lied.

"Well, if he wasn't there," I said, "how can he give Shotgun an alibi?"

She seemed thrown by that. "I guess he can't," she said slowly, "but I know he wouldn't say anything about Shotgun that would get him in trouble. If they nail Shotgun Marriott for that woman's murder, it's not going to be on account of anything Dumpster said."

Bettina was still *that woman,* I noticed. I wondered why.

"So what kind of stuff does Dumpster give Detective Morrison—as his informant?"

Franny grinned. "As little as possible. And never about anyone he likes. He has to be very careful because if those Colombians get to hear that he's an informant, I dread to think what they might do to him. So you'll keep quiet about it, right?"

I nodded.

She glanced at me. "What did you make of Shotgun?"

"I liked him," I said. "So you told Detective Morrison that your son was here with you?"

"Of course," she said, "because he was."

"And that's the story Dumpster gave to the detective about himself?"

She looked a little worried. "I wasn't there when he spoke to him but that's what he would have said, isn't it? Because it's the truth."

I gave up. She was sticking to her story so I just shrugged and said, "Now what time do you want me here this evening—for when you go out with Rufus?"

"Around seven would be great," said Franny, and as I went out the door she called after me, "I really appreciate you doing this for me, by the way. I mean *really* appreciate it."

When I went back that evening Rufus was already there, lurking downstairs in the store.

"Thanks for this," he said, giving a sheepish look. "Did you hear about Shotgun?"

"That he was arrested?" I asked. "I was there."

"Well, he'll be out on bail soon. It'll be no sweat to him to post a million bucks bail."

"Wow!" I was impressed. "By the way, thanks for those directions. You were right, I'd never have found the place without them."

"Sure," he said. "So, you're finding your way around okay?"

"I am. Tell me, have you spoken to your dad?"

"He called last night. He told me you got the job of overseeing the construction. You must be a real saint. Vanessa asked me to take care of it a while back but I passed. The last thing I want is to be responsible for a bunch of construction guys who are never going to show up. Whatever made you agree to do it?"

"Because I'm an idiot," I said. "I haven't even been by the site. Maybe we could go over there together tomorrow?"

"And maybe we couldn't." He laughed. "What's with the 'we'? You're not going to rope me in that easily."

"Well then, maybe you won't be able to rope me in for babysitting tonight."

"What's that?" Franny stood in the doorway at the bottom of the staircase. "Are you backing out already, Lee?"

I didn't answer her because when I turned to look at her, I was too knocked out to speak. She looked stunning. She had on a simple black linen shift that must have cost real money. It was sleeveless and when she turned, I saw it plunged to a deep V in the back. The dress ended midthigh and she was wearing black rope sandals with a three-inch wedge. She towered above Rufus and for an instant he looked a little nervous.

"I've fed her and now she's asleep," Franny told me. "I'm going to close the store so you can go upstairs and make yourself at home. I've left you one of Jesus's lasagnas to heat up in the microwave. You haven't lived till you've tasted it, although of course I taught him everything he knows about cooking. She's going to need feeding at around ten but I'll be back way before then." I saw Rufus frown a little. Was he hoping to score on the first date? "Here's my cell phone number. Call me if you have a problem. So Roof, your truck or mine?"

I watched her hitch her dress up almost to her crotch as she hiked her long legs into Rufus's passenger seat. It was only when they had been gone at least five minutes that I noticed she had left her cell phone sitting on the counter by the cash register.

I was slightly shocked that Franny hadn't taken me upstairs and shown me what to do with Eliza. Presumably I was just meant to sit there while she slept and there would be nothing else to do until Franny came back. Feeling a little apprehensive, I turned the OPEN sign hanging on the door to CLOSED—she hadn't even done that—and crept up the stairs to the apartment above.

It was tiny, only two rooms, and neither of them was particularly big. I saw that Franny and Eliza slept in the same room. Franny had a queen-size bed that took up most of the space. Crammed into the narrow channel between the bed and the wall, presumably so Franny could reach out to Eliza without getting out of bed, was Eliza's cot, dwarfed by packets of diapers piled perilously high on a table beside it. I checked out the other room, which served as a kitchen/living room. It was marginally bigger than the bedroom with the sink and a giant fridge against the far wall. I looked around for a cooker but saw only a microwave standing on the counter. There was a small table with two chairs and a sofa in front of a stack of electronic equipment comprising TV, DVD player, and other oblong boxes I couldn't immediately identify.

Two things were missing: a bathroom and Dumpster's bedroom.

I found the bathroom soon enough by opening a door to what I had thought was a closet at the top of the stairs. Actually, it *was* a closet but instead of housing coats or clothes, it contained a shower, a toilet, and one of those minuscule half-circle basins in which you can only wash one hand at a time unless you have unusually tiny paws. I turned back to the living room and realized with a sinking feeling that it was in fact a *sleep* sofa in the middle of the room and that's where Dumpster had to crash.

This was Franny's life. No wonder she wanted to get out. I stood between the two rooms and tried to imagine what it must be like to have to cope with a screaming baby and a teenage son playing video games in this confined space. After you'd spent a day trying to run a store where nobody appreciated what you were trying to do, after you'd undertaken such physically back-breaking tasks as chopping wood and mowing lawns—not to have even a tub in which to soak your aching muscles. What did she do to escape? Not for the first time did I appreciate how incredibly lucky I was to enjoy such relatively spacious accommodations—there was only me, after all—both here at the Phillionaire's cabin and especially in London where I had my parents' five-bedroom house to myself. And it was free. But then presumably so was this apartment, left to Franny by her aunt along with the store.

I was confronted with the biggest jar of mayonnaise I'd ever seen when I opened the refrigerator. In fact everything was jumbo size, the ketchup, the milk, the mustard, the jam, and I had to take them all out before I could get to my lasagna. I found it strange that there was no other food in the refrigerator so I investigated the freezer and found it full of pizzas and frozen TV dinners. I was depressed by the volume of Lean Cuisine meals that must be Franny's staple diet. She clearly only had time to cook fresh food for her customers. When she closed the store for the night, did she only have enough energy to haul herself up the stairs, put Eliza down, and throw a frozen dinner in the microwave before she fell asleep beside her baby?

And then, having opened the fridge and the freezer, it was as if I couldn't stop and I felt compelled to look in every cabinet and closet to see what other insights I could glean into Franny's world. But there was nothing out of the ordinary and most of the space in the kitchen was devoted to a mound of plastic bags containing Dumpster's paraphernalia and a pine chest in which I found a pathetically small pile of baby clothes together with little jars of applesauce.

Seeing these made me wonder where Franny kept her clothes

so I wandered back to the bedroom and opened the only door I could see. Franny's wardrobe seemed to imply a split personality. At one end of the closet were jeans and cutoffs and plaid shirts and sweatpants, all evidence of her outdoor life in the country. But at the other end was a small but exquisitely formed collection of fashion items, flirty "date" wear—little black dresses, tiny pencil skirts, frothy chiffon skirts, plaid miniskirts, leather pants, white jeans, lacy blouses, silk shirts. The labels alone were enough to make me draw breath. Ralph Lauren, Calvin Klein, Michael Kors, Donna Karan, and, even more impressive, Prada, Gucci, Jil Sander, and Moschino. I was up on these names—I had once ghosted a *Vogue* editor's fashion manual—and I knew what you had to pay for this kind of stuff. And underneath, row upon row of stilettos edged out the pathetic assortment of sneakers and work boots pushed to one side on the floor of the closet. Jimmy Choo, Manolo Blahnik, Chanel. Where had Franny got the money for high-end shoes like these?

Hidden in a corner was a square vanity case—Louis Vuitton, what else? I have worked hard to overcome my many vices but I don't seem to have much luck giving up snooping. I tell myself it's part and parcel of what I do, that I need to have an inquiring mind and anyway, is nosiness in fact a vice?

I flipped up the lid of the vanity case expecting to see expensive items of makeup but instead I found a pile of photographs. They were all of Franny, sometimes alone and sometimes with a well-groomed, wealthy-looking man, and not always the same one. In some of the pictures she appeared to be modeling, posing in front of a fancy car or a lake or some other exotic backdrop. Suddenly I understood that Franny had had another life in the recent past, before Eliza had been born, before she had decided to leave it all behind and move out here and try and turn a two-bit mom-and-pop convenience store into Dean & DeLuca. Had she in fact been a model? And who were her elegant escorts in the photographs?

I was so wrapped up in Franny's past I forgot I was supposed to be quiet. I replaced the photos, pushed the case back to where I had found it, and closed the closet door. With a bang.

What was I thinking? Eliza woke up gradually with a little shuffling in her cot and a whimper or two but within minutes she was thrashing around with both little arms and legs in the air, her crying increasing in volume. She stopped for a second when I leaned over the cot and peered at her, probably more out of surprise than anything else because as soon as she had got her breath back, she let rip once again. When she started to bawl, I picked her up and began to carry her around the tiny space of the apartment but she must have sensed I was nervous and unsure of what I was doing because she didn't stop crying.

I was bewildered when I laid her down on the changing table and discovered her diaper was neither wet nor soiled. Franny had said she had fed her so she couldn't be hungry. What could be wrong?

An hour later I was at my wits' end. Eliza's face was furious and desperate and a virulent shade of puce in color. I couldn't reach Franny because she'd left her cell phone behind, my mother was on her way to Venice and I couldn't think who on earth to call for baby advice—until all at once I had a brain wave and picked up Franny's phone.

Cath sounded befuddled with sleep to begin with and then she hurled abuse at me so loudly I almost dropped Eliza.

"Are you insane, Lee? It's one thirty in the morning. I was up with Marcus till about half an hour ago and I had just got back to sleep. You just don't think, do you? You're so self-absorbed, so self-indulgent, so sel"—she struggled for a second and came back with—"fish."

Well, she was right. I had completely forgotten London was five hours ahead. I was so used to picking up the phone and asking Cath for advice that I'd sort of imagined she was just around the corner as usual. I stumbled out an apology but Cath wasn't a particularly gracious woman. She was never one to brush aside your remorse and move on. She always had to make you suffer so I had to listen to more haranguing until in desperation I shifted the receiver and let her get an earful of Eliza's bawling.

When I got back on I cut her off quickly, said I knew exactly what she was going through with Marcus and then explained why, culminating in a plea for help.

"What do I *do*, Cath? Should I call a doctor? How can I get her back to sleep?"

"How long has she been crying?"

"Almost an hour."

"Is that all?" The scorn in Cath's voice made it sound as if Marcus cried for months on end. "No, I don't think you need to call the doctor just yet. Here's what I suggest, Lee, because I really don't want to get into this for too long. I need to get some sleep before it's time for Marcus's next feed. Think about it, at least you're going to be relieved later on. If you were the mother you wouldn't get off so lightly. Tell me, does this baby have a pram nearby?"

I remembered the baby carriage behind the cash register. "Yes, downstairs."

"Well, take her out in it for a while. Walk her up and down. The motion should get her back to sleep. I once took Marcus to Sainsbury's one night just before they closed and wheeled him up and down the aisles. Worked like a treat."

I thanked her profusely. I wanted to ask her how she was getting on in our house, what she had thought of the Phillionaire, I wanted to tell her about Shotgun and Franny and the little haven of paradise I'd found myself in at the beach. But most of all I wanted to ask her about Tommy.

It would all have to wait. Cath was right, and my mother had been too. I should have called Cath much earlier and maybe I should have let Tommy know I was going to America. But once again I defended my action—I hadn't canceled the wedding, he had. I might have done it unconsciously but I had wanted to punish him. I had wanted him to worry about me, to miss me. I had wanted him to be the one to seek me out—and he had but he had found Cath instead and I had no one to blame but myself.

Cath's plan worked a treat for Eliza as well as Marcus. I wheeled her out of the store in the baby carriage and up and down the Old Stone Highway where the smell of burning charcoal wafted tantalizingly from every backyard I passed and reminded me that Jesus's lasagna was waiting for me.

When we returned twenty minutes later, I knew enough to leave Eliza asleep in her pram downstairs while I rushed upstairs to put the lasagna in the microwave. Franny's extensive cable package beckoned—how much did *that* cost?—and I slumped in front of the TV, shoveled pasta into my mouth, and wondered what I'd do if Franny didn't come back till the middle of the night and I had to deal with another of Eliza's tantrums. Maybe next time I'd wheel her all the way to the beach and walk her home to my cabin by the light of the moon.

Taking my responsibilities seriously, I turned the TV down from time to time to see if she was crying. Nothing. Not a peep. Until eventually I decided to go down and see if she was still breathing.

I didn't find out whether she was or not, because the door to the Old Stone Market was wide open and the pram was gone.

HAVE NEVER MOVED SO FAST IN MY LIFE. I CHARGED out the door and skidded to an abrupt halt beside the white picket fence in front of the picnic tables where Franny served breakfast and lunch. A quick look up and down the Old Stone Highway confirmed my worst fears. There was no sign of Eliza, although I don't quite know what I expected to see—a six-month-old baby trotting down the middle of the road?

I didn't have a clue what to do. Should I call the police or go running around Stone Landing looking for her?

A car approached and I flagged it down.

"Have you seen a baby in a baby carriage?" I asked the startled driver who gawked at me suspiciously, as well he might given my demented state.

But his passenger leaned across him and said, "Well, we over-took a man pushing a baby carriage five minutes back. He's coming this way."

I thanked her and set off along the Old Stone Highway. I had been walking for about ten minutes and was about to despair when I turned a corner and ran straight into Scott Abernathy pushing a baby carriage. Eliza was fast asleep—but not for long. I snatched her up into my arms and screamed at Scott in a voice that even I could hear was shaking with hysteria.

"What are you *doing,* Scott? Just what do you think you are doing with this baby?"

"Hey, calm down." He reached to touch my arm and I literally jumped away from him. Eliza was awake now and staring at me, scrunching up her little face in that oh-so-familiar expression she adopted just as she was about to start bawling.

"I was taking her for a walk," he said. "Where's the harm in that? She was asleep, I was just giving her a little fresh air."

"But what gives *you* the right to just walk up and take her? Without telling anyone?"

"Well, what gives you?" he countered and that was when I remembered what Rufus had told me. Scott was Eliza's father. But he didn't know that I knew that.

"I'm babysitting her. Franny's out with——" I stopped. It didn't seem like the best idea to tell Scott Franny was on a date with his brother.

"I didn't know that, did I?" He sounded so reasonable. "I thought Franny was upstairs and she wouldn't mind."

"Well, she's not there," I repeated. "And the store's closed." As I said that I remembered that I hadn't locked the door behind me. In fact I'd left it wide open. Anyone could walk in and take something.

"I wasn't looking to buy anything," he said. "I needed to see Franny. She knows me. Pretty well, as a matter of fact."

The look on his face was close to a smirk and I wanted to hit him, but I restrained myself.

"But she never seems to be there," he went on. "Every time I go around there's no sign of her. What's she doing with the baby, I ask myself, out at all hours? I came by the night our parents had their dinky little ceremony and——"

I bristled silently. How dare he refer to my mother and Phil expressing their love for each other as a "dinky little ceremony."

"—admittedly it was late and I was pretty drunk but where on earth was she? There were no lights on and her truck was gone. Came back again the next night, same thing."

Well, *this* was interesting. Here was Franny insisting Dumpster had been home with her on the nights when Sean Marriott and Bettina were killed, and she hadn't even been here herself on either night. I thought about asking Scott if Dumpster had been there but then decided I didn't want to get into discussing Dumpster with Scott.

Instead I changed the subject. "I think the most important thing right now is to get Eliza home and then I think you should leave."

He threw his arms in the air in an angry gesture. "And I think you should stop being so snotty. I don't need you to tell me what to do."

He was right, of course, and that put me even more on the defensive. I wondered what on earth Franny had seen in him even if it had only been for one night. She must have been really drunk because to me he was repellent, son of the Phillionaire or not. He was so awkward, a collection of sharp angles from his curved nose and hunched shoulders to his outturned bony elbows and pigeon toes. And he had the body language to go with it. He didn't seem to be able to walk straight and he kept lurching much too close to me. I wondered how someone so seemingly uncontrolled could wield a scalpel with the precision required of a surgeon.

For some reason the image of a scalpel reminded me of his association with Bettina. Instead of an arrow flying through the air and piercing her heart, I imagined Scott plunging his scalpel into her aorta. I pictured him slicing her up into little pieces and then I stopped because the last thing I needed to do at this point was to indulge in my futile tendency to obsess about violence.

As for Bettina, I wasn't sure of my ground in talking about her with him. I had been eavesdropping when I overheard Detective Morrison tell Shotgun about Scott's dinner with her—but then it appeared most of East Hampton had seen them dining together at the Palm so presumably their date was common knowledge. I rocked Eliza who, wonder of wonders, was actually drifting off to sleep again, and looked at Scott, briefly flashing a prayer that Eliza would not grow up to resemble him in any way.

I softened my tone. "I understand you knew Bettina Pleshette?" I resisted the temptation to repeat his words "pretty well." "You must be very upset by what happened. I'm sorry."

I needn't have worried about whether I should mention him and Bettina in the same breath. It was as if I'd opened some kind of floodgate. He smiled, not exactly the reaction you'd expect from a grieving lover, and puffed up visibly with apparent pride.

"What a terrible loss," he said.

This had about as much sincerity as when he had first greeted me with "Pleased to meet you, heard a lot about you."

"You know," he continued, "I've been a terrific help to Detective Morrison. You've met Evan Morrison?"

I nodded.

"Oh yes. I told him stuff about Shotgun Marriott. You know, without my input, he'd be nowhere. I had a lot of dope on Shotgun, stuff he couldn't have got from anyone else."

"How did you know so much about Shotgun?" I was both intrigued and suspicious. Shotgun and Scott didn't seem like a good fit. "Were you and he close?"

Scott's smile faded. "Yeah, well, I never met the guy, actually," he admitted. "Bettina told me what she'd learned about him. Pillow talk." The smirk again and I gripped the handle of the baby carriage hard.

"What did she tell you exactly?"

"She was speaking to his son every day in the weeks before she died—before young Sean died." He said *young Sean* implying familiarity with Shotgun's son but I guessed Scott had never met Sean either. And as for Bettina "speaking" to Shotgun, I knew from Shotgun himself that all she was doing was pestering him on the telephone without much success. "And when she was meeting with Sean, she was getting the lowdown on the whole family situation."

"Which was?"

"An unholy mess. Sean hadn't seen his mother since she left Shotgun. He'd been raised by his father and he was a—you know, a queer."

Ah, well, what did I expect? It figured that Scott should be homophobic.

"But here's where it gets interesting." He veered toward me again and I stepped aside so that Eliza's pram was between us. "Sean told Bettina his mother had gotten in touch with him recently. He was very excited because he was going to see her again soon. He told Bettina all about it."

"He was going to London? Angela Marriott lives in London."

"I know that," Scott said quickly. "No, she was coming here. I told Detective Morrison about Bettina's meetings with Sean and he was pretty interested. He was looking for a link between Bettina and Sean's father."

"But they never met, Shotgun and Bettina," I said. "He told me."

"Yeah, well, Evan Morrison, he doesn't necessarily want to believe everything Shotgun Marriott tells him. Not right away at any rate, not without dotting every 'i' and crossing every goddamn 't' of every single word the guy says to him."

"And why do you think that is?"

Scott shrugged. "Guy's a detective. It's what they do."

"So you'll be going to Bettina's funeral?" I asked him.

He looked away. "Doubt I'll have the time. It's bound to be in California—I think her folks are there—and I don't think they've released the body yet. I'm on call for surgery at Southampton Hospital this week."

I had the impression it wasn't just his work that was preventing him from going. There was something else.

"But I'm going to have to do something about her stuff," he said.

"Her stuff?"

"She stayed a few days at my house. She'd rented this place in the woods up near Shotgun but she didn't like being there at all. It wasn't her idea of the Hamptons—north of the highway, nowhere near the ocean. She was pretty classy, she appreciated high-end living and what can I say, my house delivers. She could step out of our bedroom right onto the sand and—"

I noted a wistful air in the way he said "our bedroom." Scott had clearly been a bit smitten by Bettina. I reckoned he'd have had to be to describe her as classy.

"Her stuff?" I prompted.

"She was always on her cell phone and she'd take endless notes as she talked. It used to drive me insane, she'd scribble on whatever was close to hand, didn't matter if it was my mail or my calendar, a menu in a restaurant. She'd rip pages out and go off with them."

"How inconsiderate." Sounded just how I'd imagined Bettina to behave.

"Yeah, right. So she left all these notes—little scraps of paper—in a drawer in our bedroom along with a whole lot of beauty products in the bathroom."

"But didn't the cops come to your house too? If you were seeing Bettina, surely they must have been very interested in what she did there?"

"Sure they were. I told you, Evan Morrison and I have spent a lot of time together. But I put this stuff I was telling you about in a bag and I threw the bag in my car right away when—"

He didn't finish the sentence. When he heard Bettina was dead?

"I guess I meant to take it to the cops but I forgot all about it."

"You mean her notes are still in your car?"

He nodded. He was looking at me intently.

I decided to plunge right in.

"Scott, you know I've taken over from Bettina with Shotgun Marriott's book?"

"My dad said something about it. He called me last night, actually. I had no idea that's what you did, you never mentioned it at the wedding."

"You never asked," I said, "and you never mentioned you were seeing Bettina."

"Well, if I'd known you were in the same line of work—"

"So, I was thinking maybe I might find her notes helpful when I come to write the book. I could give her a big credit." Like hell I would!

"Hey, that's a nice gesture. And maybe you could, like, credit me too?"

"Of course." Oh boy, was he a piece of work!

"So, great." He was all smiles now, smarmy, patronizing. We were back at the Old Stone Market and he opened the door of a gleaming Mercedes sedan that was parked in front of the store and reached in to get something. "Here you are." He handed me a Citarella shopping bag and then a few seconds later I was rid of him. I knew I should be feeling relieved, even triumphant that I had lucked into what would inevitably be valuable material. But somehow I knew that by giving me Bettina's notes—as opposed to giving them to Detective Morrison—Scott would feel he had something on me and sooner or later it would be payback time.

After he left I wheeled the pram into the store and let Eliza stay sleeping in it while I perched on the stool by the cash register and fretted about the inconsistencies surrounding Franny and Dumpster's whereabouts on those fateful nights when Sean and then Bettina were murdered. When I heard Rufus's truck pull in, I raced out to meet them. Rufus gave me what I thought was quite a dirty look and I realized I'd probably scuppered his chances of a good-night kiss. And once I told Franny about Scott's visit, she barely gave him another glance. She rushed inside to see Eliza and I told Rufus about Scott coming to the Old Stone Market the night of the commitment ceremony, while he and I had been down at the ocean witnessing Sean's body being pulled out of the water.

"Oh Jesus," said Rufus, "I had a feeling he might do something like that. He was pretty drunk that night. He told me about Bettina and the truth is he was pretty hooked."

"What do you mean?" I said.

"I can see exactly how it went down. The thing about Scott is that he's pretty full of himself and this woman, Bettina, she was asking everyone a ton of questions, getting background history on the area where Shotgun Marriott had made his home. My guess is that she met Scott and asked if she could interview him, and he took it as a sign she was interested in *him*. With Scott it's always about him." Rufus shook his head but he was smiling. I sensed that his brother infuriated him but that he tolerated Scott in his good-natured way. "I think they had a bit of a fling, she spent some time at his house and found it to be more comfortable than the place she'd rented so she moved in with him for a while. Strikes me she was a bit of a user."

"He mentioned that," I said, "not that she was a user but he told me he 'delivered' on the high-end living. I think he was rather proud that she chose to stay at his house. It didn't sound like he had a clue that she was exploiting him in any way."

"Sounds like Scott," said Rufus, "pretentious as they come but naïve at the same time. Anyway, the other night, the night Sean Marriott was killed, the night before the commitment ceremony, Bettina told Scott it was over. She probably realized he didn't have much to tell her and if she went on staying at his house, he'd become a bit of a millstone around her neck. So at the commitment ceremony he's all bitter and twisted because he never saw it coming. He's like, *I thought we had something special going on.* And he was looking for someone to console him so when he'd had quite a bit to drink he started talking about going over to Franny's."

He kept glancing up the stairs, obviously hoping that the evening wasn't over, that she was going to come down and spend more time with him. But there was no sign of her.

"So anyway," he said, "I tried to stop him but once he had the idea in his head, he was determined to go there. He even started talking about Eliza as if he'd totally forgotten that he'd never acknowledged her as his child. That's typical Scott. Just because Bettina breaks up with him it doesn't stop him thinking he's God's gift to women. I guess he imagined Franny would welcome him with open arms."

For a second I wondered how Rufus thought women saw *him*.

"So did you have a good evening?" I asked him, curious about how things had progressed with him and Franny.

"Fine—till we got back here." He gave one final glance up the stairs and then turned toward the door. "I guess that's it for tonight. Everything all right at Dad's place?"

Okay, so he didn't want to talk about it.

"It's wonderful," I said. "You'll have to come over soon for dinner if I ever manage to find the time to go food shopping. Franny's warned me off this place, says I can't afford it."

"She's never going to get this business off the ground if she keeps saying stuff like that. So, give me a call and we'll get together. I'll bring take-out. From here, most likely." He grinned.

After he'd gone I went upstairs and found Franny warming up some milk in the kitchen.

"I know about Scott," I said immediately. I didn't see any point in beating about the bush. "About him being Eliza's father. Rufus told me."

"Well, God bless Rufus," she said, somewhat acidly I thought. "Good to know he's spreading my family business about the place."

"Franny, you know I wouldn't take it any further. I would never interfere. But you know Scott was pretty open with me about his involvement with you."

"There is no *involvement* with me. And yes, I know you wouldn't interfere. It's not *your* interference I'm worried about."

"You don't want Scott to see Eliza?"

Franny turned to me and I saw the anxiety in her face.

"I'm scared, Lee. He's her father and I guess Rufus told you the circumstances surrounding her conception. But the moment when he could have taken the kind of fatherly interest that I would welcome has long since passed. Now I'm kind of scared of what he might do and it's all that woman's fault."

That woman. Did she mean who I thought she meant?

"She was a damn meddler," said Franny, "couldn't keep her nose out of anything. She came around here one day and told me she was seeing Scott and that I ought to give him access to his daughter. *What business is it of yours?* I felt like saying. As if I'd ever tried to stop him! But then she started going on about how Eliza

would be better off with her father, how he could give her a better life, that it wasn't fair on a child to raise her cooped up above
a store like this. I mean, *hello,* how many children does she have
and when did she become the expert?"

Franny rolled her eyes and grinned and I warmed to her more
than ever. She was under a lot of stress one way or another and
yet she managed to retain her sense of humor in spite of everything.

"And then Scott started turning up," she said.

"Did you let him see Eliza?"

"I hid from him. He banged on the door to the store downstairs but I didn't let him in. He probably thought I wasn't here
because sometimes I let Dumpster take my truck in the evening
if I'm not using it."

"Scott told me he came round here the night Sean Marriott
was killed—and the next night when Bettina was murdered—
and there was no one here."

"Like I just said, I was hiding. Dumpster was out with my
truck."

"But Franny," I said, "you told me—and you told Evan
Morrison—that Dumpster was here with you both nights."

She turned away from me and began to walk Eliza up and
down the cramped kitchen space, rocking her and crooning to
her.

"Franny?"

"Okay, that's what I told you and that's what I told Detective
Morrison. So what?"

Her back was turned so I couldn't see her face.

"So you lied and because you lied, Shotgun Marriott's been arrested because you blew his alibi. Now were you here or weren't
you?"

"No," she said so quietly that I almost didn't hear her. "I wasn't here either night."

"So you have no idea if Dumpster was here or not? He could easily have been with Shotgun like he says he was."

"He said he was there? He told you that?"

"Yes," I said.

"He could be lying."

"You'd call your own son a liar?"

"I don't want to. That's why *I* lied and said I was here and he was with me."

"But he *wasn't* here?"

"I don't know where he was," she said. "I wasn't here because I was out looking for him. He'd been acting strange and I had a feeling he was up to his old ways again, you know, dealing. I'd withheld the use of the truck for a while, pretended I needed it, but that didn't stop him. He just borrowed one from someone else. So I put Eliza in my truck—and drove around looking for him. That's why Scott couldn't find me. I needed to track down Dumpster before Evan Morrison got to him first."

"Did you go to Shotgun's? Wouldn't that be the first place you'd look?"

"I drove to the end of the dirt track but I didn't go up to the house. I figured Dumpster wouldn't take drugs to Shotgun's, he wouldn't involve him in anything like that. I've told you, Dumpster worships Shotgun."

"And you never found him?"

She shook her head. "I thought I saw something in the woods as I drove up and I got out of the car and yelled his name but I got no response. About a week earlier he'd come home with a deer he'd shot. I was worried that he might be hunting deer on Shotgun's property, if he wasn't involved in dirty drug business again."

"Because Shotgun hadn't given him permission?"

"Because *nobody* gave him permission, Shotgun or otherwise. It's too early. The hunting season doesn't start till October."

"Franny, you have to tell Detective Morrison what you've told me. How do you know he hasn't already heard from Scott that you weren't at home those nights?"

"Oh please!" said Franny. "Don't tell me you believe what Scott tells you."

"Do it, Franny," I said, "otherwise it's going to be a whole lot harder for you later on—and for Dumpster."

"You know, I have to open the store for breakfast at six thirty, which means getting up at five thirty to prepare," she said, "and Eliza's probably going to get me up before then anyway."

She said it pleasantly enough but there was an imperceptible trace of impatience in her voice so I took the hint and left.

As I drove along the open stretch of Cranberry Hole Road that led past the cabin, I glanced in the rearview mirror and saw the headlamps of a lone car behind me. I slowed down and waited for it to overtake me but it didn't.

It was tailing me.

I veered off sharply onto the dirt road that led to the cabin, expecting it to follow me, but it continued on down Cranberry Hole Road and I sighed with relief.

But not for long.

Once inside the cabin, I brushed my teeth and flopped down exhausted and fumbled for the remote. But when I switched off the light, intending to let *Letterman* lull me to sleep once again, I saw the flickering light from the returning headlamps projected through the window onto the wall in front of me.

Why hadn't I done anything about covering the windows? Now if I went near them I would be silhouetted in full view of whoever was out there. I gunned the TV to life because I knew the sound of an approaching car would so totally freak me out that I would lose it. And maybe the sound of TV voices would make it seem there was someone here with me. And maybe I was delusional. A loud and rackety cartoon series burst into the room and I nearly fell out of bed in shock.

Was it better to watch a talk show or cartoons while awaiting my killer? Would I be attacked during a commercial break? Would the killer turn the TV off after he'd disposed of me? Would he have a shotgun? Or a bow and arrow? What in the world had induced me to stay in such an isolated place? I had been so enchanted with the idea of having such a perfect little retreat to hole up in, I hadn't stopped to think that I would be a sitting duck for a killer on the prowl.

It was no good telling myself that there was no reason why anyone would have a motive to kill me. I was all alone in a deserted place so it was a given. I slipped out of bed and went to stand beside one of the windows so I wouldn't be seen. And then, just when it seemed the car was going to crash right into the cabin, it turned around and roared away down the dirt road.

Kids, I told myself. Kids, kids, kids, just as Rufus had said. As usual I'd been imagining myself to be in danger.

The next morning I awoke bright and early and picked up the Phillionaire's land line because I couldn't make international calls on my cell phone. Cath was not as antagonistic as I had expected her to be when I called her back to apologize. It was often like this in our friendship. She would be—I felt—overly critical of me, haranguing me for something I had done, and, if I defended myself, then she was quite capable of working herself up into a storm of disapproval that could create a rift between us for weeks. But if I apologized, in other words if I acknowledged that she was right, then she was invariably all charm in twenty seconds.

"Poor little thing," she cooed when I told her about Eliza's incessant crying, "she's probably suffering from colic."

"Yes, that's it, she is," I said, although I had absolutely no idea. I just wanted to be part of the baby club too. I had to own up to a tiny niggle that had taken root at the back of my mind and was festering every day. If Tommy and I had gone ahead with the wedding, we might already be thinking about starting a baby by now, something I wouldn't have thought about for two seconds a year ago. But seeing Cath with a baby before I had left London—and now Franny—I was beginning to worry that I mustn't leave it too late.

"Then I really pity the poor mother," said Cath, not giving *me* an ounce of sympathy, I noticed. "Who is she by the way?"

I told her the whole story, how I had met Franny via Rufus and how Franny's son was working for Shotgun Marriott.

"Wait a second," said Cath, "back up. What's this about Shotgun Marriott?"

"Well, that's whose book I'm supposed to be doing. That's why I came to America in the first place, remember?"

"You never said it was *his* book," said Cath.

I could have sworn I did but then I had noticed that since she'd had Marcus, Cath wasn't as interested in the details of my life as she used to be.

"So anyway," she said, "you lucked into this job because the first choice got murdered? And now you're saying his *son* is dead too?"

"Didn't you read about it in the papers?"

"Lee," said Cath in the overly patient tone she sometimes adopted that always made me feel like an idiot, "with Marcus in my life, when do I have time to read the papers? But you working for Shotgun Marriott, I can't wait to tell Richie."

"Why? I didn't know Richie was a fan of his."

"Lee, for Christ's sake! You don't know about the groupie that was found dead on Shotgun Marriott's bed?"

"Of course I do."

"Well, don't you remember? Max Austin was working for the detective that investigated that case."

"Well, I didn't know that," I said.

Max Austin. There was someone I hadn't thought about for a while. He was Richie's boss and the detective who had been in charge of the arson murders in my London neighborhood. He was a bit of a moody curmudgeon and at first I had found him distant and a little scary. But the more I had got to know about him, the more I began to feel sorry for him. I found it particularly poignant that his wife had been murdered and her killer had never been found. He seemed to me a really sad case, still mourning his wife after five years as a widower with no one new on the horizon. I'd witnessed him starting to spruce himself up a bit—a haircut, smart clothes—and in my own dippy romantic way I had assumed he'd found a girlfriend.

I was an ostrich. I dug my head in the sand and ignored the signs. The reason Max Austin was giving himself a makeover was because he had developed a big fat brooding crush on *me* and I didn't realize it until it was too late.

"Yes," said Cath. It had been she who had pointed out to me the reason Inspector Austin was knocking on my door every day to ask yet another question regarding his investigation. "He told us all about it when we were out for dinner one night. He was pretty junior then, of course. Not the big wheel he is now. By the way, did you know he'd got a promotion? He's detective superintendent now. Anyway, he did quite a bit of the legwork, questioning the people at the place where it happened. He had to deal with the groupie's family when they all came rushing over from the States pointing the finger."

"At Shotgun?"

"Well, who else?"

"I didn't even know the groupie was American."

"Well, now you do. So tell me, how did this Franny person get you to babysit? You never helped me out with Marcus in London."

"You never asked, Cath," I protested. "I had the impression you didn't trust me with him."

Cath had been obsessively protective of Marcus, barely allowing me to hold him for more than a minute. She must be coming to the end of her maternity leave from her job as a teacher and I wondered how she would cope with leaving him in someone else's care.

"Franny's pretty relaxed about Eliza," I said and waited to see if she would rise to the bait. When she didn't say anything, I went on: "It's so ironic, she has this little white picket fence all around her store and it makes you think she must live this apple-pie American dream but I'm telling you, Cath, her life is a nightmare."

I expected Cath to ask me why and I was looking forward to a good gossip about Franny. She intrigued me and I regretted that there was no one with whom I could discuss her. Rufus was the closest bet but it was unlikely that he would have an objective take on her anymore.

"We're all surrounding ourselves with a dream to a certain extent, Lee." Oh, okay, she was in "wise Cath preaches to irresponsible Lee" mode. It was best to say nothing and just listen with one ear. "I expect you're putting up a bit of a white picket fence around your own life at the moment even though your dream's been shattered."

Was she referring to my wedding being called off?

"How is Tommy?" I asked. "My mother told me you'd seen him."

"He's in a pretty bad way. He devoted his life to two things—the BBC and you—and both of them are gone."

"Well, whose fault is that?" I knew I sounded pretty sour but I couldn't help myself.

"He was let go by the BBC and you went off to America."

"How many times have I told you, Cath, *he* was the one who put a stop to the wedding. I know I've been putting him off all these years but this time I was so ready to marry him, I really was."

Then she surprised me.

"I think he knows he made a mistake, Lee. He really misses you."

"He does?"

"He came round here to tell me he'd lost his job but once he'd got that out the way all he did was talk about you. Got pretty boring, actually." She laughed.

I didn't know what to say.

"Lee? You still there? Call him. He's dying to hear from you."

"So why doesn't he call me?"

"He told me he had."

Well, that was true enough.

"It would be so great if you two could get back together," said Cath, "but you've got to strike now while the proverbial iron's hot and your absence is making his heart grow fonder and all that crap."

"Okay." I laughed. "I'll call him." That was the thing about Cath. No matter how annoying I found her, I had to admit she always had my best interests at heart.

But every time I called Tommy, he wasn't home. I tried at odd moments throughout the day and I always got the machine. I was beginning to worry about not having heard from him. I had left a message telling him I loved him and received a resounding silence in return. In desperation I sent him an e-mail. "Did you get my message? Call me back." Tommy doesn't do e-mail if he can help it. He's a great text-messager and I had been used to constantly picking up my mobile only to read "what's 4 dinner" or "gone 2 pub" on my screen. But for some reason he finds e-mailing a big effort, too much like writing a letter.

It boomeranged back and after a second I realized why. I had sent it to his old e-mail address at the BBC and of course he was no longer there. So there was nothing left to do but wait for him to get in touch of his own accord.

When the phone rang quite early the next morning, I snatched it up thinking it would be him but a voice said:

"Lee, is that you? How is everything?"

"Phil," I clung to the phone as if he were my lifeline, "how are you?"

"I just thought I'd check in and see if you'd found out where to buy milk and cookies and stuff?"

Poor Phil. He must have regretted dialing my number by the time I'd finished with him. I chattered on and on, telling him everything that had happened, about my meeting with Shotgun, about Franny and Dumpster and—

I stopped short of telling him about Scott. I remembered just in time that he didn't know anything about Eliza.

"I still don't like it," he said.

"Don't like what?"

"You being tied in to all this business with Shotgun Marriott. You're getting in too deep, Lee. Sooner or later you're going to be implicated in some way. Can't you tell him to wait to do the book until this whole murder thing has been cleared up?"

I knew he was right. Somehow I knew the Phillionaire would always be right and I should heed his advice whenever I could. He was my new best friend and wise uncle wrapped into one.

But I couldn't get Shotgun's haunted face out of my mind and I could still hear him telling me how if I started work on the book with him, I'd be helping him more than I could possibly know. The truth is I get a kick out of being needed by someone as much as the next person. I wanted to help Shotgun, I felt I *could* help him, and what's more, I was going to.

"I know, I know," I told Phil, "but I'm afraid I'm going ahead although I haven't heard from him since he was arrested, so God knows what's going to happen."

"Well, don't go visiting him in jail. I don't want to have to deal with your mother if we read about your involvement in the papers. I like your Tommy, by the way," Phil said softly while I was still trying to picture Shotgun sitting in prison.

"You do?"

"He's straightforward and genuine and that rare thing, a stand-up guy who's also loaded with charm. Maybe he's not the sharpest tool in the shed when it comes to the world of brilliant careers but does it really matter? He's good fun to talk to and what's more, he talks a lot of sense."

"Did he say anything about me?" I asked before I could stop myself.

"Hard to say," said the Phillionaire, "we only sat up and talked about you till two in the morning. He wants to marry you, Lee, but he's apprehensive. He's not sure he's bright enough for you, he's worried you'll get bored with him in a couple of years. He's feeling pretty vulnerable at the moment, he's just lost his job, you know."

"Everyone always sees things from Tommy's point of view," I said. "I'm the one who was dumped."

"So rise above it," said Phil, "don't always make it about you. Guys are allowed to be shaky sometimes too. Tell him you feel bad because he called off the wedding, tell him you think he made a big mistake but you're willing to forgive him. Open the door a little, Lee. Although I gotta tell you something . . ." He stopped.

"What?"

"He was a big surprise to me, not at all the type of guy I'd have figured you'd be with."

"What do you mean?" I was intrigued. "What kind of man did you think I'd go for?"

"Someone more—and don't take this the wrong way—someone more challenging. I'd never have guessed a simple straightforward guy like Tommy would keep you interested but believe me, having met him, I'm delighted he has."

I was about to quiz him further but it seemed he had another agenda.

"The other reason I called," he said, "is that I really need you to go over and check on the construction. For me. I've got your mother on my back about it every day. She's a pain in the butt, we know that. But it's like with you and Tommy, I've got to rise above it and even though she's the one who said she'd take care of it, I know I have to get involved and move it along a bit. For her. Because I love her. So will you go check on it for me?"

"Of course, Phil," I said. "For you—anything." And I meant it.

For the rest of the day I couldn't get my mind off what the Phillionaire had said about Tommy being an unlikely partner for me. It resonated with me as I took my habitual walk along the beach because it was the first time anyone had registered the slightest doubt about Tommy's presence in my life.

Anyone except myself, that is.

Secretly I had always thought Tommy and I were ill-matched with him so gregarious and me such a loner. But because I had been able to dictate when and for how long we spent time under the same roof, I had been able to get the best of both worlds as far as our relationship was concerned. I had needed him desperately in the beginning when my violence phobia and antisocial issues had rendered me almost impossible to be with. Nothing I did ever seemed to get him down and his unquestioning devotion to me had enveloped me in a warm cocoon of security.

But being warm and dependable didn't make him exciting. Tommy was the sensible wool coat I put on to ward off the winter cold but every now and then I yearned to risk contracting the flu by wearing something a little more flimsy and sexy that would take me just a little closer to the edge.

I don't expect anybody to understand this—least of all myself. Because if you spend your life frantically anticipating violence to annihilate you around every corner, why in the world would you want a man who'd cause you that kind of excitement? The Phillionaire had spoken of someone who was a challenge for me and maybe that was a better way of putting it. Until he'd called off the wedding, I'd had the upper hand with Tommy and therefore he'd presented very little challenge and the more I thought about it, I wondered if maybe that had been part of the trouble between us. Because we'd had rows and mini-breakups in the past and it had always been my fault. I'd get cranky and moody with him and I'd bait him until he was forced to defend himself and then all hell would break loose between us and I'd kick him out for a week or so.

But maybe the reason I became cranky in the first place was because he didn't stimulate me. Mentally, I mean. The sex was fine. No problem there but could it be that he bored me—just a little? Don't get me wrong, it's not his fault. He is who he is. Dear sweet adorable Tommy with his gentle nonjudgmental sweetness. I love him. Yes I do. And I always will.

Yet I kept coming back to what Phil had said. Tommy had canceled the wedding because he didn't think he was bright enough for me, because he was worried I might get bored with him. I was forced to admit there was a horrible glimmer of truth lurking there. The simple truth was that I used Tommy and I hated myself for it. I used him because he let me. But over the past year I had resolved to become a better person. I had been adamant with myself that as Tommy's wife I would work harder to appreciate what he did for me and I would try my utmost to give to him in return.

Only now he had deprived me of the opportunity and I think that was what upset me the most about him backing away from the wedding. But however hard I tried, there was no getting around it: we would still be mismatched. I was fretting about this as I walked barefoot over the firm sand at the water's edge when my cell phone rang and I heard the unmistakable sound of Shotgun Marriott's soft baritone.

"I think you and I need to go to work," he said.

"You're out on bail?"

"Even better. I had my arraignment and the judge threw out the case. There was not probable cause to arrest me in the first place, at least not by the time he'd heard all the evidence. But the icing on the cake was when one of Detective Morrison's witnesses changed her story and there wasn't a thing he could do about it."

"Franny Cook?" I couldn't believe it. Franny had listened to what I had told her, she had come through.

"Right. You know her? Franny Cook, Dumpster's mother. She said she wasn't home the nights Sean and Bettina were murdered so she couldn't say Dumpster was with her. Dumpster stood up and said he was with me here at Mallaby both nights, working late, so I was off the hook, although by the look on Evan Morrison's face, it won't be for long. For some reason that man really seems to have it in for me."

"That's great news—*Kip,*" I remembered just in time. "I'll be there in the morning. What time's good for you? I'm really looking forward to getting started."

CHAPTER 7

I GOT UP AT SEVEN THE NEXT MORNING AND AFTER A quick cup of coffee, I padded off along the beach to fulfill my promise to the Phillionaire and check on the construction. It was so mild that for a second I pondered taking a dip in the bay. Franny had loaned me a swimsuit and I was anxious to get in the water before it got too cold. I had time. I wasn't due at Mallaby until ten and even if the water turned out to be freezing, maybe it would sharpen my senses for the work that lay ahead.

I mulled over what approach I should take with Shotgun. Normally when I begin work with a new ghosting subject, they have their agenda and I have mine and it is part of my job to gently coax them around to my way of thinking. Without them realizing what's going on, of course. They have to feel *they* are telling their story and that they are in control of the proceedings at all times, whereas in fact I am the one steering the course.

I compromised by taking off my shoes and socks and paddling barefoot along the water's edge, kicking pebbles to scatter the sandpipers. I had my directions from the Phillionaire—go past the Stucco House and keep going until I saw a clearing in the dunes. "By now they should have excavated the ground so you should see a giant hole and with luck a cement mixer or two," Phil had said.

What I actually saw was Rufus and several construction

workers staring into the hole and whatever they were looking at had them so transfixed, they never even noticed me walking up toward them from the shoreline.

I touched Rufus gently on the arm and he started.

"Jesus!" he said. "Don't do that."

"Sorry," I said. "You're jumpy this morning."

"Well, yes," he said, "we've all had a bit of a shock. I got a call from the contractor asking me to come right over. Take a look in the hole. They were about to pour the concrete and they saw that."

He pointed to something lying at the bottom of the pit.

It was a hunting bow and arrow.

"My God!" I took a step backward. My first thought was that it had to be the weapon that had killed Bettina and Rufus agreed with me.

"She was killed by an arrow, right?" Rufus jabbed his finger several times at the bow. "There has to be a reason someone would throw away a thousand-dollar bow that looks in pretty good condition to me. I mean, it's not like a hunter's going to be out looking for deer on the beach. And it's not as if they decided to jump into the hole to have a rest and then forgot their bow; they'd never be able to get out again without a ladder. Whoever it was just threw it in there and hoped it'd get covered by the concrete."

"But wouldn't they realize it would be seen before the concrete was poured?"

"Oh, they threw a few shovels of earth over it before they left but my guess is they did it when it was dark and they didn't realize how sandy it was down there at the bottom of the pit. The earth that covered the bow was thrown from up here and it's an entirely different color. It stuck out a mile."

"Are you going to call Detective Morrison?" I asked him.

"I guess I am," he said. "I don't like the guy but if there's any way this helps his investigation—I mean, if that arrow turns out to be the one that killed Bettina and they can track it back to the person who fired it—"

"Franny told me Dumpster hunted deer. Would he use a bow and arrow?"

Rufus looked at me, shocked. "Are you saying what I think you're saying?"

"He told me he was at Mallaby the night Sean was killed. Said he was putting up shelves but I don't know how long he stayed. Franny's pretty worried about him, generally. When the two of you went out, she didn't talk about him?" I wondered if he knew about Dumpster being Detective Morrison's informant.

"She didn't say a word about him. She only talked about Eliza and how Bettina had come over and told her to let Scott have access to her. She doesn't like my brother, that's for sure. I know she's had problems with Dumpster in the past although she's never been too specific. At one point she wanted me to give him work and I hired him for a couple of days but then he took off. Now she's got him doing the yard stuff she no longer has time for. Tell you the truth I had no idea he even worked for Shotgun, I'm not sure it's common knowledge. And now he could be implicated in the murder, what a lousy situation!"

"Poor Franny."

"You're getting along well with her?" He turned to me.

I was a little taken aback. Until he'd mentioned it I hadn't given any thought to the fact that Franny and I had got to the stage of "getting along well." But now that he had, I was surprised to find that, yes, she had become a friend in a surprisingly short space of time. It seemed my new life at the beach had broken down a few of my old inhibitions and I was beginning to open up to strangers a little more easily.

"I guess I am. I babysat for her, if that means getting on well with her. I like her. She's intriguing and she has a lot on her plate at the moment."

"How should I play it with her?"

He was looking at me intently like an anxious puppy waiting to be fed.

"What do you mean—'play it with her'?"

He was shuffling a little, clearly awkward and embarrassed to be consulting me, but determined nonetheless. "I've always had a thing for her, since I was a kid. She was my surrogate older sister, she made time to do stuff with me even though she was ten years older. She never treated me like a kid. If she was going out fishing, she'd take me along—surfing, kayaking, she even taught me to shoot. We'd go down to the beach in February and it'd be freezing and there'd be no one else around and we'd slip around on the ice and shoot skeet."

She even taught me to shoot. So *he* knew how to shoot—and so did Franny. And Dumpster. And most likely they were all pretty nifty with a bow and arrow.

And it was high time I clamped down on paranoid notions like these when they entered my head.

"What's skeet?" I asked quickly.

"Like clay pigeons. So anyway, she went away to the city and when she came back recently she was just so stunning and I was all grown up and suddenly everything changed—for me at least. I'm crazy about her and I need to know if you think I have a chance, what with the age difference and all?"

"Well, how did it go the other night?"

He looked glum. "Fine—only she acted like I was still her kid brother. I was sitting there thinking she was so hot and she was saying stuff like 'could you watch Eliza for me tomorrow, I have to go to Costco and stock up on canned goods.'"

"Rufus," I said, "she dressed up for you. She made herself look good. She could have gone out with you in her sweats or her shorts but she made an effort."

"Oh," he looked thoughtful, "you think that means she might be interested? So when do I make a move on her? Is the second date too soon?"

"When is the second date?"

"I haven't called her yet."

"Well, might that not be the first move? When she's said she'll go out with you again then call me and we'll decide how you should play it. Now are you going to tell Evan Morrison about the bow and arrow?"

"I have to," he said, "we're not the only ones who saw it. All these construction workers, they're going to talk. Word will get around. What we'd better do is make sure Dumpster knows they've been found."

"We don't know for sure they're his," I pointed out. "In fact we're going to assume they're not. And we don't even know if it's the murder weapon."

"I'm going to take a closer look." Rufus ran over to the construction workers' trucks parked at the side of the clearing and lifted a short ladder from one of them. He climbed down into the hole and bent over the bow. I watched him from above. The bow was about five feet long and shaped in a double curvature. The arrow lying beside it was almost a yard long and made of wood.

"Wow!" said Rufus. "Look at that arrowhead."

I couldn't really see it from where I was standing and I wasn't about to climb down into the hole. "What's so special about it?"

"Well, it's titanium for a start," he said, "but I was thinking about the damage it would have caused. It's got razor sharp planes and on penetration it would literally slice everything in its path—blood vessels, muscles, tendons. When they found Bettina she must have been in a pretty terrible mess."

Suddenly I felt quite sick. I hadn't exactly been Bettina's biggest fan but I couldn't help being horrified by the thought of her bloody corpse.

"I'm not going to touch anything in case I interfere with any fingerprints they might find," said Rufus, "but my guess is this bow and arrow were wiped pretty thoroughly and whoever threw them in here was wearing gloves. But I wonder what happened to the quiver."

"The quiver?"

"You know, where they keep the arrows." He mimed reaching over his shoulder and plucking an arrow from something on his back. "It's not here but my guess is there's going to be something on this bow that'll match something on a quiver in someone's possession. DNA or whatever. Do you know where she was pierced? I heard it was in her back."

"Rufus, stop it!" Dwelling on the arrow slicing through Bettina could unhinge me for the rest of the day. "I'm leaving. I have to be at Shotgun's to start work this morning. Now, what am I going to tell your father and, more important, my mother about the progress on the house?"

"Tell them the truth. You came over and they were getting ready to pour the concrete."

"No mention of the bow and arrow?"

Rufus shrugged. "Why complicate matters? I'm going to have a word with the construction workers and ask them to talk to the police but no one else. The fewer people who know about it the better. Think about Dumpster. And we don't want Scott coming over here and getting involved."

Without realizing it, I had been literally rooted to the spot with anxiety ever since I had seen the bow and arrow and when

I moved to go back to my car, I was so stiff I nearly fell over. I drove slowly, my hands shaking slightly on the steering wheel, and I arrived at Mallaby in a state of high nervous tension. So nervous that I forgot all about Rufus's suggestion that we keep quiet about the bow and arrow and blurted out what I had just seen the minute Shotgun opened the door.

I wasn't prepared for his reaction.

"Do you have his cell phone number?" he asked without even saying hello. He was casually dressed in jeans and a dusky pink velour sweatshirt and his feet were bare. It was extraordinary, I thought, how his face could appear so gaunt and strained when his body seemed so relaxed.

"Rufus's?"

"Yes, can you call him?"

I nodded.

"Do it. Now! Stop him telling Detective Morrison. Tell him to bring the bow and arrow here. Here, use my phone."

But when I reached Rufus it was too late. Apparently Evan Morrison was already on his way to the building site.

"Do you think it was Dumpster's bow? Were you going to try to shield him?" I asked Shotgun. "Wouldn't that be obstruction?"

"Let's have a cup of coffee," he said by way of answer. "Believe me, I want to find out who committed these murders more than anyone but I just wish there was someone else handling the case. I don't trust that man, Morrison. It's ridiculous but I feel I want to make life hard for him. Arresting me was just insanity."

"What happened exactly? Did they keep you in jail?"

It wasn't the most professional start to our working relationship and I wouldn't have blamed him if he'd told me he didn't want to talk about it, but he smiled and said, "Don't look so worried. I'm out now, it's okay. And of course it wasn't exactly a barrel of laughs being led into a police station in handcuffs worrying that at any second a guy from the *Post* is going to jump out and take my picture. I was stripped and it felt like every single orifice of my body was searched. And they gave me one of those orange jumpsuits and led me down all kinds of ramps and corridors and buzzed me through steel doors and all the time I knew some guard I couldn't see was watching me through a monitor. My lawyer showed up pretty quick to bail me out but they still managed to make me feel like scum."

"And what about the arraignment?" I said.

"Total farce," he said, leading me into the kitchen. "The judge more or less said as much. The minute Dumpster's mother changed her story and then he stood up and gave me a cast-iron alibi, it was all over. And now you tell me the bow and arrow's been found—assuming it's the one that killed Bettina. Evan Morrison didn't even have the murder weapon and I don't own a bow and arrow yet he couldn't wait to pin the blame on me. He'd have been closer to the mark if he'd tried to nail me for Sean's murder given that I didn't mention my Purdey was one of a matching pair."

I looked at him. He poured a cup of coffee from the pitcher in the machine and handed it to me.

"You're dying to know, aren't you?" he said. "Why I kept quiet about it. Well, I'll tell you. I gave that second gun to Sean about a month ago. I wanted him to have something of his grandfather's. I knew he wouldn't ever use it. Sean was the gentlest of creatures. He wouldn't harm the proverbial fly but I think he appreciated the gift. It was an antique of sorts, a family heirloom, and Sean was sentimental in that way, much more so than I am. He put it in a kind of makeshift display case in his room above the stables and he went so far as to invite me over to show me what he'd done and that was a pretty rare gesture on his part."

"Did you know it was no longer there—after he was killed?"

"I did. When I took Morrison to his room I saw it was missing."

"But you chose to say nothing?" I was highly intrigued.

"I thought Sean might have loaned it to Dumpster. They were close in some ways and Dumpster was pretty vocal in his admiration of the gun."

"So you were covering up for Dumpster there too? Do you really think Dumpster was involved?" I was appalled to hear this.

"I don't know what to think," said Shotgun. "I know Dumpster was at Mallaby the night Sean was killed. He was putting up shelves. But I have no idea how long he stayed. He could have been gone by eight o'clock and I wouldn't have known, the place is so huge. But I'm pretty sure he wasn't with me in the house the night Bettina was killed. He usually makes his presence known whenever he arrives and he didn't. So it looks as if he lied at my arraignment and there's got to be a reason."

I couldn't help noticing that both he and Franny were protective of Dumpster. I wanted to tell Shotgun what Franny thought Dumpster was up to, about the dealing and how Dumpster was Detective Morrison's informant, but I decided that I had said quite enough for one morning and it was high time I steered the conversation in a more professional direction. I was about to bring up his book when he turned to me.

"So are *you* going to run to Detective Morrison and tell him Dumpster was lying?" I shook my head. "No? Well, that's obstruction too, isn't it? And it doesn't really make any difference if I tell them I gave my other Purdey to Sean. They don't seem to have found any shell casings and without those they can't identify which gun fired the fatal shot. Morrison can take my Purdey that's in the mudroom, or the one he found in the woods, or any other twelve-bore shotgun and he can say 'This is the *kind* of gun that killed Sean Marriott,' but he can't prove it's the actual one. Tell me something."

I looked up, wary now that he had claimed me as his accomplice in obstruction.

"If I write this book—correction, if *you* write this book—who do you think will be the market for it? Why would anybody want to read the damn thing?"

I bristled instinctively. He was the one who had said he wanted to do a book in the first place. But then he had just acknowledged that I would be doing the writing and that was more than a lot of my subjects were prepared to admit.

"You're a world-famous musician—" I began.

"*Was* a world-famous musician," he jumped in. "I haven't had a gig in fourteen years."

"There's a big nostalgia market."

"So I'll only be read by the follicularly-challenged, hard of hearing seniors who were once my fans? There'll just be a large-print edition?"

"Is that how you see yourself?" I challenged. Was that why he had a fashionable razor cut? Had he had his once luxuriant locks shorn because he was going bald? Although whatever the reason, it suited his fine-featured face.

"I'm okay about my age," he said, "the last thing I want to do is go around in the kind of flamboyant gear we all wore forty years ago. I'm almost sixty. If I wore fringed leather jerkins and earrings and studs and long flowing scarves, I'd look grotesque. I saw a member of my old band being interviewed on TV the other night and he had hair down to his shoulders and most of it was dyed fuchsia—yet his face was lined like an old hag's. He looked ridiculous."

The time was fast approaching when I would have to come clean with him. When I would have to tell him that the only reason publishers would be interested in his story would be if he told what really happened the night the groupie was found dead in his room. Suddenly I was apprehensive. What if he refused to talk about it? What if all my time on Long Island had been spent on a wild-goose chase?

"Do you miss it?" I was too chicken to plunge right in and ask him about the groupie as Bettina no doubt had.

"Miss what? The rock 'n' roll circus I used to be part of? Not at all."

"You don't?" I was amazed.

"Oh, I miss jamming with the boys after hours, but going out on the road, the actual performing? I never really enjoyed all that like the rest of them. I was in it for the music itself, nothing else. If I could have cut the live performances and just gone into the studio to record every now and then, I'd have been happy. And as for the publicity, the intrusion into my private life, that was something I really abhorred. I"—he searched for the right word—"I *detested* it."

I could tell he meant it. So how was he going to feel about me getting him to rake up as much detail as possible about his private life for the book?

"But don't get me wrong," he went on, "I'll promote the book. I know it has to be done when you've got a product to sell. But I could never understand those guys who worked so hard to promote *themselves.* It had nothing to do with the albums they made, they just wanted to go on TV and talk about their own crass little view of the world. Anything to give their ego a boost. I'm not like that. I'll only talk about the music."

"So it's going to be a book about your music?" This wasn't looking good.

"No," he said slowly, "no it's not. Not at all. I'm going to tell my life story and sure, music's a big part of it, but I'm going to include everything that's happened right up to this very minute and beyond. The first thing you have to understand is the reason I'm doing this book. I'm not doing it to make money. I'm not doing it to try and restore my career. I'm doing it for Sean. I planned it long before he died but now that he's gone, somehow it's even more important that I set the record straight for him. When I tell you the story of my life, Lee, I'm going to be talking to Sean. No"—he held up his hand as he sensed the barrage of questions I was about to unleash—"let me finish. What I was about to say was that I know what you want me to include in the book—the full story about that girl who died in my bed. Well, you'll get that but now I also want to include the outcome of this investigation. I owe it to Sean to deal with his murder and, if possible, write about the person responsible for his death. So, Lee"— he turned to me and fixed me with a penetrating look—"we're going to work out who the killers were, you and I. We're going to be partners in obstruction and we're going to beat Detective Morrison at his own game. For my son," he said and he opened a drawer in one of the kitchen cabinets. "This is Sean," he said, handing me a photograph in a wooden frame.

I was reeling from the thrill of what he'd said—not about our obstruction but the fact that he'd promised I'd get the full story of the girl in his bed fourteen years ago. To cover my distraction I took the photograph he handed to me and pretended to study it.

But then I looked closer, because the image of Sean Marriott took my breath away. When I'd seen him dragged upon the beach, his face had been a bloated mess and I'd turned away quickly. Now I could see what it had been like before. He had the innocent look of a choirboy with shiny hair cropped short but flopping from a side parting in a slight wave over his forehead. His features were small—a perfect little straight nose, a rosebud mouth with a larger, sensual lower lip, a delicate chin—except for his eyes, which were large and almond-shaped. He looked like a softer, gentler version of his father. I couldn't see anything of the drama of his mother's looks in him.

I handed the picture back to Shotgun, still feeling uneasy. It was understandable that he would want to dedicate the book to his son but it sounded like he wanted to do more than that. He had talked about setting the record straight for Sean. It sounded like he had something he wanted to get off his chest. Had he killed the groupie and was he going to confess via his autobiography?

I snapped to attention. More paranoid notions. This was what happened when I allowed my mind to wander off on its own like an errant child. I came up with the most absurd fantasies and it always got me into trouble.

"Where would you be most comfortable working?" I said to change the subject and get things moving.

"Well, where would you?" he said. "I spend most of my time indoors in that room we were in last time you were here. The one with all the books."

"That would be perfect," I said, "so long as you're comfortable there."

But when we were settled on one of the enormous sofas, a pitcher of water and two glasses on the coffee table before us as if we were about to speak at a conference, instead of talking about himself, he began to show an enormous amount of interest in me.

"Where do you live? London? Yes? Whereabouts? Ah, Notting Hill. That's where Angie lives although she's not a Notting Hill type as I remember them. She'd be better off in Mayfair or Belgravia or somewhere where rich businesspeople hang out. Why do you live in Notting Hill?"

I told him about the house on Blenheim Crescent where I had lived virtually all my life, about the fire that had nearly destroyed it. I told him about my parents' separation and my mother's commitment to the Phillionaire. In fact I prattled on and on and on because—and I would only realize this much later—he made me feel as if he had never been so interested in anyone in his entire life. It's a gift and he had it in spades. He made me feel—and I know there must be a way to describe this that sounds less of a cliché but right now I can't think of it—he made me feel *special*. And maybe I'm flattering myself but I do believe it was genuine.

"And are you married," he said, "do you have any children? You're not wearing a wedding ring, I see, but then sometimes people don't."

And that's when I noticed that he was. He saw me looking at it.

"I never took it off after she left. After all, we're not divorced. I am still married to her." He saw my look of surprise. "You didn't know that? She doesn't wear hers anymore," he said sadly. "At least she wasn't wearing it at Sean's funeral. Anyway"—he stood up and stretched—"now I've brought that up I suppose I'd better let you turn the spotlight on me although I'd much rather go on hearing about you. Do you know, I crave the company of English people? There are things I love about the Americans—their confidence, their energy, their friendliness—but God I miss the English sense of irony. I say things and Americans look at me blankly. They just don't get it. They just don't do self-deprecation the way we do. They think we're running ourselves down and that's very un-American. We are, of course, but that's part of the fun. And the saddest thing is," the haunted look I'd grown used to seeing crossed his face again, "because he grew up here, my own son was American. I loved him but we were so different. He was one of the people who looked at me blankly. So," he turned to me and his smile was forced and pathetically bright, "how does this work? Where do you start?"

"May I use a tape recorder?" I said, rummaging around in the bag of notebooks I'd brought with me and producing my trusty little Aiwa.

He looked startled. "Must you?"

"It really helps," I said. "Speeds things up. Saves me scribbling away all the time and asking you to repeat yourself every five minutes. After a while you won't notice it, honest."

He was silent for quite a long time. Then he said: "Okay. But I'm going to have to ask you to leave the tapes here. I don't want them leaving the house."

I was appalled. "But I'm going to need to transcribe them. It takes hours sometimes."

"You can do that here," he said quickly. "We'll set you up with a workspace somewhere in the house. Lord knows, I've a ton of empty rooms. And then you can take the transcripts away with you."

He sounded paranoid. There was no other word for it. I thought about telling him that journalists all over the world walked away from interviewees with tapes full of "off the record" revelations that would destroy their careers if they were revealed. I thought about explaining that without corroboration none of it could be used. But presumably he knew all about that. Whatever he was going to talk about into the tape recorder must be seriously incriminating.

"What will be on the tapes," I said, "will be going in the book eventually and everyone will know it then."

"And by then I'll be ready," was his enigmatic reply. "Now, where do you want me to start?"

"It's your book," I reminded him, "but the beginning is as good a place as any."

At first I thought he'd fallen asleep. Because when he finally began to speak, he talked with his eyes closed and after a while I realized he wanted to pretend I wasn't even there. Whenever I shifted my position or interrupted him in any way, he opened his eyes and stared at me for a second as if he'd forgotten who I was. Normally I prompt my subject in the direction I want the story to go but I also know that at the beginning when someone is clearly delving into their memory and coming up with whatever they find there, it's best to let them keep going. Especially if the material was as unexpected as Shotgun's life promised to be. After about five minutes I closed my eyes too and just sat beside him, silently listening as the story of his early years unraveled.

"The real problem of my life was that I was born upper class and I just didn't get it. As I told you, we lived at Mallaby on the edge of the Yorkshire moors and it was pretty much on the edge of nowhere and that was fine with me. I suppose I had what you'd call a privileged childhood but if you tried to describe it to an American today, I doubt they'd see it that way. It was the fifties and we had no washing machine, no dishwasher, no central heating. And here's something that will no doubt astound you, we didn't have a television. Nobody did. It was pretty barbaric by today's standards."

I was fascinated by his account of his childhood, how he went to the local school and roamed the moors with the farm children. But his parents were "landed gentry," his father's family had owned vast spreads of Yorkshire for centuries, and in the claustrophobic and rarefied existence within the walls of Mallaby "castle" he was cared for by a succession of nannies and only saw his parents for twenty minutes every day.

He opened his eyes and turned to me. "I haven't thought about all this stuff in years. It's amazing it's all coming back so easily. I suppose it's because it's truly a part of me. We can go into all the background details you need later, okay? What the house was like, my pets, whatever you need. I was an only child, by the way. What about you?"

I nodded to indicate that I was too, but I didn't say anything. Much as I had basked in the attention he had paid me, I needed him to keep going about himself.

He closed his eyes again.

"In my parents' eyes my life was already more or less mapped out. I'd be sent to prep school, then Harrow, and then university. And along the way I'd find a suitable bride, the daughter of people just like them. I'd meet her at York Races or out foxhunting or grouse shooting and I'd woo her at a debutantes' ball—and she'd probably turn out to be someone I'd known since I was five years old.

"And I did go to prep school and Harrow and I was about to go up to Trinity, Cambridge. But I never made it because I met the girl I was going to marry and it wasn't a girl from one of the families who'd been there since the time of William the Conqueror.

"It was Angie."

I waited for him to continue but he didn't.

Suddenly he stood up and I was jolted out of the virtual reverie into which I had fallen, mesmerized by the sound of his voice.

"I'm afraid that's all I'm going to give you for today. I've changed my mind."

I must have frowned in disappointment because he reached out and touched my shoulder to placate me.

"Talking about Angie is going to be painful," he said, looking me straight in the eye, "and I think I need to sift through everything I have to tell you first. Don't be alarmed, I'm not going to hold anything back. Far from it. But I keep thinking about Sean and then I start to feel emotional and we can't have that. Upperclass Brit with a lump in his throat and all that. That would be letting the side down. My mother would turn in her grave."

"Well, could you show me where I can transcribe the tapes?" I said. I felt a little uncomfortable seeing him so disturbed. What would happen as he probed deeper into his past? On the one hand I felt he was being far too tough on himself by insisting on tackling the book while he was still grieving, but on the other I was anxious to get to work. "If I could set up the workspace you mentioned, then maybe I can go straight there each time we finish a session."

"Great idea!" He seemed relieved to have a practical task to perform. "Come with me."

He led me out into the hall and up the Jacobean staircase. At the far end of the gallery he opened a door and I found myself in a small wood-paneled room. There didn't appear to be any windows and the only light came from a computer screen glowing in the corner.

"Sean set this up for me," Shotgun said, switching on an Anglepoise lamp. "I know he thought of me as being hopelessly out of touch and he insisted way back when that I become computer literate. I'm really glad he did. He had a laptop over in his room above the stables and we e-mailed each other. I suppose it says everything about the state of our father-son relationship. We lived within yards of each other but communicated by e-mail. Anyway, will this work for you?"

I thanked him and set about familiarizing myself with his computer and starting a file for the transcriptions.

It didn't take me long to transcribe the small section of the tape he had recorded and when I'd finished, I stepped out onto the gallery and tried to figure where he'd gone. I wanted to say good-bye and fix a time for the next session.

Across the gallery a door was open and coming from the room was Shotgun's voice punctuated at intervals by the plaintive sound of an acoustic guitar.

> *"Went to bed last night, found the blues in my bed*
> *Woke up this mornin' about half past four*
> *Those blues they were a-knockin' on my front door."*

It wasn't really singing, I thought to myself, it was more like moaning. I listened as he continued the song, marveling at the way he could transform his cultured British accent into the voice of a downtrodden sharecropper from the American South with such conviction.

But then the singing stopped abruptly and I heard another sound that propelled me down the stairs and out of the house as fast as I could travel. It was the sound of Shotgun sobbing and there was nothing stiff upper lip about it. Wrenching mournful wails followed me as I made my getaway. Instinct told me that I was intruding on his grief and that he would be hugely embarrassed if he knew I had heard him. And I wondered, not for the first time, if there was anyone to whom he would feel comfortable turning for consolation or whether he was destined to live a life of unutterable loneliness holed up inside Mallaby.

On impulse, when I arrived at the dirt track off Cranberry Hole Road, I got out of the Jeep and studied the tire tracks in the sand. The Jeep's were pretty distinctive so I was easily able to distinguish them from the other set of tracks. I followed them up the sandy road to the clearing where the cabin stood. I saw the ones where the car had come up and parked halfway and the ones where it had come up and turned around. And I was convinced that I could make out a fresh set that went all the way to the cabin.

And then my heart began to beat really fast because leading from this third set of tire tracks were *footprints*.

THEY LED ALL AROUND THE CABIN AND UP TO ONE or two of the windows, as if someone had stepped up to peer in. They went to the door and then away again.

I walked slowly back up the dirt road to get the Jeep, taking deep breaths and telling myself that the footprints could belong to anybody. Rufus could have stopped by at some point to see if I was there.

But Rufus wouldn't have peered in through the windows.

I reasoned with myself. I was someone who was used to living on her own. This was the life I had chosen; having the cabin to hole up in was a golden opportunity. The fact that it was so isolated was a plus.

But the truth was I was terrified. It was all very well relishing the life of a hermit in the middle of London where in addition to the criminals I knew were waiting to get me, there were also neighbors I had known since I was a child.

Yet Rufus was close by in the pool house, I told myself. Okay, so he wasn't there all the time but he came home every night. And right now the sun was shining, there wasn't a cloud in the sky, and I had absolutely no reason to feel nervous.

I think I had been pretending to myself that now I was in America I was going to become a different person overnight. I was doing well in the social department. I had opened up—

pretty quickly for me—to the Phillionaire and then to Rufus and I didn't regret it for a second. They seemed to understand me. I had made a tentative friend in Franny although of course I hadn't as yet extended any invitations toward her. It was much too soon. I relished my privacy. It was as simple as that. I didn't like people in and out of my home all the time. I needed my space, as everyone in London who knew me well was always telling me, rolling their eyes in mock exasperation.

Well, now I had found my private space on a beautiful deserted beach but there was something missing. I needed someone there to shield me from the person who parked their car at night and watched me and sneaked around the place by day when I wasn't there.

I needed Tommy—because he had been the person who had always shielded me before. But had I not vowed to stop using Tommy in this way?

I let myself into the cabin, selected my favorite mug from the Phillionaire's collection of hand-painted Breton pottery and made myself coffee. I turned CNN on low and glanced every now and then at the news crawl running along the bottom of the screen. I was a little ashamed to admit that I found it hard to listen to the presenters talking *and* follow the crawl's headlines at the same time. I'd read somewhere that other people complained about this problem but on closer examination I had discovered they were seniors. Clearly I was precocious in my senility.

Oh Tommy! He had never called me back. What else could I do to make him understand that I really did want to reach out to him?

I could, I decided after a moment or two's thought, write him a letter. That was what I should do. I could lay it all out, calmly and rationally.

But exactly what was it that I wanted to say? That I was sorry he had lost his job? That it didn't make any difference to us? That no matter how different we were I would always love him? This was beginning to sound suspiciously like a kiss-off letter, which was somewhat ironic given we were already separated. Clearly I would need to give it some thought.

I went out to the Jeep to get a notepad I had stashed in the glove compartment and that's when I found the paper bag Scott Abernathy had given me. Bettina's notes! I'd brought them home and forgotten all about them.

Scott hadn't been exaggerating when he said she used whatever she could get her hands on to make notes. When I tossed the contents of the bag onto the kitchen counter I found old prescriptions, bills, a couple of menus, coasters, paper napkins, even toilet tissue as well as numerous indiscriminate scraps of paper torn from other sources.

I laid them out in a line and pieced together the snippets of mean, spidery writing. It was like trying to do a jigsaw. I was faced with a mass of seemingly random thoughts but after about ten minutes of fiddling I managed to shape them into some kind of disjointed narrative.

> *Shotgun's people being evasive. Get Sean to persuade his father I'm right for bk.*
>
> *Sean says he doesn't understand why his mother suddenly got in touch with him but not going to query it. Overjoyed.*
>
> *Angie Marriott alimony situation? No alimony as no divorce but does he support her?*
>
> *Meet Shotgun at house Sept 10. 7:30.*
>
> *P/up Sean 8:40 jitney. What if I'm still with Shotgun? Has Sean told Shotgun he's talking to me? How close Sean and Shotgun?*
>
> *Sean says Shotgun did kill groupie in London.*

Speak Genevieve re deal for unauthorized biog Shotgun if he won't speak to me—from Sean interviews.

Call S to explain about Shotgun canceling & Scott—apologize re missing jitney.

M saw Sean w/shotgun in woods night before Sean killed. Must have been before I took him to jitney. Where were they going?

M saw something. Meet M Mallaby beach at 9.

That was it.

Right, so what did I have here? "S" was presumably Sean.

Her note about her meeting with Shotgun, scheduled for seven thirty on the night Sean was killed, was important. As was her subsequent note to remind herself to call Sean and apologize for not picking him up from the jitney because Shotgun had canceled and she'd gone out with Scott. It confirmed what I'd already heard from Shotgun but I was further intrigued to learn that Bettina had been Sean's original ride to and from the jitney.

But the most explosive things in the notes concerned someone whose name began with "M." M had seen Sean and his father in the woods together the night before Sean was killed. In fact, according to Bettina, M had seen something and she had been going to meet M at the beach near Mallaby at nine. Nine when? The night she was killed? Was M the murderer?

"M" for Marriott? "M" for Mallaby? "M" for Morrison?

She'd say Shotgun, not Marriott, if she meant him. Mallaby was a house. That left Morrison.

Detective Morrison was a shoplifter but did that automatically make him a murderer? And would he investigate a case where he was the perpetrator? And why was I even imagining that a cop could be a murderer? Because I was paranoid, that's why, and it was high time I stopped speculating like this.

I pulled the notepad toward me to begin drafting my letter to Tommy. But before I could write anything the phone rang.

"I'm sorry I sent you away so abruptly," I heard Shotgun say, "it was just getting to be more than I could handle but I think I'm okay now. Why don't you come back and I'll make us a late lunch, then maybe we can have another session and I can tell you about Angie. If you're up for it, that is?"

I said "Yes, that's fine," flung on some jeans, and made a mad dash in the Jeep to the supermarket where Franny had told me to go to stock up on some provisions. I decided to play it safe and bought a large quantity of things like toilet tissue, paper towels, and dishwasher detergent, on the assumption that my work with Shotgun would keep me at the cabin for the long haul.

The massive front door to Mallaby was ajar when I arrived and I found Shotgun padding about the kitchen in shorts, a tee, and bare feet.

"I'm making us an onion tart," he said by way of greeting.

"How impressive," I said. And it was. The effort he was making for me at any rate, not to mention the fact that he appeared to be a dab hand in the kitchen.

"Not really." He gestured to a large skillet on the hob. "Just onions softened in butter and then I'll add some eggs and some grated Gruyère and we'll be laughing."

"No, it's the pastry that's earned my respect." I pointed to the empty pastry case.

"Oh, I cheat," he said. "It's frozen. Would you like to wash a lettuce for me and toss a salad?"

As we ate, perched on high stools at the counter, I told him about Bettina's notes.

"Did you know Angie was in touch with Sean?" I asked him.

He didn't answer. In fact he didn't say anything until I told him that Bettina had noted her meeting with him on the night Sean was killed.

"Maybe I should have seen her," he said suddenly. "Sean set it up. He wanted me to see her, became quite obsessed about it, I don't know why."

"So you knew he was talking to her?"

"Well, obviously. He was going to New York but he told me it was all arranged. She'd be coming here around seven thirty that night."

"But he didn't know you canceled her?"

"Sean? No, I don't see how he could have unless she told him. I didn't even know when he was due back."

When I remembered the next note—*Sean says Shotgun did kill groupie in London*—I lost my nerve. I couldn't ask him that straight out. Not yet. Instead I said: "There's a note that says you and Sean were in the woods together the night before Sean was killed."

He looked at me, bewildered.

"Now you're talking nonsense. Sorry, but you are. I wasn't even here the night before Sean was killed. That was a Thursday, right? I was in Connecticut. I drove to the North Shore on the Monday, took the ferry from Orient Point to New London. I didn't get back till Friday morning."

"What were you doing in Connecticut?"

He stared at me for a second. "All these questions. Not working for Evan Morrison by any chance, are you? I went through all of this the first time he interviewed me. I was visiting a guy I know who's written some pretty good songs. We were working on them together. There's just a chance—and I don't want this going in the book until I'm good and ready—there's just a chance that I may get back to recording."

He cleared my plate away and stacked it in the dishwasher.

"So I wasn't in the woods with Sean. Not exactly something we did together, go for father-son walks. Not our style at all. So I'll make us some coffee and then we'll get started, right?"

I had wanted to ask him who M might be but he had made it clear he didn't want to dwell on Bettina's notes anymore. I found this strange considering he wanted so badly to find out who had killed his son. I followed him into the little library and we resumed our positions on the sofa.

"So, Angie."

He had begun talking—eyes closed, seemingly off in another world—before I'd barely got the tape recorder set up.

"Actually I met her for the first time when I was about twelve. She was the daughter of Jack Braithwaite and if ever a man was anathema to my parents it was he. He was a mill owner, Jack Braithwaite, and he had brass, lots of brass, but it was totally unacceptable to my parents because it was new money.

"I'll never forget the one and only time my parents went to the Braithwaites whose house was brand-new and built specially for them. I have to admit it was a monstrosity—red brick, multiple garages, a swimming pool—a real eyesore that didn't sit at all well with the harshness of the moors. But it was spotless and it was warm because it had central heating, something I'd never encountered before. The living room had wall-to-wall shag carpeting and a coffee table. Well, it was too much for my parents. They never accepted another invitation. My mother dismissed them as nouveau riche when we were only five minutes out the door and we rushed home to embrace the freezing cold dilapidated chaos that was Mallaby, stinking of dogs and my father's whiskey fumes and held captive to the vagaries of outdated and malfunctioning plumbing."

I sat there beside him thinking that nowadays we looked back to the precomputer age and thought *that* was barbaric. I found it truly amazing to think that people like Shotgun—and indeed my parents, inhabitants of the twenty-first century like myself—had spent a large part of their lives without any of the appliances and modern conveniences that we take for granted today.

Shotgun downed a glass of water and closed his eyes again.

"But when I was about fourteen I learned of the existence of the guitar and then there was no stopping me. Once I escaped from the confines of Mallaby and went down south to school, I managed to save up my pocket money and buy a little turntable of my own. Then at Harrow I applied for guitar lessons and I lucked into a teacher who was a closet blues fanatic. He introduced me to Muddy Waters and Buddy Guy. I did the unthinkable as far as my parents were concerned. I sold a Parker pen they had given me for my birthday for twenty pounds, a massive amount of money in those days, and with it I bought myself a Spanish acoustic guitar and a little transistor radio. The good thing about Mallaby was that it was so vast that no one could hear the agonizing guitar practice going on in my room and the stone walls were so thick they masked the rock 'n' roll blasting out of the radio. Even when I had it at full volume, which I frequently did.

"Jack Braithwaite had big plans for Angie. He was determined to spend a large part of his money launching her into society. She was sent off to do the debutante season and during the course of it, as she would later tell me, our paths crossed several times. As the only son of good Yorkshire stock and landowners to boot I was prime husband material. But I wasn't your basic chinless wonder like a lot of my peers. I was a rough diamond in many ways and not just in my looks."

I sneaked a quick glance at him. He wasn't chinless by any means but there was nothing rough about his looks either as far as I could see. Indeed the most striking thing about his face were his fine patrician features. In many ways he was a dead ringer for the image of Andrew Jackson that I looked at every time I took out a twenty-dollar bill.

"Essentially, I was bored by the season. It was a round of endless parties at various estates all over the country. But I overrode my parents' disapproval and went to Jack Braithwaite's dance for Angie in Yorkshire.

"Two things made me fall in love with her. Jack Braithwaite's money paid for a London group to come up and play in the disco, you know, with amps and a PA, and everything was miked up including the drums. The sound was so loud it was like being at a rock concert. Most deb dances had some local band who couldn't be heard above all the Hooray Henrys and Henriettas braying at each other. A member of the band had a Gibson electric guitar and he let me have a go on it. I was in heaven and so high that I went straight up to Angie and asked her to dance and as I did so, they turned the lights down low and the band started playing 'On Broadway,' the Drifters hit.

"I held her very close and she began to sing in my ear—'They say the neon lights are bright'—and I joined in with 'on Broadway' and what can I tell you? We clicked. She was this voluptuous warm armful. For the whole season I'd been dancing with callow girls and suddenly here was someone who felt like a woman. She had big tits and they pressed against my chest and I thought I was going to go wild."

Suddenly he sat up straight and turned to face me on the sofa.

"What you have to understand, Lee, is that in those days nice girls didn't. You couldn't expect to have sex with your well-brought-up girlfriend—or even your fiancée—before marriage."

"You didn't get laid until—" I said without thinking and then blushed.

"Of course I did." He laughed. "There were plenty of girls who weren't 'nice.' But Angie was different. She was a virgin and she wouldn't do more than kiss me. When I finally realized she was dead serious it came as a big shock to find that I really respected her for it. Say what you will about antiquated sexual customs, I'm here to tell you that because I had to wait for Angie, I fell in love with her."

"So she became your girlfriend?"

Now he looked uncomfortable. "Yes—and no. There's no getting around it, I behaved like a shit towards her. I saw her on the quiet. I was part of a certain snobby set, the kids of friends of my parents, and they didn't acknowledge Angie as one of them. On the one occasion I took her to Mallaby, my parents were so patronizing, I think I would have preferred it if they had snubbed her altogether rather than subject her to such humiliation. And she was intelligent enough to understand that she was not accepted. In fact she was as angry with her father for inflicting his own upwardly mobile aspirations on her as I was with my parents for their superior attitude towards her family."

"So how did the two of you wind up together?"

He didn't answer for a minute or two. Then he said quietly, "I wish I didn't have to put this in the book but I know I have to. But I'm ashamed—ashamed that it took an act of hateful violence to bring me to my senses about Angie."

He turned away from me as if he did not want to see my reaction to what he was about to say.

"The other young 'bucks,' as Jack Braithwaite called them, my so-called friends, had her marked as an easy lay. I knew they had no concrete proof of this because she was a virgin. But, for the simple reason that she was, in their eyes, common, they assumed she was there for the taking. They referred to her as a cheap 'bint' or a 'fuckable little totty,' aping the local Yorkshire idiom. They felt she wasn't worthy of their respect and to my shame I never set them straight.

"They drank a lot—we all did and of course I was only a year or so away from experimenting with a ton of drugs. According to one of them from whom I got the whole story later on, they were drinking heavily the night it happened, revving themselves up to the point where they were like the pack of hounds they followed when out hunting. They scented blood and there was no stopping them.

"Jack and Mother Braithwaite—as he always called her instead of Vera—were away in Leeds. Angie was home alone. She let them in when they rang the bell at ten o'clock at night. Why wouldn't she? She knew them, they'd all come to her dance. There were five of them and they took turns with her, on the dining room table, in the conservatory, upstairs in her bedroom. It was like some ghastly Yorkshire variation of the girl getting gang-raped by the high school football team. They all had her except for the one who told me all about it and he came clattering out of the closet as soon as it became legal in 1967.

"She managed to get to the phone at some point and she called me and I went over there like a shot. I'd never had a boxing lesson in my life but I landed a couple of near lethal uppercuts and put at least two of them in hospital. I found myself to be capable of a violence I never knew existed within me."

He shook himself a little and turned back to me with an almost embarrassed smile.

"So there you have it, the story of Kip and Angie, part one."

"What happened next?"

"Well, we took off"—he shrugged—"don't ask me why. It just never occurred to us to do anything else. One of those monsters must have got it together to call an ambulance after we left but they kept quiet about what actually happened because no one ever came after me about it."

"What about Angie? Didn't she need to see a doctor?"

"We went to Mallaby, picked up a few things, and then we drove through the night to London, stopping at a hospital in Leicester so she could be treated. We had no intention of ever returning to Yorkshire."

"But what about her parents?"

"Jack Braithwaite's response made me sick!" Shotgun slammed his palm down on the armrest for emphasis. "He probably had something to do with the whole thing being kept quiet. When he came back from Leeds I called him from London and gave him the edited version. Angie wouldn't let me go into details but I told him enough to make him see his little girl had been ruined in the eyes of Yorkshire society. I think it says it all that he didn't care enough to go after his daughter's rapists—or that Angie felt there was no point in contacting her mother. *Vera only ever does what Dad tells her.* In her own way Angie was as alienated from her parents as I was from mine and that provided the core of our initial bonding.

"You see, in a way, by taking her off his hands I'd secured for Angie what he had always wanted for her. In his eyes, I was a lord of the manor. The only problem was that when I ran away to London, my father cut me out of his will.

"So there we were, Kip and Angie, living in a damp and moldy basement we'd rented in Earl's Court. It took a few months before she was ready to have sex with me. She was traumatized and I suppose she should have had counseling. But all she had was me and I tried to be as patient and understanding as I could—even though I was panting for her. We made love for the first time on a mattress on the floor and I swear we had group sex with a ton of fleas but it was worth waiting for."

He sighed and sitting beside him, I felt as if I were intruding on an intimate moment.

"I am never—ever—going to forget those first few years with

Angie. I don't think it's an exaggeration to say that we were both giving—and receiving—love for the first time in our lives and it was nothing less than explosive."

His voice had a longing in it that echoed the tenderness I had caught in Angie Marriott's when she had talked about him. She had called him a decent man, wonderful and kind. And I think it was at this point that I knew it was not the rambunctious life of a hell-raising rock star that I would be writing, but an intense and poignant love story.

I surreptitiously looked down to see that the tape was still running as he got up and stretched. When he returned to the sofa he perched on the armrest with his arms folded and I sensed he had turned a corner in his narrative. I shifted a little now that he had left me more space on the sofa and settled down to listen to the rest of the story.

"I only had about a hundred pounds on me when we arrived in London," he said, and I could tell he had regained control of his emotions. I made a mental note not to interrupt him unless I had to. "And although it was an absolute fortune in those days, it lasted about twenty seconds because we had to use it on renting a flat and buying food and getting established in London. We were living pretty much hand to mouth. Everything ran on a meter that you fed with coins—gas fires, electricity, phone. If you ran out of shillings, you froze. We used to go looking for empty bottles in the streets and we'd take them to pubs and get money to live on in exchange. A bit different from the life we'd been living up in Yorkshire.

"I bought Angie a battered little secondhand Remington typewriter and she taught herself to type, sitting at our rickety kitchen table till all hours of the night, bashing the keys in time to music. The faster the tempo, the faster she had to type. Sometimes I accompanied her on my guitar and she typed to that. She taught herself a kind of speedwriting too and once she was up to ninety words a minute she went out to get a job."

I reached for my pad and started to scribble a few notes, confident that he was now on track to deliver the practical facts of their life together.

"She found one right away—as a secretary to a bank manager—and there she was, going off to the office every morning leaving me to loaf around London wondering what on earth I was going to do with myself all day. There was a little record shop in a basement in Soho where they had all the American imports and I used to go there and listen to them. I drove them mad because I couldn't afford to buy anything. Finally the owner took pity on me and invited me to accompany him to R & B all-nighters at the clubs—the Marquee, the Scene, the Hundred Club—where my heroes, Muddy Waters, Sonny Boy Williamson, B.B. King, played when they came to London.

"I was always on at Angie to come with me but she had to get up to go to work the next day, she couldn't stay up till four in the morning every night. I offered her some of the speed I was taking to stay awake, Dexedrine I think it was, but she wasn't into any of that. And you know I rather liked having her there all warm and sleepy when I crawled into bed with her every morning and we had a couple of hours together before her alarm went off.

"But I wished she'd been there one night at the Marquee because the support band was the one that had played at her dance and I went up and chatted to the guy who had let me have a go on his Gibson. He told me he was about to quit the band, said he'd had enough, wanted to form his own setup. Of course one thing led to another. Instead of going home to Angie that night, I went out on the razzle with Jimmy and the next morning, when he heard me play in his hotel room, he told me I was a natural and

I should keep in touch with him. He gave me the names of a few places where I could go and sit in with a band to get some practice and pick up a few bob. Angie kept asking when I was going to get a job and I kept telling her 'I've got one, I'm a musician,' and she'd say 'Yes, but when are you going to get a real job?'

"Well, I kept in touch with Jimmy and his Gibson and when he formed a band—the Suits—I was part of it and when he OD'd from a lethal speedball a couple of years later, I moved automatically into the lead slot. Suddenly it was Shotgun Marriott and the Suits and when we released a record and it went straight to number one, Angie found herself married to a rock star."

"So was she along on the road with you or did she stay home to take care of Sean?" I felt it was time I started chipping in a bit.

"Neither," he said, "we were together for years before we had Sean. We put off trying to have a kid but then when we decided it was time, it looked like we weren't going to be able to. It was something of a miracle she didn't get pregnant when she was raped but I began to wonder whether maybe something had happened to her then—you know, to prevent her from having a child."

"So if she wasn't at home with Sean and she wasn't on tour with you, where was she?"

"Building a career for herself. Angie, it turned out, was a lot more straight than I was."

"Straight?"

"The word didn't have as much sexual connotation in those days. When we said someone was straight, we meant they didn't do drugs, they had a boring office job, they were straight-up responsible, normal people. I suppose we thought they were uncool. But Angie had a good head on her shoulders and she was shrewd about money. God knows, she had to be, she worked in it. She's a financial adviser now, did you know that? Tells people what to do with their pensions. Can you imagine anything more boring?"

"So she was a suit?"

"Totally. We always thought it was hilarious that my band was called the Suits. And of course the druggy flower power didn't come along until the late sixties. Early on she slotted in okay because everyone had boring jobs by day and went to sophisticated nightclubs at night. The class barrier collapsed and it became fashionable to be working class. Angie's Yorkshire accent was a plus."

"She sounds like she'd have been a big success in the eighties."

"Oh, she was—the nineties too. She was dot-comming it all over the place before we'd even heard of it. Poor Sean. He barely saw his parents for the first ten years of his life—Angie was at the office all day and I was away on the road or in the studio. But look, I'd better tell you about the early days, when the marriage first started to go wrong."

"When did you actually get married?"

"Not till 1980. At Chelsea Register Office in the King's Road. It was all over in a few minutes."

"Why then?"

"Sean was born. Angie wanted to make him legit. So did I, as a matter of fact. It was important to me even though things were already pretty bad between us."

"Because Angie never participated in your career? Never came out on the road with you?"

"Actually," he said, "she did in the beginning. That was part of the problem. When I began to hit the big time, she really tried. She gave up her office job—whatever it was at the time, I forget, working for an accountant or something equally boring to me— and she insisted on coming on the road."

"And she hated it."

"Absolutely right. She didn't fit in at all. She was so straight. There was me with my hair halfway down my back, a shark's tooth hanging off my ear, wearing a snakeskin waistcoat over my bare chest and high-heeled boots and God knows what else. And she'd be sitting there at the side of the stage in her tailored frock and her cardigan and pearls and an Alice band and little black shoes with grosgrain bows on them. It was a fucking joke. I mean, I was like a reptile." He grinned. "I smelled foul most of the time, all that sweating on stage. And there were all those hangers-on. We were never alone. Angie'd be sitting up in bed in our hotel room in Birmingham or Sheffield or wherever with the cocoa she'd ordered from room service, and there'd be people passing out and sleeping on the floor beside us. Not that we did much sleeping. Sometimes I didn't get any kip for as long as forty hours."

"So she gave up and went home and you drifted apart."

"Don't write her off too soon." He wagged a finger at me. "What you have to realize about Angie is that she's tough. Much more than I am. She loved me. She was in it for the long haul and she found a way to deal with it and *that's* where it all began to fall apart."

I noticed that talking about this period, he was getting quite animated. His accent was slipping into the Mockney mixed with a mid-Atlantic inflection that he normally presented to the out-side world.

"Angie decided it was a question of if you can't beat 'em, join 'em and although she'd always steered clear of it before, now she began to take speed to stay awake. Dexedrine. And she drank. Rum and Coke. Scotch and Coke. Vodka neat. She was an out-of-control lush before I'd even realized what was happening. It was—" He paused and turned away from me. "It was pitiful," I heard him say softly.

I waited for him to go on.

"I put her in rehab. It was for her own good, of course, but I have to admit that I just didn't want to deal with her. I was pretty strung out myself. I'm lucky I've never had a problem, but I was living a pretty wild life."

"Did she resent you doing that?"

"At first. But she got her act together. When she got clean she went back to work. She got *her* career in finance off and running."

"And she stayed clean?"

"More or less. We began to live separate lives. We came together in London whenever I was there—and it was wonderful. There was this incredible bond between us despite the fact that our approach to life was totally different. But I fucked it up."

"How come?"

"The usual way. You have girls screaming at you every night that you can have them whenever you want, what are you going to do? It got lonely on the road."

"Groupies?" I'd finally brought it up.

"Actually, no." He shook his head. "I didn't go in for groupies much whatever people said. I just found myself girls to keep me company. Girls I could talk to. There had to be some intelligence there."

"But there was a groupie in your bed—that night—in London?"

"Yes," he said, and I noticed his hands were clenched together so hard the blood was draining out of them. "Yes, there was."

Then, as he'd done at our last session, he suddenly got to his feet and started pacing round the room.

"I can't do it. I'm sorry. I know I said I would, but I can't. Not right now. We'll have to come back to it another time."

And that was it.

Once again I found myself driving home in a state of confusion. He'd talk for just so long and then he seemed to go into a kind of panic. I'd left the tapes lying on the sofa. He hadn't even wanted me to go up and transcribe them as we'd agreed.

I stared straight ahead with my chin up as I approached the cabin, driving slowly along the dark stretch of road with only the blinking light of the radio tower in the dunes to guide me. My resolve broke down and I glanced in the rearview mirror, expecting to see the twin circles of two headlamps following me.

But it was pitch-black all the way. I pottered about the cabin for a little while, making myself a cup of tea and heating up a bowl of clam chowder for my supper. When I'd finished it I picked up my notepad and lay down on the bed to make yet another start on Tommy's letter.

I got as far as "My dearest Tommy, I was devastated to hear about your losing" before I fell into possibly the deepest sleep I had enjoyed since arriving in America.

CHAPTER 9

THE BACK ROOM OF THE OLD STONE MARKET looked extremely inviting when I walked in the next morning. The smell of freshly brewed coffee wafted around the room and Franny had laid out a plate of doughnuts and placed a vase of brightly colored anemones in the middle of the table.

"She make coffee shop," explained Jesus, "she want people come in here, sit, drink coffee, be happy—and buy something."

It made sense to me. But I could tell the minute I walked into the store that her mood did not match the welcoming atmosphere she had created. She didn't even acknowledge me and went right on yelling at Rufus who was trying to edge his way out the door.

"Why did you have to tell him? Why? Couldn't you have just left it where it was?"

I looked at Rufus.

"She's talking about the bow and arrow," he said. "She's pissed that I told Detective Morrison about them."

"You know about this?" she asked me.

"I was there."

"See!" She advanced upon Rufus. "Lee didn't go running to the police and tell them my son's bow and arrow had been found at a construction site." She paused for a second in her onslaught. "You didn't, did you?" I shook my head.

"I didn't say they were Dumpster's," said Rufus wearily. "And he was going to find out about them anyway sooner or later. I wasn't the only one to see them."

I had an inkling of how Franny must be feeling. She was worried sick about Dumpster and the fact that she didn't know where he was half the time. She couldn't even defend him anymore. She'd gone on record at the arraignment saying she hadn't been home the nights Sean and Bettina were killed so she couldn't be his alibi.

"I gotta go," said Rufus and I followed him out the door.

"I had to tell Morrison. Didn't I?" he appealed to me.

"Of course," I said but I wasn't really listening to him. My attention had been distracted by a car that had drawn up to park alongside Rufus's truck. Louis Nichols, the president of the Stone Landing Residents Association, got out and went into the store but the person who had caught my attention was his passenger. It was the woman who had appeared on the beach in the middle of my mother's commitment ceremony. She didn't look quite the same. As she stepped out of the car I saw that her hair, which had been long and flowing as she walked along the beach, was now scraped back into a French twist. Nor was she wearing the hippie caftan I had first seen her in; she had on a crisp white shirt and jeans. Her face was tanned and weather-beaten, and up close I could see it was etched in lines that told me she was well into her fifties, but even so she was definitely what Tommy would call a looker.

She was looking straight at me but she didn't seem to register me. She went into the store and I said good-bye to Rufus and followed her, intrigued. Louis Nichols was ordering breakfast. I noticed he followed Franny as she moved about the store doing a stock check, trying to engage her in conversation. The woman I had followed went straight to the back room and poured herself a cup of coffee but instead of sitting down at the table, she stood before the notice board, studying it intently. I moved up to stand behind her and saw her remove the card about the wedding dresses and slip it in her pocket. Was she someone who was interested in buying a wedding dress—or was she the person who had put the card there in the first place?

She was the latter, I discovered with a little frisson of excitement when she sat down at the table and smiled at me, patting the bench beside her. I was a little taken aback. I had come in to get breakfast, not to socialize, loner that I was, but before I could politely decline, Franny came over.

"You two should get to know each other," she said. "Lee, this is Martha Farrell. Martha, this is Lee Bartholomew. She's the daughter of the woman Rufus's dad married."

"They weren't married," I said automatically.

"Yeah, well, whatever." Franny didn't look convinced. "But Martha, Lee here is a writer. I mean, a professional writer. She's published, unlike most of the folks who hang out in writing groups around here and never get anywhere."

"Like me," said Martha, giving me a wink. "Only I don't even go to groups. I just slave away on my own, getting nowhere."

"Well, anyway, I just thought you guys might have something in common." Franny was edging away. Louis Nichols had followed her to the table and was sitting down to eat his breakfast. I saw Martha Farrell's fingers reach out in a fleeting, stroking gesture to his hand on the table. And I noted the way he quickly snatched it away.

"So what do you write?" asked Martha.

I explained about being a ghostwriter and then asked about her work.

"I'm trying to write a novel and the truth is I need guidance," she said. "I have a confession to make. Franny already told me about you, said you often came by the store in the mornings and maybe I could run into you—you know, accidentally."

"Ah." I wasn't sure I liked the sound of this.

"I was kind of wondering if you'd read my manuscript, give me your take on it. I'd pay you, of course," she added quickly.

"I'm not a novelist," I pointed out, "or an editor."

"It doesn't matter," she said. "I'm desperate. I just want it read by a professional."

It was a pretty outrageous request and I cursed Franny silently for setting me up like this.

"I saw you take your card off the notice board," I said, stalling for time. "Why did you do that?"

"Why? Do you need a wedding dress?"

"I don't know. Maybe. Who knows?" She had caught me by surprise with the question.

"Doesn't sound like you'd be my best bet as a customer. Actually, I took the card down for two reasons. I'm not really selling my dresses anymore." She made it sound as if they were her own wedding dresses. "And the other reason is a little darker. Franny said you're going to be working with Shotgun Marriott on his book. Well, Sean Marriott's body was found in one of my dresses and I'm not wild about anyone being reminded of the fact that I once sold them."

"He was wearing one of *your* dresses?"

"When they pulled him out of the ocean, yes."

Louis Nichols had been listening silently beside us. Now he finished his breakfast and prepared to leave. Martha clasped his forearm as he stood up. I noticed he looked rather uncomfortable and didn't return the gesture. "I'll see you later," she said. And when he didn't reply, "Won't I?"

When he'd gone she turned to me.

"Do you have wheels?"

I nodded. "Do you need a ride?"

"I don't have a car." She laughed. "I never learned to drive. Where are you staying? If it's anywhere near me, it'd be great if you could drop me off."

When I told her she clapped her hands and said, "Yes, that's not far away." She lived farther along the bay.

"Yes, Sean was wearing one of my dresses," she resumed when we set off in the Jeep.

"You were there when they pulled him out?"

"I was over by the ocean that day. There was a big storm and I love walking by the ocean when the sea's rough and seeing the breakers. It's exhilarating. Earlier in the day I'd been walking along the bay and there was a wedding in progress, can you believe it? They went ahead with the weather like that. I like to watch weddings and see what the brides are wearing. This was an older woman—"

"That was my mother," I said.

She turned in the Jeep and looked at me. "You know, I knew I'd seen you somewhere before. Your *mother* getting married, you'll have to tell me that story. Sorry to gate-crash the ceremony but weddings at the water's edge are perfect. There's no law to stop me walking along the beach providing I keep below the high-water mark but I'm afraid it's got me a bit of a reputation. They say I was jilted at the altar and I go to other people's weddings because I never had one of my own."

Her cackle reverberated against the canvas roof of the Jeep. I wondered what on earth I was doing with this woman. Was she a nutcase? I suspected her nonstop chatter masked a bundle of nerves.

Of course I knew the answer to my question. I was with her because Sean Marriott had been wearing one of her dresses when he died and because her name began with "M." *M saw something.*

M saw something. M saw something. The words repeated themselves over and over in my head as the Jeep hurtled down Cranberry Hole Road. *Meet M Mallaby beach at 9.*

"Anyway, yes," she said, "I walked along the bay all the way to Lazy Point and the Shellfish Hatchery guys were there with this veil that had become entangled in a clam raft they were towing. Everybody was standing around and going *ooh* and *aah*. What was a wedding veil doing floating in the bay? It was drenched but I recognized it immediately as one of mine. Then we got word that a body had been pulled out of the ocean so I called Louis Nichols on my cell phone and asked him to come and pick me up and drive me over there."

"But how come Sean was wearing one of your wedding dresses?"

"Because he used to come over and borrow them. He liked dressing up in them. He'd go for walks through the woods in them and I'm here to tell you—he made a seriously beautiful bride."

"When did you give him that particular dress?"

"Oh, I don't know. About a week earlier. Wait a minute, slow down, you make a left here."

She directed me to take a turn off Cranberry Hole Road not far from the one that led to Shotgun's house. Like the dirt track going to Mallaby, this road ran through woods, but instead of leading to a proper driveway, it petered out into a sandy lane. We arrived at a clearing in the beach grass on which stood two beaten-up trailers.

"Here we are. Home sweet home."

"You live *here*?" I said before I could stop myself. What was a woman like her doing living in a makeshift trailer park? "Sorry, that was rude. I just expected—"

"You just expected me to live in a fancy Hamptons home.

Well, get real. There's plenty of us who live out here who don't have a bean to our name."

"Do you own this land?"

"Not an inch of it. It belongs to the town, although I got this spot from an old fisherman I met when I first came here. He leased it. He came back from several years working on long-liners or gillnetters or draggers or whatever work he could find and discovered his little shack had fallen down, been blown over in a hurricane or something. So he took off again—but not before he'd told me I could do whatever I wanted with his spot. See, we're on Lazy Point here—"

"We are?" I looked along the bay and recognized the inlet where I'd gone after my first visit to Shotgun.

"—and as I said, this old bayman, he doesn't own the land. The town does. At the end of WWII the town fathers divided the beach around here into various lots and assigned leases. You could own a house but not the land. The town kept that. And you can only sell your house, catch-22 style, to someone who already lives at Lazy Point. So when his shack fell down, the old guy didn't really have anything."

"So these trailers?"

"I found them, had them towed to the lot and deposited right onto the beach. I scoured all the yard sales and the dump for a mass of broken-down furniture and then I found someone to fix all of it. I talked a ship's carpenter I knew into working for next to nothing alongside local plumbers and electricians and pretty soon I had a home. Come on in and take a look."

She opened the door to the first trailer and it was like entering another world. Right in front of us was a wood-burning stove, the chimney going out through the roof of the trailer. There were no chairs, only benches built into the wall around a table that was nailed to the floor.

"For when the next hurricane hits," said Martha ominously.

In the window of the trailer overlooking the water there was a big ship's wheel and a telescope.

"In the eyes of the town these trailers are his so I kind of wanted them to have a masculine, seafaring feel." Martha stood behind the wheel. "See, it's like you're steering a ship, looking out to sea. I figured if he ever came back, he'd feel right at home."

"How long has he been gone?"

"Oh, about twenty years. He's probably dead." The infuriating cackle again.

"So the town could turn you out at any time?"

Her laughter subsided instantly. "You've got it in one," she said. Her manic self-assurance faltered and for a second I saw a vulnerable middle-aged woman of no means whatsoever.

At the other end was a kitchen area. All the appliances were pretty basic with the exception of a giant stainless-steel fridge that dwarfed the rest of the confined space.

"Isn't she a beaut?" said Martha. "Just got her in a sale. Now come and meet my girls."

Did she have daughters stashed away somewhere? Cats?

The trailers stood opposite each other, leaving a sandy patio in between. There was a screened-in porch attached to the back of one trailer.

"See, I've got a little fridge set up out here and a grill. This is my summer living room." She pointed to a little card table and some wrought-iron weatherproof beach furniture. There were little feminine touches here and there, window boxes with geraniums, brightly colored cushions, displays of conches and other shells.

The layout of the other trailer was weird. We walked straight into a primitive bathroom—a shower and loo behind a curtain. To the left was Martha's bedroom—a double bunk bed built into the wall covered with a patchwork quilt, a little rocker, and another wood-burning stove. Were they her only way of heating the place? High up, just underneath the ceiling, bookshelves ran around the walls but when I glanced up I saw they were crammed with magazines, not books. I looked closer and saw they were all back issues of *Brides* magazine. A tiny feeling of unease began to work its way around my head.

"Isn't it great?" she said. "I can lie in bed and listen to the waves lapping away outside."

"What about in the winter? Doesn't it get a little bracing out here on the beach?"

Her enthusiasm evaporated in a second. "It's a nightmare," she conceded. "And it can be pretty terrifying. Of course it's calmer over here on the bay side but there are times when I think the waves are going to rise up and obliterate me. The tide comes up underneath the trailers and I just sit in here and quake."

Suddenly I realized she was in a far more precarious state than I had begun to imagine. Whatever image she tried to present to the world, by living here right on the beach she was bordering on bag lady status.

"But hey!" she said, the smile returning. "It's free and you know what? I could put up with everything if it wasn't for the wind. Wind destroys me, it always has. It's not just my arthritis, it's what it does to my head. Sometimes I think I'm going to go crazy. I know it looks cozy in here but the wind always finds a way to get to me."

"I hate the wind too," I said. "I can't write a word when it's howling outside."

"Me either," she said, pointing to a corner, and I noticed a little laptop set up on a makeshift trestle table. I couldn't help but admire how organized she was.

"So, time you met the girls."

Her "girls" were her wedding dresses. They were in the other end of the trailer on the far side of the bathroom. A tiny portion of the area housed Martha's own clothes in a built-in closet and a chest of drawers, while the rest of the room was given over to racks, the kind they use in garment districts to wheel clothes up and down streets. And hanging from them, encased in transparent plastic covers blurring the sight of them and rendering them as lines of girlish wraiths, were wedding dresses. There must have been at least fifty and they spooked me because they looked like an assembly of reproachful brides who had been put in storage and forgotten.

"Aren't they just the most beautiful things you have ever seen?" Martha plunged into them, unzipping the covers and fingering the lace or the satin or the silk. "So your mother got married in a short dress. Makes a change. What happened to your dad?"

"She's still married to him." The look on her face when I said that made me rush to explain about the Phillionaire. Then I asked her flat out. "Why do you collect wedding dresses?"

"Well, it's a long story but, you know, there's no smoke without fire." She led me back outside to sit in the screened-in porch and I was relieved. I really couldn't wait to get away from the wedding dresses. I felt they were *watching* me.

"You want some lemonade?" She took a pitcher out of the little fridge and poured me a glass. "You see, I *was* jilted a long time ago right before the wedding and it nearly destroyed me. But you know, I'm from an era when women didn't give in to their neuroses, didn't fall apart and start spouting a lot of self-help claptrap like they do now." She reached across and patted my hand to show she didn't mean me. "So I pulled myself together and I decided I wouldn't become bitter and twisted. I would start over and somehow I would make something out of what had happened to me. So I moved out here and all I had left was my wedding dress. I was an actress back then and I was working off-Broadway. I was moving around all the time, wherever my work took me. I really didn't have that many possessions. It was June. I went for a walk along the beach. I walked by three weddings and I thought to myself, this is big business out here."

"You gave up acting?"

"There wasn't much to give up. My acting career was going nowhere. I told myself, *Girl, there are three things that you do well. You can act but that didn't work out. You can write*—and that's where you come in." Another pat on my hand and I folded my arms to ward off any further attempts. *"And you can sew.* Under the bench in the trailer back there is a Singer. You'd be amazed how many girls who think they're going to hang on to their wedding dresses forever wind up getting rid of them. The marriage goes sour, what are they going to do? They're going to offload them onto me for a knockdown price and I'm going to remodel them into amazing gowns I can sell to gullible new brides."

"Where's your showroom? The beach?"

"Don't knock it," she said. "What better place? Most of the weddings take place there anyway. But no, you're right. Actually I go to their houses for the fittings."

"And Sean Marriott modeled for you? How did you meet him?"

"Hah!" She slapped her knee. "That's a good one. I met him right here on the beach. It's secluded down here. No one's ever around and there were these guys, they had a ceremony like your mother's only they were gay. I made the bride's dress. Sean came to the 'wedding' and I showed him my collection. After that he borrowed dresses one at a time, at least once a month."

"And that's how he came to be wearing it when he was killed?"

"I wondered if maybe he was returning it to me when he was attacked? I wasn't here. I had a big problem that night. I'd had a ride earlier in the day to Sag Harbor where I had an appointment with the foot doctor there. Have you ever had an ingrown toenail? It's the worst. And then I did a little shopping; there's a health food store where I can get the short-grain brown rice that I like. I browsed in BookHampton and I walked over the bridge to North Haven to catch the sunset. And then I did something quite unusual for me. I stuck out my thumb and hitched a ride to the Shelter Island ferry. It's a really special place, totally unspoiled."

"Did you really?" I was impressed. I would never in a million years hitch a ride from a stranger. I always imagined they'd strangle me as soon as I got in the car.

"So I went to Shelter Island—it's only a five-minute hop and I wandered around there as far as I could get on foot but then, of course, I couldn't get home. I had my cell phone but I didn't know the numbers for cabs on Shelter Island. And when I finally knocked on a door and asked for a number, there were no cabs available. No one wanted to drive as far as Lazy Point."

"So what did you do?"

"I went and stood by the ferry until I found someone who was coming this way. I didn't get back until nearly midnight by which time, from what I can make out, poor Sean was already floating in the bay."

So much for *M saw something*.

"You said you lived near Mallaby? It's close to here?"

"Just along the bay and through the woods over there." She nodded behind her.

"So the next night—Bettina was killed very near here?"

"And I was over by the ocean watching them haul poor Sean out of the water."

"And then? You said you were with Louis Nichols?"

"You don't miss a trick, do you? I went home with Louis,

spent the night there. He lives within walking distance of the Old Stone Market."

"He brought you to the market this morning?"

She looked at me quizzically. "Yes. He did. We're an item, as they say, only he's not too keen to make it public. Doesn't really like us being seen as a couple. I think he's got a crush on Franny Cook and he never likes me cramping his style when he goes to the Old Stone Market."

"Surely not?" I tried to make it sound as if I didn't believe what she was saying but I recalled noting Louis Nichols's interest in Franny at the Stone Landing Residents Association meeting, and the way he had followed her around this morning was revealing.

"Stands to reason. She's a beautiful creature who's at least twenty years younger than I am." Once again the vulnerable side of her filtered through a chink in her buoyant and theatrical armor.

I wondered who had jilted her all those years ago. However much she might claim she had put it all behind her, her confidence was clearly still pretty shaky where men were concerned. Louis Nichols would be a good catch. His money would get her out of her precarious trailer existence.

I was uncomfortable in her presence. Was it because I felt sorry for her? Was it a case of it takes one to know one and having been jilted by Tommy, I knew how she felt? Was I worried that at the rate I was going, I too would wind up one day living on the beach like this eccentric old maid?

"I'd better be going," I said, getting to my feet.

"What about my manuscript?" she asked. "I've got it right here."

There was a pleading note in her voice that got to me. I knew how important it was to get feedback on your work. Whenever I finished a book I'd ghosted, I sat around biting my nails until I had first the publisher's and then—twice as nerve-racking—my subject's reaction.

I thought quickly. By all accounts, Bettina had interviewed several people in the area while researching Shotgun, Sean Marriott included. I wouldn't be able to talk to Sean for obvious reasons but access to someone who'd known him might prove to be valuable.

"Okay," I said, "let me take it with me but I have to tell you, I'm not sure how much time I'll have."

"Listen," she said, "take your time. Here's my number, just give me a call when you're ready to talk about it. If it's a nice day I can walk to you along the bay."

It was only as I was driving home that I realized she knew where I was staying.

There was a message from Cath on the Phillionaire's answering machine and it was highly intriguing to say the least.

"Hey, Lee, it's me, Cath. Where are you? Out on the town with Shotgun Marriott? Well, guess what? Angie Marriott's in my AA program right here in Notting Hill. Apparently she stopped coming to meetings for a few years so I never saw her until now. But she's back—and I tell you, she looks a wreck. So anyway, I told her, I went up and said I was a friend of yours and you were working with her husband and she said yes, she'd met you out there. And she wants to talk to you. That's what she said. She told me to tell you that she's changed her mind. So call me soon, okay?"

No word about Tommy, I noticed.

As I got into bed that night and prepared to fall asleep, I thought about how it would be to talk to Angela Marriott now that I knew so much more about her. I couldn't stop myself thinking that it would be some kind of betrayal to Shotgun to talk to her about him.

Yet nothing was going to stop me.

When the phone rang again in the middle of the night, I fumbled for the receiver in a befuddled state, thinking that it was Angie who had tracked me down and wanted to talk *now* and I wasn't ready.

But Rufus's voice said: "Lee, sorry to wake you but we've got a problem. Dumpster just called. Franny's been attacked at the store. She needs to get away from there fast so I'm going to go get her and bring her over to the Stucco House. Can you meet us there? Dumpster says she won't say who it was but she might open up to you. Lee, are you there?"

"I'm here," I said. I was wide awake in a matter of seconds. "Give me twenty minutes and I'll be there."

I THREW ON JEANS AND A SWEATER, GRABBED A FLASH-light and left the cabin. As I ran down to the water, I was aware of agitated rustling in the tall beach grass on either side of the sandy trail. I glanced behind me, looking beyond the cabin to Cranberry Hole Road. The darkness seemed to stretch for eternity but for once it was welcoming because the lack of headlamps meant no one was lying in wait for me in a car.

Unless it was already parked out there in the darkness. The beam from my flashlight would send a signal of where I was going. What if someone came after me along the deserted beach? Maybe I should have taken the Jeep and driven over to the Stucco House but that would have meant going up the dirt road in the dark and confronting whoever was out there. *If* they were out there.

As I walked along the shoreline, shining the flashlight over the murky water—there was no moon and everything was pitch-black—I began to imagine horrible creatures clambering out of the sea to claim me. As far as I knew, there were no alligators in the Hamptons, but there was always a first time. For all I knew, there could be a posse of them on their way up the Eastern seaboard from Florida eager to gobble me up.

As I neared the Stucco House, the dunes were illuminated by the glare of Rufus's headlamps approaching from the opposite direction. He had those lights on the roof that shine down on everything in a truck's path, perfect for hunting at night, I assumed. With a bow and arrow. Or a shotgun. Oh *stop!*

I waved my arms in the air to show him I had arrived and he leapt out as soon as his truck came to a stop.

"I don't know what the hell's going on," he muttered to me. "There isn't a mark on her and she hasn't said a single word since I picked her up. Eliza's been yelling her head off and Franny's used it as an excuse to ignore all my questions. But Dumpster was pretty hysterical when he called me and Franny couldn't get out of the place soon enough when I turned up. Something happened to her but so far it's all a mystery to me. Anyway"—he patted my arm—"thanks for coming over. I'll go on in and sort out a room for her."

I took Eliza from Franny while she climbed down from the truck and she followed me into the house.

"What are you doing here?" she asked me, almost grabbing Eliza back from me. It didn't signify much gratitude on her part but at least she was speaking to me.

"I'm living just along the beach, didn't I tell you? Rufus thought you might want someone with you."

"This is Lucia," Rufus told Franny as Lucia emerged from the kitchen in a quilted robe.

Franny shrugged and said nothing. I wanted to shake her and tell her to be more gracious.

Lucia tried to take Eliza from her, making soothing baby noises, but Franny screamed and backed away from her. "Leave my baby alone!"

"Franny," I said, with mounting impatience, "let her take Eliza. She's only trying to help."

Miraculously, Eliza fell into almost instant silence once Lucia was cradling her. In Franny's arms she had picked up her mother's tension and it had frightened her. Franny followed Lucia and Rufus up the staircase. On the landing Rufus surprised me by rattling off some Spanish at Lucia.

"I've told her to put Eliza in the crib in the old nursery. I don't think it's been used in forty years but she'll be safe there. Franny, you can sleep in the room next door. I'm going to shoot off now because I have to get up and go to work in an hour and a half. Tomorrow we'll go get your stuff. Okay, Franny? Say something, *please!*"

"How am *I* supposed to get to work in the morning?" she said. "I'll have to be there by seven to start serving breakfast."

Rufus looked at me.

"I'll come by and get you," I said. "No problem."

"Thanks," said Franny and began to follow Lucia down the long corridor, leaving us standing at the top of the stairs.

"I'll talk to her in the morning," I said.

"I just want to know who it was who gave her such a scare that she won't sleep in her own bed," said Rufus. "Do you think it could have been my bastard of a brother? It might explain why she's so reluctant to talk to me."

"Scott?" I was shocked at the thought of it but it was a possibility. "What did Dumpster say?"

"He says when he came in, he went upstairs to bed and fell asleep immediately."

"I think Dumpster sleeps in the kitchen," I said, "which isn't above the back room so he probably couldn't hear anything once he was upstairs."

"Whatever," said Rufus, "he woke up around two thirty when he heard a car door slam outside his window and he went down and found Franny in a bad way."

"Bad way, how? Was she injured?"

"He didn't go into specifics. All he said was that she was

slumped at the table in the back room crying and she wouldn't tell him what had happened so he called me. She didn't *appear* to be injured as such when I got there but she was shaking all over. Anyway, see what you can get out of her in the morning. By the way," he called back to me as he walked toward his truck, "my dad called last night and they're on their way home. He said he's going to get out here as soon as he can."

Back at the cabin, I didn't even bother to take my clothes off. I set the alarm for six thirty, lay down on the bed, and when it went off, I leapt up, brushed my teeth, and set off in the Jeep.

When Lucia answered the door, I wondered if she'd even bothered to go back to bed. She had Eliza in her arms once again.

"I'm going to leave Eliza with her for this morning," said Franny. "I've told him to tell Lucia I'm going to send Jesus back with all her stuff. I only brought a couple of feeds with me."

I think I'd known from the beginning that Franny was a pragmatist but until that moment I don't think I'd fully understood just how much of an opportunist she was. Last night she had been unwilling to let Lucia even touch Eliza but only a few hours later she was entrusting her to the woman's care. Franny wasn't about to overlook the fact that she had found a haven with a built-in babysitter.

"So how long are you planning to stay?" I asked her as we set off along Cranberry Hole Road.

"How is it living in the cabin?" she asked me by way of reply.

This was crazy. Was she going to pretend last night had never happened?

"*Franny!* You got Rufus and me out of bed in the middle of the night to rescue you from a situation and now you won't tell us what it was."

"I never got *you* out of bed. Don't put that on me. It was Rufus who called you. Anyway, sounds like you already know what happened from my son."

And that was all I could get out of her before we arrived at the Old Stone Market and she hailed Jesus with, "I'm moving out of the apartment upstairs. I'm going to need you to go over to Napeague with our stuff, once we're done with the breakfast shift. Is the coffee brewed?"

I helped myself to a cup of coffee and marched up the stairs to Franny's little apartment where I found her packing up Eliza's paraphernalia into canvas holdalls.

"Okay, Franny. The game's up. I want to know exactly what you're playing at." I kicked the door shut behind me to show her I was angry. "I'm not leaving until you give me the real reason why you're too scared to stay here at night."

"All right. All *right!*" She threw down a baby's rattle on the bed so hard it bounced onto the floor. "I was going to tell you anyway. I sort of feel I can trust you not to tell anyone mostly because who are you going to tell? You barely know anyone. But Rufus is another story. I just don't want him scattering my business all around the neighborhood."

"Oh, he wouldn't do that. He—"

I stopped short. I was going to say, *He loves you.* But I didn't feel I quite had the right to speak for Rufus just yet. Instead I said, trying not to sound too judgmental: "But you're happy to accept his hospitality and allow him to shelter you."

She had the grace to look ashamed. That was the thing about Franny, I was beginning to realize. She could be arrogant and outspoken one minute and modest and contrite the next.

"He's a darling, isn't he?"

"You really think so?" I smiled.

"I like him quite a lot." She sat down on the bed. "We haven't had another date as such but he comes in here all the time and it's changing between us. For the better. I'm comfortable around him because we've known each other for so long."

"And he's cute?" I said with a grin.

"Not only that," she was suddenly serious, "he's kind. I haven't had a lot of that with men. And most important—Eliza likes him. She's quite a handful as you may have noticed but when she takes to someone, that's it. She's the proverbial putty in their hands—like she was with Lucia."

"Well, I'm afraid I'm not on that list," I said and then I flinched at Franny's next words.

"Nor am I," she said. "I'm beginning to think I'm a terrible mother. I don't seem to have any control over Dumpster. God knows what he's up to every night. And I can never get Eliza to settle down the way Lucia did last night."

"It's not about control, Franny," I said. "I think it's about love."

"But I love my kids desperately," she protested, and there was a break in her voice. "You have to believe me when I say that. I truly, *truly* love them. They're everything to me."

"I do know that," I said, putting my arm around her shoulders and feeling how bony they were. She was whippet thin, probably because she raced around expending more energy in a day than most women do in a week. "So what happened last night?"

"Evan Morrison," she whispered. "That's what happened. He *said* he dropped by to speak to Dumpster about the bow and arrow in that pit. And while he was here he decided to make it clear to me that I had no chance of hiding anything from him."

"He was threatening you?"

"Oh, he did more than threaten me. He pushed me up against the wall and thrust himself against me and reminded me that he only had to say the word and Dumpster would be arrested—just like that." She clicked her fingers in the air.

"Did he speak to Dumpster?"

"I wouldn't let him. Dumpster was upstairs asleep."

"He really wants to nail Dumpster and he's using you?" I asked.

"No. He's using Dumpster—and me—to nail your guy, Shotgun Marriott. He's obsessed with pinning at least one of those murders on Shotgun and he's determined to get some kind of evidence via Dumpster."

"He wants Dumpster to lie to frame Shotgun?"

"Pretty much. He hasn't exactly come out and said the word 'lie' but he's come close. And he wants me to lean on Dumpster. And that's not all he wants."

"What do you mean? What else does he want?"

"Sex." Her voice was flat and devoid of emotion. She might have been telling me he'd asked her to pour him a cup of coffee. But I sensed that this was the only way she could keep a lid on the turbulence that had to be churning up inside her. I admired the way Franny refused to give in to her problems. Grim determination to avoid freaking out at all costs seemed to be her stock in trade, even if it meant driving the rest of us crazy by keeping us out of the loop. "And," she continued, "he made it clear last night that he'll hold the threat of turning Dumpster in over me until he gets it."

"Franny, you have to tell someone—someone who can deal with him."

"I'm not telling anyone and neither must you. I don't want anything to happen to my son. That's why I won't tell Rufus. He'd go after Detective Morrison right away. Promise me you won't tell him. Promise me."

She was clinging to me. Jesus was calling to her from down below in the store and she slowly released me and went to open the door.

"I'm coming!" she shouted and looked back at me. "Well?"

"Okay," I said, "I'll keep quiet. But not for long."

I was so wound up when I left that I knew I couldn't just go back to the cabin and wait for something to happen. So I drove to Mallaby and took the unprecedented step of calling on Shotgun unannounced.

The big front door was open and there was loud music blaring out from the house. I went in and shouted that I was there but there was no way anyone could have heard me unless they were standing right beside me.

I followed the sound of the music down a long passage leading away from the hall in the opposite direction to the one that led to the kitchen. And it delivered me to a sound studio with all its walls crammed with recording equipment and a glassed-in booth at the far end with consoles covered with those knobs you slide up and down.

The lights were dimmed but there was a spot on Shotgun. He was standing at a microphone on the soundstage and belting out a raucous song I didn't recognize.

After a few seconds I realized he was lip-synching and the song was blasting out of the huge speakers either side of him.

This was not a Shotgun I'd seen before. He was wearing skintight red velvet trousers tucked into snakeskin boots with two-inch heels and a black leather waistcoat over his bare chest. He had chains around his neck hanging down between his nipples and a white-spotted navy bandanna tied around his head.

He was dancing as he sang, moving around, jutting out his hips, banging a tambourine, and sweating profusely.

And he looked utterly ridiculous.

"That was my first number-one record," he said, grinding to a halt as the song came to an end. "They screamed for it at every concert, right up until the end, and I was thinking if I do this book—and it's a best seller—I can use it to get myself back onto everyone's radar."

I wasn't quite sure what to say. Why was it that men invariably assumed that when they wrote a book it would be a best seller? Everyone always hoped it would work out that way—myself included—but men, far more than women, always thought it was automatic.

"You know, to get everyone's attention when I make a comeback with my music"—he paused—"I'll be doing concerts and they'll want to hear this. So I thought I'd come down to the studio and give it a dusting off."

Suddenly I felt very depressed. How could I tell him that he looked like an old has-been, that nobody dressed like this now, that even I—who was pretty hopeless when it came to rock music—could tell that his moves were dated. And his upper body, while pretty impressive for a man of his age, was just not in good enough shape to display like this. And what had induced him to dig out his old gear? Hadn't he been the one to condemn the pretensions of the old rockers he saw on TV? What had happened to his minimalist approach to clothing that rendered him so elegant?

I didn't really need to ask myself the question; I knew the answer. I could hear it in his voice, see it in his face. He had succumbed to insecurity. He was appealing to me. *I've still got it, haven't I? I can still do it, can't I? They'll still love me, won't they?*

Was *that* the real reason he was doing a book? To hang his comeback on its success? I realized I was incredibly disappointed. I had thought Shotgun had drifted into middle age with a rare and impressive gracefulness, that he had resisted the temptation to imagine his golden years could continue unabated. Apparently not.

And then, as he came closer to where I was standing by the

door, I realized he was drunk. He wasn't lurching about the place and his words hadn't really been slurred but there was a loony grin on his face that told me he was under the influence of something.

"I'm sorry to drop by unannounced," I said, "but I wanted to transcribe the tape I made of you last time. I was wondering if we could set up a system whereby I came by and went straight up to your office without disturbing you."

"You can disturb me any time you want," he said, throwing an arm around my shoulders as we walked back down to the hall.

"Is this what you used to wear onstage?" I asked him, thinking I ought to show some kind of polite interest in what I'd just witnessed.

He paused and looked down at himself as if he'd only just noticed what he had on.

"Well, it's what everyone used to wear, innit?" Did he sound defensive or was it my imagination? "And before you say anything, it's not what I'll be wearing if I go out on the road again."

"No?" Maybe I had misjudged him.

"Not at all. Do you want to know the real reason why I'm togged up in my old gear and singing my old songs? Well, I'll tell you. I know I've got to give you the story of what happened that night with the groupie and the truth is I needed a little help to get me started down that particular memory lane."

"You don't want to go there, as they say?" I thought I'd keep quiet about the fact that it was clear the most help he'd sought had come in the form of a bottle.

"Got it in one. But I will!" He stepped ahead of me, turned and wagged a finger at me. He was an irritating cliché, a bad comedian's portrayal of a drunk. "I'm going to give you the goods. I promise. The tape is in the machine right by my computer, by the way, all ready to roll."

But when we got upstairs he seemed to forget about me and wandered off down the corridor to another part of the house. I walked around the landing and found the office where I booted up his computer, put on the headphones, pressed PLAY and went to work.

As I listened to his voice, I realized that today he had slipped once again into the phony Cockney of his rock star public appearances. I wondered to what extent he had been playing a role during his years as a performer and how much it had taken its toll on him.

And then I gave myself up to the transcription of the tapes, letting my fingers dart about the keys and working up to a rhythm whereby it was almost seamless the way he narrated his story into my ears and it came out on the page. I was so caught up in it, mesmerized, yet again, by the story of his early years with Angie, that I didn't hear him come in and stand behind me.

When he touched my shoulder, I jumped and typed gibberish for several seconds.

"I went and had a little rest," he said, "and while I was lying there, I thought to myself, *I'm going to do it now, while she's here, while I'm all worked up to talk about it.* So what do you think?"

But he didn't wait for me to answer. As I sat there with my fingers poised above the keyboard, he began to speak.

"By the 1980s we weren't touring nearly as much, maybe only every two or three years, and by 1990, when the groupie died, we hadn't been on the road in five years. So it was something of a comeback tour and the audiences were crazy in their anticipation. I'm not sure it happens anymore but if you were old enough to remember, the rock concerts of the sixties and seventies were sheer mayhem when it came to the fans. That was our heyday but even at the later shows it was still bedlam. Those little girls packed in shoulder to shoulder, crushed up against the stage below me, it was thrilling and horrifying to me all at once. And what you have to remember is that at this London concert in 1990, I was forty-fucking-five! But the fans seemed younger than ever.

"They kept fainting and my natural inclination was to jump off the stage and go to their rescue but I couldn't do that, of course. It would have made matters fifty times worse. There was no way the ambulance people could get to them through the crowd so they had to be hoisted up and passed horizontally over the audience to safety. Half the time it looked as if they were dead.

"At the end of each concert they rushed us out round the back and into waiting cars—or helicopters if we were playing a stadium—before the fans could get to us. But sometimes the security was rubbish and some of the more persistent girls would break through and come after us, jumping onto our car as it was moving away. Of course quite often the other members of the band looked down at them from the stage and cherry-picked a few to help them make it through the night. They'd send Freddy, our roadie, to bring them round the back. I never did that, you know? I really didn't. If I was at a party or a club and I was so out of it, I didn't know what I was doing, then yes, there were times when I succumbed to temptation. I mean what guy wouldn't when it's handed to him on a plate and he's had a few? But I wasn't proactive about it. I didn't point them out to Freddy like the others did and say 'Get me the redhead with the big knockers.' "

He'd been standing by the door and now he slid down the wall and sat on the floor, his long legs stretched out in front of him, his back resting against the doorjamb. He'd changed out of his rock star gear and was wearing just a toweling robe, knotted firmly around the waist. The hairs on his legs were fine and blond and his toes were as long and tapered as his fingers.

"I first saw her at the De Montfort Hall in Leicester. She was pathetically small and I couldn't stand the way she was being jostled by the crowd. She went down a few times but she was a game little creature, she was on her feet again in no time. And she was always smiling at me.

"Then I began to notice her at every gig—Birmingham, Sheffield, Liverpool, as well as down south in places like Brighton and Reading—always in the front line. And then finally in London what I'd always dreaded, happened: She was pinned up against the stage and I suddenly noticed that she was flailing her arms around and she was trapped. She was pressed so hard against the stage she couldn't breathe. She was literally getting crushed to death right in front of me.

"So I had them lift her onto the stage and they took her round the back to revive her. Of course when she recovered, she took it as a sign that I'd asked for her and she was waiting for me in the car. I was quite surprised to find she was American. She'd seen us on our last tour there and she'd followed us to England. Followed *me,* I should say. After what she'd been through, I didn't like to have her thrown out so I let her ride back with us to the hotel.

"And there I made my escape because what she didn't know was that I wasn't staying at the hotel with the rest of the band. I had an apartment off Queens Gate that I always went to when I'd finished a London concert. The home I shared with Angie always had a throng of fans outside and if I went there after a concert it was sheer bedlam all night and we never got a wink of sleep. And of course I was getting on a bit by now, I needed my sleep!

"I was so dead beat that night that I went straight back to the apartment to get some kip. But she was more crafty than I'd bargained for. Apparently she worked on one of the band until he was drunk enough to tell her where I'd gone. Before I'd even taken my clothes off, there was a knock at the door."

Even before he told me, I knew there was no way someone with Shotgun's impeccable manners would shout at her—*Fuck off out of here, you little slag!*—which would have probably been the only way to get rid of her. Sure enough, he said, he invited her in and made her a cup of tea.

"Nothing stronger. I really was concerned about her age. She said she was twenty-one but I didn't believe it for a minute. Then of course I couldn't get rid of her. We didn't have cell phones in those days and I couldn't reach Freddy to get him to come and cart her off. He was probably passed out in some club. So she followed me into my bedroom and she wouldn't leave.

"So I did. I must have been out of my mind to just walk out and leave her there but I swear, at the time, it struck me as the easiest thing to do. I waited until she was in the bathroom and then I ran down the stairs and out of the house. I ran into one of the people living in the apartment above mine on the way out. He was coming in and I could tell he was quite surprised to see me, probably hadn't realized he had a celebrity neighbor. He acted pretty cool, just nodded to me as if he saw me all the time. I walked the few blocks down the road to our house. I thought if by some miracle there was no one outside I could spend the night there. But of course the usual hard core of fans had settled down for the night in their sleeping bags. I had taken care to keep to streets that weren't too well lit. If anyone had realized Shotgun Marriott was walking around unattended, I'd have been mobbed.

"Having got that far, I took a risk and sneaked round the back of our house to a gate that led into our garden. It was locked but I had a key. I actually had quite a nice time. It was the summer, it was a warm night, the moon was shining bright, la-di-da-di-da, and I stretched out on one of the sun loungers and had a snooze. Actually it was more than that, I was out for two or three hours and the girls round the front had no idea I was even there. There were lights on upstairs and I could have woken Angie but if you really want to know I was quite enjoying the adventure of camping in the garden.

"The only problem was when it got a bit nippy and I did want to go inside, Angie wouldn't answer the bleeding back door. She more or less used to barricade herself inside the house when I was doing a concert in London. I mean, I don't blame her. It was four in the morning and she probably thought it was one of the fans.

"So I had to walk back to the apartment. I got a bit lost and I asked a policeman walking his beat where I was. I thought I could rely on him not to mob me and as it turned out I wound up relying on him for much more than that.

"The girl was still there when I got back. I had assumed she would leave when she found I was gone but she had got into my bed and was fast asleep. And it wasn't as if I could sleep on a couch or something. This was just a place for me to crash after concerts so the place was totally bare of furniture except for the bed. By this time I was too tired and exhausted to do more than climb in beside her and go to sleep myself. It was probably the most idiotic thing I've ever done in my life but at the time I just thought it was the easiest. We'd both get a few hours' kip and by the morning I'd have the energy to deal with her. I think I even envisaged having some kind of wise-uncle chat with her in the morning about the error of her ways.

"When I woke up in the morning and tried to rouse her, I discovered she was dead. And if you've done your homework and read all the press clippings, you'll know what happened next. The police were all over me and the only reason I'm not doing twenty-five to life is because of that copper I spoke to. He'd recognized me, of course, and when they did a postmortem they put the time of death as being while I was gone. The neighbor who had run into me on the way out couldn't wait to tell anyone who'd listen that he'd seen me go out and the copper confirmed where I was three hours later. And while I had no one who could say I was in my own garden for most of the night, they had no one who could say I wasn't."

I remembered the headlines now. PILLOW TALK was the one they used the most. The girl had died of suffocation. Someone put a pillow over her head and held it there and they had found that there was one pillow missing from Shotgun's bed.

Suddenly I realized something. I hadn't got a single word of this on tape. I started typing furiously, trying to remember word for word what he had said. I'd done it in the past when I'd been doing an interview and the tape recorder had gone on the blink and left me with nothing. If I allowed nothing to distract me, I had probably unconsciously retained enough to recapture the gist of what he had said. And then I'd get him to sign it—or read it into the tape recorder.

It didn't take me that long—it was only about four pages—but when I turned to hand it to him, of course he had gone. I was frustrated beyond belief. We always got so far and then he opted out. I needed to take it further, to ask him for more detail. Had he been the only suspect?

But when I went looking for him, racing around the landing to where I'd seen him disappear before, I was stopped dead in my tracks by the wailing sound of a harmonica. Then it stopped and once again I marveled at Shotgun's authentic rendering of the blues.

"Got plenty muddy water, don't need no water t'all
All I need's a sweet mama, to hear her daddy call."

But I left before I could hear the sound of him breaking down into heartrending sobs. Once was quite enough. God knows how he would cope when he had to talk about Sean's death for the book.

This time I had a little trophy to take away with me. My right hand thrust into my pocket was clutching a disk onto which I had copied the transcriptions. Now I could get to work on the beginning of the book in the cabin. In the Jeep I laid it on the passenger seat beside me and then snatched it up into my pocket again as I looked through the windshield and saw a car parked at the end of the dirt road and leaning against it was Detective Morrison.

Had he come to pursue his persecution of Shotgun? Ought I to rush back and warn him? I drove past him, ignoring his wave to me over the steering wheel. As I approached the flat terrain surrounding Cranberry Hole Road that I now found so threatening, I wondered if I should have reported my nighttime prowler to him. But then I remembered what he had been doing to Franny and I knew that he was the last person to whom I would feel comfortable entrusting my safety.

CHAPTER 11

MIDWAY THROUGH THE MORNING OF YET ANOTHER glorious day, I realized with a certain amount of satis-faction that even though I had been at the cabin for less than a week I had already created a nest just like the one I had in London. I could come in, close the door, and dismiss the world outside. No one bothered me apart from a few squawking seagulls, but if I felt like company, I could pop over to the Old Stone Market and visit with Franny or pick up the phone and speak to Rufus.

And there was another reason why I was suddenly so content in my surroundings, one that I had a little trouble coming to terms with. I was on my own again. To be translated: Tommy wasn't around. It was a bit of a shock but I had to admit that while I thought about him quite a bit, I didn't actually *miss* him as much as I had thought I would.

Of course there was the trivial little detail that two grisly murders had been committed less than half a mile away and I had my very own personal nighttime prowler but you can't have everything. And in the meantime I had a job to do.

I spent the day setting up my "office" in the desk area of the cabin and making notes on how to structure Shotgun's story. I drove to East Hampton and bought the reference books without which I could not work—a dictionary, a thesaurus, maps—at

BookHampton and I called Staples and ordered a printer, a supply of typing paper, and all the other stationery I needed. I was, as they say, all set.

I had planned to spend the evening preparing a leisurely supper of clams (provided by Rufus) and a tomato salad made with local tomatoes from the farmers market and fresh basil, and then I was going to tackle Tommy's letter.

So when Martha appeared in the doorway brandishing a bottle of wine, I wasn't happy.

"I'm not disturbing you, am I?" Whenever people said that, you could bet on it that they knew perfectly well that they were. "It was so good to talk to you the other day, I kind of hoped I'd find you here. And of course I wondered if you'd had a chance to—"

The look on her face was eager and pathetic and it infuriated me but I reminded myself that Martha had known Sean Marriott and I needed to keep her sweet. The one thing that could encourage me to be social was if it had something to do with my work. Yet why did she have to come and ruin my evening?

"I was just about to give the place a good clean," I said in an attempt to steer her away. A total lie. I was hopeless at cleaning. Vacuum cleaners always saw me coming. I swear the minute I switched one on, it turned its suction off and began to shoot dust balls *out* all over the place.

"Oh, it's too beautiful an evening for housework," she said. "Why don't we take a few chairs outside and have a drink there? Then we won't have to look at whatever mess you were going to clear up.

"That's the problem with living in a small space," she went on, "you really have to keep on top of the clutter. I tell you, living in those trailers sure keeps me on my toes."

As I remembered, the inside of the trailers was immaculate.

Maybe she had her "girls" trained to pop out of their plastic covers and run around with a duster every day.

"No," she said, "domesticity's not my bag at all. That's why I'm working on Louis. Have you been to his home?"

I shook my head. "I don't really know Louis," I said, wondering what "working" on him entailed.

"Well, he's got money—a housekeeper *and* a maid, you know? The whole bit. If I married him, I wouldn't have to lift a finger."

"You and Louis are getting married? I had no idea."

"I said *if* I married him. He hasn't exactly asked me yet. You know I've always envied my women friends who were married to rich men." Martha seemed to be in a confiding mood. "I don't really need to live a fancy lifestyle but I do like to be pampered now and then. You have no idea how much I yearn to be whisked away for a romantic weekend, wined and dined. I want someone to buy me jewelry, clothes, to put me on their health care plan, and set me up with a nice little bank account."

"Don't we all?" I said. "Doesn't Louis do all that for you? Sounds like he can afford it."

"No," she said sharply. "Oh, he buys me a hamburger every now and then wherever there's a movie ticket included in the price of a meal. And he talks about taking me away somewhere but somehow he never seems to get around to it. Have you ever been married?"

"No," I said and left it at that. I didn't want to get into a discussion about Tommy with her.

"I've come close more times than I care to admit," she said, "but somehow it never happens and I just don't understand why. Here I am in my fifties, still hoping that one day I'll go out with a guy and it will automatically lead to the altar. I mean, it's not like I'm unattractive."

As we carried the chairs outside I studied Martha out of the corner of my eye. She was certainly good-looking. I wondered if maybe she was the kind of woman who heard wedding bells the minute she started having an affair with someone and never realized they were only viewing it as a fling.

"So how's it going with Shotgun Marriott?" she asked when we were settled. Mercifully she had not mentioned her manuscript again.

"Fine," I said. "What about Bettina Pleshette? The woman who was murdered—she was originally going to work with Shotgun. Did you know her?"

"Never met her," she said.

"And Shotgun?" I said, deciding to turn the tables on her and see where it got me. "Did Sean ever take you up to Mallaby and introduce you?"

"No, he didn't," said Martha and I could tell she had been disappointed. "He said his dad didn't really like him taking people up to the house, that he'd become a real recluse. Shame," she added reflectively. "I mean he would have been the perfect catch. All that money from his rock 'n' roll days, there must be some of it left."

Something told me that she wasn't quite as mercenary as she made out. Of course her age and circumstances had probably made her paranoid about how she was going to support herself for the rest of her life but there was something about Martha Farrell that made me think that wasn't the whole story. At a guess, I'd have said what she was really desperate for was warmth and affection from a red-blooded male.

"Maybe you could introduce me?" she said casually and then warmed to her idea. "Now *there's* a thought. How could we do it, do you think?"

"We couldn't, I'm afraid," I said firmly. "Sean was right. Shotgun Marriott keeps himself to himself. Besides I thought you were *working* on Louis Nichols." I smiled.

"Yeah, but at my age I can't really afford to put all my eggs in one basket." She laughed again. A softer sound than her previous cackling. Maybe that had been a nervous tic and she was beginning to relax with me. "And I haven't really noticed him *working* on me in return."

"Besides," I said, without thinking, "I think Shotgun's still in love with his wife."

Now why had I said that? I didn't have anything to go on other than the way he had spoken about his early years with Angie.

"Really?" Martha sounded very interested. "Are they getting back together?"

"Did Sean talk about his mother?" I asked, ignoring her question.

"All the time," said Martha.

I turned to her, surprised. "He did?"

"Well, of course he did. He was getting ready to get out of here and go and be with her in London. At least that's what he told me. And he was excited about her coming here."

"Angela Marriott was due here?"

"Sean was thrilled because he believed she was going to come and confront Shotgun about Sean's living with her in England. Sean was proud of his mother, that she had the guts to come and discuss it with his father face-to-face. He'd always thought his mother didn't care about him and the fact that she suddenly wanted to reestablish her relationship with him made him so happy. So it was just tragic that he died before he got to see her. Just tragic," she repeated and for a moment I thought she was going to break down.

"Anyway," she said, recovering, "I'm not so sure I want to meet Shotgun. Not if Sean was so anxious to get away from him."

"Is that what he said—that he wanted to get away from Shotgun?"

"Well, what's Shotgun's side of it? What's he going to put in this book of his?"

"Martha." I hesitated, trying to hang on to my patience. So far I'd been amazed that Franny and Rufus hadn't pressed me for gossip about Shotgun. I'd known it was only a matter of time before someone like Martha Farrell stuck her nose in. "I'd love to tell you but I really do have to keep everything confidential at this stage. I'm just starting to get some rather delicate material out of him. I really couldn't jeopardize our relationship—"

"*You* have a relationship with him?" She jumped on it.

"A professional relationship—"

"But you'll tell me later? When you can? We're going to see a lot of each other. We're virtually neighbors, I can just walk up the beach and—"

I had a mild panic attack at the thought of Martha descending on me at unexpected moments but before I could think of a tactful way of dissuading her, she had disappeared back to the cabin.

She reappeared almost immediately and I nearly groaned out loud.

She was carrying her manuscript.

"I saw this on the counter," she said cheerfully. "You haven't started it, have you?"

I opened my mouth, searching around for an excuse.

"Don't worry," she said, "I understand. Here's what I'm going to do. I'm going to give you a taste of it. I'm going to read you the first chapter." And she positioned herself in front of me so that she was outlined against the crimson sun as it began its descent into the bay.

"You'll see why I wanted you to read this," she said before she began. "As soon as Franny said you were English I knew you were the reader I wanted. My story is about two Englishwomen in an uneven and destructive friendship"—she looked at me—"that ends in tragedy."

I was a captive audience and all I could do was take a large slug of wine and pray that it would soon become too dark for her to see.

Which it did, but that didn't stop her. She just carried her chair indoors and continued reading. And to my utter amazement, by that time I was hanging on her every word.

It was melodramatic but from the first page it succeeded in moving me. It was narrated in the first person from the point of view of a nervous schoolgirl whom I suspected was based on Martha herself. It described her first meeting with another girl, someone with a much stronger personality who was clearly going to dominate the "Martha" character in a powerful and twisted way. I felt a shiver run through me. Stories of female friendships were strong commercial bets for the women's market and as I listened I had a hunch the time would come when I would be telling Genevieve about Martha.

But there was something else about Martha's reading. The former actress in her had come to the fore and she had given it everything she had—in a British accent. And it was brilliant! I closed my eyes at one point and it could have been an Englishwoman sitting beside me.

"What do you think?" she said when she'd finished the first chapter.

"Martha, I think it's spellbinding." I was embarrassed to see her face break into a look of such pathetic gratitude that for one moment I thought she was going to leap up and embrace me. "You've succeeded in carrying me right up into your story from the first page and I can't wait to read more."

I was so impressed that for half a second I actually contemplated inviting her to join me for supper. But the last thing I wanted to do was to set a precedent and have her thinking she was going to hang out with me all the time. In any case she seemed to realize her visit had come to an end, if only for different reasons.

"I'll leave you to get on with it," she said, "and I'd better make a move before it gets too chilly to walk home along the beach. I didn't bring a sweater."

Not long after she left I happened to glance out of one of the back windows of the cabin. What I saw caused me to lean over the counter and sink my head in my hands in despair.

There were headlights halfway up the drive again. They weren't moving, which meant someone was parked, watching. And I was fully illuminated. There was no point pretending it was Martha come back for something she'd forgotten because she couldn't drive.

It was the fact that someone was out there watching me that got to me. I think I would have even preferred it if they had shown themselves. Suddenly I needed to see exactly who—or what—I was up against.

And then the headlamps went out and I screamed involuntarily. Now the voyeur was totally invisible—and possibly creeping up on me.

I dialed 999.

Nothing happened. I waited for a voice to say "Emergency—police, fire, or ambulance?" but there was complete silence.

Then I suddenly remembered. They didn't dial 999 in America. It was something else. I rushed to the cupboard in the kitchen where the Phillionaire kept a set of phone books and was frantically flicking through the pages at the front when a figure went past the window.

I screamed again, grabbed a bread knife, and rushed to hide

behind the shower curtain. It was thick and expensive and double layered so providing I kept the light off in the shower, I should be hidden from view. My heart was pounding in my chest as I waited.

And then there was a knock on the door.

What did he expect me to do? Answer the door so he could shoot me at point-blank range?

But I'd left the door open and I heard the handle being turned.

I raised the bread knife high above my head, trembling all over. But my hand was shaking so hard I dropped the knife and it clattered onto the tiles.

The curtain was yanked open and I stood face to face with Detective Evan Morrison.

He looked at the knife in my hand.

"I didn't know who you were," I said in a terrified squeaky voice I didn't recognize as my own. "Someone's been parking out there at night and watching me."

"Really?" He sounded almost amused.

And suddenly a horrific thought popped into my head. It had been him spying on me? He had turned up at Franny's late at night. What was there to stop him doing the same to me?

"What do you want?" I said brusquely. "What are you doing here? Have you been here before?"

"You mean have I had you under surveillance?"

From his tone of voice, I knew that one way or another that was exactly what he had been doing. Either he had been tailing me or sitting parked outside watching me, or he had told someone to keep an eye on me.

"Ma'am, I'm here to ask you some questions about Shotgun Marriott."

"It's a little late." I couldn't look him in the eye.

"And I apologize for not calling first."

I didn't want him inside the Phillionaire's special space. I didn't want him here at all and I was nervous about him being so close to the Stucco House while Franny was there. I picked up the knife, stepped out of the shower, and walked across to the kitchen. Then I leaned against the counter and confronted him. I couldn't bring myself to invite him to sit down.

"It's a great spot you've got here," he said. "Belongs to Philip Abernathy, I believe. You friends with the Abernathys for long, Miss Bartholomew?"

"My mother and Philip Abernathy are partners," I said, surprised at how easily the description of their relationship came to me now.

"Partners." He let the word hang there for a beat as if he were slightly disgusted by the thought of it. "No one gets married anymore. Men, women, they're all—partners."

"Are you married?" The last thing I wanted to do was to let the conversation take a personal turn but I couldn't resist it. And I wished he'd stop smiling. I hated people who smiled *all* the time because generally these were the insincere kind of smiles that never reached the eyes.

He held up his left hand by way of reply. No wedding ring. "So you've been hired by Shotgun Marriott to help him write his autobiography?"

I nodded.

"How does that work?" He leaned forward and his belly flopped over his belt, straining at the buttons of his shirt. I think what I hated most about him was that he was so *fleshy*. I remembered what Franny had said about him pushing up against her and I felt sick.

I described the process of interviewing subjects, transcribing the tapes, and roughing out a first draft that I then reworked with them. "It's a collaborative process," I explained, "most of the time anyway. Occasionally people leave it all to me, never even read the finished book, but that doesn't happen very often."

"When did you start work?"

"Last Saturday."

He looked surprised. "Really? Not till then? Didn't I see you at his house earlier?"

"That was the first time I met him. We hadn't started on the book then."

"But you have now?"

I nodded. I didn't want to look at him and I didn't want to speak to him any more than I had to.

"So is he talking about his son's murder? What has he said about Bettina Pleshette? And what made him want to write his memoirs now, after all this time?"

It was a very good question and one that I didn't yet have the answer to. Shotgun had said he was writing the book for Sean but why now?

"I never reveal what my subjects tell me until we're done," I said. "Everything that isn't in the final book is confidential. It's a rule of mine."

"And anything you don't tell me that pertains to the case will be regarded as obstruction," he said, leaning over to put his face very close to mine. I leapt away from the counter, shaken, and backed away from him. I wanted to run away, to race out the door and down to the beach and plunge into the water. I wanted to swim out to sea following the path illuminated by what I thought must surely be a full moon. But at the same time I knew that it wouldn't help Shotgun if I antagonized Evan Morrison. I searched frantically for the best way to handle him. I decided to take a chance that he might be susceptible to flattery. Maybe instead of revealing what I knew about Shotgun, I could merely *appear* willing and at the same time cajole Detective Morrison into telling me how his case was progressing.

"This assignment is unusual." I gave him such a blazing fake smile that I succeeded in making him recoil a little. "Obviously the fact that his son has been murdered makes Shotgun Marriott a little different from most of my subjects. I'll try to be as helpful as I can."

He seemed to relax a little and took out a notebook. He asked me routine stuff: I lived in England? Where exactly? London? Oh, he'd been in London once but he hadn't liked it much. How long had I been a writer, had I known Shotgun before taking on the job, had I known Bettina? Oh, we had the same agent? He hadn't known that.

"So where were you the night Sean Marriott was killed?" The question shot out of his mouth like a rattle of gunfire. "Were you already in America?"

"I was still in New York," I said and explained how I'd come out the next day for my mother and Phil's commitment ceremony. He nodded, yes he knew about that, and he couldn't resist a smirk. A *commitment* ceremony! "And I was at the party after the ceremony while Bettina Pleshette was . . ." I paused. I had been about to say "getting killed" but that sounded callous.

"Being sliced to pieces by an arrow?" He reached out suddenly and tapped me on my back and I jumped. "That's where it got her. Boy, I'm telling you, she was a real mess. Viewer discretion advised. The arrow went in between the ribs and the side of the spine and that's where you've got your big arteries, your aorta, and a couple of kidney arteries. If even one of those got hit she'd have been dead in less than sixty seconds."

I was shaken by his coarse description of her injuries. The nature of his line of work probably gave him more immunity than the rest of us to having strong reactions at the sight of slaughtered bodies but couldn't he at least show a little more respect when talking about them?

"So you don't think they were killed by the same person?"

"You probably know Shotgun Marriott better than I do by now. You think he would kill his own son?"

I didn't answer. I was too busy thinking that he had just nominated Shotgun as Bettina's killer.

"So this party after the *commitment* ceremony, as you call it, where you say you were at the night Bettina Pleshette was killed, took place where exactly?"

Damn! I didn't want to draw attention to the Stucco House.

"At Philip Abernathy's house but around eleven his son took me over to the ocean where he was going to surf. And we saw Sean Marriott's body being pulled out of the water." I said this to distract him. "You might have seen me there. Of course we thought he had drowned."

"What makes you think he didn't?"

"It was all over the papers that he was shot," I said innocently, "and I was there when you brought Shotgun's Purdey to his house and arrested him for Bettina's murder. Shotgun's prints were on it, I suppose, since it belonged to him. Anyone else's?"

He ignored my question as I had assumed he would. But when he did speak again, I was stunned by what he said.

"You're English, right? You were around when Shotgun Marriott killed that"—he hesitated—"that girl in London?"

"What?" My heart was banging against my chest again. "What makes you say *that*? He was never convicted."

"We've got Sean Marriott's laptop. Mostly it's just full of e-mail exchanges with his boyfriend in New York, where they're going to meet, what they're going to do to each other when they do." He shuddered and I prayed he wouldn't offer any further comment. "And there was some stuff from his father. 'Want to get together for dinner tonight?' That sort of thing. No sign of Sean ever replying. Pretty sad if that was the extent of their communication. But there were plenty of e-mails from his mother referring to the fact that Shotgun Marriott murdered someone in London fourteen years ago."

"They never proved that," I said quickly. "What about Shotgun's computer? What's on that?"

He looked at me for a second, probably trying to gauge if I already knew the answer to the question I had just asked and was only trying to find out what he knew. The truth was I was so utterly computer-hopeless most of the time that it had never occurred to me to look beyond the documents I had set up for the transcriptions.

"There's nothing on Shotgun's computer apart from his e-mails to his son and a couple to the guy he was working with in Connecticut," said Evan Morrison. "He didn't seem to use his computer for anything except making arrangements with people."

"What about Sean's boyfriend?"

"We've talked to him and we've established that he stayed in New York the night Sean was killed so he's in the clear. He said Sean was becoming obsessed with the fact that his father had killed this girl. I'm saying that Shotgun Marriott is a killer and while I don't really like him for his own son's murder, I'm not ruling it out because I think the intended victim was Bettina Pleshette and Sean Marriott was killed by accident. When he didn't get Bettina the first time, Shotgun lured her to his home the next night to kill her. He didn't want her digging into his past."

I listened to him and I hated what he was saying, hated it because there was a trickle of doubt that was beginning to worm its way into my head. Earlier in the day I had told Martha Farrell that Shotgun still loved his wife. And from the brief contact I had had with Angie Marriott, I could believe that she still loved him. And this might well be the reason she had never turned him in for the killing of the groupie. But would she leave her son with a murderer?

I was shocked that I was even allowing myself to process these thoughts. I was supposed to be trying to help Shotgun.

"But Detective Morrison, you're forgetting one thing." I turned to him.

"What's that?"

"Whatever might have happened years ago in London, Shotgun Marriott has a cast-iron alibi for the nights that his son and Bettina were killed. Dumpster has sworn on oath that he was at Mallaby both nights and Shotgun was there." Even as I said it, I recalled Shotgun himself saying Dumpster was lying about the night of Bettina's death.

"Dumpster?" Evan Morrison looked confused.

"Dumpster Cook. Franny Cook's son. He works for Shotgun."

"Oh, you mean Martin Cook?"

Did I? I had never thought to ask Dumpster's real name. And suddenly it all made sense. *M saw something.* "M" for Martin. Dumpster was at Mallaby at least the night Sean was killed and who knew? Maybe he had been out in the woods when Bettina died.

As if he were reading my mind, Evan Morrison said: "Whatever he wants to call himself, Martin Cook's in trouble. He swore under oath at Shotgun Marriott's arraignment that he was with Shotgun both nights. Well, okay, he may have been over at Mallaby but I know for a fact that he went out to hunt deer the night Bettina Pleshette was killed. Quite apart from the fact that he shouldn't have been hunting at all, he hasn't been able to show me his bow and arrow since that night. Says it went missing. Looks to me like either he perjured himself at the arraignment or he did something with that bow and arrow that he's not telling anyone about."

I didn't like the sound of this one bit. And it got worse.

"So my guess is he was Shotgun Marriott's accomplice. That's why he's covering up for him. But I'm working on him. He's the one who'll help me nail Shotgun, I'm counting on it, and then I'll be back with another warrant for his arrest."

I had heard from Rufus that Detective Morrison had conducted extensive interviews with a mass of people in the area but he seemed determined to pin the murders on Shotgun no matter what. But if anyone was in immediate serious trouble it was Dumpster. And suddenly I realized I might know something Evan Morrison didn't: that Bettina had had an assignation with M at Mallaby beach at nine the night she was killed. But if M turned out to be Dumpster, I was going to keep this knowledge to myself until I had spoken to Dumpster.

"So where's his mother?" Evan Morrison leaned in close again. "I hear you two were getting pretty friendly so maybe you can tell me where she's at. She's not at her store and no one seems to know where she's gone."

I shook my head. "Can't help you."

"Can't help me or won't help me? Remember what I said about obstruction."

I just looked at him.

"Maxed out on helping me, huh? Just how much do you know about Franny Cook? Scott Abernathy told me quite a few interesting things about her. That's his kid, that baby, did you know? Bettina Pleshette set him straight. She had info on Franny from the city. Wasn't pretty. So now will you tell me where she is?"

"I can't tell you," I said. I was telling the truth. I couldn't tell him not because I didn't know where Franny was but because I couldn't betray her. *And what was the "info" Bettina had on her?* I wondered.

"So you're going to be difficult. Fine, now let me see your passport," he said. He had me by the arm and on my feet. It was more of a suggestion than a forceful move, nothing I could complain about, but I felt distinctly threatened.

"My passport?" I moved away from him. I couldn't see the connection.

"Just let me take a look. Formal ID. I'm not going to take it from you. You can hold on to it and turn the pages for me if you're scared I'll run off with it.

"See this?" he said when I'd handed it to him and he had flipped over a few pages. "See this white card? This is your I-94. They've given you only a month to be in the country. You'd better be out of here in two weeks otherwise you've overstayed Uncle Sam's welcome."

And you can count on me to let them know if you're still here was what the look on his face told me.

I was pretty shaken by just about everything he'd said and I had a strong feeling that was his real motive for paying me a visit: to rattle me. But it was his parting shot that unnerved me the most.

"By the way," he said as he set off across the dunes to his car, "I know it was Shotgun Marriott. I've got it from the horse's mouth."

"Who's that?"

"His wife. She was one of the first people I spoke to right after the funeral. She told me about what happened in London long before I read her e-mails to her son. And while she didn't have any concrete proof, she as good as pointed the finger at him for Bettina Pleshette's murder."

So that was how the land lay. Angela Marriott was gunning for her husband.

I waited a good twenty minutes after I'd seen Evan Morrison drive away down Cranberry Hole Road. Then I raced out of the cabin and along the beach. Franny's car was outside the Stucco House and I burst into the hallway without bothering to ring the bell.

"Franny? *FRANNY!*" I yelled. "Franny, I need you."

She appeared above me at the top of the stairs.

"Where can I find Dumpster? Is he here? I need to speak to him right away."

Franny gave me an odd look. "Why are you looking for him?"

"I'll tell you later. Just tell me where he is, I really need to get hold of him."

"Well, that's just it," said Franny, coming down the stairs. "I don't know. He's taken off somewhere. A bag and most of his clothes are gone from the apartment above the store and he left me a note saying he was leaving and he'd be in touch. He left early this morning before I got to the store and I've called everyone I can think of but no one's heard from him. So it's weird that suddenly you rush in here desperate to find him because basically"—she sat down in a heap on the bottom step and put her head in her hands—"Dumpster's gone, Lee. He's totally disappeared."

CHAPTER 12

THE PHILLIONAIRE WAS KILLED INSTANTLY WHEN HIS car came off the Long Island Expressway and careered across the hard shoulder to hit a tree at seventy miles an hour. The irony was that despite Phil's own history of heart disease, it was his driver who had the heart attack at the wheel just past the sign to Shirley and Wading River at exit sixty-eight, even though he had passed his recent physical with flying colors. Even worse was the fact that the Phillionaire's Sikorsky helicopter had been standing by at the Chelsea helipad in Manhattan ready to take him out to East Hampton. But he had apparently had an early morning meeting on Long Island and it was surmised that because it was such a beautiful day, he must have acted on impulse and told his driver to just keep going out to the Hamptons.

Rufus broke the news to me in person, which was thoughtful of him. My knees turned to jelly with the shock and I sat down with a bump and began to bawl my head off. He exercised such extreme gentleness in comforting me that it was a good thirty seconds before two things struck me. First, it was *his* father who was dead and I should be comforting *him*. And second, much too late, I asked:

"My mother?"

"She wasn't with him. She's in New York and I've come to take you to her. I'm driving in now."

"Was it—?"

"They told me it was instantaneous and that he wouldn't have felt a thing and right now I'm going to believe them because I have to keep it together," said Rufus. "But I know I'm going to wake up at three in the morning and start imagining what happened to him in all its gruesome detail."

He left me to pack a bag and I forced myself to calm down. Rufus was absolutely right when he spoke about keeping it together and I had to think how much my mother was going to need me.

I was in the process of closing all the windows and throwing out the milk when Martha Farrell appeared in the doorway.

"Knock, knock," she called.

I stared at her in horror. It had come true. What Rufus had told me about how people believed that if she turned up at a wedding, it wouldn't last. My mother's relationship with the Phillionaire was over because he was dead. By turning up at their commitment ceremony, Martha had jinxed it for them.

"What's the matter?" she said. "You look terrible."

Sometimes a crisis can turn a relative stranger into an instant best friend and even in my distress I was aware that as Martha put her arm around me and began to console me in a soft and urgent voice, a bond was being established between us. She knew exactly what to say. "Just remember," she hugged me to her, "I'm here for you. Call me anytime. Sometimes the wind coming in off the beach makes it hard to hear anything when I'm in the trailer but try me anyway. You're in for a rough time and I know what that's like. I lost my father when I was twelve and I still don't think I'm over it. I don't subscribe to this *time heals everything* crap. You cared about this man—I can tell by the way you talk about him— and you're going to suffer. I only wish you weren't. But everyone's going to be focusing on his sons and your mother so just know that I'll be here for *you*."

It was exactly what I needed to hear. I had to face up to the enormity of it all and deal with it and it helped to know that someone understood how I was feeling.

Rufus told me to look the other way as his truck passed the wreckage of his father's car on the LIE. Apart from this brief exchange, we made the trip into New York in almost total silence and for this I was grateful. I think we both needed the space to come to terms with what had happened. Franny had come over to the cabin when Rufus had picked me up and I had been struck by the tenderness between them. She had held his face between her palms and bent down to kiss his brow and for a second he had buried his head in her breast. I had seen him heaving with muffled sobs and I had heard Franny's almost inaudible parting words: *I love you*. And I was pleased that Rufus had managed to establish this closeness to her so that he had someone to lean on.

Because it became abundantly clear as soon as we arrived at the Fifth Avenue apartment that he couldn't count on the remaining member of his own family for support.

"Mr. Scott's upstairs," said the doorman.

"He is?" I could tell Rufus was surprised. "I must have spoken to him half a dozen times on the phone today. He never said he was in New York. I just assumed I was speaking to him in Southampton."

Rufus escorted me into the elevator and when we stepped directly into the apartment, Scott emerged from the library, a large Scotch in his hand. He presented an extraordinary sight because he still had on the bottom half of his green scrubs with a sweatshirt on top. He'd clearly been called out of the OR and I wondered whether his patient was still lying there waiting for him.

"She's in Dad's bedroom," he said shortly. No other greeting, and not *their* bedroom, I noticed.

I found my mother on her knees on the floor of the Phillion-aire's dressing room. The doors to the hanging closets all around the room were open and row upon row of his immaculate tai-lored suits were hanging before her. Before she registered my presence I found it heart-wrenching to see her reach up and stroke the sleeves of the jackets, murmuring to them as if the Phillionaire was still inside them. She was as groomed as ever in black pants and a black silk shirt and not a hair out of place but when she turned her head I was shocked to see that tears had wrought havoc with her makeup.

"I must call his tailor," was the first thing she said to me. "He saw him when we were in London last week and ordered four more suits and now he won't need them."

A chill iced through me. Her tone did not match the devasta-tion etched on her face. She was in control of her emotions, as practical as ever, and in fact there was an almost aggressive edge to her voice. It didn't take me long to realize what it was.

Rage.

She allowed me to hug her for a fraction of a second before pulling away.

"Did you see him?" She jerked her head in the direction of the reception area of the apartment and for a second I thought she meant the Phillionaire. "Scott? He arrived here a couple of hours ago. If Pedro hadn't called on the house phone and told me he was on his way up in the elevator, I doubt he would have even come to find me. When he walked in and I started to talk about Phil, he just grunted."

"He didn't comfort you?" I was horrified.

"Nothing," she said. "To give him his due he was in a terrible state himself. I think we were both trying hard not to cry but he looked so awful that I started whimpering just at the sight of him and he couldn't get away from me fast enough. He went straight to Phil's bureau in the library and broke open the drawer where Phil kept his will. *Today!* Within hours of his father's death. *Hours!* I hadn't even thought of it."

By this time she had got to her feet and I led her by the elbow to the bedroom and persuaded her to lie down on a chaise by the window. I covered her with a shawl and perched on the end by her feet.

"Before he opened it, he turned away from me as if he expected me to peep over his shoulder. Do you know what he said? I just could not believe it. He said 'I suppose you want to see what's in here. Well, just remember something, you're not Vanessa Abernathy. You never became his wife, you're still Vanessa Bartholomew. And you won't be living here much longer.' He was actually telling me in so many words to get out of the apartment. On the day Phil died."

Rufus and I could not have got there any faster than we did but I found myself wishing that we had arrived first. But Southampton was that much closer to Manhattan and Scott had beaten us to it. It sickened me to know that he had raced to the apartment not to take care of my mother but to look at the will before Rufus got there.

"Well, whatever he found in the will it won't be much use to him," said my mother. "Phil told me he saw his lawyer and changed it right before we left for Europe. Even I don't have a clue what's in it now."

Outraged, I went in search of Rufus but when I found him, I backed away in confusion without saying anything. He was sitting on the end of a sofa in the foyer of the apartment with Scott slumped at his feet. Scott's awkward frame seemed to be hunched around his brother's knees as he uttered awful choking sobs. Rufus was patting the back of his neck and telling him it was okay and "Dad loved you" over and over again. When he saw me he gave a little wave and mouthed "Later?"

I crept away and sought refuge in the kitchen. But I walked straight into a huddle of maids in the pantry and they all turned and looked at me expectantly and after we had stood there in silence for a beat or two, I realized with horror that they were waiting for instructions and I didn't know what to tell them.

I wandered back through the cavernous apartment and found a phone to call Shotgun. I got the machine and left a message explaining what had happened and saying that I would be in touch on my return. I added the suggestion that if he felt like making a few tapes on his own, that would be great. I imagined him sitting on the sofa with his eyes tightly shut, talking to an empty room with the tape recorder whirring beside him. It created such a lonely image I almost called him back and told him not to bother.

I went to check on my mother and found that she had emerged to be with Rufus. Scott had recovered and they were all seated at the dining room table making plans for the funeral. I sat quietly beside them for a few minutes observing that my mother appeared to be in command of the proceedings and that she and Scott were at least being civil to each other. There was a moment of tension when Scott said that his father should be buried beside his mother in the family plot in Amagansett. But Rufus said he was pretty sure that the Phillionaire would want to be cremated and have his ashes scattered over the bay. My mother exercised surprising restraint and stayed silent but I piped up like an idiot and said I agreed with Rufus.

Scott turned on me. "You keep right out of this. You do not belong in this discussion." And the lump in my throat returned. "Anyway," Scott went on, "I've got the will right here so maybe he left instructions." Whereupon my mother broke her silence and informed him of the existence of the new will and he erupted again.

I turned my head and whispered to Rufus, "Do you need me here?" And he whispered back, "No, you take off. Probably better we sort this out on our own. Don't worry, I'll root for Vanessa." So I slipped away and took the elevator down to the lobby.

Aching with unhappiness I went for a long walk in Central Park and when I returned, I found the foyer in almost total darkness and Scott and Rufus ensconced in a heavy drinking session in the dining room.

"Where'd you go?" said Scott. "We've been looking all over." He said this in a way that made me think he hadn't even noticed I'd been gone. Rufus said they'd given the staff the night off to mourn their father and sent out for Chinese and I was welcome to help myself. He gestured to the little cartons scattered all over the table. "We ordered some for your mom but she went to bed so there's plenty."

I reached for a pair of chopsticks and began to root around in the cartons. Much as I loathed Scott, I was pleased to witness a brotherly bonding between him and Rufus. I ate in silence listening to them reminiscing. "Do you remember the time when he . . ." and "I'm never going to forget the look on his face when you . . ." But it wasn't really the Phillionaire I had known and after about an hour or so, I crept away to my room.

Hours later I awoke and acting on instinct, I got up and went in search of my mother. I found her curled up in the middle of the vast bed she had shared with the Phillionaire, clutching a pillow. She was snoring gently and I went and lay down beside her, remembering with affection how Phil had once told me that she snored almost melodically, even, on one occasion, giving a passable rendition of "La Vie en Rose." I could tell what he meant. There was a soft underlying hum to her snoring that made it sound as if she was trying to sing in tune. As I lay where he had lain every night in the short time he had known her, I blessed him for bringing at least a brief period of joy into my mother's life.

I thought about what a simple and genuine man he had been despite the unbelievably sophisticated life he must have led. And after I had leaned over and given my mother a gentle kiss on the forehead, just as I imagined he might have done, I closed my eyes and said my own silent good-bye to the Phillionaire.

The next day it was decided that I should take the jitney back to Amagansett because there was only room for one passenger in Rufus's truck and he was driving my mother out. Scott had made it clear that he intended to take root in the apartment and my mother had caved.

"It's not as if I have any particular affection for the place now Phil has gone," she said, sounding frighteningly cool and pragmatic although her drawn face betrayed her. "And apart from the funeral, I want to be as far away from Scott as possible. I need to be with you, Lee. You'll take me in, won't you?"

But when I began to describe the Phillionaire's cabin and the fact that there was only one bed and one shower behind a curtain, she changed her mind about moving in with me before I'd even finished the sentence.

"I'm not sleeping in the same room with you, darling. No offense but you snore."

I almost smiled.

"Could you live with a room at the Stucco House until you decide where you want to be?" suggested Rufus. And of course it was the perfect solution. We were all being very careful not to mention that she couldn't really make any decision until we had heard what provision the Phillionaire had made for her in his new will.

The man sitting next to me on the bus looked familiar. He kept glancing at me with a half smile as he pretended to read his *Times* in a way that I found quite disconcerting. But then he stuck out his hand as we pulled out of Manhattan along the stretch of road that rises high above a cemetery—a sight that filled me with renewed gloom—and said "Louis Nichols. We met at the Old Stone Market and you're Vanessa's daughter, aren't you?" and I realized that it was just because I was seeing him out of context that I hadn't been able to place him.

The president of the Stone Landing Residents Association. And Martha Farrell's lover?

"Yes. I'm Lee Bartholomew. You know my mother?"

"My condolences," he said immediately. "I am just devastated by what's happened and I can't imagine what she must be going through. Phil and I were classmates at Harvard together," he explained. "And I grew up with Alison. His wife," he added when I looked blank. "Rufus and Scott's mother. I introduced her to Phil."

I didn't say anything. I hadn't figured him for being the same age as Phil. For all his immaculate grooming, Phil had seemed older than this man. Was it because his role in my life, though brief, had been caring and avuncular whereas at close quarters there was the faintest hint of flirtatiousness in Louis Nichols? He was certainly attractive, I could see how Martha had become smitten, yet he was too smooth for my taste, and a little too pleased with himself.

"You've been to see your mother." It wasn't a question. "How are Rufus and Scott doing?"

"Rufus better than Scott," I said, wondering how much I should reveal to this man. "Scott is staying in New York till the funeral but Rufus is coming out today. He's bringing my mother. The funeral's on Friday."

"Yes, I know," he said and I wondered how. "Your mother called me on my cell just before I turned it off. Tell me, you've become quite a good friend of Franny Cook's, haven't you?"

I nodded.

"How serious is it between her and Rufus? It's okay." He held up his hand when he saw the look on my face. "As I just said, I went way back with Phil and he used to talk to me about his concerns for the boys. Phil saw it coming a long time ago between Rufus and Franny. Rufus was besotted with her when he was a boy but then she got involved with the guy in New York and it looked like whatever torch Rufus had burning for her would have to be extinguished. But then she came back and even though Rufus was jumping on every good-looking girl on the East End of Long Island, Phil knew it was only a matter of time before he threw his cap at Franny again. Except now that she's gone and had Scott's baby it all gets pretty messy."

"Phil knew about Eliza?"

"Of course he did, although he never told Scott or Rufus he knew."

"And did he ever see her? Or Franny?"

"The baby? That I don't know. He knew Franny as a kid, of course, when she used to hang out with Rufus. He had a soft spot for her."

"I'm pleased," I said.

"Yeah. Too bad what happened later on."

"What do you mean? Dumpster?"

"That's the boy? Yes, well, there was his drug problem but Franny got in with a pretty bad crowd herself for a while. I'm not sure Rufus even knows about it. I hope not."

I didn't like the sound of this.

"You didn't know about her past?" He looked at me.

I was annoyed with myself. I didn't want to gossip with this man about Franny but I was itching to know about her.

Louis Nichols hesitated for a fraction of a second. Then he gave a little shrug that caused the sleeves of the cashmere sweater looped around his shoulders to untangle and flop down his chest.

"Okay, I'll tell you. But Franny Cook needs a friend around these parts, so just don't go judging her too harshly, okay?"

Now it was my turn to shrug. Hadn't he just established that I was Franny's friend?

"It wasn't really that bad. She had men and, I don't know any other way to say this, they paid her."

"For sex? She was a call girl?" My shocked reaction was involuntary but it was there all the same.

"In a way but it was all pretty high class. Men dated her—publicly—they took her to dinner, the theater, even the opera, showed her off all over town—and believe me, she was worth showing off—and they had affairs with her and they paid her. It works like that with most relationships except women get paid in kind—gifts of jewelry, clothes, or foreign travel. The only way it was different with Franny was that she got hard cash. And a lot of it. For services rendered."

Suddenly I had a horrible thought: *Had Louis Nichols been one of those men who had taken advantage of Franny's "services"?* I banished it immediately.

I didn't say anything. I didn't want to dignify what he had just told me with a comment, although a quick flash on the high-end contents of Franny's closet and the box of photographs I had found told me there might be some truth to what he said.

And then I had another unsettling thought. Had Bettina known about Franny's slightly murky past? Had she threatened Franny in some way? Maybe she had told Franny that Scott knew and that he would use the information to help him gain custody of Eliza in some way?

"What about Eliza?" I asked Louis Nichols. "What will happen to her?"

"As I said, it's messy. It all depends what provision Phil has made for her in his will, as his only grandchild. If it's substantial in any way, then you can bet your life Scott will want to play a bigger role in her life."

That was it, I thought. Scott had to be aware that his father had known about Eliza. Maybe he'd known for some time and that was why he was suddenly taking more interest in Eliza.

"By the way, I've become friends with Martha Farrell," I said, to see what sort of reaction that would get. "I'm reading the manuscript of her novel for her."

"Really?" Louis Nichols sounded surprised. "Who'd have thought Miss Havisham would have it in her. A woman of many talents."

I didn't quite like the patronizing way he said it.

"You knew her when she was an actress?"

"Well, I've known her since she first came to live out here. I wasn't aware she was ever an actress although I suppose it's possible. Tell you the truth, none of us knew where she came from when she arrived out here. She kept pretty much to herself in the beginning and we all let her have it that way. That's one of the things you can count on, being left alone to do what you want. It's the reason some people come here in the first place—it's the end of the road in more ways than one. You get people who ride the Long Island Railroad all the way out to Montauk, check into a motel room, and *boom!* It's all over. And no one ever hears the shot."

Surely that wasn't what he was saying about Martha?

"No," he went on, "I never knew Martha was an actress. When

she first came out here, all she ever did was fish. She set herself up in those damned trailers and she was out in her boat on the bay at first light along with everyone else. We thought we had a born-again Bonacker—that's what we call the locals, people who live around the Accabonac Harbor—but then she got involved in all that wedding dress crap."

"You see quite a lot of her now, don't you?" I wanted him to know that I knew about him and Martha.

"Oh Lord, what's she been saying?" He smiled in what was intended to be a charming, throwaway manner. But his next words made my blood run cold. "Sure, I see Martha from time to time but I have no intention of getting any more involved with her than I am now. I mean"—he shrugged again, an irritating habit he had that indicated he didn't want to take anything too seriously— "it's Martha. Come *on!*"

I was still finding all my spare thoughts directed toward memories of the Phillionaire and I think I would have forgotten Louis Nichols's chilling dismissal of Martha sooner rather than later had she not been standing on the shoulder when the bus drew to a halt in Amagansett. I knew immediately that she had come to meet him, to surprise him, but when she saw me get off the bus ahead of him, she rushed to embrace me and he used this to slip off toward his car parked farther up the road.

"Louis!" she called. "Here I am."

"Oh hi," he called back, "how are you? I would have given Lee a ride but it's great you've come to meet her."

He knew exactly why she was there and it killed me to see the look on her face.

Just as it killed me to see how valiantly my mother was trying to keep it all together when Rufus deposited her at the Stucco House that evening. I was touched by the way Rufus included her in all the decisions that were made over the next few days for the simple service that was to take place on the beach at the end of the week. But when the time came, for all that we'd spent the week discussing how it would be, I wasn't prepared for the devastating sight of the Phillionaire's coffin being held aloft above the high beach grass as it was carried down to the beach.

We were to gather at the very same spot where the commitment ceremony had taken place, only this time the weather was the kind you prayed for if you were having a wedding. I was in the process of trying to steam the creases out of a black linen shift in the shower—the Phillionaire hadn't deemed it necessary to keep an iron at the cabin—when a shadow fell across the open doorway. I looked up and screamed.

But in surprise not fear.

Dumpster stood there, his lanky frame towering above me as he stepped into the room and looked around. "You're alone, right? I need to speak with you."

CHAPTER 13

Y MOM TOLD ME YOU WERE LIVING HERE," HE said, eyeing me warily. "You guys hang together, right? You've become friends?"

I nodded again, yes. I was horrified to see what a terrible state he was in, a far cry from the outgoing, rosy-cheeked youth I had encountered at Shotgun's. His hair was matted and gave new meaning to the term "dirty blond." His clothes were filthy and I knew that if he came any closer I'd get a nasty whiff of his unwashed state. He looked disheveled and hollow-eyed from lack of sleep.

"I have to see her," he said, "my mom. I know she's living over there"—he jerked his head in the direction of the Stucco House—"but there's cars parked everywhere. I don't want to run into anyone else. I saw just your Jeep here so I took a chance you were on your own."

"You want to see Franny?"

He nodded. "Can you go get her? Bring her back here?"

"Dumpster, I don't really have time. We've got a funeral service starting in twenty minutes down on the beach for Philip Abernathy and—"

"Yeah, I heard he died. I'm sorry. But you know"—he looked at me helplessly—"I really do have to see my mom."

"Where have you been?" I asked him. "She told me you just took off."

"I had to get where *he* wouldn't find me."

"He?"

"Detective Morrison. He's got me all tied up in knots so I can't move. He wants me to retract what I said at Shotgun's arraignment. To say that I wasn't with Shotgun the night Bettina was killed. He's going to make my life hell—and he's going to make my mom's life even worse—until I go along with what he wants."

"Well, were you there or not?"

"Not really."

"Dumpster!"

"Okay, okay. I was there, I was at Mallaby but I wasn't at the house. I was out in the woods with my bow and arrow, I had plans to hunt deer."

"So Shotgun doesn't really have an alibi?"

"Not as far as I know. But he does have me. I'm not going to change my story again. Then I'd get done for lying at the arraignment. And I'd get my mom in trouble because she changed her story for me. But it was my bow and arrow they found, I know it. I left them in my truck at the end of the dirt road round about eight thirty that night, I had to go meet someone, and when I got back they were gone."

"You went to meet Bettina at the beach?"

He looked astonished. "How in the world did you know that?"

"Listen," I said to him, "I'll go and get your mother but in return I want a guarantee that you'll answer a few questions for me. Like how come Bettina Pleshette had an assignation with you the night she was killed? Maybe you're saying you were with Shotgun not only to give him an alibi but to give yourself one as well. Maybe Shotgun's *your* alibi instead of the other way around."

"I thought you were my mom's friend," he said, backing away from me. "That's why I came to you. I thought I could trust you to bring her to me without anyone seeing me. But now you're pointing the finger at me. Okay, that was my bow and arrow in the pit but I swear to God, I don't know how they got there. I'm backing up Shotgun because I like the guy. I want to help him. It's that simple. I haven't done anything wrong."

"Except lie all over the place. Dumpster," I said gently, "I know what the deal is with Evan Morrison. Your mother told me all about it, how you have this arrangement with him and—"

He broke in. "That's why I took off. That's why I'm on the loose. I can't handle that anymore. So far I've been making stuff up but I'm running out of stories to give him and I don't want to have to rat on my friends. Plus the guy won't leave me alone. He keeps putting the pressure on me to say I wasn't with Shotgun. It's like he *knows* I'm lying. He wants to nail Shotgun so bad, it's scary and I don't want to be a part of that."

"And you think running away is going to make it any better?"

"*No!*" He was yelling at me now, totally distraught. I hated provoking him like this but I wanted to scare him into telling me the truth. "No," he quieted down a little, "but I just can't handle it anymore."

"You know Evan Morrison thinks you might have been Shotgun's accomplice?"

I stood back, ready for the outburst that I felt was sure to come, but he just looked sad.

"Well, then I don't have a prayer, do I?" Now he looked totally helpless.

"But what was the meeting you had with Bettina all about?"

"The meeting I didn't have with Bettina, you mean. She was killed before I saw her. I asked her to meet up with me down at the beach by Mallaby, told her I had some stuff to tell her."

"Which was?" *M saw something.*

"Oh, it was just a way of getting her to meet me."

"Why did you want her down at the beach—alone—at nine o'clock at night?"

"I wasn't going to kill her, if that's what you're thinking. Although I might have come close."

"You didn't like her?"

"I didn't really know her but I hated what she was doing to my mom. She was always trying to talk to me because she knew I worked for Shotgun. But I knew he didn't want to deal with her so I kept out of her way as much as I could. But there was one time when she cornered me as I was coming out of the Old Stone Market. She started asking me about the life Mom and I had led back in the city."

So I'd been right about Bettina knowing about Franny's past.

"She asked me who my father was," he went on, "and when I didn't answer, she started making these *insinuations*—like my mom had had way too many men in her life and maybe—I mean, she was making slurs on my mom's character that I just did not care to hear. And I sort of knew I wasn't the only one she was talking to." He shook his head. "I got the feeling it was only a matter of time before she started telling my mom's customers at the market about her life in the city. So I felt I had to do something to shut her up. I thought if I made her think I had some information about Shotgun, I could hold it over her until she promised to stop bad-mouthing my mom."

"You gave her information about Shotgun?"

"That's why I called her and told her to meet me at the beach."

"What did you have to tell her?"

But he was eyeing me suspiciously. "What does it matter?" he said evasively. "I never saw her."

He was standing right in front of me, blocking the door, his fingers drumming against his thigh, but I wasn't remotely threatened by him. He was just a boy acting big, protective of his mother, protective of Shotgun, and utterly, utterly confused.

"Did you see anything out there in the woods, Dumpster?" I stepped forward and stared straight into his face.

"Oh *man!*"

What was that supposed to mean?

"Well, did you?"

"So what if I did see something the night Bettina died? Or the night Sean died for that matter. I'm not going to say a word. Whatever I say it's going to get me in trouble with someone. Shotgun, Detective Morrison, Mom. That's why I'm going to keep quiet. That's why I need Mom to give me some money so I can get out of here. If I don't tell anybody, they won't know, and believe me, it's better that way."

"Dumpster, we're talking about murder here. *Two* murders. You have to tell what you saw. I'll go and get your mother and leave you here together while I go to the funeral on the beach. No one's going to come near here while that's taking place. Then I'll come back and you and I will talk. And you'll tell me everything and then we'll find a way to make sure nothing will happen to you."

Even as I spoke I wondered if I would be able to guarantee this. I had no idea what he was going to tell me. *If* he agreed to tell me anything.

"You're scared, Dumpster," I said, "and I can see why. The real problem here is that we don't want to talk to the very person we ought to be helping, the person who's supposed to be clearing everything up. I can understand why you need to get free from Evan Morrison's power and I'm going to help you do that."

Exactly how, I had absolutely no idea and I knew what I really ought to do was go straight to Evan Morrison and tell him what Dumpster had told me.

But I knew I would never rat on Dumpster. I couldn't do that to Franny.

"But my mom?" he said. "I keep saying I'm not going to say what he wants me to say but then what's he going to do to my mom?"

"I know. But she's safe over there. Do you like Rufus?"

He shrugged. "I guess."

"Well, he'll take care of your mom. We'll just have to let him in on the whole story so he knows it has to be extra special care from now on. He's a pretty good guy and you can trust him. But are you quite sure getting away from here is the best thing?"

"Absolutely," he said. "I need to clear my head."

"And you don't think you ought to tell your mother everything when she comes over?"

"I don't want her involved. I said that already. She's had enough going on, she needs a break."

"Okay." I nodded. He could get it all out of his system with me, whatever he had been carrying around that had got him in such a terrible state. This was one way I could help Franny. But what would I do with whatever he told me? Would I go to Detective Morrison? Because the only thing I could tell *him* and walk away unscathed was that Shotgun was the killer—and that was the last thing *I* wanted to hear.

But in the end I heard nothing because Franny wasn't at the Stucco House when I raced over to get her, having told Dumpster to wait at the cabin. My mother opened the door and when I saw her I realized she was desperately in need of moral support. I think up to now she had been in shock and it was starting to hit her what had happened to Phil, just when she needed to find the strength to get through the funeral.

Lucia came rushing up and began to dab at us with a clothes brush, flicking away imaginary fluff from our dark clothes. I knew she was trying to be helpful, to offer some kind of consolation, but it felt intrusive. And when we stepped outside we found a long black funeral car had drawn up to the Stucco House ready to drive us down to the beach.

"Oh no, this is all wrong. It'll get stuck in the sand. We'll walk," my mother told the driver.

She took two steps off the porch and her heels sank into the sand and then to my amazement she stopped and kicked off her shoes.

"Let's go barefoot," she said, "you know, like the last time."

So I slipped my arm through hers and together we set off barefoot down the sandy trail to the beach. I sensed someone behind us and turned to see Evan Morrison.

"I'm sorry to intrude at this time," he said, "but I understand Franny Cook is living here. I need to see her and ask her where her son is. And of course I want to pay my respects—"

I was speechless. My mother was smiling uncertainly. She had no idea who he was. And then the most surprising person came to our rescue. Scott was running down the trail toward us and when he reached Evan Morrison, he placed his palm flat against the detective's chest and pushed him away.

"You should go," he said, "and you should leave my stepmother alone. This is family only."

Evan Morrison looked at me but Scott was still backing him firmly away and unless he wanted to fall flat on his back into the dunes, he had no option but to turn and leave. Scott took my mother's other arm and the three of us continued slowly on down to the beach. I had noted the reference to his "stepmother" and I wondered what my mother had made of that. And my mind was racing about Evan Morrison. *Please God, do not let him walk over to the cabin and find Dumpster.*

It was a glorious day and tiny dots of sunshine were dancing all over the bay. I didn't know whether to be glad about this—the sun was shining as a mark of respect for the Phillionaire—or resentful because it appeared to be taunting the gloom that pervaded a funeral.

Rufus and his surfer gang were standing around the coffin although this time they had their surfboards pointed down away from them. The tears started in my eyes and the service passed in a blur. I barely registered what was being said. I just gripped my mother's arm, ostensibly to stop her from falling but in actual fact I know I was hanging on to her partly to hold myself up. Scott read something in a flat monotone and Rufus talked about what his father had told him of his surfing days. Louis Nichols spoke quickly about Scott and Rufus's mother, glancing at mine from time to time, but then he went on to describe how the last few months of the Phillionaire's life had been blessed with the joy of being with Vanessa.

"What happens now?" I whispered to my mother as the short service came to an end. "Where is he going to be buried? Is it far from here?"

"He's not," she whispered back. "He's going straight to a crematorium—they wanted us to have the service there but I couldn't face it. And then we'll be given an urn and Rufus is going to take Scott and me out in his boat and we'll scatter his ashes over the bay. Darling, I'm sorry"—she gripped my arm a little tighter—"there won't be room for you in the boat. I'd rather it were you and me and Rufus but Scott has to come."

"I understand," I said. But I was miserable. I wanted to be there, to be part of the family, a stepsister—even though I wasn't.

Midway through the ceremony I had noticed a tiny dot of a figure approaching along the water line from far up the beach. After a while I realized with a shudder that it was Martha. Was she going to jinx the funeral too? Or was she just stalking Louis Nichols? She materialized now at my side as I began what I had anticipated being a lonely walk back to the cabin from the Stucco House.

"Not going with them?" She put her arm around my shoulders as I shook my head and explained why. "It doesn't matter," she said. "I'll take you out in my boat another time and you can take something from his cabin and throw it in. Same thing. Do you want company now or shall I leave you alone?"

"No, please come back with me." I didn't want to wallow in my grief all alone. I really needed her.

"Thank you for your support," I said. "I tend to find it awkward showing people how much I appreciate the things they do for me. I like to think I don't need anyone but every now and then I really do and you seemed to know that without my telling you. I think that's what I'm really grateful for."

"Oh stop!" she said. "Just remember it's a two-way street if it makes you feel any better. I need your help with my writing."

"Oh," I said, when we walked into the cabin and there was no one there. Had Dumpster got fed up with waiting and left or had Evan Morrison found him here and taken him?

"What's up?" said Martha. "Were you expecting someone?"

I explained about Dumpster, expecting her to share my concern but to my surprise she just nodded.

"Oh, I expect Evan's got him."

"I don't feel I can trust him for some reason."

"You can't?" She was surprised. "Because he's new around here? Why would that bother you? You are too. But you haven't come from the South Bronx like he did. He must think he's died and gone to heaven working out here in the Hamptons. It's a far cry from patrolling the public housing projects he started out with, all those dealers lurking in stairwells, watching the action in the streets for hours on end, crouched on a tar rooftop till he could barely move, finding dead junkies in burned-out houses."

"He was a narc? Sounds like you've talked to him quite a bit."

"He was a narc. I talked to him quite a bit," she repeated. "Last night, as a matter of fact. He came by the trailers and we walked on the beach."

"Why did he come to see you? He'd questioned you before now, surely?"

"Of course he had. With me living so close to where the killings took place, he wanted to know if I'd seen or heard anything."

"And had you?"

"Well no, but then I remembered that I'd seen something the night *before* Sean Marriott was killed. I saw him walking through the woods with a shotgun."

M saw Sean w/shotgun in woods night before Sean killed. Bettina had meant Sean was with the Purdey *shotgun,* not with his father, Shotgun, as I had assumed. And this "M" wasn't Martin, it was Martha.

"And you told Bettina this?"

She looked at me as if I were crazy. "*Bettina?* I didn't know Bettina. No, I followed Sean because it was such a strange sight. He was the least likely person to use a shotgun. I wanted to see where he was going with it and he went straight to this little blind Dumpster's got set up in the woods, the place he goes when he hunts deer. Sean left the shotgun inside—for Dumpster, I guess."

"Shotgun told me they were friends," I said. "In fact he said that when he saw the Purdey was missing from Sean's room, he figured Sean must have loaned it to Dumpster. But surely you're not suggesting that Dumpster killed Sean?"

"Actually, I am. By accident," said Martha. "And the real tragedy is that he probably did it with Sean's own gun. He saw a shadow in the woods and he thought it was Bettina."

"But he knew Bettina wasn't coming. He told me he overheard Shotgun talking to her on the phone, telling her not to come."

"But he told you that *afterwards,* right? He could have been lying. Maybe he didn't know Bettina wasn't coming and he was waiting in the woods for her."

"But why would he be waiting for her?"

"To kill her, for Shotgun. Evan Morrison and I worked it all out as we were walking along the beach. Here's what happened. Are you okay, by the way? I didn't plan on coming over here and getting into this. I'm supposed to be consoling you and—"

I nodded yes, I was fine—although I was a little shocked to realize I hadn't thought of the Phillionaire for several minutes.

"Shotgun Marriott wants to get rid of Bettina because she knows something about what happened to that groupie in London. Sean's mother as good as told him that his father killed the girl. Shotgun is scared Bettina either knows what happened or she'll uncover the truth as she digs into his past for the book. But he doesn't want another murder on his hands so he talks Dumpster into killing her for him. Sean left the first murder weapon in Dumpster's blind and the second, Dumpster's bow and arrow, were found in that construction pit. It doesn't look good for the kid."

I didn't say anything because as much as I tried to dismiss it, it was beginning to sound like a plausible scenario. Dumpster had as good as admitted to me that he had been lying about his whereabouts on both nights. He had told me he had been at Mallaby but he hadn't been at the house—which meant he *was* out in the woods. Had he been lying about his bow and arrow being stolen from his truck? Had the meeting with Bettina in fact taken place? Was Shotgun covering up for him, or was he covering up for Shotgun—or both?

"I'm with Evan Morrison on this," said Martha. "His theory is the only one that pans out. There's no one else around here with a likely motive for killing Bettina. Whether he actually pulled the trigger or not, Shotgun did it."

"Did what?" said a voice behind me and Martha gasped.

She had gone very pale. She was on her feet and moving past me out the door before I could say anything.

Shotgun looked after her, puzzled.

"Look, if it's not a good time? I just wanted to come and tell you how sorry I am about Philip Abernathy. For you I mean. I didn't know him. But that woman who just rushed out of here, I think I've seen her somewhere before. Who was she? And what am I supposed to have done?"

He was looking immaculate in freshly pressed linen pants and a crisp white shirt. His only concession to the fact that he was in a beach environment was a pair of rope-soled espadrilles in a virulent shade of purple. Didn't he ever wear beat-up shorts and sneakers like the rest of us? What was the point of living at the beach if you didn't get down and dirty in the sand once in a while? He appeared more formally dressed than I was and I had just been to a funeral.

"We've just had Phil's funeral," I said, "down at the beach."

"Yes, I saw them packing up on my way over here—oh, sorry," he looked mortified for a second, "that makes it sound like you just had a picnic."

"I know what you mean." I smiled. "They're taking the coffin to a crematorium and later they're going to scatter his ashes over the bay. Did you walk over here?"

He nodded. "Dumpster told me where you were staying. He said it would be a short and beautiful walk and he was right. I just wandered down through my woods and there I was. I really have to get out and about more. I've become such a recluse."

"That's what they say about you round here—that you're a total hermit. No one ever sees you and the only way people know you're here is that you hire local people to work at the house and *they've* seen you. Like Dumpster." I looked at him. "Dumpster told you where to find me? So you've seen him around Mallaby lately?"

"Sure," said Shotgun, "like half an hour ago. He came by to take care of a few things around the house, in Sean's old room above the stables as a matter of fact. He's helping me clear the place out and maybe I'll let him move in there permanently. He seems to be sleeping there most of the time anyway."

"He's hiding out with you?"

"Hiding out?"

"As far as his mother's concerned Dumpster's disappeared."

"Is that right?" said Shotgun. "Well, maybe you'd better keep quiet about the fact that Dumpster's with me."

Shotgun was shielding Dumpster.

"So who was that woman who just left? She didn't exactly act like she was one of my fans."

"On the contrary," I said, thinking of Martha's remark about me introducing Shotgun to her as a rich and eligible suitor, but I thought better of mentioning it. "That was Martha Farrell. She's lived round here for—what?—twenty years? So you've probably caught sight of her at some point—on one of your rare excursions outdoors during the daytime."

"Martha Farrell," he repeated it slowly. "She said 'Shotgun did it.' What am I supposed to have done?"

"You mean you really don't know?" I forced myself to continue the banter between us and hoped he'd let it go at that. "So, when would you like me to come over for another session? I think I'm ready to go back to work—now that we're past the funeral."

He didn't answer me. Instead he seemed preoccupied with something he could see through the open door.

"Shotgun? Kip, I mean?"

"Look," he said, turning around suddenly, "this is awkward. I really did come over to offer my condolences about Philip Abernathy but there's another reason I wanted to see you. I'm through with the book. I don't want to go on with it."

I was staggered.

"But you were doing it for Sean."

"I was. Only for Sean," he confirmed. "But I've changed my mind. No more book."

"But why? This is very sudden." I couldn't understand it. All his talk about tying the book into his music comeback. "What about the cross-promotion of the book and the concert tour?"

"I'm just going to work on the music. No book. I've been thinking it over and it's too much to do all at once. I just don't have the energy. I'm not as young as I once was."

He gave me a weak smile.

It had to have something to do with what he'd raked up out of himself about the night the groupie died. Could it really be that he had something to hide about what happened that night, something a prying investigative writer like Bettina would uncover? But hadn't I gained his confidence in the short time I had known him? Hadn't he said he had a story that he really needed to tell and he needed me to help get it out of him?

Suddenly I felt immensely depressed. On top of the agony of the Phillionaire's death, now my work looked like it was going to evaporate into thin air. Tears welled up in my eyes and I looked away from him quickly.

But he saw and he came over and before I could move away, he put his arms around me.

"I'm sorry. I really am, I'm sorry. I didn't come over here just to tell you that. I wanted to help you get through your loss. Dumpster told me you were pretty close to Philip Abernathy. I mean, I know how it feels."

Well, that was true, sure enough. He was still mourning Sean's death.

"Of course you do," I said as gently as I could. "You've lost a son. I only knew Phil for a few weeks but still I—"

I couldn't help it. The sadness had lodged itself inside me now and I felt myself heaving. I expected him to pat me on the back, embarrassed—what had he got himself into with this hysterical woman? But instead he drew me closer to him, brought my head to rest against his shoulder, and soothed me with the kind of murmurs one would use to comfort a baby or a high-strung animal: "There there, it's all right, easy now." And I began to relax safe in the knowledge that it was okay to let go like this, I was with someone who was going through the same thing, someone who understood.

Maybe I relaxed too much because I have no idea how it happened. One minute I was snuffling quietly against his shoulder, deep in my own thoughts about the Phillionaire, and the next he had eased me gently away from him to bring his face to mine and we were kissing.

I think what surprised me the most was that I didn't stop. I didn't leap away from him and go *Whoa, what are you doing, stop that!* I let it go on and on because he was a wonderful kisser, the kind that makes you feel as if he has all the time in the world and there is nothing else he wants from you. *This kiss is not a means to an end, I'm just enjoying it for what it is and I'm going to go on and on until you're the one who starts begging to take it a stage further.*

"Uh-oh," his lips left mine long enough to murmur into my ear, "we've got company."

I backed away from him, as much from the shock of hearing his voice as from what he actually said. My instant assumption was that it must be Martha who had thought better of her hasty exit.

But there was no one at the open door and I stood waiting for Shotgun to explain, not looking at him and wondering if he could hear my heart thundering in my chest.

"It was a bloke," he said, "big hairy guy. Anyway, he took off like the proverbial bat out of hell when he saw us."

Of all the big hairy guys in the world—and there had to be zillions, literally—I knew instantly who it was. I dashed outside but the only person there was Franny. She pointed to the bay where a figure was beating a lumbering retreat down the sandy trail to the beach. He had his battered old knapsack that had been falling apart for years on his back and he had abandoned an equally dilapidated suitcase on wheels that had become entrenched in the sand.

"TOMMY!" I yelled after him. "Tommy, come back here. *Please!*"

CHAPTER 14

AS I STOOD SHOUTING AT HIM TO COME BACK, I could already see the reproachful hunch of his shoulders rising with each shambling step. I could almost hear his thoughts. *I just caught you kissing some bloke and if you think I'm going to turn around and trot meekly back to you, you've got another think coming.*

"Franny," I said, turning to her, "you brought him here?"

"He turned up at the Stucco House in a cab. He said he knew your mother and Phil and he'd come to Amagansett and everyone had told him where the funeral was taking place."

"He came for the *funeral*? He barely knew Phil."

"Who is he?" said Franny.

"He didn't say?"

"Well, he gave me his name, Tommy Kennedy, and he said he was looking for you too, so I brought him over here."

"Nothing else?"

"What else is there?"

"I'm sorry to blurt this out in a rush, Franny, but right before I came out here, he and I were going to be married and then he backed out. Now he picks this moment to turn up just when I'm kissing another man."

"You are? I mean, you were? Who?"

"Shotgun Marriott."

"You're not serious?" Franny looked extremely impressed and I wanted to throttle her.

"It didn't *mean* anything. We were just comforting each other—for his son's death and Phil's."

"Yeah, right," she said, still grinning.

"It's true," I said although it wasn't, not entirely, and I was still trembling inside with the memory of Shotgun's kiss. "But Franny, whether you believe me or not, I need you to do something for me. Please would you go after Tommy and persuade him to come back. Tell him I really want to see him. Tell him anything you like but get him to come back here."

"Why can't you go tell him yourself? You'll catch up with him easy. He's not exactly making a speedy getaway."

That much was obvious. Tommy looked to be in even worse physical shape than when I'd left. Even though he was out of earshot I could hear him huffing and puffing along the beach just by watching him. He was a perfect example of an overweight Englishman whose shorts were too long and too baggy to be cool, whose lager paunch was not quite covered by his flapping T-shirt, and whose flip-flops appeared to be rubbing and hampering his every step. His sweaty progress as he lumbered along the water's edge could not have been more removed from the sleekness of Shotgun's perfectly laundered linen.

"Because he's not going to listen to me. He's going to make me pay. But if there's even the slightest chance that he actually does still want to see me, he might just listen to you. So, Franny, *please*—"

She took off without another word.

I returned to find Shotgun had settled himself in the Phillionaire's kitchen. He was perched on a stool at the island, pouring himself a glass of San Pellegrino.

"You don't mind?" He held up the glass. "I helped myself. This is a quaint little place you've got here."

Suddenly I was furious with him. Irrational, of course, as only I could be, because of course I was furious with myself more than anything. Shotgun hadn't really done anything wrong. He had offered comfort and I had accepted it. The comfort had just evolved into something I hadn't been prepared for but which I hadn't exactly resisted. How long had he wanted to kiss me? Had it been a spur-of-the-moment thing? Was this the real reason he was canceling the book? Did he want to avoid mixing business with pleasure?

"Could you please—like—leave," I said to Shotgun, awkward and abrupt in my urgent need to have him gone before Tommy reappeared. *If* he reappeared.

Shotgun was on his feet in a second. "My God, of *course*. Do forgive me. I'd no idea I was intruding." He spoke with an exaggerated politeness, almost mocking me. No allusion to the fact that just a few minutes ago I'd been perfectly happy to be ensconced in a passionate embrace with him.

I decided to stick to as much of the truth as I was capable. "I'm sorry. It looks like a friend has turned up from England earlier than I expected. He knew Phil and—"

"Don't say another word. I don't know whether to say something like *It's been nice working with you*—" I couldn't believe it. He was actually holding out his hand as if nothing had happened. I shook it nervously but to my relief I felt none of the electricity his kiss had transmitted.

Of course as he was going out the door he ran straight into Tommy and Franny.

"Hello, Kip Marriott. I'm sorry for your loss." Shotgun held his hand out again to Tommy.

Tommy just stared at him open-mouthed and I could have killed him for being so gauche. He wasn't normally impressed by celebrities. Maybe he just felt awkward being greeted by a man he had just seen kissing me.

"Is that your real name? Kip?" said Franny. "I'm Franny Cook by the way, Dumpster's mom."

"Oh, I know who you are. I owe you a debt of gratitude," said Shotgun, all charm now. "Dumpster does incredible work for me at Mallaby, plus I'll never be able to repay you both for speaking up at my arraignment. You must be very proud of him."

"I'd welcome the opportunity," said Franny, as she followed him out of the door, "I never see him. He's taken off, disappeared. Actually, you know? I was going to come by and see if *you'd* seen him."

"Was that who I think it was?" was the first thing Tommy said to me when Shotgun and Franny had left.

"Shotgun Marriott," I said, "the man whose book I'm doing. *Was* doing," I corrected myself.

"Oh yeah?" said Tommy. "Your kisses not up to snuff? He's broken up with you, has he?"

"I'll ignore that," I said. "And although I don't feel I owe you any explanation, you should know that the kiss you just saw was an accident."

"Like he was on his way to the bathroom and you were in the way?"

"Don't be crass, Tommy. His son was murdered, I'm upset about Phil's death. He was comforting me or I was comforting him, whichever way you want to look at it. And it must have looked to you as if we were kissing *that* way."

"You *were* kissing *that* way." We were standing about two feet apart and I could reach out and touch him if I wanted. It was incredible to me that even though we had been about to marry—and had not seen each other for several weeks—as yet we had had no physical contact. He was still sweaty from his exertions along the beach and the paunch and the floppy shorts were still very much in evidence. But all I saw in front of me was the tousled little-boy look that had always been one of my biggest weaknesses when it came to Tommy. He generally presented himself this way when he was not at all sure of his ground and somehow his vulnerability was irresistible.

"I know how you kiss *that* way, remember." He almost stamped his flip-flop in his frustration. "I came all the way here from London to kiss you in the *other* way, to console you about Phil. I read about his death and I knew you'd be devastated. I called his apartment in New York and they told me your mum had left for the funeral and it would be in Amagansett. I planned to— you know—surprise you. Only you're the one who gives me a surprise. I turn up and find you snogging away with that creep of a has-been."

But however much I want to let it all ride over me, something about Tommy's needling always gets to me. I think it has something to do with my stupid pride. I stared at him standing before me all puffed up with resentment and I told myself firmly: *He's hurt and disappointed as he has every right to be. I should be sweet and understanding with him and I should rise above my irritation at his petulance and bend over backward to make him feel that I need him and want him and I'm unbelievably touched that he's come all this way to be with me.*

"Oh fuck off, Tommy!" I said. "You know absolutely nothing about Shotgun Marriott. You walk away from our wedding for no reason, you humiliate me and hurt me, and instead of hanging around and whining, I pick myself up and get myself a pretty impressive assignment far away from you so you won't be embarrassed by me hanging around. And what do you do? You come over here and start slinging mud. Well, you can fuck off!"

So much for sweet and understanding!

"I heard you only got the job because his first choice got herself murdered."

Trust Tommy to ignore everything else and hone in on the one thing I said that wasn't quite true.

"And——" he said, backing out of the door and returning a few seconds later, lugging his battered suitcase behind him——"and, as I said, I came over here because Phil Abernathy bought the farm, no other reason."

"What does 'bought the farm' mean?"

"Kicked the bucket."

"So if that's the only reason you're here why have you packed for a six-month stay?" I pointed to the vast suitcase. "And why are you bringing that in here?"

Tommy started shuffling his feet a little. I knew the signs. If I kept up my shrewish tone with him, he'd give in eventually and tell me why he was really here. He always caves before I do because fundamentally he's a nicer person than I am. He can't sustain confrontation the way I can.

"You got any beers in that fridge?" I knew what this was. He was proffering an olive branch. Why oh why did I feel compelled to ignore it?

"No." I glared at him. "Just milk."

"And cookies? Phil told me you two sat up one night with milk and cookies and put the world to rights. I must admit, I became quite jealous listening to him talk about you." Tommy was smiling now, tentatively, and he had taken a step or two toward me.

"He was like a father to me," I said, not looking at him. "Or an uncle, more like. He listened to me and he gave me good advice. He seemed to really care about me, I don't know why."

"Because in spite of the fact that you try to present yourself to the world as this incredibly capable and independent woman who doesn't need anybody to lean on, those of us who care about you know it's all a front. We can see perfectly well that you're a neurotic and pathetic old duck who worries and frets herself into the ground and it's blindingly clear that the only thing that'll keep you on an even keel is a round of milk and cookies. So if that's all you've got, I suppose I'll have to settle for that."

He started to walk over to the fridge, glancing warily at me out of the corner of his eye as if I were a rabid dog that might fly at him at any second. Which I was.

"You're a silly goose, you know that?" said Tommy affectionately as he slurped his milk. He had an uncanny way of sensing just when my anger toward him was beginning to evaporate.

"Am not." Now I was the one beginning to sound like a petulant child. I got a grip on myself. "Actually, Tommy, I want to apologize. I really appreciate that you've come all this way." I was aware that I was sounding a little stiff and formal. "I mean, you could have given me a bit of warning so I could have washed my hair but I suppose that was too much to ask." I smiled. *I'm trying, Tommy, I'm trying.*

"Wanted to surprise you. Thought I said that." He was looking at me suspiciously as he always did when it seemed I was deliberately trying to be nice to him.

"And you certainly did! So have you heard all about the murders?"

He nodded. "Sounded pretty hairy."

"Well, I'll tell you all about it but first I want to say that I heard about you losing your job at the BBC."

He tensed.

"And it's all right. I mean it's not all right for you, it's awful, and totally unfair, but what you need to take on board is that we're both in the same boat now. You just saw Shotgun kissing me, okay? He was comforting me but he was also kissing me good-bye. He was essentially firing me. He doesn't want to do the book anymore so we're both out of work now."

"Bloody hell!" said Tommy. "So what are we going to live on?"

For a fraction of a second my old indignation surfaced. I'd just commiserated with him about losing his job but instead of telling me he was sorry about me losing mine, his first thought was— but then I caught myself. *What are* we *going to live on?* I should focus on how I felt about the reemergence of the *we*.

"We'll manage, Tommy. Genevieve will find me another assignment. She always does." Even as I tried to reassure him I knew it was the wrong thing to say, that he needn't worry, as usual I'd solve the problem, nobody needed to rely on him. "And you'll find something when we get back to London."

But it was too late and also, as it turned out, not what he had in mind.

"I thought I might have a better shot of getting some work out here," he said gloomily. "I had it all worked out. You were here. I'd try my hand at something completely different. Fresh start and all that."

So he hadn't come here just to comfort me. "What kind of something completely different did you have in mind?" I said carefully. Had he never heard of visas and work permits and green cards?

"Well, I was just talking to your friend Franny and I asked her if maybe I could help out at her store."

Oh, great! Tommy with fifteen-odd years of valuable experience as a radio sound engineer was now about to become Tommy the illegal immigrant stocking shelves in a grocery store. Besides, he hadn't known Franny when he decided to come to America so clearly he hadn't had a plan at all. Spur of the moment Tommy strikes again.

"Well, that might work for a while but then what?"

But Tommy's eternal optimism was another thing I loved him for. "Dunno," he said. "Something'll turn up. America, land of opportunity and all that. So anyway, what do you do with yourself all day?" He looked out the window. "Must be handy having the beach so close. Quite fancy going for a dip, what about you?"

I gave up. If I'd had a bucket and spade I'd have handed them to him, made him some of his favorite cheese-and-pickle sandwiches, and packed him off to the beach for the afternoon with a warning not to go in the sea without his water wings.

But when I stepped behind the shower curtain in some ridiculous show of modesty to change into my swimsuit, he followed and peeked through the curtain. And when I was naked he picked me up in his arms and carried me back to the bed. He might be unfit but he was pretty strong. I tried not to giggle as he wriggled out of his shorts in a sort of elephant shimmy and flopped down beside me.

And passed out.

I lay beside him, prodding him every now and then in an attempt to wake him up, but he was out for the count. *He's just got off a plane,* I told myself, *he's exhausted.* He didn't even wake up when the phone rang right beside the bed.

"Lee?" It was Rufus. "Okay, we just cremated Dad. Sounds awful but I don't know any other way to say it. Look, I just wanted to say I'm really sorry we can't fit you in the boat when we go out on the water to scatter his ashes. There's just no room. But there is something happening tomorrow where I really do need you to be present."

"What's that?"

"The reading of the will. Dad's lawyer's coming out and we're going to do it at the Stucco House at ten A.M. Does that work for you?"

"Sure," I said, "but why would you need me there?"

"You'll see," he said mysteriously.

Tommy was out for the count so I left him a note on the pillow telling him to help himself to whatever he needed, and said that I was going over to the Stucco House to be with my mother and probably wouldn't be back that night. I imagined he would have likely reduced the place to chaos by the time I returned but I felt it was important to keep my mother company.

I found her in the kitchen, sitting on a barstool and staring into space. I was still grieving for the Phillionaire but for my mother it must be a different kind of pain altogether. What would it be like if I lost Tommy? And not just if he died but if he had died when were still in the throes of the almost unendurable passion that had accompanied the first eighteen months of our relationship? A passion that had subsided over the eight years we had been together until I had begun to wonder if we could ever recapture it. That we did, and that it had led to my finally wanting to marry him, was something of a miracle.

But then as I tiptoed around my mother, not wanting to break her trance, I wondered if it was possible to experience this kind of passion when you were in your sixties. Suddenly my mother looked up.

"What makes this harder than anything I've ever had to bear is that I know Phil really loved me." The tremble in her voice was unmistakable. "He was the only person who really loved me in my life and now he's gone."

I was stunned. "I love you, Mum. And I'm still here."

"Not the same," she said flatly. Once upon a time hearing something like this from her would have hurt but since my father had left her, our relationship had changed. She had become more needy and I was able to look past the sometimes blunt and insensitive woman to the complicated person underneath. I knew what she meant about it not being the same love as that for a child or a parent. But what did it say about her relationship with my father?

Then I remembered what Rufus had said: that his dad seemed determined to help her learn to love herself and express her love for others.

"Mum, just keep the memory that he loved you—and that you loved him. And how lucky you were to find each other, if only for a short time."

"That's just it," she said, looking even more distraught, "that's what's really haunting me. I don't think I ever really made him understand how much I loved him. He died not knowing what he meant to me and I just can't bear to think of it. I just took from him. Money, time, affection. What did I give back?"

"You," I said simply. "That was all he wanted. He knew you loved him. Phil and I used to talk quite a lot, Mum. You know we used to plot how we were going to creep in under your defenses when you weren't looking and get you to come right out and *say* how much we meant to you."

I held my breath because I had never spoken to my mother like this before, and because I was including myself in the equation. I was giving her a chance to acknowledge that she loved me as well as Phil. Deep down I knew she did—in her way—but suddenly I felt as if I needed her to voice her feelings, for the Phillionaire's sake as much as my own.

"Oh, don't talk such nonsense," she snapped, and after the initial blow I smiled because it was the first sign that she was returning to her old self. "What defenses? I don't hide anything. I'm as open as can be. I just don't think it's necessary to vent one's feelings all over the place."

"But you just said you should have *told* Phil you loved him, *really* loved him."

"Quite true. But I wouldn't have slobbered all over him. I'd have told him—I was *going* to tell him—in a different way. My way. More dignified."

"Not very romantic, Mum."

"Well, that's the way I am."

I laughed. I had to. She would never budge and I don't know why I had even thought she might. She was who she was and even though she hadn't said she loved me, I knew that just by talking to me in this way she was taking infinitesimal steps to opening up. And I knew I had to keep burrowing away in an attempt to get through to the still very lonely person locked inside.

When I told her that Tommy had turned up, her face softened in a momentary smile.

"Dear Tommy," she said. She had always liked him. In fact they were two of a kind, gregarious, outgoing, everything I was not. "So what does this mean—for the two of you?"

"Your guess is as good as mine," I said.

"But you won't send him away again? You'll give him a chance? Try to be gentle with him, Lee. You're always so tough on him."

"Mum, I never sent him away in the first place." Why did everyone always think I was the one who had called off the marriage? "He walked away, not me."

"And you're surprised? Like I just said, you're always too tough on him. Men need to be handled sensitively. Why *are* you so tough on him?"

I clamped my lips firmly together so I wouldn't come out with the retort that was forming in my mind. I didn't want to argue with my mother tonight of all nights.

But I knew the answer to her question and the fact that his sudden reappearance in my life had done nothing to banish my qualms about the uneven nature of our relationship only made me even more uneasy. And what would my mother say if she knew that earlier in the day I had been locked in a passionate embrace with another man? Because this was what was causing me the most unrest: the fact that I had found it so easy to kiss Shotgun Marriott.

But by eleven o'clock the next morning I'd almost forgotten that Tommy was now just up the beach in the cabin, so stunned was I by the contents of the Phillionaire's will.

As expected, Scott and Rufus were to share the bulk of his billion-dollar estate between them. But it was in dividing up his American real estate property that the Phillionaire had made the changes that had been added just before he left for Europe. My mother was to have the land and the new house under construction to do with whatever she wanted. She could continue building herself a beautiful home by the water or she could sell. Scott got the apartment in the city and Rufus the Stucco House with the proviso that it be put to some kind of charitable use.

"Rufus, it's almost as if he knew he was going to die," I whispered to him. "Are you okay with this?"

"From what I understand Dad changed his will every couple of years," he said. "He was always talking about putting his affairs in order, as he called it. I guess I'm going to have to do the same. The property's just a tiny part of it. You just cannot imagine the amount of money we've been left in other areas. I think Dad always knew I'd have a problem dealing with being fantastically wealthy—that's probably why he gave me a direction like turning the Stucco House over to a charity."

Franny was sitting on his other side and I noticed he was holding her hand. He nudged me and lifted her ring finger to show me the cluster of diamonds on it. I had no idea when he had proposed to her but I was stunned—and thrilled—and I reached over to clasp her hand. But Scott had cut Franny dead when she had walked into the reading of the will on Rufus's arm and as it turned out, there was more to Scott's hostility than the fact that she was engaged to his brother.

The Phillionaire had left the cabin to Eliza, with the proviso that Franny be its custodian until Eliza turned twenty-one.

And he had added a last minute codicil stipulating that until that time I be allowed to live there if I so desired.

Quickly I put two and two together. Once he found out that his father knew about Eliza's existence, Scott must have realized Phil would include her in his will, just as Louis Nichols had said. Well, he could still sue for custody but Franny would soon be a legitimate member of the family and on much stronger ground.

As for me, I could hardly wait to get back to the cabin and start planning my future life there—except when I walked in and saw the appalling mess Tommy had managed to reduce the place to, I almost changed my mind.

It had taken him less than twenty-four hours to cover the entire floor area with his stuff. What could only be described as sheer dread crawled all over my body when I looked in his suitcase and saw the terrifying amount of junk he had brought with him.

"Tommy, what's this?" I asked, plucking a small brown jar from amongst his briefs.

"Marmite."

"I can see it's Marmite." A salty yeast extract spread that Tommy liked to smear on toast. I studied the label. "This jar contains approx 62 servings." Which meant approx twelve in Tommy's case, he spread it so thickly. "I'm familiar with Marmite but what I want to know is why you packed it in your suitcase."

"Someone said they don't have it in America."

And he couldn't live without it.

"But, Tommy, they do have toothpaste." I pointed to an industrial-size tube protruding from a pouch.

"Wasn't sure if they had Macleans," he mumbled. By now he wasn't looking at me and no wonder. He had packed at least six months' supply.

He promised to leave everything in the suitcase because, as he could very well see, the cabin did not have sufficient storage to accommodate my stuff, let alone his. But every couple of hours he would feel the need to retrieve something from the very bottom and this would necessitate ferocious burrowing until he found it, resulting, inevitably, in most of the upper items in the case being deposited around the room. What infuriated me most of all was that this burrowing took place as I was trying to fill him in on the details of the murders of Sean Marriott and Bettina. And then, just as I was about to speculate on the possible suspect, and ask him what he thought, he sat back on his haunches and looked at me.

"But why are you still fretting about all this stuff? It's not like you're going to be involved anymore. Shotgun Marriott's toast as far as you're concerned. No more book, right? Get over him."

I ignored the slight edge to this last remark. *Get over him.* To my surprise, the memory of my moment with Shotgun had not lingered. If anything I was having a much harder time letting go of his book than his kiss. The disk that I had placed beside my laptop had gone and the realization that Shotgun must have pocketed it without telling me really stung. Maybe he had done it while we were kissing to distract me, the rat! And as for being able to walk away from the murders, what on earth was Tommy thinking?

What he was thinking became abundantly clear as soon as he heard about the Phillionaire's will.

"Well, that's fantastic. That really is fantastic. What a great bloke. What a sweet thing for him to do. He must have really got the point of you, Lee. Look at that beach, you couldn't ask for a better neck of the woods to shack up in, could you, Lee? Perfect place for you to write your books and stuff and it's safe as houses. You're not going to tell me you're frightened of seagulls, are you? Bloody fantastic, eh?"

"Fantastic," I agreed, "and no, I'm not frightened of seagulls. I'd be amazed if they committed the murders that took place only five minutes' walk up the beach from here."

But Tommy was undaunted. "But I'm here now. I'll protect you. Not sure where we'll put my mum when she comes to stay, but I'm sure we'll find somewhere. Can't wait to tell her. She's never been to America. I've only been once before, for that matter. Can't remember much, mind you."

"That's because you only came for the weekend when you were eighteen. You told me you came with Shagger and the two of you were blind drunk the entire time. I'm surprised you even remember going."

"Shagger sends his love, by the way. He's got a new girlfriend. She's got hair down to her bum and she's Czechoslovakian."

"I thought Shagger's girlfriends were all inflatable."

"Same thing," said Tommy and I was amazed. Normally I was never allowed to utter the slightest criticism of Shagger, who had been Tommy's best mate since he was about two. Occasionally, *very* occasionally, when I had the flu and couldn't get my head around anything more substantial, I entertained myself by trying to imagine what Tommy and Shagger talked about when they were on their own. Apart from football, that is. In all the years I had known Tommy I had never heard Shagger say anything more demanding than "All right, are you?" or "Sun's coming out." But, as Tommy never failed to point out, Shagger didn't have a malicious bone in his body and that was the main thing. Or a sober one, was my response but I kept it to myself.

"No, I mean she doesn't speak English and nor could the inflatables."

"I don't know how you're going to fit yourself in here let alone anyone else." I pointed to his paunch. "If you want to move in with me, you're going to have to lose weight. No more Marmite. What have you been living on since I left?"

"Turkey Twizzlers," he said cheerfully, "and I've brought some with me. They must be in here somewhere." He started burrowing again until I leaned over and gently closed the lid of the suitcase. "Oh," he said and looked at me in slight reproach for a second. Then he bounced back. "So what's it like in winter?"

"I doubt I'll ever find out," I said. I hadn't actually got as far as working out what use I was going to make of the cabin from now on. But I was beginning to get the distinct feeling that Tommy thought we were going to move here lock, stock, and barrel. Quit London. Set up home—and office—together in a tiny beach retreat, and act as if nothing had happened. And the very thought of it terrified me.

What was the matter with me? Only a few weeks ago I had been miserable because Tommy had pulled the plug on our impending marriage. Now here he was seemingly ready to re-ignite the relationship and I was the one getting ready to balk.

"Why's that?" he asked. "Where are you going in the winter?"

"Well, it all depends where we find work," I said, silently congratulating myself on both answering his question and evading it. "Tommy, I really am sorry about you losing your job. Why didn't you tell me earlier?"

"Oh, it really wasn't an issue. It was high time I moved on. They did me a favor actually. I was totally ready to do something else, totally ready." Now he was the one being evasive.

"Like what?"

"Like coming to be with you in America and getting a job. What sort of work can you pick up easily round here?"

"Fishing maybe. Cooking, waiting tables. Bar work. Real estate, landscaping, construction. You're not exactly fit, Tommy. I'm telling you, the men I see round here are unbelievably strong. I saw the guy who came to pick up the garbage at the Old Stone Market and I realized the true meaning of the phrase 'single-handedly.' He emptied two garbage cans and lugged three hefty bags to his truck with one hand while talking all the while on his cell phone."

"Who says I want to collect garbage?" Tommy shook his head at me. "But I'd make a terrific landscaper."

"A window box in the middle of London with a geranium that died because you didn't stop watering it for twenty-four hours does not exactly constitute landscaping, Tommy."

"So maybe I'm a bit green about the gills instead of the thumbs. Don't start nagging, I'll find something. You'll see. And I may not be as fit as I once was but what makes you think I'm not strong?" And he wrapped his arms around me and lifted me bodily off the ground.

I had to admit it felt good. I could always be reassured by the sheer bulk of Tommy's body but there were moments when I wondered what it would be like to inhabit his world. A strange thing for someone's partner of eight years to speculate on maybe, but we were so different I never ceased to marvel at his insouciant attitude to life. Tommy's world was like a child's, constantly reduced to simple things. His biggest problems in life appeared to be Chelsea losing on a Saturday afternoon, and running out of Marmite. In a nutshell, he was rarely anxious.

Anxious was my natural state of mind. Or fretful, as Tommy called it. "Don't fret," were probably the two words he had used most in my presence during our eight years together. Or rather *not* together, living at opposite ends of London while I refused to commit to marriage. Until it was too late.

The difference between Tommy and me was that he woke up every morning anticipating a carefree day whereas I opened my eyes and immediately started counting imaginary problems. "What would I do if I didn't have problems?" I had asked Franny only the other day. "I guess you'd have issues instead," she'd replied with a wry smile that showed she was beginning to get my number. And she was right. I *created* problems. Right now, I could feel the anxiety as to how I was going to deal with letting go of Shotgun's book rising to the surface—not how quickly would I find another job although that would undoubtedly materialize at a later stage. Nor did I seem to be worrying about the abrupt severance of my relationship with Shotgun. I liked Shotgun, admired him even. He was charming and it was a genuine charm, not put on for my benefit. And for a split second I had found him physically appealing. But there was also something creepy about the way he holed himself up in his reconstituted moorland castle. However romantic it appeared from the outside, there was a gloom that pervaded the interior and I suspected it was perpetuated by Shotgun himself—and for good reason. Yet I sensed that there had been an undercurrent of sadness permeating Shotgun's life long before the death of his son. And although I'd never met him, I felt sorry for Sean. Now I was forced to distance myself from life at Mallaby I began to understand why he had retreated to a room above the stables and escaped to Manhattan whenever he could.

No, what was beginning to bug me was that my work on the book was being cut off before I was ready. I hated unfinished business and where Shotgun's book was concerned I felt totally unfulfilled. It wasn't my fault but I felt I had failed. He had ended it but I couldn't understand why and I knew that until I discovered who had killed Sean Marriott and Bettina, my assignment would not be completed and I wouldn't be able to go on to another job, no matter what Genevieve came up with.

And the more I thought about it, the more I realized that like Bettina before me, I was determined to write Shotgun's book whether he was involved or not.

CHAPTER 15

BUT HOW COULD I EVEN THINK OF WRITING A book with Tommy constantly under my feet? That was the question that presented itself time and again over the next few days as I picked up various items of clothing off the floor and attacked the piles of washing up he left in the sink. At night, he always managed to redeem himself by holding me in his arms and gently stroking my hair as if I were an agitated dog until I relaxed.

It had always been like this. He seemed to know just how to drive me to distraction and then wait until my resistance was low enough that he could totally disarm me.

Just as I was at my wit's end the problem resolved itself in a way I would never have envisaged. Tommy and Rufus became instant best friends. They were introduced—on the beach where we ran into him and Franny—and within minutes they had disappeared together.

"It's a bit like we're their mothers and we've brought them together for a playdate," said Franny. "Now we can relax because they're going to play well together and we won't have to entertain them."

I didn't say anything for a second. I was too busy wondering if that was how Franny felt most of the time—like Rufus's mother. And if Rufus might somehow be more comfortable with people older than himself because Tommy had to be at least fifteen years older than he. But the friendship between them developed so fast I began to wonder if I ought to call Shagger and warn him that he had competition. Over the next couple of days Rufus appeared to take Tommy to every bar on the East End as well as to a Mets game at Shea Stadium, clamming in the bay, and windsurfing. When there was talk of skydiving farther up the island, I put my foot down.

"I doubt there's a parachute that will hold you up," I told Tommy. He glared at me but I could tell he was relieved about the skydiving ban. Frankly I was amazed that he'd got it together to go windsurfing.

But the unlikely bond between them developed beyond the personal to a professional relationship.

"Rufus is hiring me as his mate," Tommy announced one day, "heavy lifting and that wherever he's working. See, I told you I'd find a job."

When he proudly presented himself the next morning in a pair of rather snug shorts and a brand-new tool belt strapped around his hips, the maternal instinct Franny had alluded to washed over me in waves. He had a baseball cap perched jauntily on his head and a pair of strapping work boots on his feet and he could hardly contain his excitement. As I made him a couple of rounds of Marmite sandwiches and packed them in the lunch box with the Stars and Stripes on it that he'd picked up at the hardware store, I felt like a mother preparing to send her son off for his first day at school.

"Just remember, Tommy, you may be strong but Rufus is in far better shape than you," I warned him. "Be aware of your limits. Don't do anything stupid and land yourself in the hospital. We neither of us have health insurance over here."

But in fact the only stupid thing he did was to take his T-shirt off and allow his pale flabby skin to get disgustingly sunburned so that if I accidentally brushed against him in bed, he screamed in agony.

In American.

His accent seemed to become more transatlantic by the hour. He began to answer virtually everything I said to him with snappy phrases like "Got it!," "Gotcha!," or "You betcha!" He began to bore me to distraction by drawing my attention to the difference between English and American.

"They say 'al*oo*minum' instead of 'aluminium.' And 'trunk' instead of 'boot.' '*Zookini*' instead of 'courgette.' 'Shrimp' instead of 'prawn.' I mean, that's not right, is it? Shrimp are tiny and prawns are big, that's how you tell 'em apart." I couldn't help noticing most of his examples were food related. "But even if the bleedin' word's the same, they pronounce it all wrong," he complained. "They say 'depot' to rhyme with 'deep' instead of 'death.' And the one that really gets me is 'clerk.' They rhyme it with 'jerk' instead of 'ark.' And if it's words of more than one syllable, they put the emphasis in the wrong place. They say '*in*surance' instead of 'in*surance*,' '*dee*-fense' instead of 'de*fense*.' Someone ought to set them straight."

"Well thank God you've arrived to do just that, Tommy." I had forgotten his ability to soak up language like a sieve. I recalled how astounded I had been when I had discovered he spoke French fluently with no trace of an English accent. I had been less impressed by the discovery that this had come about via an affair with a French woman working at the BBC. Still, this constant ability to surprise me had been one of the things that had made me sit up and decide that I should marry him before someone else did.

But his instant American makeover was a little too sudden for me. I couldn't quite cope with him becoming Tommy the Marlboro Man overnight. Rather grudgingly, I noted that he did have rather a good American accent—Franny said he sounded New Jersey and rather late in the day I realized he was aping one of his heroes, Bruce Springsteen—but I found I missed his guttural North London mumbling.

Anglo-American language was on my mind. To avoid having to deal with the void left in my life by the absence of work on Shotgun's book, I had decided to read Martha's manuscript. One of the first things I noticed, before the real horror of the story hit me, was that as well as setting her story in a 1960s English boarding school, Martha had adopted English spelling. "Neighbour" instead of "neighbor." "Travelling" instead of "traveling." "Centre" instead of "center." I reveled in it—or rather I *revelled,* being an English woman—because when reading American books there was always a split second when I thought that U.S. spelling was an annoying misprint before I remembered it was correct American usage. And I marveled, *marvelled,* at her consistency. But wait a second. When she had read her first chapter out loud to me she had done so in an impeccable English accent. Had Martha spent time in England? And wouldn't she have mentioned it if she had?

Her novel was narrated in the first person and the shy, tentative voice was that of Kit, a fourteen-year-old girl from a quiet unassuming background. She was the daughter of a schoolmaster and his librarian wife, academic bookish clichés, strapped for cash, and anxious that their only child should receive the best education. So when Kit's wealthy godfather offered to pay for her to be sent to an elite little academy in twenty acres of Sussex parkland they accepted with alacrity. There Kit found herself a forlorn and indigent duckling amidst the other students arriving in Daimlers and Rolls-Royces when her parents drove up in their chubby little Austin A30 and deposited her in the car park on the first day of term.

She was thoroughly shunned and derided by her snotty classmates and just when she was on the point of begging her parents to take her away from St. Mary's, Martha gave her Iona.

It was a cloudless day and because it was also completely still, with not a speck of wind to blow away the pages, I was reading on the beach. Every two or three chapters, I anchored the manuscript with a rock and wandered into the clear glasslike water that was blissfully warm even though it was the end of September. I didn't swim because I could wade halfway across the bay and still not be in above my waist. The tide had furrowed the seabed into row after row of sandy ridges that fitted snugly into the instep of my bare feet and I decided wading in the water was the perfect workout.

Iona Crichton Stuart didn't arrive until after half term because she had been away on a cruise with her parents in the Caribbean. Her family, Martha informed us, divided her time between a six-bedroom Belgravia town house in London and a vast estate in Scotland. I scrabbled around in my beach bag for a pencil and began to scrawl frantically in the margin because although she mesmerized the reader the second she appeared on the page, Iona's over-the-top character, as depicted by Martha, was in danger of becoming a caricature.

When she first arrived, Iona treated Kit with disdain. In the dormitory she was given the bed next to Kit's and dispatched her to run errands like a slave. *Make my bed for me, will you, while I clean my teeth. Can I crib your French prep? I'll never be able to finish it and play tennis. If you get me an A+ I'll let you wear my angora cardigan. And by the way, I'm sorry but I finished that fudge your mother made. Can she send you some more?*

Not that she treated the rest of the girls any better. Iona seemed to regard herself as being a cut above everyone else and it was with a certain amount of satisfaction that Kit observed her classmates vying in vain for the newcomer's attention.

So when she became the Chosen One, selected by Iona to be

her pet, Kit's world exploded into a galaxy of unadulterated bliss. One rainy afternoon she was the helpless little field mouse on which Iona pounced out of sheer boredom, offering the callow girl her first cigarette, taking her through the steps for the latest dance crazes, the twist, the Madison, and the hully-gully, and showing her the juiciest passages in a well-thumbed unexpurgated edition of *Lady Chatterley's Lover*. But, as I noted in the margin, we did not see Kit's reaction. Nor were we party to what must have been her agony when Iona ignored her for the next four days before returning to toy with her again.

"Let's hear the dialogue between them during their burgeoning relationship," I wrote, "and how does Kit describe Iona to her parents when she writes to them? What is their reaction to the growing influence of this exotic creature on their precious daughter? Will their concern hint at the corruption that will follow?"

Martha plunged her novel into more sinister waters without warning. A bizarre scenario unfolded one morning over the breakfast table where a hundred and fifty girls erupted in raucous clamor until they were silenced to listen to the eight o'clock news on the radio turned up to full volume to reach the entire length of the cavernous dining hall.

A man was to be hanged at two minutes past eight at Bedford Prison. James Hanratty had been given a sentence of execution for the murder of a man in a parked car on the A6 road in Bedfordshire, although he bore little resemblance to the picture of the alleged killer. Two cartridges from the murder weapon were found in a hotel room used by Hanratty the night before the murder.

Martha timed the scene to perfection with the girls half-listening to the broadcast until suddenly the airwaves went quiet and they realized this was the moment he was being hanged. And Iona, sitting beside Kit, began to whisper in her ear.

"The noose is covered in leather." She said it so quietly that Kit was not even aware that Iona was talking to her until she felt the gossamer touch of Iona's fingers on her arm. "They're putting a cotton hood over his head while they adjust it around his neck." There was a pause and Kit held her breath. "Now his legs are being pinioned with more leather straps. And now"—Iona gripped Kit's shoulders tightly—"the executioner is removing the safety pin from the base of the lever and he's pushing it away from him to open the trap. It's too late to stop it now, Kit. Hanratty's legs are dangling, his feet are twitching and he's dying, Kit, he's dying."

By now Iona's hand had moved up to caress Kit's neck and—

Kit screamed and so did I. A mosquito had attacked my left forearm but it could just as easily have been because of what I was reading. Hanging had been abolished in 1964 just before I was born but I knew about the Hanratty case because it was thought to have been a miscarriage of justice. Another man, who had rented the room where the shell casings were found the day *after* the murder, had subsequently confessed.

And then it was the end of term and the girls dispersed to their various homes for the holidays. Martha had Iona register shock at Kit's nervous invitation to accompany her home to meet the schoolmaster and the librarian. Instead she turned the tables and steamrollered Kit up to Scotland with her, thrusting her headlong into Highland society and lending her appropriate clothes for every occasion. Now it was Kit's turn to be the caricature—the plain Jane struggling to keep up with every snotty nuance.

But she was also the observer and what she witnessed over that summer, on the grouse moors and in the ballrooms, prepared the ground for the horror that was to follow. Iona set her cap at a boy who stubbornly resisted her temptations. Instead he was besotted with another girl who, as luck would have it, was also a student at St. Mary's. Back at school for the autumn term, this girl wasted no time telling everyone about Iona's humiliation, flaunting the letters the boy wrote to her at every opportunity.

And that was when Iona murmured casually to Kit as they were walking into the gym one day, "Of course you don't have to cover the noose in leather. All you need to hang someone is rope."

Martha didn't explain how—or indeed why—Iona came to know so much about hanging and I scribbled more notes in the margin. However, in the buildup to the book's grisly and melodramatic outcome, Martha handled Kit's mixture of sheer terror, blind submission to Iona's malevolence, and growing excitement with brilliant sensitivity. Through Kit's eyes the reader was led through every harrowing step as the girl who had stolen the object of Iona's affections was lured to the gym on the pretext of a midnight feast, intoxicated, and hanged.

It was Kit who befriended the girl at Iona's instruction and it was Kit who suggested the midnight feast to her, leading her by the hand through the pitch-black of the gym to the picnic she had prepared at the far end. It was Kit who motioned the girl to sit cross-legged on the floor, with her back to the place where Iona stood, waiting in the shadows beside the noose hanging from the bar. It was Kit who lighted the candle and encouraged the girl to eat the sausage rolls and Crunchie bars that Kit had sneaked out of the school to buy, and to drink glass after plastic glass of vodka and Coke from Iona's secret stash of alcohol.

Iona might have masterminded the murder but Kit was every inch her willing accomplice, helping to heft the drunken girl onto the chair and holding her steady while Iona secured the noose.

Iona might have been the one who kicked aside the chair but Kit cleared away the picnic and wiped the chair clean of prints like the good little slave that she was. It didn't matter if they left their mark on the rope, said Iona, it was a climbing rope they had touched legitimately many times before in gym class.

And then I cursed Martha out loud to the surprise of a passing seagull waddling along the water line. The end of the book was missing. The story stopped dead after the body had been found, the detective had arrived, and Iona appeared to be on the brink of pointing the finger at poor little Kit.

I stomped back to the cabin in a rage and called Martha. There was no reply and I left a message on her machine. "Martha, the end of your book is missing. I need to know what *happens*! Call me as soon as you can."

But she didn't call back and the next day I woke up thinking I would drag Tommy along the beach to her trailer for an early morning walk. I'd beard her in her den and make her hand over the final pages. But when I rolled out of bed I stepped on Tommy's passport. Distributing the contents of his suitcase around the cabin was clearly not enough for him. Now he had up-ended his knapsack on the floor beside the bed in search of God knows what and his passport had somehow landed over on my side.

I picked it up and flicked through it to look at his photo—as you do—and blinked. I found myself staring at a moody and expertly lit head shot of the hulk whose bloated seminaked body was rising and falling under the covers beside me. Lying on his stomach, he had a pillow over his head and all I could see was a bit of stubbled chin resting on one of his huge paws.

I looked again at the picture. There were shadows in the hollows below his cheekbones and you could see every single one of his incredibly long eyelashes. It wasn't that I didn't recognize him. I'd seen him look like this—hair immaculate, freshly shaved, a suit and tie—but only at weddings and funerals and Very Special Occasions. This wasn't a passport photo, it was a glamour shot.

I whipped the pillow off his head.

"Oy!" His arm shot out and grabbed it. "What the bloody hell are you doing?"

I put his passport photo within an inch of his nose. "Where on earth did you get this taken? Doesn't look like it comes from one of those little booths the rest of us go to when we need a passport photo."

He sat up and gave me a grumpy look. "Those places make you look crap."

"Tommy, it's a passport. Everyone looks crap in their passport photo."

"Not if you have a proper photo done. It's important what you look like when you go abroad."

"Ambassador Kennedy?"

"Stop taking the piss. We're all ambassadors for our country."

"God, you're pompous this morning." Tommy was not normally vain. For some reason it irritated me that he should care so much what he looked like in his passport photo. Probably because I knew I looked so utterly dreadful in mine.

Which reminded me. My visa. What had Evan Morrison said? They'd only given me a month? What was today? September 28 or 29? Oh shit. My time was running out.

I flicked through Tommy's passport again till I found the little white I-94 card.

"Jesus, Tommy, they've given you three months to stay in the country."

"Is that all? I told them I'd be here for a long time."

"What do you mean, is that all? They only gave me a month."

"Can we have pancakes for breakfast?" He was out of bed and padding naked toward the bathroom, scratching his tummy. "Franny made Rufus pancakes the other morning when I was over there. That's what they do in America, pancakes."

"Tommy, we are trying to *de*crease your stomach, not—"

"Okay, okay." He stopped scratching,

He disappeared behind the shower curtain and I sat down heavily on a barstool.

"You'd better give Rufus a bit of warning that you're not going to be around for a while," I shouted to him. "We're going back to London as soon as I can book a flight. I need to renew my visa."

"Well, I don't," said Tommy, reappearing with a towel wrapped around his waist. "Mine's good for another three months, as you've just pointed out."

"But don't you want to come back with me?"

"What's the point?" he said. "Bit pricey hopping back and forth across the Atlantic. Might as well get my money's worth and stay here. Besides," he grinned, "I like America."

He wasn't the only one who had no plans to return to England.

To my amazement my mother announced that she wasn't going to sell the unfinished house Phil had left her. She would continue building it in his memory.

"Maybe there will be some things you can do for me while you're there," she said when I told her I was going back to London.

At that point I fled. The last thing I wanted was to be given a list of repairs to deal with. I called the airline and booked myself on a flight leaving three days hence. I was procrastinating as usual, delaying my departure, but constantly running through my head was the distinct feeling that I had a load of unfinished business to attend to before I left.

And then Shotgun suddenly appeared on my doorstep again.

He was looking very English in a cream linen blazer over a white shirt, a pair of floppy navy linen trousers, and a pair of plimsolls—the canvas shoes we used to wear at school before they invented trainers. All he needed was a panama hat or a boater to complete the picture of an English village gent. But his face was wretched. Dark shadows beneath his eyes and hard lines had suddenly appeared running down either side of his mouth.

We stood facing each other in awkward silence for about twenty seconds until I remembered my manners and gestured for him to come inside.

"Cup of tea?" I said. "Marmite sandwich?" I held up Tommy's jar.

He smiled and shook his head. "I won't stay long. I wanted to ask you if you took away the disk you were working on the last time you left Mallaby? I thought it was beside the computer but it's gone. I found the tape but I couldn't find the disk. Do you have it?"

"Well, yes, I did," I said, startled at the reminder of how paranoid he was about anything leaving his possession. "I sort of got the idea you were a bit clueless when it came to computers. I thought if I took the disk, then I could begin work on the book here—on my laptop." I pointed to it.

"But you're not going to be working on the book anymore so I need it back." He spoke with exaggerated patience but there was a distinct edge to his voice.

"I don't get it," I said. "Surely you took it the other day when you were here?"

"No," he said, shaking his head at me, "I didn't."

"Well, it's not here. When I looked for it, it was gone and it was right after you were here so I assumed you'd taken it. I'd labeled it with your name so I thought you must have seen it and pocketed it. I was rather annoyed that you didn't say anything, to tell you the truth."

"Try to get it through your head," he was on his feet now, "that I did *not* take it. Someone else must have and that's a bit of a disaster. The last thing I want is for some unauthorized person to be in possession of the transcripts of everything I said on those tapes. It's a *disaster,* Lee. You had absolutely no right to take that disk."

I was beginning to get angry so I went on the defensive. "Well, perhaps I've just mislaid it but I have to tell you, Shotgun—I mean Kip—that anyone writing a book on a computer needs disks so I was completely within my rights to take it. What's more if I find it I'm going to hang on to it. I've decided I'm going to do a book on you whether you cooperate or not. It'll be a favorable portrait, I promise you. And I won't turn it in until I have all the facts about the murders. All of them," I added. "The murder of the groupie in London *and* what happened to Sean and Bettina."

"*Cooperate?*" Shotgun virtually spat out the word. "What do you mean 'cooperate'? It's my story and if anything I would enlist *your* cooperation in telling it, not the other way around."

"No, you don't get it," I said, exasperated, "I'm going to do *my* book now. I'm willing to ghost your story for you but if you're still refusing to continue with that then I have no option but to do my own book. And I'll hunt down the facts on my own."

"You can't!" Now he was totally enraged. "Don't you understand what I've been trying to tell you? I thought I was going to be able to, I *did* want to do a book, I swear to you I did, but I've changed my mind." He looked at me suddenly and the expression in his eyes unnerved me for a second. "For your sake," he said, "I'm canceling the book for you."

"For *my* sake?" I was mystified. "But why?"

"You can work it out," he said, softer now. "Bettina was all set to do the book even without my cooperation and look what happened to her. I've grown fond of you, Lee. Don't worry"—he must have seen the look of alarm on my face—"I'm not going to make any more moves on you—unless you want me to, that is—but I don't want anything to happen to you. I think you should just walk away from this project and anything else that has to do with me. Go back to London—for your own good."

"I am going back to London," I said slowly, not looking at him. "My visa's run out."

"Well, don't come back. Believe me, I'm not happy saying this. I'll miss you. I'd have liked to have the chance to see a lot of you. But you have to get away from me. And if that disk turns up," he was standing very close to me now, "destroy it."

And then he leaned forward, gave me a lingering kiss just above my left ear that sent an electric shiver through me, and disappeared out the door. I watched him through the window as he hurtled through the beach grass, his long legs striding up and down the dunes until all I could see was the top of his head receding down the bay.

Would I ever see him again? I wondered. Why had he pulled the plug on the book at this late stage? Was he covering up for Dumpster? I didn't like any of it, least of all the implication that Bettina's fate awaited me if I continued with the book. Was that a threat?

Whatever it was I was going to ignore it. I needed something practical to do to calm my quaking nerves so I set about searching for the missing disk. But after twenty minutes I was forced to admit that it was nowhere in the cabin.

But who on earth could have taken it?

Martha still hadn't called me back by lunchtime so I set off along the beach to seek her out at the trailers. It was a gray overcast day and the wind rippled the waters in the bay and caused the beach grass to rustle all around me. How did Martha survive out here in winter, I wondered, when the bay was an expanse of ice, the snow had piled up on the beach, and there was a gale howling so loudly she probably couldn't hear herself think? No wonder she was trying to find a rich savior.

Tommy's take on Martha had disturbed me in its vehemence.

"She sounds like a nutter," he said after I had described her to him in bed the night before. "I don't know why you're hanging out with her."

I was astonished. "What makes you say that? You don't even know her."

"Dunno. She sounds weird. What's she doing out here anyway?"

And of course when I told him about her "girls," the wedding dresses in whose company she spent most of her time, he punched the air above him.

"What'd I tell you? She's been living out in those trailers with forty-mile winds doing her head in for years on end. Stands to reason. She's loony tunes." He tickled me and I yelped. "Of course you know what they say, takes one to know one. She took one look at a neurotic old bat like you and thought *There's my soul mate*. You never had a prayer."

I'd thrown a pillow at him and he'd pounced on me and within minutes we were enjoying the best sex we'd had in months, literally. And now, I thought as I walked along the water's edge, skipping out of reach of the incoming tide, I was leaving him.

Martha wasn't at her trailers. I banged on both doors and peered through the windows and then I got a shock.

Inside, the place was totally bare. All that remained was the built-in bunks and appliances. All Martha's belongings were gone. And it was when I saw that the eerie silhouettes of the wedding dresses were no longer hanging in their plastic bags that I knew she had gone for good. Martha would never leave her girls behind.

I backed away so quickly I overbalanced onto the sand.

And felt something hard under my right buttock.

I rolled onto my side to see what it was. At first it looked to me like hard sand. I was at a part of the trailer nearest the beach where the water ran underneath it at high tide. Then I noticed little specks of something dark protruding here and there. There appeared to be an object buried under the sand that the tide must have gradually uncovered. Or maybe it was something that had been tossed into the sea and then washed up on shore.

I scrabbled away at the wet sand until I had exposed it.

"Need a hand there?" I looked up quickly to see Louis Nichols standing above me. "What you got there?"

"Oh, nothing," I said as he helped me to my feet.

I kicked sand over the quiver quickly, thinking right away that Dumpster must have come here to bury it after throwing his bow and arrow in the cement pit along the bay. I had serious difficulty in accepting that Dumpster was involved in either Sean or Bettina's killing yet there was no denying the facts were mounting against him. And Shotgun appeared to be covering for him. He had made no secret that he was harboring him at Mallaby.

"I came here to look for Martha," I said to distract Louis Nichols's attention from the quiver.

"Me too," said Louis. "I've been trying to reach her for a couple of days."

"Well, it looks like she's gone," I said. "There's no sign of her belongings."

"You're kidding?" he said and he looked so alarmed that I began to feel anxious.

"No, I'm not. Take a look."

"I came here to apologize," he said. "There's no other way to put this but I dumped her the other night. Said some pretty awful things as a matter of fact. Told her she was becoming like an albatross around my neck and that we should maybe cool it for a while. She took it pretty bad."

"And you're surprised?" I said bitterly. Poor Martha. She probably had been a bit clingy but I imagined he must have been pretty rough on her.

Once again I dismissed the thought that I should go straight to Detective Morrison and tell him about the quiver. I had to get it back into Dumpster's possession before Evan Morrison got hold of it.

"Do you want a ride?" said Louis. "It's getting pretty bleak out here."

"No, I'm fine," I told him. "I'm just along the beach."

"Okay," he said. "If you hear where Martha's gone, I'd appreciate it if you'd let me know. I just hope she hasn't gone and done something stupid."

"Like what?" I had been wondering if the old fisherman had come back and reclaimed his lot on the beach from Martha. Or maybe the town had finally figured out that she had no right to be there.

"She could work herself up into a pretty emotional state when she got upset," said Louis. "She never actually said she was going to kill herself but I always thought she was the type."

I said good-bye to Louis and watched him drive away. I was horrified by his words but I had to admit they had a ring of truth. Desperate, unstable, and disappearing without a word, Martha was a prime example that life in the Hamptons was not always a walk on the beach. As I made my way back to the cabin, with the quiver bundled up in my sweatshirt, I looked out over the bay and prayed that she too would not be dragged from the water in a wedding dress.

CHAPTER 16

TOMMY DROVE ME TO THE AIRPORT WITH MUSIC BLAR-ing all the way. I had thought we might use the journey to have a serious talk about our future but I couldn't compete with his favorite tape of the Blues Brothers blasting at full volume, followed by Gretchen Wilson, his new country music passion.

"Now I'm in America," he yelled above the music, "it's probably only a hop, skip, and a jump to Nashville."

"Planning a visit to the Grand Ole Opry?" I said, burrowing in my bag for my passport. I'd been known to leave it behind before.

"Well, that too, but I thought maybe I could do a bit of singing myself. Something I've always wanted to try, you know, Lee?"

"Tommy, you can't—" I was about to say *You can't sing,* because no one in their right mind would call the tuneless moaning he emitted in the bath every morning singing. But the little boy side of Tommy with his hopeless dreams had always been the part of him that I loved the most. I needed his eternal optimism to balance my crabby neuroses and keep me on an even keel. So I couldn't pour cold water on his ludicrous assumption that he might have a chance at being a country singer. I just couldn't.

"You can't go to Nashville now," I said instead. "What would Rufus do without you?"

"No, you're right," he said, "thanks for pointing that out. But it'd be great, wouldn't it? You writing best sellers all day while I mind the house and in the evening you'd come out and sit by the stage at my gigs. Hey, maybe Shotgun Marriott could give me a few tips on how to get started."

I was still contemplating his fantasy of our life together— what were the groupies like in the country music scene?—as I settled into my aisle seat on the plane. Who knew if I would even return to Long Island? And yet how could I not when I had so much unfinished business there?

And then I started thinking about Franny and the growing unease I had about her role—and possibly Dumpster's—in the murder of Bettina Pleshette. I couldn't get out of my mind the look of shock on her face when I had turned up at the Old Stone Market with the quiver. I didn't need to tell her who I thought might be the owner or what that meant. She took it from me quickly and thrust it under the counter.

"Where did you find it?"

"Lazy Point," I told her.

She looked sad.

"I was there the other day," she said. "That's where Rufus proposed. It was so romantic. We were in his truck and he drove all the way to the end of Cranberry Hole Road and just kept going until we were parked right out in the middle of the lagoon. It's so shallow around there. Then he produced the ring. We just sat there in the truck and held each other till the sun went down and even then we stayed awhile. He turned on the headlights and we watched the water by moonlight. And all that time"—she shuddered—"this thing was buried just a few feet away. So what were you doing at Lazy Point?"

I told her and asked her if she knew where Martha had gone.

"I have no idea. I didn't know her too well." Already Franny seemed to be speaking of her in the past tense, I noted, with a sense of dread. "And I didn't realize she and Louis had something going on."

"Speaking of Louis Nichols," I said, "I sat next to him on the jitney and Franny, I think you should know, he told me all about—"

Suddenly I didn't know how to put into words what Louis had told me about her life in the city. "He knew what you did, you know, when you lived in Manhattan."

"Oh my God!"

"But as far as I know he hasn't talked to anyone else. He spoke to me because he knew we had become friends. But he was asking if Rufus knew."

Franny shook her head violently.

"But Franny," I said, "I think you should tell him. I don't think it would make any difference. Rufus loves you, he's not going to care what happened in your past. And it's not as if his life out here has been exactly virginal by the sound of it. But it would be awful if he heard about your past life from someone else."

"It's not just Rufus," she said, "it's my reputation as a whole. It's about the Old Stone Market. I'm having a hard enough time as it is getting established. There's such a backlash among the older members of the community about what I'm doing to the place. I don't want my past raked up, that would make it even worse. I've come back here so Dumpster and I can start afresh. And most of all," I could see she was on the point of tears, "it's about Eliza. I don't want her growing up here with people pointing the finger at her mother."

"Franny," I said, "just discuss it with Rufus. You have to, for your own peace of mind."

"I don't!" she yelled at me suddenly. "He doesn't have to know and if you say a word to him, you'd better be careful." She was advancing on me now, coming around the counter into the main area of the store, and her amazing stature seemed to make her tower over me. "I warned Bettina to keep out of it."

"You *warned* Bettina?"

"When she came around to see me about Eliza, that was the blackmail she used. She knew all about the"—Franny hesitated—"the men."

"But how did she find out? And by the way how did Louis Nichols know?"

"Louis? You never heard this from me but Louis could quite easily have been one of my 'escorts.'" She waggled her fingers in the air to form quotation marks. "He knew plenty of other girls who were doing what I did so he probably heard about me from them. And Bettina? She was a busybody. She poked her nose in everywhere. Who knows where she got it from. All I know is that she threatened to use it against me and after she left, I just got to thinking—I thought if I went looking for her and told her the kind of trouble *she'd* be in if she—"

She stopped abruptly.

"You went looking for Bettina? When?"

"I just wanted to stop her—"

"Franny, *when* did you go looking for her? Did you find her?"

But she just shrugged and turned the conversation around to me.

"So Rufus and I are getting married. What about you and Tommy?"

Now it was my turn to shrug. "Who knows?"

"What do you mean? I thought the fact that he'd come over here to see you meant you guys were going to work things out."

"Franny, it's not that simple," I told her and before I knew it I was telling her about my misgivings and how I was beginning to wonder if Tommy and I would ever be really compatible.

"But you love him?" said Franny.

"Yes," I said slowly, "but I don't really want to *be* with him, not all the time—like you'd have to be in a marriage."

"You can't really see him as a husband?"

"Yes," I said, "oh, yes, I can definitely see him as a husband. He'd be a perfect husband. He's supportive and caring and almost too good to be true. I just can't see him as *my* husband."

"You know what, Lee?" Franny had a slightly quizzical look in her eye. "Maybe you just can't see any man as *your* husband. Ever thought about that?"

"You think I'm blinkered? That I don't really appreciate what a prize I have in Tommy? Because I do. I totally do."

"Oh, I'm sure you do. Just like I know what I've got in Rufus. The difference is that I know I want to be with Rufus all the time. I'm unhappy when I'm not with him. And I also know that I want to be part of a couple. But I listen to what you say and I think about what Rufus tells me, of what Tommy tells him, because they talk to each other, those two, oh yes they do. And Tommy tells him about how you used to send him away every now and then, how you needed your space over there in London, just like you hide away in that cabin over here all on your own, and I'm wondering, Lee, maybe you don't need to get married at all. Not to Tommy or to any man. It's what usually happens to people but there ain't no law that says you *have* to get married. Maybe you just think you *ought* to marry him because he's such a sweetheart and you'd be a fool not to. But think about it, Lee. There shouldn't be any *ought to* about getting married!"

I couldn't believe it. She'd hit the proverbial nail on the head. I was so grateful to her for having the perception to understand who I really was that I did something totally out of character for me. I reached out and gave her the hug I'd evaded from her when I'd agreed to babysit for her.

"You're so right, Franny. Tommy and I always used to have this joke that I'm an undercover polar bear. The male and the female don't live together, you know, they only come together to mate. Ideally, that's how I'd like it to be with Tommy. But that's not a marriage, is it?"

"Not really," she agreed sadly. "Maybe you'd better remind him that you're a member of the Polar Bear Club before things go too far."

And that was where we had left it. Now trapped in the plane, when I wasn't fretting about when it was going to plummet into the Atlantic, I worried about what would become of her while I was gone. Of course I would be coming back, I reasoned to myself, to see her, to see Rufus, to see my mother—and Tommy. But when, I did not know. It all depended on what happened in London. I would discuss with Genevieve whether to continue the Shotgun book but if we wound up scrapping it and she found me something else in England, then there would be no need to go back to America. So what would Tommy do if I stayed in London?

I picked up the notepad I always carried with me and began yet another attempt at a letter to Tommy, although this time I knew what I wanted to say.

Dearest Tommy,

It's tricky what I want to say to you and that's why I'm writing a letter. I can hear you telling me—whenever I had a hard time making you understand something important I wanted to get across—"Write it down, Lee," you always said, "you're a writer. That's what you do. Write it down instead of spluttering away at me." And you were so right. So here's a letter to try and get across what I have to tell you.

You're not going to like it but please don't jump off the handle right away. Hear me out. I think it's time I reminded you that I am a member of the Polar Bear Club. You must never ever think that

*this means that I don't love you because I do. But I have been
thinking for some time that I might not be able to live with
anyone—not even you—for a sustained amount of time. There was
a moment a few months ago when we were planning our wedding
that I thought I could change. And believe me I wanted to—for
you. But I fear now that I would probably wind up making you
very unhappy and that is the last thing I want to do. Where we go
from here, I do not know but*

And that was as far as I got before I fell asleep for the rest of
the flight. When we landed on a cold October London morning,
I treated myself to a cab into Notting Hill even though I didn't
have much luggage with me and arrived home at Blenheim Crescent at about ten o'clock in the morning.

It was the first time I'd been away from home for so long and
I was struck anew by the massive size of our four-story Georgian
house. It was almost indecent that I should have had it to myself
for as long as I did until I moved Tommy in to live with me.

I dragged my suitcase up the steep flight of steps to the front
door, knowing the lazy sod of a cab driver was enjoying watching
my exertions before he set off in search of his next fare. I was anticipating the sight of Marcus's paraphernalia cluttering up our
hallway as my mother had warned me it would be but when I let
myself in, I reeled in astonishment.

I barely recognized the place. It was immaculate with glisten-
ing polished floors and surfaces, everything stored away in cabinets and no sign of a baby's presence anywhere.

And there, sitting at the kitchen table in a silk dressing gown,
eating a perfectly formed triangle of whole wheat toast, was my
father.

"Ed!" I gasped before I could stop myself. I had never called
my father Dad or Daddy, except when talking about him to

other people. It had been my mother's newfangled idea when I was little that I should call my parents by their first names. I think she thought it would make them appear younger. However it was she who quickly tired of it and requested "Mummy," which I detested. We settled for Mum but somehow my father remained Ed.

He was a bit of an Ed somehow, tall and thin and lanky, the perfect clotheshorse for his stylish wardrobe and his vanity. The thing about my father was that he had always been a bit of a blank canvas, a listener rather than a talker, someone who encouraged you to talk but rarely revealed anything about himself. He adapted his mood—and, I noticed sometimes, his views—to whomever he was with and in this way he had been the perfect foil for my mother's whirlwind ambition. That is until he had absconded with a young French divorcée.

He stood and embraced me and lowered his head so that his lips collided with my forehead in a kiss. "What are you doing here, Nathalie?" A greeting that more or less summed up our father-daughter relationship. Suspicion and interrogation rather than unconditional welcome.

"I live here, Ed. It's my home. What are *you* doing here?"

"It's my house," he said.

"But what are you doing in London?" I persisted. "And where's Cath? I expected to find her here. And Richie. And Marcus."

"Well, you won't," he said. "I called before I arrived and asked them to move out, and before you start yelling at me"—he held up his hand—"the renovations to their flat were finished. It was all ready for them to move back into. Cath said you were in America. I'd no idea you were coming home. How long will you be here?"

"Why are you asking something like that?" I stared at him. "I live here, Ed. You know I do. It's my home. It always has been." I was starting to feel panic rising. I spent more time at home than almost anybody I knew. If I didn't have a base to which I could retreat and in which I could hide from the world, I would come seriously undone. It was no good, people like Tommy and Cath and anyone else who said they cared about me telling me I needed to face up to the demons I imagined lurked just the other side of my front door. Deep down I knew I'd always need a place where I could hole up and take stock. The Phillionaire had known that instinctively about me, and that was why he had introduced me to the cabin. But my father wasn't the Phillionaire and suddenly I realized I was comparing them in a way that I knew couldn't possibly be healthy.

"Nathalie," said my father gently, "I'm not asking you to go. I'm just inquiring how long we might be able to spend some time together. Because I'd enjoy it, no other reason. It's been a long time and you're my favorite daughter, don't forget."

It was an old joke between us. I was his only daughter, his only child. And suddenly I felt terrible for thinking he had any ulterior motive for asking what he had.

"So what about you, Ed? Why are you in London?"

"Exactly what it says on the packet," he said cheerfully, "this is my house and I've decided to come back to London and live in it. Who knows, I may even go back to work in the shop."

My father had inherited money as a young man and had indulged in what my mother always referred to as a "dusty" profession. Edward Bartholomew Books was a tiny stall tucked away in Portobello Market dealing in antiquarian books. My father had sat there happily losing money every Saturday until my mother had yanked him off to France, at which point he'd turned his space over to a young whippersnapper who now used it to sell punk memorabilia.

"Your mother's got this new life in New York," he said, "so she really doesn't need it. Although as soon as she hears I'm here I expect she'll want it back," he added ruefully. "Why are you looking at me like that?"

As he was speaking I realized with a sinking feeling that he didn't know about the Phillionaire. And why would he? Nobody had thought to call him, buried as he was in the depths of the French countryside, least of all my mother or me.

I made a fresh pot of coffee to stave off my encroaching jet lag and talked him through the events of the last month culminating in the Phillionaire's untimely death. To my surprise he looked unbelievably sad.

"I must call your mother," he said. "This is the worst thing that could have happened to her. It really sounded as if she had found someone who could get through to her."

I don't think I could have been more amazed if he had said he was sprouting wings underneath his dressing gown.

"Don't look so stunned," he said. "Your mother and I have had a few conversations since she met him—in fact I'm a little sad she didn't call and tell me he had died—and I could tell by the way she talked about him that she loved him. And it sounded as though she actually believed that he loved her, not like—"

He stopped suddenly and I wasn't sure what to say. Surely he hadn't been about to tell me my mother didn't believe my father's love for her.

Apparently he had.

"I mean, I should never have married her," he went on and I held my breath. He was musing to himself, almost as if I were not even there beside him. But then he said something that told me he was very much aware of my presence, more than at any other time I could remember.

"I'm like you, Nathalie. I like being on my own. I had absolutely no intention of getting married. Ever. It's a rare thing but there really are a few people who are better off going through life on their own. I'm one of them and I've always suspected you are too. But then I met Vanessa and she was this stunning, exciting creature. I was seduced by her energy, her wonderful ability to embrace life full on. She literally swept me up in her wake and it wasn't until I was totally smitten that I discovered how complicated she really was."

"Complicated?"

"She was needy in a way I hadn't anticipated. She was so desperate for us to get married that I found I couldn't resist her, even though I knew I should. Yet she couldn't seem to accept the fact that I really loved her. Nor did she ever really say she loved me. She smothered me with attention but she always seemed to back away—mentally—when I tried to express my feeling for her. She was—I don't know any other way to describe it—she was awkward."

I knew exactly what he meant. And so had the Phillionaire.

"But you loved her, Ed?"

"Always. But I didn't need to be married to her. Still, as you can imagine, that's the last thing I could have told her given how insecure she was about my love for her. I just went ahead with it and hoped for the best. As you probably noticed, I had a hard time keeping up with her."

"Join the club," I said and he laughed. It saddened me to realize what had happened. He had retreated into himself, worn down like everybody else by my mother's hyperactive personality. I recalled a conversation I had had with her shortly after she had told me they were going to separate, when she had made a remark that I realized now had probably been fueled by resentment. She had told me that once the initial passion of their married life was over, she had decided my father was boring and had no conversation. But sitting here in the kitchen with him, I sensed that in the same way I had begun to access my mother's more vulnerable persona, I would now unearth a long repressed side of my father that was far from boring.

I stayed awake as long as I could, given part of my body, and indeed my mind, was still entrenched in Long Island. But after my father and I had shared an early supper of a mushroom omelet and a frisée salad, expertly prepared by him, I made my excuses and escaped to bed. Before I went, however, I called my mother, chatted for a few minutes, and then handed the phone to my father. Then I went upstairs to take a bath and slipped into bed. But as sometimes happens when you are desperately in need of it, sleep wouldn't come and after about an hour, I slipped downstairs to make myself a milky drink.

And to my amazement I could still hear my father talking in low urgent tones to my mother.

It was a little weird having him back in the house. I woke up the next morning and suddenly realized I wouldn't have the place to myself like I used to. When I went down to the kitchen to make myself a cup of coffee, there he was, sitting at the kitchen table with a pile of bills laid out before him and his checkbook.

"I don't think your mother's paid a single bill since she took off for New York," he said. "So unlike her."

"Ed," I said, sitting down beside him, "there's something I want to ask you. Mum's never said anything to me about the divorce, like how far along you are, who's getting the house, stuff like that."

"Nathalie, I already told you," said my father, not looking up, the merest hint of steel in his voice, "it's my house. I know your mother always behaved as if it belonged to both of us, or even just to her, but the deeds are in my name. The place in France is hers."

"But when you took up with Josiane, Mum left you there and came back to live here."

"Ironic, isn't it?" he said. "And as for the divorce, I never wanted one. She started proceedings."

"And?"

"And," my father repeated, "that's where it stands. *And*. She met Philip Abernathy and got herself so distracted, everything seemed to grind to a halt. Again, ironic. But that's your mother for you," he said, scrawling his signature across a check in such a wild flourish that it seemed to me the end of "Bartholomew" landed on the table.

The phone rang and it was my agent, Genevieve, who never seemed to be able to wait until she got to her office to call me.

"So, you've arrived. Good. We need to meet. Flight okay?" She was as brisk as ever.

"Yes, thanks, Genny. How are you?"

"Busy as a busy busy bee and very happy to be so. When are you going to come and see me? I've got a new assignment for you."

"You have?" This was exciting.

"I don't know what's been going on but no sooner does Shotgun Marriott say he doesn't want to continue with his book than his ex-wife decides she wants to tell *her* story. And of course she wants you to do it with her. I've had her on the phone three times in the last two days. Wants to see you as soon as possible."

"I don't believe you," I said, stunned. "How does she know I'm here?"

"Your friend Cathleen Clark told her you were coming to London and suggested she call me to set up a time. So when can you come in and see me?"

I said I'd be there that afternoon and then I called Cath.

"I gather you've been telling all and sundry I'm back in town."

"Yeah, so? I told Angie Marriott, where's the harm in that? I already told you I knew her from AA and that she wanted to talk to you. I didn't think you'd have a problem with that. Anyway don't get your knickers in a twist about it, just come to dinner tomorrow night. Come around seven. I want you to see your godson in his bath before I put him to bed."

My mind was in a turmoil as I set off a couple of hours later on a short walk around the neighborhood. I'd called an immigration lawyer to inquire whether there was any point applying for a long-term visa to America. The trouble was I just didn't have a clue what the future held for me. If I was going to continue with the book about Shotgun, then I would need to go back indefinitely. But if I wound up working with Angie Marriott instead, then how long would I be staying here? I had absolutely no idea. Nor did I feel entirely comfortable with the idea of suddenly switching to Angie's story. But no doubt Genevieve would make up my mind for me as she always did.

The hustle and bustle of Notting Hill, where I'd lived all my life, was quite a shock to the system after the idyllic beauty of my Long Island beach existence. Ugly housing projects rose cheek by jowl with elegant Georgian mansions and brightly colored Victorian terraced houses. Running through the center of the area like a cheerful, nonjudgmental artery was the Portobello Market where the hip and the affluent jostled for their fruit and veg with drug dealers, street kids, and Irish and West Indian immigrants who had lived there for forty years. Crime was rampant now and for the last ten years I had holed up in my parents' house, terrified of what might be happening outside in the streets, and emerging only under cover of daylight.

And yet within hours of escaping to the relative safety of Long Island I had been catapulted into the midst of not one but two murder investigations. I could already hear Cath admonishing me—*For God's sake, Lee, get a grip! You're paranoid, you really are!*—

but I was seriously beginning to believe that wherever I went I would encounter violence.

Later in the day on my way to Genevieve's office in Covent Garden, I found myself thinking about what my father had said. *I had absolutely no intention of getting married.* As far as I knew Genevieve had never been married. Maybe she was another member of the Polar Bear Club. As I climbed the steep flight of stairs to her tiny office I wondered how she would react if I broke our unspoken rule that we didn't discuss our personal lives. What if I asked her if *she* thought I should marry Tommy. But as I reached the top step, slightly out of breath, I was hit with the sudden realization that I was back where I had been a couple of years ago. I was no longer fretting about the fact that Tommy had decided he didn't want to marry me. Now I seemed to be more interested in trying to decide whether *I* wanted to marry *him.* Or, more to the point, whether I wanted to get married at all.

In any case Genevieve was all business when I walked in. She waved at me and smiled but didn't get up to embrace me. Just as well because the differential in our height meant that her face always landed in my chest and I was left pecking the air above the top of her head. She always sat firmly behind her desk and I suspected it was because then you couldn't see the way her body spread out below the waist, giving her the look of someone wearing a crinoline.

"One way or another you've got a book to do," she said, getting straight to the point, "whether it's for the husband or the wife."

"Or for myself," I said. "Shotgun doesn't want to go ahead. My plan is to write my own book even if it's an unauthorized version."

"Hmmm." Genevieve didn't seem too keen on that idea. "Won't sell as well. You know what I think you should do? Put the whole project on the back burner for a while till they convict someone for those murders. You can't really do anything until you have the whole story, can you? Just assemble your notes and prepare what you might write should you have to write it."

"What about Angie Marriott?"

"Shotgun's is the story that will sell but Bettina always did say that the wife was the key and if she could get her to talk, she'd have Shotgun over a barrel."

Genevieve lumbered to her feet and tottered over to a cupboard where she kept a kettle. I looked down at her minuscule strappy sandals with their three-inch heels and wondered how on earth they supported her.

"I'm on the fruits of the forest infusion," she said, "it goes with my outfit, but you can have a coffee if you'd prefer. Nothing? Anyway, Angie Marriott; I think you should at least go and see her. Whichever book you wind up doing, it's surely going to be a big plus to have access to her."

She was right. It was just there was a part of me that didn't relish discussing Shotgun with her. For some curious reason I felt a kind of weird loyalty to him. But I was also aware that such hesitation was about as unprofessional as you could get. After all, I was going to be putting everything in a book for the whole world to read eventually. I reminded myself that Bettina would have been around there like a shot and held out my hand for Angie's number.

"I'll call her," I said.

"And you might as well have Bettina's file. She lodged a whole lot of stuff with me for safekeeping. She dug up such a lot of dirt on people that she became a little paranoid, if you must know. She always thought people would be after her tapes and the names of her sources so she'd send me these sealed packages to store for her. But there's one marked 'Shotgun Marriott' so I

292 ⏤ *Hope McIntyre*

think you might want to take a look at what's inside, don't you? It's not like she's going to be needing it anymore."

I carried it home wondering how long Genevieve had been planning to sit on it. When I walked into the house my father was on the phone. "I need to call someone," I mouthed at him. "I won't be long," he mouthed back and after a second or two I realized he was talking to my mother again. As I went upstairs I heard him say: "Vanessa, I've always wanted to live in America."

News to me.

"Nathalie," I heard him shout a few minutes later, "I'm off the phone and your mother sends her love. Sorry she didn't have time to speak to you but she was just rushing out."

Nothing changes, I thought as I dialed the number Genevieve had given me.

"Hello?" The sound of Angie Marriott's throaty mid-Atlantic drawl took me straight back to our meeting at the Old Stone Market.

"It's Lee Bartholomew," I said. "I'm in London and my agent said you wanted to get together."

"I certainly do," she said.

"I understand you want to do a book now?" I said.

"I'm certainly thinking about it," she said. "It's taken me an awfully long time to come to this decision but I feel I have no other option. I have to tell my side of the story and I'm ready to tell the world what really happened that night."

"What really happened," I repeated.

"How my husband killed that girl. I was there. I saw it all and I'm going to talk. Come and have a drink tomorrow and I'll tell you everything."

CHAPTER 17

THE FOLLOWING EVENING CATH OPENED THE DOOR to me in her bra and knickers.

I was shaken at the sight of her in a state of undress—I could have been anybody—and my face must have registered my disapproval because she laughed.

"Oh, come on, don't look like that. Relax, Lee. I took a look through the peephole before I opened the door, saw you standing there."

I bristled. *Relax, Lee.* Cath never missed an opportunity to have a go at me but that was part and parcel of our friendship.

"Anyway, come in, come in. I don't want to be caught standing here in me undies if one of the neighbors comes by. I strip down whenever Marcus has his bath because I always get soaked. By the time he's finished there's always more water outside the bath than in. You might think about doing the same."

"I'll just stand in the corner and watch," I said.

"Oh, come *on,* Lee. You've got to get into the spirit of the thing. Sometimes I even climb in with him. Think of it as practice for when you have your own. You and Tommy made any plans in that direction yet?"

Oh, great, jump right in and put me on the spot, why don't you, Cath? I was about to tell you of my doubts about my future with Tommy and ask your advice but, oh no, you have to go right past the finish line and start talking about kids.

"I told him, Lee. Once I'd persuaded him to get up off his butt and go to America and be with you, I said to him, what she wants is a baby, Tommy. And he'd be a terrific dad, you know he would. Hasn't he been on about settling down and having kids all these years he's been with you? So now he's got the chance, what does he do but run a mile in the opposite direction. Men! Typical!"

"Hold on a sec, what do you mean you persuaded him to go to America to be with me? Didn't he want to?"

"Of *course* he wanted to, stupid. Just like he wants to marry you more than anything else in the world. He just doesn't *know* it. He needs telling, that's all."

"And you told him?"

"I did. I said 'Tommy, this is your last chance. You don't marry her now, she's going to give up on you once and for all.' Never mind he's been the one been pestering you to get married for umpteen years and you've been the one running in the opposite direction. You've got to make them think they're losing their control over you and then they try to assert it all over again, the nitwits. So he goes 'Right, I'm on it' and the next thing I know he's running round showing me moody head shots for his passport photo. 'Which is my best profile, Cath? I think the left, don't you?' I ruined it all by telling him he needed to be face-on for a passport photo. So has he put the cork back in the champagne bottle and repopped the question yet?"

"I was the one who popped it in the first place," I said.

"Well, it's his turn then. Now take off your top at least and come and help me try and wash Marcus's filthy little feet."

Watching her with Marcus—a scrappy little toddler with Cath's carrot-colored hair—I saw how having a baby had softened her, just as being around Eliza seemed to take the edge off Franny Cook's bravado.

"By the way," she said, winking at me and squeezing the water from a sponge over Marcus's head, causing him to squeal in glee and beg for more, "we're trying for another."

"What about your teaching?" I said and realized immediately it was the wrong thing to ask. But Cath had been obsessive about her work before she got pregnant.

"Well, I'm not going back, am I?" she said, smiling at me. "It'll be a bit of a scrape making ends meet but Richie seems prepared to have a go. Having Marcus changed everything for us. That's why I'm telling you, Lee. You and Tommy should get started. You're going to be forty next birthday, if I'm not mistaken?"

I was about to start fretting about when I would be able to have a baby when the front door banged and Richie's voice shouted up the stairs.

"I'm home! Max is just parking the car. He and Paula'll be here in a jiff."

I looked at Cath and she made an *Oh dear!* face.

"Sorry, should have told you straight away. I invited Max Austin to join us for dinner. Did I tell you about Paula?"

"No," I said, feeling suddenly numb, "you did not."

"His new girlfriend," she said, winking again, "not that he ever had an old one." She paused. "Except you, I suppose."

"I was never his girlfriend," I said. "There's this bloke called Tommy Kennedy, remember? Been hanging round my neck for nine years like an overweight knapsack until he fell off of his own accord and now I can't seem to straighten up without him."

"Yeah, yeah, yeah. But in Max's mind you were his potential girlfriend. He had the mother of all crushes on you. Don't tell me you've forgotten?"

I hadn't forgotten. Far from it. In fact I couldn't understand why I was experiencing this sudden feeling of outrage that he had found someone new. I should be pleased for him. His wife— by all accounts a colorful character and not just because her Jamaican skin had been café au lait—had been murdered. The ultimate irony for Det. Insp. Max Austin in charge of the arson/ murder investigation that had swept through the Notting Hill area barely two years ago. Until he fell for me, he had not looked at another woman for five years.

It was a case of unrequited love, I hasten to add. He was a moody piece of work, probably understandable under the cir- cumstances, sometimes downright caustic and dismissive. Yet he was pretty interesting in the looks department, very much the type I went for—dark, deep-set brown eyes, straight nose. Brood- ing, tendency to give you mocking looks and then disarm you with a flash of wit or unexpected flattery. It was the unpre- dictability that I liked. You never knew where you stood so it woke you up, kept you on your toes.

Tommy, by contrast, was a big blond bear by whom I had always been able to set my clock—until it came to the most im- portant thing of all, our wedding.

So why was I so irritated that Max Austin had found someone? Because I was complacent enough to still think of him as mine and I was no good at being competitive. I was already dreading holding my own with Paula because she had to be smart and chal- lenging to keep him interested.

She wasn't.

She was a silly little creature with a tinny high-pitched giggle and somehow that made it even worse. It brought out the snotty side of me and I could see Cath beginning to look very worried as we heaped taramasalata onto our pita bread and sipped our Soave.

Max Austin looked daggers at me when he walked into Cath's

living room and picked his way around a pile of building blocks, a giant stuffed panda, and a plastic crate of assorted toys that signified Marcus's total rule of the apartment. If I hadn't known him better I'd have been worried, but a glare from Max could easily mean *Fuck! I'd forgotten how much I'm attracted to you and how much you mean to me.* He did nothing to introduce Paula but it didn't matter because she introduced herself and didn't stop talking.

"You and Maxie know each other, do you? Funny, he's never mentioned you but Cath and Richie, they talk about you nonstop. So what's it like living in the Hamptons? Do you see movie stars all the time like they say? Have you been to any of those parties we read about? The girl who did my pedicure last week, she was working out in the Hamptons at one of those spas on the ocean last summer, said it was chockablock with celebrities. I keep saying to Maxie that he needs a holiday. Maybe we could come and stay?"

I was still trying to get my head round the "Maxie." The amazing thing was he didn't appear to mind. I had to admit she was engaging with her streaked blond hair tied back in a ponytail that seemed to bob with excitement as she chattered. She had wide apart gray eyes and a cute little turned-up nose covered in freckles. But the best thing about her was her smile, because I could tell it was genuine. She was a good-natured airhead and I was a miserable old has-been.

Stop it! I told myself. *You never wanted Max when he wanted you so why should you deny him Paula?* In any case it wasn't as if there was even room in the cabin for me to have them to stay.

"Jesus!" I whispered to Cath when I followed her into the kitchen to help serve the fish pie. "How do you put up with it?"

"Oh, she's harmless enough," said Cath, "and it's all about sex, isn't it? Poor old Max didn't get any for five years after his wife died and now he's getting shagged senseless every night, proba- bly every fifteen minutes for all we know. He doesn't know what's hit him."

Richie, bless him, eased me into the conversation over the coffee.

"So, I told you about Lee working with Shotgun Marriott, sir."

"How many times have I told you not to call me sir when we're off duty," said Max.

"Call him Maxie like I do," Paula giggled. I derived a small amount of satisfaction from seeing Max look at Richie in alarm and shake his head.

"Hell of a thing his son getting killed," said Max, looking directly at me for the first time. "You were there when that happened?"

I nodded. "And Bettina Pleshette. Her body was found in the woods, on Shotgun Marriott's land."

"You don't mean *the* Shotgun Marriott? And you're involved in a murder in the Hamptons?" Paula's eyes had opened very wide. "Maxie's been holding out on me. Tell us everything. Don't leave nothing out." She reached across the table and patted my arm. "Go on."

And then Max surprised me. "Not now, Paula. She's working on a book. It's like my investigations, she can't talk about it." His voice was gruff and a flicker of hurt crossed Paula's face. I felt sorry for her. In my experience Max had never bothered much with tact or sensitivity and it was clear that he shut her out of his professional life. I saw Richie and Cath exchange glances and then Cath asked Paula if she'd tried the new Safeway that had opened up in her area. Richie asked me if I was still in touch with Selma Walker, the soap opera star whose autobiography I was working on when Max had been investigating the arson murders in the Notting Hill area, one of which had taken place at the bottom of our garden. Max was silent while I filled Richie in until Paula picked up on what I was talking about and wanted to know all about Selma.

"Why don't you just read her bloody book like everyone else?" Max snapped at her.

Why did he do it? I wondered. He was a tough detective, his heart long since hardened to granite against the murderers he hounded. But outside of his job I recalled touching glimpses of a rather vulnerable person, a helpless widower trying to cope with his laundry and preparing solitary meals without his wife to look after him. I'd braced myself once or twice against the aftereffects of his sharp tongue but more than anything I had felt sorry for him. Because of this I had been unable to think of him as anything other than a sad suit when he'd tentatively voiced his feelings for me.

"So you're a writer then?" said Paula. "You must be so clever."

I saw a harmless way to keep her enthralled and launched into a series of behind-the-scenes anecdotes of some of the celebrities whose books I'd ghosted. After all, I was only repeating what was already in the books, which clearly she was never likely to read.

But when the evening broke up I was in for another surprise. Max said his good-byes, ushered Paula out the door ahead of him, and then turned back to me.

"I'd like to hear about the Shotgun Marriott case," he said to me almost under his breath. "Fancy getting together in the next day or so?"

He was looking right into my eyes, and I looked right back at him and nodded.

"Right then," he said loudly. "Good to see you again, Lee." And then he mouthed "I'll call you tomorrow" and was gone.

"I saw that." Cath was standing right behind me. "Looks to me as if his torch is still burning."

*   *   *

I went home and dreamed about Max and woke up with violent feelings of guilt that prompted me to call Tommy as soon as I'd made myself some coffee.

"Know what I've been doing to keep me busy in the evenings and stop me from feeling a bit lonesome? I've been cooking," said Tommy cheerfully, "practicing for when you come back. I've decided I'm going to take care of you while you write. Your idea of cooking is to open a can of tuna and that's not good enough, Lee. I'm going to *nourish* you properly," he was literally savoring the word "nourish," "so I'm trying out some recipes while you're away."

I've got nothing to write, I'm probably not coming back, and I've been cooking perfectly well for you on and off for the past nine years, I mouthed silently down the phone. *And if you're eating the fruits of those recipes all by yourself then you need to stop right now, Tommy, you're too bloody fat as it is.*

"So when *are* you coming back?" His voice was a little more tentative now. "Because I miss you. I thought I'd let you know that."

I thought I'd let you know that. What was that supposed to mean? You didn't spend time sitting around *thinking* you were going to tell someone you missed them. You came right out and said it—spontaneously.

But I recognized the tone of his voice. He was unsure of his ground. He wanted me back where he could look into my eyes and see just what state I was in. If I was neurotic and crabby and standing right in front of him, it was a piece of cake as far as he was concerned. He knew just how to handle me. But he was no good at dealing with me over the phone.

"Tommy," I said, "just don't make too much of a mess. *Please!*"

I hung up on the sound of him spluttering at the other end of the line. It sounded like he'd just stuffed something into his mouth and was trying to speak at the same time.

Max called me about an hour later and suggested we meet for lunch at a Thai restaurant I'd never heard of. It was called Number One Café and turned out to be a stone's throw from Wormwood Scrubs prison. When I asked him why he had dragged me up to that neck of the woods, he didn't answer and it dawned on me that he must be conducting a murder investigation nearby.

It took us a moment or two to settle down at the table he selected by the window. He sat down opposite me and stretched his legs but there just wasn't room under the table to accommodate them. Max is a beanpole. His feet shot into my shins, causing me to yelp in pain. We both shifted instinctively to another chair and the same thing happened again. Finally, in desperation, I got up and went around the table to sit beside him but when he decided to take off his jacket, his long arms flailed and he narrowly avoided digging his elbow into me.

I returned to my original position and placed myself at an angle. He had hung his jacket over the chair and I saw the label: Ralph Lauren's Polo. A designer label but this jacket was seriously dated. He'd probably bought it at a cancer research charity shop in 1988. He saw me looking at his tie, a garish lapping tongue of maroon and white against his gray shirt. Undoubtedly a gift from Paula. It was a warm day for London and he removed the tie, undid the top button of his collar, and rolled up his shirtsleeves, exposing unusually hairy forearms.

They had an unsettling effect on me, along with his brown eyes, soft and liquid one minute and boring into me like an eagle's the next.

"Nice evening last night," I commented, hiding from his gaze behind the menu.

"What do they think of Paula? Have they said?" He leaned

across the table and I signaled the waitress for a beer while I tried to think what to say. "They don't like her much, do they?"

"Actually," I said carefully, "I think they do. More important, do *you* like her?"

"I have no idea," he said and I looked at him in astonishment. "I mean, I just haven't really stopped to think. I got so fed up with people trying to fix me up with bitter middle-aged divorcées, I told myself the minute a youngish, single, reasonably attractive female presented herself, I'd go for it just to knock the bloody matchmaking on the head. There's a bonus," he fingered his shirt and gave me a sheepish look, "she takes care of my laundry."

I laughed. There had been a time when I had felt so sorry for him, *I'd* done his laundry at Blenheim Crescent.

"Anyway," he said quietly, "you were spoken for. I thought I'd just better get on with it. Can't hang around being a moody old misery all my life waiting for you to notice me. Although Richie said you didn't get married after all, ran away to America instead."

It wasn't a question. He'd done his usual trick of leading me down one path—*no point pinning my hopes on you*—and then abruptly switching tracks—*but you didn't get married after all*—and catching me unawares.

I took a swig of my beer and eyed him down the side of the bottle.

"Tommy canceled the wedding, not me."

"Why on earth did he do that?"

"I have absolutely no idea," I said.

"Well," he said slowly, "let me know when you do. Or don't."

He'd never actually come out and told me that he liked me, fancied me. Never flattered me, bought me a gift, or romanced me in any way. His behavior, as befitted the professional relationship that we had—he was investigating a murder and I was one of the people helping him with his inquiries—had been impeccable at all times. Yet it was clear to Cath—and ultimately to me—that he was besotted with me.

I wanted to tell him that if he were to have any hope of success with me he would have to be much more assertive. I was too shy to take the initiative myself. I needed him to be the first to make physical contact, to clasp my hand across the table, to flick an imaginary crumb away from the side of my mouth. In the past, apart from a quick peck on the cheek I'd given him without thinking, we'd barely touched.

And that was when I realized that if he ever did reach out for me, I might not be responsible for my actions. He had done absolutely nothing a man normally did when he was attracted to a woman. He had merely offered a few half-baked intimations that he was interested in me and seemed to expect that that would do the trick.

Yet my reaction to Paula's presence in his life had shown me that I was a little more interested in him than I had bargained for.

I forced my thoughts to turn to food before I gave myself away. I ordered what I always ordered in Thai restaurants—chicken satay and pad thai—and then left them congealing on my plate as I talked him through the events surrounding the murders of Sean Marriott and Bettina. I talked for a long time, taking care to include every single detail. I was aware of him finishing the contents of his own plate and reaching across the table to pluck a few mouthfuls from mine.

"I don't like Shotgun Marriott for those murders, not at all," he said finally, when we had ordered coffee.

This gave me a jolt. "You don't? Why not?"

"Well, do you?"

"Well, no. Not really."

"Why is that then?"

I looked at him. "If I tell you, promise not to tell me I'm pathetic?" He didn't say anything. "It's just that—I liked him," I continued. "I can't see him killing someone."

"Well, there you are," said Max. "That's my instinct too. I met him, don't forget. Long time ago but I remember him pretty well. I liked him too. Not what I was expecting."

"But surely in your"—I paused, wondering how best to describe hunting down cold-blooded killers—"in your line of work you must come across loads of people who seem really charming. And then they turn out to have—I don't know—cut someone up and buried them in the garden."

"Oh yes," said Max, smiling at me in the rather patronizing way I remembered so well, "at least two or three before lunch every day. No, the thing is that they might be charming as hell but I've never *liked* a killer, personally I mean. It's one of the hunches I try to stick to. Arrogant maybe, complacent, but you have to have something. And I think if you liked Shotgun Marriott too, for what it's worth, that doubles the odds in his favor in my book. Innocent, I mean."

"Well then, how do you work this out?" and I told him about Angie Marriott wanting to tell her story.

He stared at me for quite a long time. "And she requested this meeting?" I nodded. "Well then, I'm going to have to go away and think about that for quite a while and get back to you. And someone's going to have to have a little talk with Mrs. Marriott. She and Shotgun, they both said independently that she was asleep all night at their house. The whole point of Shotgun having this separate apartment was that it was somewhere he could go after a concert and then she wouldn't be disturbed." He was getting pretty worked up now.

"Didn't you talk to her when you were on the case?" I asked him.

"My superior interviewed her. And Shotgun. I was in the room. I was pretty junior back then, you know? She must have lied through her teeth, said she was tucked up in bed at home, never went near her husband's apartment. Beautiful woman," he added after a second.

I interlaced my fingers tightly under the table. He'd never told me I was beautiful.

"Of course we found her prints all over the place but she said she'd been there earlier in the day to check everything was okay for him. I have to say I thought that was a bit odd at the time. When we went to the house, the place was swarming with hired help. I was smoking in those days and there was one flunky following me around to catch my ash, you know, holding out an ashtray whenever the buildup looked like it was going to fall on the carpet. I remember wondering why she felt she had to go check out the flat herself when she had maids coming out of the woodwork."

"What's more," I said, "she mentioned on the phone that she thought Shotgun might have killed their son. Her theory is Sean's death was an accident. Shotgun mistook him for Bettina and he wanted to kill *her* because she was going to unearth the truth about the groupie murder in her book."

He looked skeptical. "Did he have an alibi?"

"For Sean, yes. For Bettina, no. At Shotgun's arraignment, Dumpster lied and said he was with him at Mallaby both nights but strictly speaking, he wasn't. Dumpster told me he was there the night Sean died. He was putting up shelves in the kitchen and he overheard Shotgun canceling Bettina. She went out to dinner with Scott Abernathy instead. Shotgun omitted to mention to the detective investigating the case that he canceled Bettina. He says it just slipped his mind, but who knows?"

"Sounds like a man who's got something to hide—in the past or the present. Didn't he realize Dumpster was around?"

"Maybe not. It's a big house. And he doesn't have an alibi for the night Bettina was killed even though Dumpster lied at his arraignment and said he was at Mallaby that night too. He was— but he wasn't at the house. He was out in the woods, hunting. He kept quiet about that because he shouldn't have been. The hunting season hadn't started yet."

"For Bettina's murder, Shotgun has possible motive, no alibi, and plenty of opportunity. And his wife says he's committed murder before."

"But we both like him so he's innocent," I said.

"Until proven otherwise," said Max. "It's not looking good for Dumpster either. He was out in the woods the night Bettina died and you say he was due to meet her on the beach. And there's his bow and arrow to take into account. Opportunity, yes, alibi, no, motive? He wanted to get rid of Bettina because of what she had over his mother? Possible. Did he strike you as a hotheaded young man?"

I thought about it. "Not really," I admitted. "Not *that* hotheaded."

"Yet he was a hunter, he was familiar with those woods. And he knew Sean Marriott pretty well. I just don't see him killing Sean; he sounds too experienced to have shot him by accident although he did have opportunity. He can't have been putting up shelves all night. Pity about the storm destroying all the evidence before they even found the body washed up on the beach. There was a cab driver said he dropped Sean off at the edge of the woods and saw him walk into them so that's where he was shot. I suppose the cab driver's got an alibi for the next few hours? Who else lives around there? What about that weird Martha woman you mentioned?"

"She didn't know Bettina so what would be her motive? She knew Sean and he was wearing one of her wedding dresses when they fished him out of the ocean. But she had an alibi for both nights."

"You know," he took a slug from his beer and looked at me sideways, "there is one person I have a few concerns about— among the people you've mentioned."

"Who's that?"

"Franny Cook."

I didn't say anything. Hadn't I had my own moments of unease about Franny? But she was Eliza's *mother*. And soon she would be Rufus's *wife*.

"You don't look too happy about that," said Max. "I sense that you really like her. She's become a friend, yes?"

I nodded.

"A friend like, say, Cath in this country? If you stayed out there on Long Island—I mean you're not going to, are you?" He looked worried at what he had suggested. "But if you did, hypothetically, would Franny Cook become your best girlfriend? Were you becoming that close to her?"

Was Franny my American Cath? It was a very odd notion but there was some basis to it. They were both blunt, outspoken women with troublesome pasts. In their different ways they both made me feel a little inadequate but that was probably my fault as much as theirs. But this wasn't really what Max had been asking. He'd wanted to know if I felt really close to Franny, as close as I felt to Cath. It was a tricky question. I'd known Cath virtually all my life. She knew me better than I cared to admit and even though I didn't always relish what she told me about myself, I trusted her and felt her to be an integral part of my life. Did I feel the same about Franny? No, I did not.

But thinking about this made me realize there *was* someone to whom I had become enormously attached in a short space of time. Rufus. He was in a way all I had left of the Phillionaire and I really did think of him like a brother. Rufus had introduced me to Franny. Rufus loved Franny. And because of *that* I felt close to Franny.

"It's not quite the same thing," I said, picking my words carefully. "I've known Cath since we were kids. But the thought of Franny murdering anyone—"

"Okay, you like her. But *I* don't know her," said Max, "and I can look at her overall picture objectively. She's tall, she's Amazonian, she's strong. She grew up there, she knows the territory, she could have gone hunting with the guys."

"Rufus told me she taught him to shoot," I said.

"There you are," said Max, "and although it doesn't necessarily follow, if she knew how to handle a shotgun, she could have been familiar with a crossbow. And she's got a past Bettina knew about and it's really in Franny's interest that people don't get to hear too much about it. She's trying to set up a business, raise a kid respectably, and marry a local millionaire. And she admitted to you that she was out on her own both nights driving around looking for her son. She doesn't have an alibi—for either night."

"I can't argue with you," I said, "but I can't help feeling that Dumpster knows more than he's telling anyone. Bettina's notes: 'M saw something.'"

"And Dumpster's her son. You think 'M' is definitely Martin, as in Dumpster?"

"Well, who else would it be? He was going to meet Bettina the night she died."

"So of course he'd run a mile rather than tell anyone he saw his mother commit murder," said Max.

"I have so much trouble with Franny as the killer," I said, "just as I can't see Shotgun murdering anyone. Especially," I added, thinking about it and realizing I felt quite sure about this, "a woman. He's not the kind of raucous, hell-raising type you associate with rock stars, at least not anymore. He's quiet and thoughtful and cultured, he's a *gentle* man. I just can't imagine him exerting any kind of violence on a woman. Of course he may have been different back then but he claims he let the groupie sleep in his bed beside him rather than turn her out into the night. He felt it was the easiest option. Were you there that morning? Did you go to the apartment after they found her?"

He shook his head.

"So you never saw her. For some reason I've always been curious about what she looked like." I had been carrying around a picture in my mind of Shotgun waking up beside a tiny waif of a creature but I realized I couldn't put a face to her.

"You want me to describe a corpse in the morgue? Because that's the first glimpse I got of her." He shook his head. "But I tell you what I can do," he went on. "Believe it or not, I've brought along some photos from the time." He pulled out an envelope from his jacket pocket. "Look, here's one of Shotgun. I wanted to ask you what *he* looked like now. I don't have any pictures of the groupie—her name was Anna di Santi, pretty name, I never forgot it—but here are some of her family. They came over from New York, the Bronx I think it was, to claim her body and I had to look after them. I didn't know what to do with them. They had never been to London and so I showed them a few sights while we were waiting for the forensics to be dealt with and the body to be released. It was harrowing beyond belief. They had thought it would be better than sitting weeping in their hotel room but of course it was worse. I'll never forget, they asked me to take a picture of them at the Tower of London and then weeks later, long after they'd gone back to New York, I got this in the mail."

I stared at the photograph of a group of dark-haired Italian-looking people huddled together with the Tower of London rising above them. Not surprisingly, not one of them was smiling, a fact that was emphasized by the grinning face of a Japanese tourist standing to their right.

But it was the figure on their left that caught my attention. I held the photo in front of Max and pointed to the man. He seemed to be with Anna di Santi's family and yet he was standing slightly apart from them.

"What in the world is he doing there?"

The picture had been taken fourteen years ago and since then he had filled out considerably, but I had no difficulty recognizing the young man with the groupie's family as Evan Morrison.

CHAPTER 18

"Oh, he wasn't part of the family," said Max.

"I know that," I said. "I know who he is. But what was he doing *there?*"

"He was Anna di Santi's boyfriend. He came over with her family and he was even more distraught than they were, if that was possible. I talked to him a bit because he was at the police academy in New York. It was clear he didn't like her going to concerts the way she did. Not that I can blame him given what she got up to. But he was devastated by what happened and he arrived in the country out for blood."

"How do you mean?"

"He wasn't exactly pointing the finger at Shotgun but he wanted us to find someone he could blame, someone he could take his misery out on."

"Max," I said, "listen to me. That's Evan Morrison."

"That's right," he said, looking at me in amazement, "that was his name. I remember now. How do you know him?"

"Because he's the detective investigating the murders of Sean Marriott and Bettina. He's the one who is totally obsessed with pinning the murders on Shotgun. I told you, it's like he won't even consider anyone else."

"It's hard to credit it, isn't it?" Max glared at me as if it were my fault. "But I suppose it's a form of vengeance. He's had fourteen years to fester. It's the reason he's been so blinkered about this case but by God, he needs a wake-up call."

The revelation about Evan Morrison seemed to galvanize him into action. He called for the bill, paid it, and was marching off down the street, waving good-bye before I'd even realized what was happening. Feeling suddenly totally deflated I wandered off in search of a cab. I searched for a taxi rank although why I expected to find one outside one of London's major prisons was beyond me. I was just about to give up and call my father to come and pick me up when Max appeared at my side and grasped me by the elbow. He stood right in front of me looking straight into my eyes and my heart began to pound. He was going to do it. He was about to kiss me. Was this the point of no return?

"What are you staring at?" he said testily. "Can you save me some time and give me a contact number for Evan Morrison? Angela Marriott too, if you've got it."

"I don't have it with me," I said, aware that my face was going red, "but if you want to give me a call later—"

"Suppose I'll have to," he said. He sounded so ungracious that I barely recognized him as the person with whom I had just had a very enjoyable lunch. But as we set off once again in opposite directions, it didn't stop me turning back once, twice, and then a third time for one last look at him. How could it have happened? A year ago I had spent a lot of time with this man in close proximity—on a professional basis, true—and more than one person had explained to me that he was mine for the taking. Yet I had not for one moment been attracted to him.

Or had I? Had the longing I felt for him now been lying dormant in my subconscious? Had there just been too much else going on in my life at that time for me to recognize that Max Austin was exactly the kind of edgy challenge I'd told myself I needed? Well, whatever comatose state I had been in then, I was wide awake now and I had to do something to regain his attention.

And by the time I'd got home I knew the perfect way to do it. I'd get Angie Marriott to spill the beans to me about Shotgun and then I'd invite Max around for a drink to tell him what I'd discovered.

To my amazement I had found that Angie Marriott lived just around the corner from Blenheim Crescent and she had suggested getting together for a preliminary drink to discuss her plans for a book. I had about a half hour to kill before walking over to her house so I tipped the contents of Bettina's file onto the kitchen table. Immediately I understood why Genevieve had not done anything with it. There were pages and pages of unmarked transcripts, endless interviews with no indication as to who was talking to whom. I recognized them as such only because I used a similar format for the initial rough transcriptions of my own interviews. Get it all down on paper and then see what you've got. I would say one thing in Bettina's favor: She had meticulously labeled each folder of transcripts by subject and date and I flipped through a pretty impressive list of bold-faced names before I came to the one I was looking for. Shaking slightly with anticipation I opened Shotgun's folder.

And swore out loud.

There were just a few sheets of paper in it headed by a name, "Mike Molloy," an address, "3 Queens Gate Mansions," a time but no date.

I was aware that my heart had started beating quite fast. Shotgun had told me his apartment all those years ago had been in Queens Gate.

I began to read.

MM: Oh, I didn't live there long. A month maybe. I'd come over from Sydney for a conference and when that was over, my wife and I drove around the West Country a bit visiting her family. She's English, you know, not Australian and—

BP: You saw Shotgun Marriott in the lobby?

Bettina really was meticulous. She had transcribed what she said as well as her interviewee's content. Not something I ever bothered to do.

MM: Oh, yes, sorry. We rented the flat so as to have a base in London. And as I said, I left Shirley down in Somerset with her rellies one week and came back up for some meetings. Can't recall it too clearly but I think the traffic was bad so I didn't get there till around one in the morning and there he was coming out of the building, none other than Shotgun Marriott. I mean it's not what you expect, is it? I was a huge fan and suddenly he's right in front of me. I was tossing it up in my mind, could I ask him for his autograph or should I— Anyway in the end I just nodded at him and he went out and I rang the bell for the lift and that was that.

BP: But then?

MM: The lift was slow. It took forever. You know how they are when they're old? And then when I got upstairs—we were on the third floor—I remembered I'd forgotten to pick up the mail. We were given a little box in the lobby and I was expecting a document that I knew I ought to look over before my meeting the next day so I had to go back down again, didn't I? At least the lift was right there. But once I was back down in the lobby and standing in front of the bank of mailboxes with my key all ready, I couldn't remember which number to open. It was the number of our flat. So guess what?

BP: You had to go all the way up again to look.

MM: That's right. It was number three. Well, it would be, wouldn't it? It was on the third floor. What? Oh, yes, sorry. You want me to get to the bit where I saw his wife. Well, of course I didn't know it was his wife. I'm not sure I even knew he was married. I'd just picked up my package when this woman comes running in through the front door and she's in the lift before I can even close the mailbox and I shout out to her, "Stop, wait! Hold the door." Because I don't want to wait for that lift again, do I? So we ride up together but she stops at the second floor and out she gets. She was good looking, dark. I smiled at her but she wasn't very friendly. She didn't smile back.

BP: And it was Angela Marriott?

MM: Well, as I say, I didn't know who it was and I didn't think anything more about it until I saw her on the television news a couple of days later. I recognized her.

BP: And you didn't do anything about it?

MM: Like what?

BP: Tell the police you'd seen her.

MM: They never asked. They'd already spoken to me and the truth is, I forgot about her. They were very interested in hearing that I'd seen Shotgun Marriott go out because of course I gave him a bit of an alibi. And when I saw her on the TV, I didn't really think anything of it beyond "Oh, that was his wife I saw." It seemed only natural that she was going to their apartment.

BP: So what you're saying, Mr. Molloy, is that when Angela Marriott arrived at the apartment that night her husband wasn't there?

MM: Don't see how he could have been. I saw him leave the building and I didn't see him come back in with her. No, she was on her own when she went up in the lift with me.

I turned the page but there was no more transcript, just a note in what I assumed was Bettina's handwriting. "Telephoned Shirley Molloy, Sydney, August 1, 2004. Mike Molloy died 2003." August 1. Bettina must have followed up as recently as this summer once she learned that she might have another chance to do Shotgun's book.

Shotgun had not mentioned Angie being at the apartment that night. He had given me to understand that the whole point of having the apartment was so that he could go there after a concert and leave Angie at their house to sleep undisturbed. What he had said was that she had barricaded herself into the house and if she had heard him banging on the door, she had probably not answered because she had thought it was one of his fans.

But what if she hadn't been there?

Now I couldn't wait to go around and see her.

She opened the door to me in what was obviously her version of mufti—a white polo shirt and lime green capri pants. On her feet were spangled flip-flops and her toenails were painted the same bloodred as her lipstick. It didn't really go with the lime green but you can't have everything. Her dark hair was tied back in a long braid that fell over one shoulder. It was unwashed and greasy and I realized it was dyed. It didn't do her any favors; it made her strong face look hard and unforgiving.

Her house was a bit of a bombshell. When I arrived at the address she had given me I thought I must have misheard what she'd said. It was just off Portobello Road, a shabby nondescript door in a rather beat-up terraced house. More ordinary you could not get and it had to be one of the noisiest locations in Notting Hill. They started setting up the stalls for Portobello Market every morning around five o'clock and the racket was unbelievable. But then maybe Angie Marriott was one of those driven, edgy people who never slept.

But once inside I got the picture. The place had been gutted and given a mega makeover. I was standing in a kitchen with marble countertops and an impressive display of status appliances that would have given the Phillionaire a run for his money. The place was like a giant loft and I'd stepped directly into it, there'd been no hallway, no staircase. Suddenly I realized the ceiling was exposed to the rafters and the kitchen seemed to take up the whole house. There was no upstairs. So where did she sleep?

"Cath's lovely, isn't she?" said Angie, taking out a bottle of rosé and offering me a glass. "It's all right," she must have noticed my concerned look, "I'm on the pomegranate."

"They say it's the new cranberry juice," I said.

"Do they indeed? Let me just throw some snacks together and then we'll go and sit down. I only just got back from work."

"Which is?"

"Oh, sorry. Don't you know? I have a financial advisory service. Our main office is in London, in Chancery Lane actually, but we've got another one in Kent and I seem to have been running nonstop between the two recently. Suddenly the world is full of people who've just realized they haven't given enough thought to their pension requirements—all those irresponsible baby boomers—and they want me to invest twenty pence for them. Still, it does me good to keep busy after what happened to Sean. By the way, what provision have you made for your old age, Lee?"

Give me a break! I hadn't come over to be sold a pension plan.

"Do you use the name Angela Marriott at work?"

"I don't use it at all, anywhere. I've been Angela Braithwaite for years. Ever since—well, you know. Come on, let's go and make ourselves comfortable. Could you take these?" She handed me a bowl of crisps and the bottle of rosé. "And I'll bring the rest."

I couldn't help noticing she picked up my glass of wine and hers of pomegranate juice and then she grabbed a third glass by its stem. Who else was she expecting?

"Oh, by the way," I said, "has Max Austin been in touch with you?" Only a few hours had passed since lunch but I knew Max never wasted any time. He hadn't called me for Angie's number but that didn't mean he hadn't got it from another source.

"Who?"

"Detective Inspector—well, no, hang about, he's a detective superintendent now. Det. Supt. Max Austin. I saw him today and I told him what you told me, what you said about—about Shotgun killing the groupie. Back then he was working for the man who led the investigation, I don't know his name."

"Frank Shaw," she said as if it were a name engraved on her memory for a lifetime, "Det. Insp. Frank Shaw. He's retired now."

"Right. Well, I saw Max Austin and I told him what you said about Shotgun. I was going to call and warn you he'd be contacting you."

She looked at me for a long time. Then she said slowly, "You know, you shouldn't have done that. Not without checking with me first." Her eyes were wary. "Did he believe you?"

It was an odd question but in fact a perfectly reasonable one. Because *I* hadn't believed *her* when she'd told me on the phone. Not because I didn't think she was telling the truth but because I hadn't *wanted* Shotgun to be guilty. There was a difference. Wasn't there?

"More or less," I said. And that *was* the truth.

"Well then, that's that," she said and suddenly she was sad and deflated. "One way or the other, Kip'll go down now."

"And there's something else," I said, wondering if it was a good move to let everything come rushing out like this but unable to stop myself, "I didn't believe you at first but now I know you were there."

She dropped a glass in shock. It slipped from her hand and clattered onto the floor.

"You do?"

As she kicked the broken glass into a corner and went to get another, I explained about Bettina's tape.

"So you've been quite busy since you arrived. How long are you over?"

"I don't know," I told her and explained why.

"Well, you *are* going to be finishing the book but it'll be my book instead of Kip's so that's answered that question. You won't need to go back to Long Island because I can tell you everything you need to know from now on."

"Except I've left my fiancé over there," I said, "and he doesn't sound very keen to come back. I may have to go back and drag him across the Atlantic."

"My goodness," she said, "when's the wedding?"

So then of course I had to tell her that it hadn't happened and there was no firm guarantee that it would.

"Man trouble," she sighed and opened the kitchen door, beckoning me to follow her. "A woman without it in her life is a woman who can get away with murder. And now you've got Max Austin to add to your problems."

Now it was my turn to stare at her.

"You blushed bright red when you said his name," she said and laughed. "Come on, let's go flop in the living room, and have a girly evening together."

If there was anyone with whom I could feel less comfortable about spending a girly evening it was Angie Marriott but I followed her meekly out of the kitchen.

And then I gasped.

We were in a glass-roofed passage leading across a courtyard to a totally separate house—a town house, four stories high. She laughed again when she saw my face.

"You didn't think I lived in that little hovel?" She jerked her head back to the kitchen we had just left. "No, that address is just a front for deliveries. No one ever gets to see beyond the kitchen. And the entrance to this house in the street around the corner is boarded up. It looks as if no one lives there. I only let my nearest and dearest through to where I really live."

I wasn't quite sure what to make of this.

"Don't look so surprised, Lee. We may not know each other very well yet but I've told you the biggest secret of my whole life, haven't I? The one I've been carrying around for fourteen years. If that doesn't make you eligible to enter my private domain, I don't know what does."

She unlocked a tall iron security gate that led to the front door and let it clang shut behind us so loudly I felt as if I was entering an episode of *Law & Order*.

"When I'm in here no one can reach me. No one even knows I'm here."

She was almost purring but to me it seemed as if she were making herself a prisoner in her own home. She led me into a sumptuous room, wood-paneled and rich in color with tapestries and velvet-covered sofas and heavy curtains complete with corded tiebacks. The atmosphere was almost medieval except for a giant flat screen TV in a prominent position on the far wall.

I looked around the room. There were photographs of Sean everywhere, in silver frames, in wooden frames, and some just snapshots propped up on the bookshelves. As I took in the poignancy of this display of the son she had not raised and would never see again, something registered with me. These were all recent photos of Sean. Sean as a young man, clearly taken in the last two or three years. Who had sent her these pictures?

"Have a seat," she said, flopping down onto one of the sofas. "So, this is a little weird. I guess you know all about me from Kip by now. So what did my old man have to say about our marriage?"

She wasn't stupid. Talk about blunt and direct! Okay, so she was determined to be in control of the proceedings from the word go. What should I tell her about my meetings with Shotgun? Well, the truth would be the simplest route to go. Not only that but past experience had taught me that the more forthcoming I was, the more that approach persuaded my interviewee to open up.

Only right now I wasn't quite sure who was interviewing whom.

"He told me everything." Let her make of that what she wanted.

"All about his other women? All those little girls on the road and then the real threats that came along once I started drinking? Can't blame him, I suppose. I wasn't much use to him in those days." I saw the unmistakable pain in her eyes before she carried on without giving me a chance to answer. "Oh, I'm sure he didn't tell you the whole story. In fact, I know he didn't, otherwise he'd be locked up by now. And it's my own fault. I could have picked up the phone and told the police everything I know any time I wanted." She looked hard at me. "But I didn't, did I? Because I still love Kip, as you've probably guessed, and I couldn't do that to him. That's why I want to do a book. It's the only way I'll ever be able to tell the truth, that I went round to the apartment that night because I wanted to be with him and I walked in on him with a girl—just as I had so many times before. Only this time he was holding a pillow over her face, smothering her. He looked at me the whole time—while he was squeezing the life out of that poor girl, Lee, he was looking at me. I saw her legs twitching, her hands. She was lying there on the bed putting up a pathetic struggle but she was a tiny little thing. She was no match for him."

It took a moment for me to register what she had just told me and I began to feel slightly sick at the thought of having to accept once and for all that Shotgun was a killer. But the intensity with which she had just described the killing told me she really had been in the room.

"You saw him and you didn't call the police?" I looked at her.

"Terrible, isn't it?" She nodded her head several times, agreeing with me. "But I could never have done that. What you have to understand is that Kip and I loved each other with an intensity you just wouldn't believe and that's why I had such a hard time turning a blind eye to his other women. He always said they didn't mean a thing, they were just evidence of a weakness in him and he had absolutely no feeling for them, they were just about sex. But I couldn't handle it."

"You've lived with it all this time?"

"Yes," she said, "I've been in my own form of hell."

"You left Shotgun—"

"I couldn't stay with him after that—"

"But you left your son. How could you leave Sean—with a murderer?"

"I told myself I wasn't leaving him with a murderer. I was leaving him with his father. Because Kip gave me no choice. He said he was taking Sean as a hostage; if I ever breathed a word of what had happened, he'd—"

"He wouldn't harm his own son?"

"I had no way of knowing what he would or wouldn't do but

he said if I tried to get custody of Sean, he'd drag up all my drinking and prove I was an unfit mother."

"But he let you go—that night. And he stayed—with the girl?"

"Probably sounds weird that he didn't get as far away as possible but we agreed he would appear less guilty if he stayed and said he'd found her dead beside him when he woke up. And that's when we made the pact to keep quiet about what really happened. Forever."

"But you left later on, because you weren't there in the morning."

"Right," she said quietly, "I went back and said good-bye to Sean. I mean I didn't actually say the word 'good-bye,' I just crept into his room and sat by his bed watching him sleep. In any case it was sometime after that that I actually relinquished him. We wanted to make it seem like a natural turn of events prior to a divorce, like it tied in with Kip moving to the States. But I think that night was when I forced myself to acknowledge that I would be losing Sean. I'll tell you something"—she looked hard at me for a second—"but I don't want this going in the book. Okay?"

I nodded, wondering how many more off-the-record revelations there would be.

"It wasn't *that* hard. It wasn't like I was a born mother. I was selfish—still am, actually—and I resented the demands a child made on my time. I think there are probably quite a few women who feel this way only they'd never admit it."

She turned to face me head on and she was smiling at me, appealing to me. *You agree with me, don't you? We're becoming friends, right?* I felt edgy. I had no desire to bond with Angie Marriott. I was here on a professional basis. I wondered how close she had become to Cath. Had Cath been invited back to her hidden retreat?

"I loved my son," said Angie, "I really did—but at a distance. I had a baby for Kip. I loved *him*. I would do anything for him and that's what he wanted—a child. I've thought a lot about it and I've worked it all out. I remember one awful moment when I was pregnant. I actually found myself thinking of Sean as a fashion accessory—you know, got the rich rock star husband, got my own successful career, got the perfect house, all I need now is a baby. And when he arrived I was proud of him, he was such a beautiful little boy. Delicate. People went *ooh* and *aah* when they saw him and he had impeccable manners. I'm a disgusting person, aren't I?" Again she seemed to be imploring me to condone her view of herself. "I'm really telling you everything. I don't know why, Lee, but I need to open up to someone. Just hear me out, will you?"

Her eyes were filled with tears but her voice was still strong.

"You have to understand that I'm telling you how I was *then*. But when he died, when I first met you in that store right after the funeral, I discovered something about myself. I realized that of course I loved Sean, I mean *really* loved *him,* even though I didn't know him. I cared about him in retrospect. Isn't that awful? I didn't know myself back then and I just slotted him into a compartment in my emotions. I didn't acknowledge what he meant to me. But since then I've come to terms with who I am, with everything that's happened to me, the gang rape, Kip, *every*-thing. I've learned to accept myself and somewhere along the journey I realized I had to get Sean back. You understand what I'm trying to tell you, don't you?"

All I understood was that I felt nauseous. There was some-thing appallingly claustrophobic about being shut up in this pri-vate retreat with Angie intent on baring her soul. I needed to get out for some air if only for a few seconds.

"Could I use your loo?" I smiled to show I was sorry to be in-terrupting her story.

"Out the door, down the passage, and it's the first door on the left at the bottom of the stairs," she said without getting up.

But the door was locked and from the inside I could hear water running. Someone was in there.

I should have waited but I was pretty desperate. So I tiptoed upstairs assuming I'd find another bathroom. And of course it gave me a chance to nose around a bit.

I glanced through a door at the top of the stairs and saw a bedroom. In fact it was more like a wood-paneled womb with richly textured fabrics and a four-poster bed piled high with velvet cushions. I saw a bathroom leading off it and rushed in.

Coming back into the bedroom, I flicked on the light switch and stopped dead.

The room was a shrine to Shotgun. Every inch of the walls was covered with photographs and memorabilia. Shotgun on stage, microphone in hand and standing in a pool of spotlight. Shotgun with the band, arms around their shoulders. Shotgun with celebrities. I moved closer to scrutinize each picture. His eyes gave him away. He looked trapped, nervous, uncomfortable.

I turned to the photos in frames on the various surfaces. On each of her bedside tables she had giant portraits of him smiling wistfully at her. Smaller heart-shaped frames showed him cradling Sean as a baby, kicking a football to him as a young boy.

It was an old house with generous sash windows and the deep sills were the perfect place to display pictures. I crossed the room to study the group amassed on the far windowsill and found they were all—predictably—of Shotgun but here there was a difference. Like the ones of Sean downstairs, they were recent pictures taken on Long Island—and it was clear he had not known he was being photographed. I recognized the beach below Mallaby and here and there a shot of him in the woods near the house itself. When had these been taken? When she was over there for Sean's funeral? But as I looked closer, I could make out Sean in some of the long-distance shots hovering near his father with Mallaby in the background. Whoever had taken these pictures had been spying on them from the woods.

There was a wooden frame at the back hidden behind the others and I reached for it. This was an older picture, a blurred amateur image of two girls in school uniform.

"We haven't changed a bit, have we?" said a voice behind me and I turned around to see Martha Farrell smiling at me nervously.

And behind her stood Angie with a twelve-bore shotgun hanging loosely in the crook of her arm.

CHAPTER **19**

"IT'S OKAY, I'M NOT GOING TO SHOOT YOU." ANGIE'S
smile was almost gracious. "At least not in here. Think of
the mess! If I used this thing in this confined space you'd be splat-
tered all over the room." She actually laughed. "Martha heard you
come upstairs and actually it's rather cozy in here. Martha, why
don't you go down and get our drinks. We'll have a little party
right here in my bedroom."

I couldn't move and I couldn't speak. All I could do was keep
my eyes fixated on the barrel of the gun. I didn't know anything
about shotguns. I didn't know anything about *any* gun. I had no
idea how to tell if it was loaded. When Martha began to walk
across to the door I was convinced the vibration of her weight on
the floorboards would cause the thing to go off.

"I had a secret nickname for her when we were at school together," said Angie when Martha had left the room. "You know
what it was? Putty. Because that's what she was in my hands. I
could get her to do anything I wanted. In an instant. All I had to
do was throw her a smile every now and then. And here she is
today, alive and well and still ready to do whatever I ask her."

I wanted to ask her if she knew about Martha's novel because
as Angie was speaking I had realized instantly that the fictional
monster Martha had created in Iona was of course based on

Angie. But I dared not move, not even to open my mouth. I was like a statue planted in the middle of her bedroom.

"You know I was all set to do a book," Angie went on, "I really was. I knew I had to point the finger at Kip before he broke his silence about me. I knew it was only a matter of time before he told someone even if he did it inadvertently."

No, I wanted to cry out to her, *no, he protected you to the last. He thought he'd be able to tell what really happened but at the last minute he backed out and now I know why. He still loves you. He'll keep your pact to the end, I know he will.*

But I had convinced myself that if I opened my mouth it would cause the gun to go off, so I maintained my rigid and silent stance and the only change was that I was now blinking away tears of terror.

"And then it would just be a quick step and a jump to him telling the world how I smothered the groupie in his bed. I'm telling you, if it hadn't been her it would have been another one. I'd had enough. I knew Kip took girls back to that flat. I got up that night after the concert and went round there. I assumed I'd find Kip there with someone and I was just going to confront him. But he wasn't around, there was just this girl asleep in his bed. I was enraged—" Angie paused and shifted the gun to her other arm and I knew the true meaning of the expression *I thought I would die.*

"At first," she said, shrugging casually in reflection, "I think I just meant to hit her but then her eyes opened and she began to sit up. I grabbed the pillow from under her head and smashed it down on her face. I held it there—she was a tiny little thing, too skinny to be attractive, but Kip had all sorts of girls, you know? He told me it was all in my imagination, his womanizing, but I kept thinking about it, seeing him with them, and the images would fester in my mind, Lee. Have you ever been jealous?"

She was appealing to me and coming toward me with the shotgun. I wondered why I did not faint with fear, my knees were shaking so hard and my teeth were clacking away like a rattle.

But she moved past me to stand the gun against the wall as Martha came back into the room and handed her the pomegranate juice. I burst into tears in relief and Martha put her arm around me.

"Poor duck," she said, "here, sit down and drink your wine. It'll calm you down. You're in a real state, aren't you?"

"Leave her be, Martha. I'm telling her about that groupie nightmare. It's true, that girl really did look as if she were asleep. I got out of there fast, leaving a mass of evidence, I imagine. Which is why I was so amazed when they went after Kip. Everything I told you downstairs, about the two of us making a pact to keep quiet, was a bunch of lies. I never saw him there. He must have come back, found her dead, got rid of everything that would incriminate me, like the pillow I used to smother her. He must have known it was me because I was the only other person with a key to the place."

She took a sip of pomegranate juice. It was dark red, almost black, the color of dried blood.

"But he would never—ever—talk to me about what happened. When I saw him he said right away he did not want to discuss it. All he did was make me promise that I would never tell anyone. And he said he wouldn't either. But it was an order from him, not a mutual pact. And then he left and took Sean. We agreed that he would say that I was leaving him but of course it was the other way around. And that was where we left it until Bettina started nosing around. They had no firm evidence that Kip had killed that girl, no witnesses, and both the policeman and the Australian had seen him outside the flat around the time of death.

"So," she said, flashing me a grim smile, "when you told me you knew about Bettina's meeting with the Australian, I realized it was all over. You knew I went to the flat that night so you were going to be a problem. Just like Bettina, you had to go too far, didn't you? It's a shame you had to blow it because up to then I could have let you go. I know Kip didn't tell you anything. I've got the disk of all your transcripts. Quite touching, some of it."

I stared at Martha. It was *she* who had taken my disk from the cabin, not Shotgun.

"You know, I always thought I'd get Sean back one day but when Martha told me Bettina had arrived on the scene I realized things were going to get rough. I remembered what a nightmare she had been the first time she'd tried to do a book with Kip. I knew if she got another chance, she'd dig deep and I couldn't allow that to happen," said Angie. "So we hatched a little plan, didn't we, Martha? When Kip decided to go and bury himself in the back of beyond out on Long Island, Martha was the first person I thought of. She was living in Manhattan, trying to make a go of it on Broadway or some such fantasy. Total waste of time, she was a useless actress. Don't look at me like that, darling, you were hopeless, you know you were. I told her to stop trying to achieve the impossible and move to the Hamptons to keep an eye on my son for me. We thought about changing her name in case Kip heard about her, but in the end we decided it would be too much aggravation. Martha and I had been friends at school but, although we kept up by phone and letter, we didn't really get together that often once I was in London. She was never part of my life with Kip. I don't think he even met her." She looked at Martha, who shook her head. "I did the right thing, I sent her money. Well, she couldn't live on what she made from those silly wedding dresses, could she? And she sent me news of Sean as he was growing up, pictures.

"When Kip called me to tell me Sean was dead he had no idea I was already on Long Island, just down the beach from him in Martha's trailer. He was calling me on my cell phone and he thought I was still in London. I'm still waiting for that incompetent Detective Morrison to ask me what I was doing in America *before* Sean's funeral. He must have learned from Immigration that I was there and he's asked me a lot of stuff about Kip but he's never asked me *that*."

Because Evan Morrison wouldn't have wanted you to be the killer whatever evidence he had, I thought. He had been determined to convict Shotgun no matter what. What would he do when he found out Angie was the killer?

If he found out. What was going to happen to me? I knew as much as Bettina and Angie had killed *her*. Wasn't that what Shotgun had intimated when he had tried to explain why he no longer wanted me to do his book? He hadn't named Angie but had he known she was responsible?

And now here I was at Angie's mercy. Stupidly I didn't have my cell phone with me. I could visualize it lying on the kitchen table at Blenheim Crescent. Had I mentioned to Max when I was seeing Angie? I didn't think I had.

"It doesn't matter if you told anyone you were coming here," said Angie with an uncanny insight into my thoughts. "I'm assuming you told that agent of yours. If you suddenly disappear, Martha will be my witness. She'll tell them she was with me tonight and that you turned up for a while—your prints are all over the place—but that then you left. She's useful that way, aren't you, Martha?"

I looked at Martha and I opened my mouth for the first time.

"What happened to you, Martha?" I asked. "You left without saying good-bye, without telling anyone." Some instinct told me to be gentle with Martha, to pander to her like a child but not in the arrogant, patronizing manner Angie adopted with her.

"Her so-called boyfriend dumped her," Angie laughed, "so she came running to me."

"I know," I said. "Louis. I saw him, Martha."

Martha's eyes widened with a pathetic glimmer of hope. "You did?"

"At your trailers. He'd come round to see you but you'd gone. I found something, Martha. A quiver, buried in the sand. Probably the one that held the arrow that killed Bettina."

"But I didn't know it was there," said Martha, anxiety making her voice rise. "I swear I didn't. Tell her, Angie."

"Calm down, for God's sake. Lee, she had nothing to do with burying that quiver. I killed Bettina."

"And Sean?" I looked her in the eye for the first time.

"Oh, I didn't kill Sean," said Angie. "My own son, are you crazy?" She came over to clasp me roughly by the arm. I pulled away from her in panic and she snapped at Martha, "Don't just stand there. Help me! I want to put her next door."

I could see Martha was reluctant, apprehensive even, but she dutifully took hold of my other arm and the two of them propelled me forward. I contemplated trying to struggle free but it was two against one and Angie was surprisingly strong.

They led me out of her bedroom across the narrow landing at the top of the stairs and into what appeared to be nothing more than a small box room. There was no furniture, just bare floorboards. Its message was unmistakable. It was a cell and I was to be the prisoner.

But it was what was lying on the floor in a corner that made me begin to struggle frantically in their arms. A coil of rope—with the end fashioned into a noose.

With almost superhuman strength, Angie flung me onto the

floor and before I had time to move she was kneeling over me, holding me down while Martha bound my wrists and ankles.

"I'm not sure whether we can use that here." Angie had followed my terrified gaze to the noose. "You need a high beam of some kind. But I've got to hand all credit to Martha. I got the idea from reading her novel. I found myself getting hooked on that story she wrote. Quite ingenious, I thought, what about you? I told her, didn't I, Martha? I said, stick to writing. You're a darn sight better at it than you were at acting.

"But anyway, the noose is an option providing we can find the right place. I'll be moving you to a different location tomorrow but I'm going to need a few hours' sleep before I take to the road."

"Where are we going?" asked Martha.

"Like I'm going to tell you, now, in front of her." Angie's tone was contemptuous. "I'm not going to go into any overdramatic details but I think we all know what's going to happen. But right now I'm exhausted so I'm just going to leave her in here."

She knotted a scarf around my face and then she pushed Martha out of the room and locked me in.

I lay there listening to the sounds of them moving about the house. Was Martha staying here? My mind was racing with the realization that she had deceived me right from the start. Who knew whether anything she had told me had been true. *M saw something.* Yet I could not accept that Martha was as deranged as Angie although she was clearly in thrall to her in a way that was very scary. Didn't I have to take her novel into account? By having me read it, had she not been trying to tell me something? Yet surely she must have known it would be too much of a stretch. I had thought the story was autobiographical in some way but there was no way in which I could have made the leap from those destructive schoolgirls in the book to two crazy menopausal huntresses in the Mallaby woods.

Because I was assuming Angie had involved Martha in Bettina's murder in some way.

And I was right, as I found out a few hours later in the most unlikely way I would have dreamed—from Martha herself.

I didn't sleep, not that I expected to for a second, so wound up was I by the events of the evening. I was still awake when they started setting up the market in the early hours before dawn. I could hear the cautious rumbling of the carts of produce being trundled over the cobbled streets of the mews nearby, coming closer and closer. I lay there stiff and aching and wondering what my father would do when he discovered I hadn't been home for the night. He'd call Cath before he called the police and she might mention it to Richie and he might say something to Max who might guess I'd gone to see Angie. Or he might call Genevieve first but had I told Genevieve *when* I was seeing Angie? As far as I could remember, I hadn't said a word to anyone.

And then, over the muffled clattering of the stalls being put up outside, I heard the sound of someone coming up the stairs. Was this it? Had the time come for me to be taken away to my fate?

I heard the sound of the key being turned in the lock of my room—slowly, as if the person didn't want me to hear.

Or didn't want Angie to hear, as it turned out, because Martha crept into the room and with the help of the moonlight shining through the window I could see she had her finger to her lips. I made a sound through the scarf and she clamped a hand over my face.

"Shhh! Keep absolutely quiet! She's right across the hall. She's asleep and the door's closed but the walls aren't too thick," whispered Martha. "If I untie the scarf, you have to promise to keep your voice down."

I nodded my head frantically and she released the scarf from my face.

"What about my hands and feet?" I said. "Please, Martha."

But to my utter astonishment she shook her head. "I came to ask you about Louis," she said. "I need to know what he told you. You said he came to find me?"

It was beyond belief. She wasn't here to help me escape. She just wanted to find out if she still had a chance with Louis. She was a pathetic and pitiful creature but she was, as I realized in a moment of desperate lucidity, my only hope.

So in hushed tones I told her what she wanted to hear, that Louis had regretted what he had said to her and that she would undoubtedly be reunited with him when she returned. And when I sensed that I had her complete trust and attention, I asked her again.

"Martha, *please!* You have to set me free."

But she shook her head. "No point," she said. "You'd never get out of here. I'm as much a prisoner as you are. Don't you understand? This whole place is boarded on the street side. The only way out is through that steel gate you came through and only Angie has the combination. You can open the windows up here but it's a sheer drop to the courtyard. I wouldn't risk it."

"So why aren't you tied up too?"

Martha's answer filled me with dread.

"Because she knows I would never leave her."

"Martha," I said as gently as I could, "did you help Angie kill Bettina in any way?"

She shook her head again. "No," she whispered, "I wasn't there that night."

"And Sean? Did Bettina kill Sean?"

She hesitated.

"Martha?" I whispered, trying to keep a check on the frantic urgency I could feel mounting inside me.

But she shook her head again. "No, Bettina didn't do it."

"So who did? Do you know?"

She didn't say anything.

"Martha?"

"Yes. Yes, I know."

"So who was it?"

"I killed him." She mouthed the words at me.

"It was an accident," she said, raising her voice to an alarmingly high level when she saw the expression of shock on my face. She clutched me and thrust her face in front of mine to make me pay attention to her words. She manipulated me like a puppet because I was still tied up. "And that's why I'm here," she hissed at me. "She called me and said she'd tell the police I killed Sean unless I came to London to be with her. She said she needed me."

"You'd better tell me everything, Martha," I said. "Start at the beginning."

She was silent for a few seconds then she began to whisper urgently, "Here's what happened. When Bettina suddenly appeared in the Hamptons in August and started going around asking questions about Shotgun, I contacted Angie and she went ballistic! For the first time since she'd asked me to keep an eye out for Sean, she said she wanted to get in touch with him herself."

"So you set it up?"

"I gave her his e-mail address and she took it from there. Then she called me and said she was coming over. She said Sean had mentioned Shotgun had given him one of his grandfather's Purdeys and I had to get hold of it."

"Did Sean know you knew his mother?"

"Of course not. I had to engineer a conversation with him

about shooting the next time I met him on the beach and he said he'd bring the Purdey to show me. I think he was a little frightened of it, to be honest, but he was proud enough of it to want me to see it and admire it. He came looking for me with it before he went to New York the night before he died."

M saw Sean w/shotgun in woods. I remembered Bettina's notes. Dumpster must have seen him.

"I had arranged to meet him in the woods. We often used Dumpster's hunting blind as a meeting place. But I didn't see him and I found the gun in the blind. I caught a glimpse of Dumpster's truck in the woods and I was worried that he'd seen me take the gun," said Martha. "Of course it was covered with Shotgun's prints. Then Angie flew to New York and came out to hide in my trailers."

"Before Sean was killed?"

Martha nodded. "The day before. Sean told me he was going to the city and that he would be back the following night. He said he had arranged for Bettina to meet with Shotgun at the house at seven thirty and then come and meet him, Sean, off the jitney at around eight forty.

"I was in Sag Harbor and Shelter Island that Friday, just as I told you, and Angie drove over there in a rented car and picked me up about six thirty. We were back in the Mallaby woods about seven fifteen. It was just getting dark. We left the car quite a long way away and found a place to wait in the woods. Angie had learned to shoot when she lived on the Yorkshire moors. She had Sean's Purdey that I had passed on to her and she made us both wear gloves. She wanted me to help her carry Bettina's body. Once she'd shot her, she planned to take her out into the middle of the bay in my boat and dump her in the water."

I wondered if Martha realized she was revealing herself to be an accomplice in Bettina's murder. She was on her knees beside me with a wide-eyed look on her face that belied the horrific details coming out of her mouth.

"But seven thirty came and Bettina never arrived," said Martha. "I wanted to leave but Angie said that even though the meeting with Shotgun clearly wasn't happening, there was still a chance that Bettina would pick up Sean from the bus and drop him at the house—and we could get her on the way out.

"It was pitch-black, just starting to rain, and nearly nine o'clock when we glimpsed a figure coming through the woods—on foot. It was very sudden and we weren't prepared. I had assumed we'd have the headlights of the car to give us warning and that then there'd be a few minutes while she dropped Sean off. I suppose we never stopped to wonder why Bettina was on foot. Angie had stood the Purdey up against a tree and I reached for it, intending to hand it to her. I had never shot anything in my life. The shadow was upon us so fast and I panicked. The gun was loaded. Somehow I lifted it up and it went off."

She looked at me expectantly. "See? That's how it happened that Friday."

"It was Sean?"

"The figure fell instantly and we waited to see if it would stir. When it didn't we rushed over and discovered what I'd done."

She was terrifyingly calm, I noticed, as if she had already divorced herself from the proceedings in her mind.

"It was my idea to use one of my wedding dresses as a shroud," she whispered proudly. "We carried him down to the beach and I made Angie help me drag him into the shallows and I opened his shirt and washed the blood from the hole in his chest where he'd been blasted by the shotgun. I stuffed an old cloth into the wound to stop the blood seeping out. Then I rowed out into the bay and we tossed his body into the water. Angie wanted to say a prayer but there wasn't time." Martha was quite matter-of-fact now. "I insisted she drive me all the way back to Shelter Island so I could establish an alibi. My story of having been on Shelter Island would have to stick. Angie dropped me off and I went around asking for a ride home from Shelter Island so the guy who drove me all the way back would remember me. I didn't get back to the trailers till almost midnight."

"And the next day, Saturday, Angie killed Bettina."

"When I left my trailers on that Saturday, she told me she was only going to go out to get rid of the Purdey. She said she was going to bury it in the sand just along the beach near Shotgun's property. When she'd done so, she said, she saw movement in the woods. So she started back the way she'd come, but using the woods as cover, and she came across a truck. She found this bow and arrow in it and then this figure appeared out of nowhere. It was almost a repetition of the night before. It was a woman and she came toward Angie and started waving at her as if she knew her. It was Bettina and she'd recognized Angie but then as she grew closer she saw Angie had a bow and arrow pointed right at her so she turned and ran. And Angie shot her in the back."

"So where were you, Martha?"

"You know where I was," said Martha, looking at me with reproach. "You saw me, remember? Earlier, at your mother's ceremony on the beach. And then I had a date with Louis."

She sounded like a lovesick teenager whenever she mentioned his name and suddenly I saw a way to get through to her.

"Martha, you have to get out of here and go back to Louis. I told you, he came to find you."

There was an element of truth in what I said. He had gone looking for her but before she could ever be reunited with him, she'd have to talk her way out of her role in two gruesome murders. But I had to bank on her apparent failure to realize this.

"But how can I get out of here?" she said. "Angie would never let me leave."

"That's right," I said patiently, "that's absolutely right. Martha, you know Angie won't let you out of here alive."

"But she asked me to come here."

"To kill you," I said brutally. "I'm sure of it. Which is why you have to call for help—you have to find someone to get you out of here, away from Angie."

"But I don't know anyone in London anymore."

"Call the police," I said simply. "Call them and tell them where you are and ask them to tell Det. Supt. Max Austin of New Scotland Yard that you're here with me and he needs to come get us. Okay? Can you repeat that back to me?"

I made her say it several times, repeating his name over and over again. I persuaded her to at least untie my feet and when she let herself out of the room and I heard her tiptoeing down the stairs, I could only pray. Pray that she would make the call and that they would hear the urgency in her voice and pass the message on to Max.

As it began to get light I heard sounds coming from Angie's room, footsteps crossing the landing, and then the door was unlocked.

"How did you get the scarf off?" she said immediately. "And who untied your feet?"

She locked me in again and I rolled over to press my ear to the floorboards. I heard the sound of her voice raised in anger downstairs and Martha wailing in response. Then there were footsteps thundering up the stairs and Angie was crying out: "I'm going to get the gun."

I squeezed my eyes tight shut and waited for the inevitable.

But the next voice I heard, coming from downstairs, was Martha's.

"I'm in here. HERE!" I heard her screaming and then the sound of footsteps on the cobbles. I rushed to the window and looking down through the glass-roofed passage I saw Max shaking the steel gate.

"Smash the window!" he yelled to Martha and I heard the sound of shattering glass.

I could hear Angie on the landing and through the door I made out the unmistakable click of the gun being broken open and the shells being loaded into the chamber.

The gun had not been loaded. I need never have been threatened by it and now it was too late.

"Put down the gun. Do not move," I heard Max's voice say.

Even though I couldn't see anything through the door the scene was brutally vivid to me as if I were right there with them. Max was at the bottom of the stairs and Angie was on the landing at the top of the stairs with a loaded shotgun.

There was an eerie calm for about twenty seconds as I pressed my head against the door. Then I recoiled violently at the sound of the gun going off in my ear.

THE FOLLOWING SEPTEMBER, ALMOST A YEAR AFTER
Sean Marriott's body, swathed in its saturated finery, was
found washed up at the water's edge, Franny and Rufus's wedding took place farther up the beach at Lazy Point.

They were married in fits and starts due to the fact that at the
last moment Franny had insisted that Eliza be her flower girl.
Eliza was barely eighteen months and she toddled after them,
clutching her little posy of daisies, for all of fifteen seconds before veering off in search of distraction and falling over in the
sand. At which point the preacher came to an abrupt halt as
Franny abandoned the ceremonies and rushed after her.

When the service was interrupted for the third time, my
mother stepped forward and intercepted Eliza on her way down
to paddle in the water. Eliza's mouth puckered in automatic re-
flex but then she looked up at my mother and wisely thought better of it, allowing herself to be carried back up the beach to sit
on my mother's lap. Not that I was remotely surprised. My
mother had spent the last three months stage-managing every
minute detail of Franny's big day—from the daisy chain around
Eliza's neck to the gold silk Indian-style wedding dress with its
wraparound skirt and cropped top that exposed the diamond in
Franny's navel, a wedding gift from Rufus. She wasn't about to
have it ruined by the antics of a wayward toddler.

The preacher stood with his back to the water, Franny and Rufus before him, and the rest of us perched on spindly gold chairs rooted in the sand. Behind him, parked in the bay, was Rufus's truck bedecked with flowers, a reminder of the day when Rufus had proposed and another indication of Franny's newfound romanticism.

It was a gorgeous day with a cloudless royal blue sky above us, and the sound of the water lapping gently only added to the serenity of the moment. Yet I couldn't relax.

Throughout the ceremony I was miserably aware that we were but a stone's throw from the site of Martha's trailers. If I turned my head slightly I could make out their silhouette in my peripheral vision. Martha wasn't there, of course. She was in jail somewhere awaiting her fate. I had heard she had been promised some kind of deal in exchange for a confession to being responsible for Sean's death and for testifying about Angie's orchestration of what had happened those fateful nights a year ago. I wondered what had happened to her wedding dresses. In my head I began to hear them rustling and whispering, taunting poor Franny while she was blissfully united with Rufus at the shoreline. When I found myself wondering if the dresses had inherited Martha's ability to jinx weddings I rapped myself mentally over the knuckles.

Apparently I did not do it silently, for my father, sitting between my mother and me, glanced quickly at me. He had accompanied me when I had returned to Long Island almost a year ago. He claimed it would be a surprise for my mother but when I witnessed their reunion my mother behaved as if she had been expecting him for some time.

I had been so wrapped up in writing Shotgun's book for the past few months that I had not really monitored my parents' tentative reestablishment of their marriage. But I had heard from my father that Vanessa had marched him straight into couples therapy.

"What happened?" I asked him, intrigued.

"What do you think?" He smiled. "She talked nonstop and neither I nor the counselor could get a word in edgeways. But it worked, because after I don't know how many sessions of listening to herself, she decided that we should give it another go."

I was pleased, of course, but I would never stop mourning the loss of the Phillionaire, and thinking that he might have been the one person who could have penetrated my mother's emotional defenses once and for all. Still, as my father pointed out rather wistfully, "What is marriage if not a friendship? And that's the thing about your mother and me, Lee. We've been friends for a long time. Whatever else happens, it makes sense for us to renew that friendship."

Scott stood up for Rufus, as they say. I figured Rufus had to ask him. I watched as he lurched forward with the ring, body rigid, shoulders hunched, his demeanor more fitting for a funeral than a wedding. There would always be a certain amount of tension between the two brothers in regard to Franny and Eliza but there were two things that had gone a long way to smoothing the relationship. Scott had moved his practice into Manhattan and himself into the Fifth Avenue apartment. And no one could be impervious to Rufus's good-natured charm forever. Scott was still Eliza's father but once he moved away, it became clear that he had no real interest in adopting that role in her life. He seemed happy to pass that responsibility on to Rufus, who was only too glad to step up to the plate. Franny was aware that the problem of Scott hadn't gone away entirely—how could it? He was Rufus's brother—but for the time being they had arrived at an acceptable compromise. Until, I imagined, Eliza started asking who her father was.

As for Dumpster, who had just given Franny away, leading her along the beach to the tip of Lazy Point to hand her to Rufus, I just didn't know what to think. It wasn't just a case of *M saw something*. As it turned out, M had seen everything.

What had come to light in the wake of the investigation was that on the night Sean was killed, Dumpster had been driving through the woods around seven o'clock on his way to put up Shotgun's shelves at Mallaby, and had seen Angie and Martha go past in the car. He had caught only a glimpse of Angie but it had been enough to start him wondering where he'd seen the face before. When his memory was sufficiently jogged to send him up to Sean's room to take another look at the picture he'd seen on the inside of the closet, he realized it was Angie. And then he called Bettina and suggested a meeting at the beach. As he'd told me at the cabin when he'd come looking for Franny just before the Phillionaire's funeral on the beach, he had lured her to the beach with the tantalizing bit of information that he had just seen something he knew would interest her. He planned to tell her about Angie's arrival and offer future snippets in return for her silence about his mother.

But he never got to speak to her. Instead he witnessed her murder.

He had intended to go hunting that night but the weather was so bad he had abandoned the idea pretty early on in the evening. He had tried to call Bettina to postpone the meeting at the beach but had not been able to reach her because her cell was turned off. So he had parked his truck—with his bow and arrow inside—and set off through the woods to meet her as planned.

Instead he saw her shot with an arrow in the back by Angie. It did not occur to him until he returned to his truck, after racing through the squelch of the rain-soaked leaves, that his bow and arrow were missing and they had been used as the murder weapon.

I learned all this from Shotgun while we were working on his book and the first question I asked Shotgun was why Dumpster did not report what he saw.

And this was when I received the biggest shock.

"He did," said Shotgun. "He came to the house in the middle of the night and he told me."

I gasped. "He told you what?"

"That he had seen Angie kill Bettina and throw the bow and arrow in the pit. Then he followed her back to Martha Farrell's trailers and saw her bury the quiver and let herself into one of the trailers."

"What did you do?"

"I told him to get right back out there and get his truck off the property as quickly as he could before anyone saw it. It wasn't a problem if they found tire tracks because he had a legitimate reason to be driving to and from my house, but it wouldn't have helped if anyone had seen him there that particular night."

"But why didn't Dumpster report what he'd seen to the police?"

As I asked the question I already knew the answer I would get from Shotgun—*Because I asked him not to*—and suddenly everything fell into place with a sickening lurch. Shotgun had asked Dumpster to keep quiet about what he had seen. Shotgun had known about Angie's involvement in two murders fourteen years apart, and he had covered up for her for both of them. All that stuff about pretending not to know why Dumpster had lied at the arraignment—Shotgun had lied to *me*. He had covered up for Angie regarding Bettina's murder because whatever might have happened between them he still loved her and would shield her no matter what.

"I was telling you the truth when I said I wanted to do the book for Sean," Shotgun told me. "I made a kind of maudlin New Year's resolution at the beginning of this year that I would set the record straight for him once and for all. There had been times when he'd asked me what had happened and I just hadn't had the guts to tell him. How *do* you tell your son that his mother was a murderer? But I just knew it was going to come out one day and that it was better he hear the truth from me than from anyone else. And of course I would have broken the news to him before the book came out."

"But you changed your mind?"

"I owe you the biggest apology, Lee. I should never have even started work on the book with you. Once I heard that Angie had killed Bettina, I knew you were in danger. The problem was I didn't know who had killed my son. I couldn't believe Angie had had a part in that and I thought you might uncover something there for me. Of course I should have gone to the police as soon as Dumpster told me about Angie in the woods. But I couldn't be the one to turn her in—and especially not to that bastard Evan Morrison."

"Do you suppose Dumpster told his mother?" I asked Shotgun.

"No. He told me he didn't want her involved any more than he could help. He was very shaken when she changed her story at my arraignment but he had to be my alibi. He could have told Evan Morrison what he'd seen Angie do at any time but he had promised me he'd keep quiet. I owe him a lot."

And in a way this proved to be the saving grace for Dumpster. He was finally out of the woods—an appropriate enough expression—and Shotgun had taken him on full time to be the caretaker at Mallaby. He had given Dumpster Sean's old apartment above the stables. They would continue to cover for each other about the events of the night of Bettina's death. To all extents and purposes Shotgun had become the father Dumpster never had and if Franny had a problem with this, she kept it to herself. All she asked of Shotgun was that he keep Dumpster clear of any drug activity.

Despite her new role as the fiancée of a millionaire, Franny still turned up to run the Old Stone Market every day and whenever I went there, I thought of my first meeting with Angie Marriott. Over the past nine months I had spent a lot of time trying to get Angie Marriott out of my head and wondering over and over again if she had planned the final outcome of what happened that night at her house off Portobello.

Following the deafening blast of the shotgun on the other side of the door, I had held my breath for as long as I could before rushing to rattle the door handle in panic.

"Let me out! Please, let me out of here."

And then I heard Max's voice. "Lee, don't move. DO NOT MOVE!" I heard him running up the stairs and then the sound of the key turning in the lock. I rushed to the door but he only opened it a crack. He was leaning in and pushing me away.

"Stand back. Move right away from the door. Go on," he said as I struggled to get out. "You're not coming out. You're staying here."

What was he *doing*? He had to let me out. Was he trying to hold me prisoner too? And then I looked down and saw the bloody footprints made by the soles of his shoes and I began to shake. He pushed me firmly away from the door and locked it from the inside.

"You're staying here, Lee. Do you understand? I do not want you to see what's out there. We'll get a ladder up to the window and take you out that way."

"What happened?" I whispered, almost paralyzed with fear. "Did she shoot Martha?"

"She shot herself," said Max. "She sat down on the top step, rested the shotgun a few steps down with the barrel pointing up into her mouth and fired. Her brains exploded all over the landing."

"You just stepped in them," I said, staring at his bloody shoes.

"I had to tread in them to get to you and you will too if you go out there." He threw open the window and leaned out to yell down to the courtyard, "Up here, we'll need a ladder soon as you can. The entrance is round the corner in Westbourne Park Road."

"So," he turned back to me, "what happened?"

I told him, speaking very fast because it was the only way I could stop myself from breaking down in tears. When I'd finished, a smile began to spread across his face. All the brooding tension that was part and parcel of his normal expression seemed to dissolve as his features relaxed. For one memorable instant he looked genuinely happy and I barely recognized him.

I yearned to be able to capture this softer side of Max and bottle it so I could produce it to offset the grouchiness he normally presented to me. Was this the only thing that put him at ease? The solving of a murder?

"Wait till Frank Shaw hears about this!" He punched the air with an uncharacteristic show of excitement. Then before I knew what was happening he had gathered me up in a spontaneous hug that was so forceful I felt the tip of my nose being abraded by the scratchy tweed of his jacket and I pulled away.

"Oh, sorry," he said and the scowl was back.

"No," I said and pointed to my nose. "Your jacket's like a Brillo pad."

He took it off and flung it on the floor. Then before I could say another word, he brought me back into his arms and lifted my chin so that my lips met his.

His lips were unbelievably soft and his tongue explored my

mouth slowly and carefully as if he were investigating it for evidence. I reached up with my arms above my head and stretched myself against him. He ran his hands down the sides of my body to the bottom of my thighs and up again and then he lifted me up and held me high above him as if I were a feather. He brought me down slowly to reengage his mouth with mine.

It was all over in seconds—suddenly there was a tap on the window and I saw a hand reaching up. Richie's head appeared at the top of the ladder. I felt Max freeze in my arms before he sprang away from me.

"I'm sorry," he said curtly, "I don't know what came over me. I'm truly sorry."

Richie was standing there on the other side of the glass, trying in vain to open the window from the outside. Max signaled to him to go back down again.

"I'm not remotely sorry," I said quickly. "I'm very pleased and happy and excited about what just happened and I'd like it to happen again. Do you understand what I'm saying?"

He didn't give me an answer, just opened the window and beckoned me to climb out onto the ladder.

We had several meetings after that, about the investigation and nothing else, and he made sure that each one took place in an interview room down at the station. It was sheer agony for me to sit there, separated from him by a metal table with Richie parked beside him like a chaperone. At one point our knees touched and I became electrified. I contemplated reaching out with my foot although where exactly I intended to aim it, I wasn't too sure. In any case there was a chance I'd start stroking Richie by mistake and make things even worse.

Max's eagle eyes bored into mine during the interviews but the minute they were over, he stood up and barely looked at me again. And then he disappeared off my radar altogether. Cath told me he and Richie were caught up in a horrendous case investigating the murder of a four-year-old girl and that Richie was so strung out he was coming home and not speaking to her all night. She didn't say anything about Max and me and I began to think that maybe Richie hadn't seen us kissing, or if he had, he hadn't said anything to Cath.

Or maybe he had. Because Cath didn't stop going on about Tommy and when was I going to go back to America? And then Genevieve got in on the act and reported that Shotgun had been asking about me. In the light of what had happened, he wanted to return to the book.

"Oh, I don't know, Genevieve," I said. "I'm wondering maybe if I'm not too close to this whole thing."

"Well, that's why you have to see it through," said Genevieve, matter-of-fact as ever. "Or shall I look for someone else to take over?"

I was like a rat out of a trap. "Absolutely not! If Shotgun's asked for me, I have to go back, don't I?"

If Genevieve was surprised by my abrupt change of mind, she didn't show it. At some point in the last few months it seemed I had learned—at this late stage in my life and career—to be competitive.

Even though it was some time before Shotgun came through with his startling revelation that he had known all along that Angie was the killer, the minute I walked back into Mallaby, I knew there was an unbreakable bond between us. As a ghostwriter I am often party to confidences pertaining to my subjects' lives that are not mentioned in the book. As Shotgun and I went back to work, I sensed a tacit understanding between us that he was going to have to tread very carefully as to what he put in and what he left out. He didn't know how much I knew. He didn't know exactly what Angie had told me about the night the groupie had died and gradually I enlightened him.

"You knew," I said, looking directly at him and speaking in a tone that brooked no evasion on his part, "you knew it was she who killed the groupie. There must have been some clue. You removed the pillow she used, *something.*"

But he'd had fourteen years to perfect his story.

"It was a long time ago," was all he said and later on in the book he left out the fact that Dumpster had told him what he had seen so he wasn't implicated there either.

It was collusion on my part too. Shotgun was taking a big risk. I could easily report what he had said to me but I knew that I never would. Apart from the fact that I would be done for obstruction, it was as I had told Max—I liked Shotgun. And for Franny's sake, I would keep quiet about Dumpster too.

Shotgun and I established a routine whereby I arrived for work at ten each morning and stayed there the whole day. As a result we were able to get the book done in six months and it was due out before Christmas. The buzz was already growing and Genevieve was beginning to make the kind of clucking noises she emitted when she sensed a best seller in the offing.

As for Tommy, he and I had managed to coexist at the cabin surprisingly well but this was because we hardly saw each other. Tommy had become a workaholic. He left the cabin every morning around six thirty to hook up with Rufus and four evenings a week he was out till 2:00 A.M. embarked upon his new career.

For in my absence in London, Tommy had become a karaoke DJ.

He had discovered it at a bar in Montauk where he proved to be an instant hit with the crowd. He sang all his Johnny Cash favorites—"Ring of Fire," "I Walk the Line"—and apparently they loved him. The photos he produced with great pride showed him dressed in black from head to toe and in a video he insisted I watch, I had to concede that his voice wasn't as bad as I expected. He would be performing later on at Franny and Rufus's wedding party, for which Shotgun had given them permission to use Mallaby—a clear sign that he was emerging from his reclusive state.

The ceremony was over now and as we prepared to follow the rest of the guests in a procession along the beach to Mallaby, Tommy took my hand and whispered.

"So, could this be you and me soon? Shall we get married on the beach too? Hey, I just had a thought? Will our kids be American?"

"You mean if we were to be married on an American beach?"

"Ha-ha! No, I mean if we bring them up in America."

"Well, no, they won't," I leaned in closer to him, "because I'm going back to England now I've finished the book."

Tommy raised his head to a passing seagull. "I don't know," he said, "what would you do, mate?" Then he gave me a squeeze. "Well, I guess they'll have to be mid-Atlantic kids because I'm staying here. I love it in America. Give me one good reason why you would want to go back to London when you could have all this?"

Later that night as I watched him in his element setting up his karaoke equipment—and thinking that being a DJ was the perfect follow-up for a sound engineer—I thought about his question. It would be wonderful to get married on a beach. And my parents looked like they were going to settle in New York for a while. Genevieve had reported lucrative assignments were being rumored for me in America and she seemed convinced that once Shotgun's book came out, I would be the hottest ghost in town. In fact every time I turned my mind to it, I came up with another reason to stay.

But then I would remember the letter already in an envelope

with Tommy's name on it, the one I had begun on the flight to London almost a year earlier—*It's tricky what I want to say to you and that's why I'm writing a letter*—and which I had finally finished a few hours before Franny and Rufus's wedding. Franny had it safely stashed under the counter at the Old Stone Market and she was under instructions to give it to Tommy when he contacted her after he'd discovered I'd gone. And she and Rufus would be there for him, to help him understand.

Because by this time tomorrow I would be on my way to the airport because there *was* one good reason for me to go back to London. Just one, and it was an insane reason given that I had never heard another word from him, but it was the only one that mattered.

Max was there.